Blood at Dawn

Jim R. Woolard

BERKLEY BOOKS, NEW YORK

BLOOD AT DAWN

A Berkley Book / published by arrangement with
the author

PRINTING HISTORY
Berkley edition / February 2001

The Penguin Putnam Inc. World Wide Web site address is
http://www.penguinputnam.com

ISBN: 0-425-17861-7

BERKLEY®
Berkley Books are published by The Berkley Publishing Group,
a division of Penguin Putnam Inc.,
375 Hudson Street, New York, New York 10014.
BERKLEY and the "B" design
are trademarks belonging to Penguin Putnam Inc.

PRINTED IN THE UNITED STATES OF AMERICA

10 9 8 7 6 5 4 3 2 1

To my brother Bryan . . .
. . . gone too soon but never forgotten

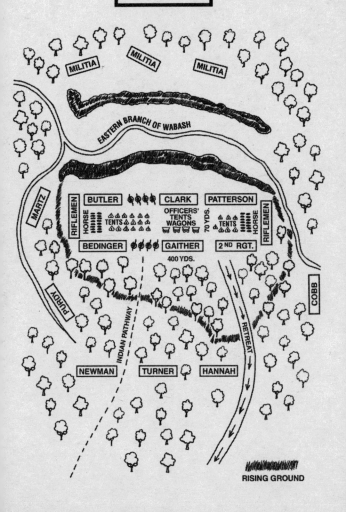

Prologue

Eden's Fork, Ohio
18 November 1821

It is hard for an old soldier preparing to meet his maker to silently abide what he has done in the past, rightly or wrongly, that disappointed those about him who deserved better.

Guilty memories are like sores that fester and won't heal. Dwell on them too long, and they turn an aging man raw and cantankerous, making him fit company for only those like himself—beings so close to the grave they could kiss the cheek of the devil and feel uplifted by the momentary touch of warm flesh.

I have started on many previous occasions to confront my past sins and omissions, and always, I have permitted something of lesser merit to blunt my will. Trust me, nothing is harder to face than the slighting of those who were closest to you . . . and loved you the most.

It is no excuse for my inaction that many others who were also there chose to quickly and forever forget the precise details of that savage, bloody dawn, 4 November 17 and 91, when hundreds of white soldiers and militia died under the strike of ball and tomahawk. For who desires to recall the most glorious day in the history of our red enemies? Who desires to recall how, from commanding general to the most spurious of contract suppliers, we so carelessly and foolishly helped the enemy defeat us? No force of arms has ever had more it should want to forget than those who marched with St. Clair.

Yet, for all the blame that can be parceled out for our

horrendous defeat, there were those, both men and women, who stood firm and stout that inglorious early morning. Their story, unfortunately, has gone untold. To date, thirty years to the month after the battle, only the selfish ramblings of our haughty commander, General St. Clair, have been made public. And, as Tap Jacobs observed when we finished perusing that document, never have a pair of fallen breeches been recovered so rapidly and cleverly as those of our disgraced leader.

After St. Clair published his personal posturing as a private citizen in 18 and 12, I expected either Denny or Sargent or Miles Starkweather, all of whom were present and kept daily journals, would tender a more balanced account of our 17 and 91 campaign. But none was forthcoming, perhaps because those three officers retained lengthy loyalties to our former general when he was allowed to continue as governor of the Northwest Territory. I fault them not, for no matter how righteous the cause, it is difficult to later turn on anyone who offers you a seat at the table in lean and dangerous times.

I am, therefore, resolved that lest I make the effort, no firsthand recounting of the St. Clair debacle will ever be recorded. It deters me not that scant few will take notice of my completed memoir now that the Injun and Redcoat Wars are well behind us. If I faithfully retell the particulars of that autumn march and resulting battle as I know them, I will at least pay homage long overdue to men such as Bear Watkins, Tap Jacobs, Miles Starkweather and, most importantly, my father, Caleb Downer. At the same time, I will reveal how one can find enemies about your own fire as dangerous as those in the opposing camp, enemies frequently harder to kill than the painted redstick.

It is only fair to warn the reader that my recounting will hold no appeal for the squeamish or the faint of heart, for the harshness of some of my recollections wears heavily upon me to this day. I will simply swear here at the outset that what follows will be the truth as best I can render it, and I will suffer the judgment of others as to my veracity accordingly.

Given aloud this date to a clerk in my pay,
Colonel Ethan Downer

Part I
Fort Hamilton

Chapter 1

Every now and again, if you suffer a misstep at the outset, the events that follow such a blunder seem to slide from bad to worse as if they have a will of their own. Never was this truer than throughout my experience with the St. Clair campaign, for I found myself in great danger even before I laid eyes on any of the general's forces.

My first inkling of trouble came in the deep hours of night. Hardy Booth and I were working ten head of riding stock up the Great Miami River, bound for the general's newly built Fort Hamilton, and had camped at dark below where Blue Rock Creek joined the river from the east.

I wasn't certain at first what had awakened me in my blankets, but once propped on an elbow and listening, I was immediately aware we were no longer alone in the shadowy river bottom. To the north, on the same bank of the river as our camp, plumb where the Blue Rock joined the Miami, hooves struck rock and splashed water.

Somebody was moving horses, and moving them fast!

That realization routed the sleep from me. It didn't take any more brains than those necessary to tell right from left to reckon no one of the same skin color as Hardy and me would be moving horses under cover of darkness. We white folks unfailingly trailed in full daylight when we didn't run the risk of injuring our stock and could keep a constant watch roundabout. So, if it wasn't our kind out there shoving for the Miami jack quick, it was those we dreaded meeting the most . . . the redstick enemy.

I pulled my flintlock from twixt my thighs and shook

Hardy's ample shoulder. He awakened with a puzzled grunt. I clasped a palm over his mouth and spoke softly into his ear. "Quiet now, there's Injuns yonder hazing a sizable bunch of horses."

Hardy was a jovial soul, prone to fun anyone, anytime, anywhere, but he wasn't prone to foolishness of any stripe if his scalp might be at stake. He curled fingers 'round his own long rifle and stared past me toward the creek. The whites of his straining eyes were faint smudges in the shadowy night.

"What are we to do, Ethan?"

Hardy was two years my senior, but he would look to me, as Paw had put me in charge of our sojourn south into Kentucky to purchase mounts for General St. Clair's officers. And when Caleb Downer said how it was to be, everybody in his pay done as he was told. Paw might forgive a man 'most anything else. Never would he brook insubordination.

I rose to a knee, Hardy crawling alongside of me. "We can't let 'em come onto us. Get over to our animals and watch for sign they've heard what's happening at the creek."

"What do you intend for your ownself?" Hardy asked in a whisper.

The moon slipped clear of the clouds left from the afternoon rain, and four-legged shapes, a few bearing hatless riders, sprang into view forty-plus yards upstream. The river valley ran flat to the west in the direction the Injuns were traveling. On the near bank of the Miami, wooded hills swept down within a few rods of water's edge, hiding all but the mouth of Blue Rock Creek from our sight.

"I'm gonna skirt along the hillside and get a count of how many horses they're making off with. Paw will likely want to report what we're seeing to the general and his staff."

Hardy stiffened. "It ain't important enough to get killed over, for chrissake," he contended. "A damn good guess would do just fine."

"Never you fear," I quietly assured him. "They're in an all-fired hurry, and I ain't aiming to draw a step tighter to 'em than necessary. They won't spy us back here in the willows less'n we attract their attention. Besides, any of them inch our way, I'll scoot back here like a spooked rabbit. Now, ease back down the bank, and keep our own stock quiet."

For a usually bumbling fellow, Hardy slipped through the willows sheltering us slick as a prowling weasel. I looped the shoulder straps of my shot pouch and powder horn over my head, then held fast a brief spell, gathering my nerve. I was no stranger to Injuns. I had, in fact, faced them painted and screeching in the loft of our family cabin. But that experience had put a fear of them in me steady as I sucked wind. You reached near a blazing flame, you took every caution lest you might get burnt terribly bad.

Once free of the willows, I angled uphill, seeking solid footing on the high side of the looming tree butts. What undergrowth that couldn't be avoided rustled gently against my leather leggins and linen frock, sound too faint for distant ears. I stalked as Paw had taught me, head level and steady, knees bent, each stride a deliberate step, feeling with the toes of my moccasins for anything that might snap or roll under my weight. Maybe I wasn't stealthy as a woods panther, but two-legged game seldom heard me approaching. Years of laying the sneak on your own wily brothers can be downright helpful once you're somewhat growed.

As I gingerly crested the hilltop separating me from a look-see into the creek bed where all the commotion was occurring, the moon ducked behind a thick cloud. My brief glance before the moon disappeared left me with the disturbing notion it was riding stock the Injuns had stolen. If that were true, given their large number, more than a few of General St. Clair's mounted cavalrymen were perhaps going off to war afoot. On the opposite hand, if those were pack-horses wending past beneath me, the blow to his campaign was damaging but less severe. No matter how much gold or federal scrip you had in your fist, good riding mounts were much scarcer than toting animals south of the Ohio. Either way, the general would welcome an accurate report of his losses, the sooner the better.

I slipped over the crest of the hill. Problem was, the lower I descended twixt the thick beech and oak trunks, I still couldn't see a whit better in the dim, murky light. The ground leveled at the bottom of the hill, and the brush thickened as I neared the creek. Fearing I'd arrive too late for my look-see, I forged ahead, trusting to the darkness, the splash of water under pounding hooves, and the yipping of the horse-hazing redsticks to mask my presence.

The moon suddenly reappeared, and to my right, at the outer fringe of the brush overgrowing the creek bank, not four paces from the muzzle of my rifle, rode an Injun. My innards tried to climb into my throat, but I stifled the fright welling inside me with a forceful swallow, halted in midstride, and hunkered down in the screening brush. Not a part of me moved afterward except the balls of my eyes.

Curiosity replaced surprise when I saw the rider hadn't spotted me, for he was a most peculiar specimen of enemy. His chest wasn't bare and painted. He wore instead a wide-sleeved, ruffled, satiny white shirt with large pewter buttons. A flat-crowned hat covered the top of his skull where heathens always displayed roached topknots. And lo and behold, wasn't that a braided pigtail of hair descending well below the nape of his neck? A good goddamn if it wasn't.

I resisted the urge to scratch myself somewhere. Injuns shunned hats when on the warpath and rarely, if ever, wore their hair long and braided on such ventures. I stuck my chin forward and peered harder. Best I could tell, what with how the rider was holding the reins so awkwardly in front of his fancy shirt, his hands appeared to be tied at the wrists. What I next made out popped my jaws apart. Be damned if a leather gag wasn't tied over his mouth. My heart thudded and thumped.

I had stumbled upon a white captive!

What followed shocked even me. I suspect the taking of my ten-year-old brother Aaron by the Shawnee from the sleeping loft we shared, never to be seen by kin again, had much to do with it. So did the fight that broke out among the stolen horses farther downstream. Squeals and whinnies rent the night air, drawing the rearmost Injuns past their prisoner to the Miami and leaving him untended for a scant minute smack in front of me.

Whatever blunted what little sense I possessed and goaded

me into action, soon as the unexpected opportunity to attempt a rescue presented itself, my feet were moving almost before I realized what was happening. And once I stepped forth into the chill waters of the creek, there was no retreating.

Standing as I did within two inches of six feet, it was no great challenge for me to rise on my toes in the shallow Blue Rock and wrap an arm 'round the waist of the Injun captive. With a hefty tug, I yanked him toward me. Thank the Lord his legs weren't bound in any way. He came clear of the saddle without hanging up in the stirrups, the gag in his mouth muffling a yelp of alarm.

Not wanting to tarry for a second, gentleness was the last thing on my mind. I took full advantage of the lightness of the body I held and lunged for the protective cover of the creek bank. I extended an arm in front of me, parted brush with the barrel of my flintlock, and without hesitating, scampered for the hillside and its beckoning woods, my freed captive bouncing on the point of my hip with each jolting, stretching stride.

The ruckus downstream at the river was petering out by the time the ground began slanting uphill. By then, too, my rescued captive was squirming and kicking, undoubtedly from my rough handling. His protests threw me off balance, and to avert a nasty fall for the both us, I cast him nose down at the base of a massive tree trunk.

I let him lie there while I listened for any pursuit and regained my wind. When he didn't stir whatsoever, I grew concerned that I had done my new traveling companion harm. Stepping across his prone body with my right leg, I reached under his chest to roll him over and got the biggest surprise yet of what was proving to be the most unusual night of my young life. My fingers hadn't grasped the hardened muscle of a male rib cage. They were folded around a female breast large enough to fill my entire hand.

My clutching grip froze in place. God's bones, a woman! How the devil had a woman become prisoner to Injun horse thieves? And more astounding, why had they burdened themselves with her while fleeing in the depths of the night?

My subsequent squeeze to make certain I wasn't mistaken was my undoing. The bound hands resting on the ground above the former prisoner's now hatless head flew upward in a blurring arc. Bent over as I was, I made a perfect target. Flesh slapped bare flesh, and heat blossomed on my cheek.

Stunned though I was, I'd survived enough brawls with my male counterparts to know what was coming next. The slap had turned her onto her backside and, sure enough, the knee I quickly raised caught her kick short of my vitals. It was mean and had to hurt, but I lowered my weight onto her legs, pinning them flat before she tried the same with her other foot.

Damn vixen, she'd been fooling me all the while!

I lay hold of her lashed wrists, then bent over her again till my lips brushed the leather gag covering her mouth. The curve of her cheekbones gleamed in the moonlight. The memory of that firm breast still fresh and vivid, I can't claim I didn't wonder how she would look with the gag removed. But I'd no intention of untying it any time soon.

She stilled completely, eyes boring into mine. "I'm white and a friend. You understand what I'm saying here?"

When I got not a hint of a yea or nay from her, my temper grew foul. "Nod or I'll slap you liken you did me. Damned if I won't!"

She nodded sharply.

"Good girl," I acknowledged. "There's horses and more help just over this hill. It may not suit you, but I'm gonna lead you there just as you be so we won't get separated in the dark. An' we'll leave that gag stay put, too. Thataway, you take a spill, you won't yell out and tell the Injuns where we be. You understand?"

Her head cocked to one side and I swear I saw red darken those gleaming cheekbones. She didn't like it even a little bit. I straightened, raised an open palm in a threatening manner, and without further delay, she gave me the nod I sought.

It crossed my mind that it would be a right smart idea if I were prepared for an assault by tongue and anything handy that she could throw whenever I did cut her loose. I suspected this particular female wasn't inclined to suffer insult easily under any circumstances.

Injun calls in the creek bed floated to my ear. They had discovered their captive was missing. They would search close about, then upstream since that was the quickest escape route for anyone fleeing them. And while the redsticks nosed around a tad and moseyed the wrong direction, we would sally over the hill, rejoin Hardy, and withdraw a distance down the Miami. The enemy wouldn't hunt futilely for long, for St. Clair's troops might be in rapid pursuit of their lost mounts. They'd want to be across the river and well westward come daybreak.

Fortune seemed to further favor us, for the moon found another cloud to slide behind. I stood in the welcome darkness, pulled my hot-tempered mistress upright, and hiked for the safety of the far hillside.

It took only a few uphill strides for me to appreciate the litheness of my new companion. She clung within a half step of my heels and sustained without hint of a solitary falter the rapid pace I set. Whenever I halted for a quick glance and listen to the rear, she nimbly crouched out of my line of sight as if she had a string attached to my thinking. She was a girl who hadn't spent her days tied to a hearth cooking and baking.

Fresh shouts in Injun tongue echoed twixt our position and the creek. They had undoubtedly found sign of our passage. Tracks would be almost impossible to discern in the continuing darkness, the same with slightly disturbed brush. That left only one solid possibility—my companion's missing hat. Cursing myself for an oversight that could result in our deaths, I resumed our upward climb.

I kept an ear cocked best I could over my labored breathing. We had one distinct advantage in our rush to escape. The Injuns believed they were seeking an unarmed captive. Otherwise, they would have hunted silently rather than giving away their locations by yelling aloud to each other.

Beyond the crest of the hill, I broke into a run. Down we plunged, making surprisingly little clatter for our haste. At the bottom of the incline, I stopped once more to listen. The brief respite also gave me time to slash the leather thongs binding my companion's wrists with my knife, for if she were soon to sit a horse, I preferred she could mount on her own if need be. The gag I left to her.

"Follow me less'n you want to travel with your Injun friends again," I whispered hoarsely while gasping for breath.

I was turning away to lead off along the riverbank when her loosened gag hit my hat brim and sailed past me into the darkness. "Don't worry, you big oaf, there's no danger of you outrunning me."

I took her at her word. With nary a peek her direction, I zigzagged through rocks, reedy bogs, and willows across the clearest path to where Hardy Booth waited. The complete absence of Injun sound behind us, instead of heartening me, made speed seem even more paramount. Tap Jacobs was always reminding us Downer boys that it was too late after you were dead to try and explain how you had underestimated the cleverness of the Shawnee and the Miami.

It was Hardy Booth's forethought that gave us any chance of escape at all.

We came up to him on the dead run, and he was waiting with our personal mounts saddled and the horse string tied nose to tail and lined out down the riverbank. For all the merriment Hardy provoked, he could show an uncommon amount of sense in a tight situation.

The moon bathed the river bottom with a new wash of light, and the waiting Hardy stood out like a Bible-thumping minister poised before his flock on a bright Sunday noon. His stammering, "What the hell!" at the spectacle of a strange white girl dogging my heels was overwhelmed by Injun war whoops that flowed from every quarter. A plume of red flame spewing yellow arcs of burning powder shot out of the willows flanking the horse string. At such close range, the instantaneous boom of the large-caliber musket was deafening. The ball hit Hardy twixt the shoulder blades, and he lurched toward me. His outthrust hand, reaching desperately for help, thumped limply against my chest. Then the narrow trace threading the willows erupted into a nerve-jangling jumble of whinnying, kicking, bucking horses and howling brown bodies charging from our rear brandishing spiked clubs and war axes that killed swift as any bullet.

How many of them there were in total, seen and unseen, I was never to learn. There was no time to think. No time to scheme. No time to mount any defense. There was time for only the simplest of recourses—flight, swift and bold. And flight by foot would be too slow. It was ride out of there or die.

I grabbed a fistful of fancy white shirt and slung my rescued captive ahead of me, straight among the neighing, bucking horses. A war ax, spinning end over end, whipped by within a finger's width of my shoulder. The weapon's blade, equaling the length of my forearm, struck the haunch of a panicked paint horse and sliced through hide and meat to the bone. The pain-maddened animal reared, front hooves flailing the air, and toppled over backward. I darted forward, and the tumbling paint smashed into the redsticks charging from our rear, scattering them willy-nilly like thrown sacks of flour.

"Mount and ride, mount and ride!" I screamed.

It was an unnecessary command, for mistress whatever-her-name needed no urging from me. Ignoring our attackers with the steadfastness of a veteran dragoon, she untied a sorrel gelding nearly as calm as herself from the middle of the horse string, grabbed his mane with both hands, bounced nimbly on one leg, and mounted Injun fashion from the right side. A slap of the rump and keening yell later, she was off into the night.

Feeling decidedly lonely of a sudden, I bolted after her. A screeching savage burst from the willows, tomahawk raised high above his blackened countenance. Without breaking stride, I jabbed backhanded with my rifle, and the barrel snagged his slashing hatchet, sparing me a fatal wound. Then somehow, with those weapons locked together, my knife was in my other fist and my sweeping stab buried its razor sharpness to the hilt in the savage's bare belly. I shoved his collapsing body aside with the knife still in place and ran on, amazed that the confines of the trace had in a flash grown utterly silent. It was as if the enemy, though superior in number, had paused to regroup.

Hardy's dun-colored mare proved my salvation. Where she had been since the initial shot of the ambush felled her master, I knew not. But when she veered into my path, confused and unsure which direction to flee, I seized her trailing reins and was up and into the saddle before she could shy away from me. And once she felt my weight on her back, her training came to the fore. I swear, one rap of the heels and that old girl was into a gallop.

A musket roared, and the ball slivered leaves above my head. Branches of the close-set willows flailed my hat and shoulders. Praying the mare's hooves found nothing that might imperil her legs, I flattened my flintlock against her neck and let her gallop all out 'round a long, tapering bend of the river. Well beyond the bend, with her wind starting to fail, I sawed her down to a fast walk and had me a gander back the way we'd come.

Trailing hoofbeats brought my rifle to bear at full cock, but the five approaching animals were without riders. They had followed after the mare. Last in line was my own personal mount, a blaze-faced roan of three years and much speed.

The roan's arrival put a whole new slant on things. He could outdistance anything on four legs north of the Ohio . . . or damn near. I still had my rifle, my shot pouch, and my horn. And, most importantly, I still had my hair. To say I felt a heap better about my prospects of gaining Fort Hamilton alive than I had mere minutes ago wouldn't have done justice to the elation coursing through me right then. All I had to do was straddle Blue and light a shuck directly away from those murdering redsticks.

That's all I truly had to do to ensure my own safety: mount Blue and light a shuck. But that wasn't in the toss of the bones for me, leastways not for a while yet. Hardy Booth, who'd been my best friend forever, was dead because I had chosen to play the hero. And if I was ever to enjoy a peaceful night's sleep the balance of my days, I owed that man more than a cold grave I didn't dare dig. I needed to complete the rescue I had undertaken that had cost Hardy his life. I needed to see mistress whatever-her-name got home wherever she belonged, or if not that, at least to Fort Hamilton where she would fall under the protection of St. Clair's army.

That decided, I stroked Blue's forehead and pondered the question now of utmost importance to me: Just where the hell was mistress whatever-her-name any-by-God-how?

Chapter 2

Dawn till Dusk, 4 October

When I forswore going off half-cocked and did a little thinking, I conceded that my missing female hadn't shown a hindering lack of brains during our flight from the redsticks. She would, therefore, pursue the course of action most likely to protect her from harm, that being to put as much distance twixt herself and the enemy as fast as possible. And the best route for that was due south along the river trace on which I stood, the opposite direction the savages had been traveling.

The moon tailed off to the west. The first gray fingers of morning fog poked among the willows. I checked the priming in the firing pan of my flintlock, lined out the extra horses, mounted Blue and, keeping an alert eye on my back trail, set off due south my ownself.

I watched left and right as well as ahead, and it didn't prove any great chore to locate mistress whatever-her-name. It was that fancy white satiny shirt that fixed her location for me. Hell's bells, it had probably appeared bright as a five-candle lanthorn to the redsticks during our moonlit rush to rejoin Hardy.

That notion pinked my dander nicely, and I deliberately rode past the large beech trunk from behind which part of a billowy white sleeve protruded. As I anticipated, she came charging after me once she was certain who I was.

"Whoa up, mister! Whoa now!"

Though no less concerned than before that the savages might be hot on our trail, I nevertheless didn't get in any hurry reining to a halt. I turned slowly in the saddle and, bless me, she was already within a yard of Blue's rump. She stopped beside my stirrup, and let me tell you, in the yellow tinge of the emerging dawn, her beauty, seen for the first time full blown, dampened my anger powerfully quick.

The braided pigtail so dark in the night hung from hair no red sunset could match for brilliance. And if her hair didn't freeze a man's gaze, the features below it certainly would have. High cheekbones lightly dusted with freckles and arching brows framed eyes blue as the summer sky after a clearing rain. A finely bridged nose flared outward above lips full and nearly as afire as her hair, and skin as delicate and unlined as that of her cheekbones covered the slant of her tanned jaw and slightly square chin.

The balance of her also passed muster with plenty to spare. Substantial breasts bowed the front of her shirt. The span of her waist didn't exceed what both my hands could circle, while the girth of her hips rivaled that of her chest. At her nether end, past the full-length breeches encasing her legs, slim ankles disappeared into beaded moccasins.

It didn't sway my opinion any that the sleeve of her shirt was frayed at the seam or that the garment showed much wear and considerable abuse. Neither did the bagginess of her breeches, which indicated they might have once belonged to someone else. She was, to quote Tap Jacobs, a female of such uncommon beauty she could, without trying overly much, have you talking to yourself while you drowned in your own drool.

Not me, I vowed silently. I spoke before I felt my lips getting wet of their own accord. Besides, much as I was enjoying it, we couldn't spend the morning staring at each other. "You got a name?"

My gruffness wrung a frown from her. "Green. Erin Green," she answered, defiance edging her voice. She wasn't about to be bullied. "And who might you be?"

"Ethan Downer," I informed her. "Where do you hail from?"

My lack of manners didn't set well with her, but I was mighty anxious to get moving. "I was taken near Fort Hamilton."

"Good. I'm bound there with what's left of my horse string. I'll see you home."

"Oh, I'm not from this part of the country. My family's traveling with General St. Clair's army."

"That's even better. These horses," I said with a sweep of the arm behind me, "or what's left of them, were Kentucky-bought for the general's officers. Where's the sorrel you rode off astride?"

"Tied in the trees where I hid him."

"He pull up lame on yuh?"

"No," she responded. "I saw no reason to run him to death and leave myself afoot."

I couldn't argue the sense of that. She was obviously no stranger to horses. "Get your sorrel an' we'll make tracks on down the trace."

Her brow furrowed deeper than before. "That's the opposite direction of the fort! Why that direction?"

My face grew hot. I wasn't accustomed to women challenging me as to the best means of fleeing Injuns, no matter how beautiful the female. "There's a heap fewer savages to treat with if we travel south, that's why."

Her eyes bored into mine as they had in the dark last night. "The Shawnee won't stay after me. They took me 'cause my red hair fascinated one of them. His fellows fussed, but my admirer must have been in command. He glared good and hard at them, and they tied me on a horse and away we went. Now that you've freed me, I doubt they'll persist in chasing after me. They were pushing those stolen horses mighty fast."

I leaned my face closer to hers. "Since you've already got everythin' figured to the nubbin, what should we do next, Colonel Green?"

She returned my slight full bore. "Well, Private Downer, we might wait here for an hour or two till the Shawnee carry off their dead and drive their stolen stock west of the river. Then we can travel north past Dunlap Station, the shortest route to Fort Hamilton. We could be there by dark, we don't malinger."

"Sounds as if you know this country. Or is it just what you've overheard?"

"My mother and I were aboard one of the boats that ferried the lumber up the Miami to complete the fort. That was just two weeks ago."

I studied on what she'd said. For a girl, she reasoned right fine, whether I liked the idea or not. She had sand in her craw, this one did. She showed not the slightest blush or hesitation when it came to speaking her mind. And she had a temper best left unprovoked.

Damnation, I hated backing water a single finger length. But if we waited for the Shawnee to clear out as she suggested and went north, she'd be safely home at her mother's fire by nightfall . . . and out of my hair.

I straightened in the saddle. "All right, we'll risk the Injuns following us and have a go at it your way. I'm near to starved, anyhow. I'll fetch the sorrel and tend to the animals. You'll find victuals in the saddlebags of Hardy's dun mare."

With neither the haughty gloat nor gleeful smile of triumph I expected, Mistress Erin Green nodded politely and walked down the line of horses to the mare. Being male through and through, I couldn't help but take serious notice how smoothly her hips moved, even in those baggy pants. Fortunately, I took after the missing sorrel before she spied my gaping mouth or I fell off Blue and declared myself a total fool. She could put a sweat on a man like no woman I'd ever seen or heard tell of. She made those handsome Carroll twins from beyond our ridge look like woods hogs covered with warts.

Dawn light slanted through red and yellow leaves. A light breeze curled the morning fog in gray swirls low to the ground. The air smelled of rain, same as yesterday morning. I led the horses through a narrow break in the bank willows and watered each in turn, flintlock clutched in off hand throughout. Watering completed, I tied the remainder of the string in the order they would travel. Then I let myself think of victuals.

Mistress Green, wrapped in a woolen blanket from either the night gear of Hardy or myself, was seated atop a fallen sycamore. She clutched the muslin sack in which Hardy toted his trail mixture of parched corn and lumpy brown sugar. Her jaws were grinding away with a seriousness that bespoke considerable hunger. My tin canteen rested against her hip on the log, wooden stopper hanging by its cord.

"Pretty tasty, ain't it now? You find the venison jerk, too?"

She reached beside her feet and tossed me the longish leather bag. "I don't believe I've ever been so famished," she observed.

I braced a leg on the sycamore, a position that allowed me to maintain a watch upriver along the narrow path of the trace. I chewed a strip of the smoke-dried meat and helped myself to some water.

The mistress's chewing halted. She swallowed and drank before saying, "I'm afraid I appear ungrateful without meaning to. I'm very sorry your companion was killed over me, and that you had to leave him unburied."

I didn't doubt her sincerity. But mourning over Hardy wouldn't start him breathing again or put him under the ground. And it was too late for any meaningless crying. "Can't nothin' help him now," I concluded.

She flinched at my bluntness, blue eyes softening. "He must have been a very dear friend."

"He was . . . that he was," I admitted, wondering at the ease with which she understood so readily the way it had been with Hardy and me.

I was suddenly afraid of tearing up in front of her. Locking my gaze on the trace, I hastily asked, "How'd the heathen lay their paws on yuh, anyhow?"

She was a while answering, as if she was afraid of embarrassing herself. "I had gone into the woods to see after myself. They jumped me on my return. It was near noon, and nobody would have missed me for a spell. And given the horse and cattle lots that surround the fort, tracking after me would have been a fruitless venture, too much of a miracle for even Mr. Jacobs."

Relieved she had provided something else to talk about, I flashed her a brief smile. "That wouldn't be Tap Jacobs by any chance, would it?"

Her blue eyes sparkled. "It would be if your Mr. Jacobs is completely bald, combs his scruffy beard with his fingers every whipstitch, and can hold a pickle barrel twixt his knees without hardly trying."

She had described the aging border scout perfectly. "It's the same Tap for certain. I bet he sought you out the first day he passed within a half mile of your supper fire."

Erin Green's laugh was cheerful as swift water foaming around rocks in a brook. "Oh, Lordy, but didn't he. My mama warned me your Mr. Jacobs is a hound whose nose never lifts from the scent once he sights a pretty face."

"Has he been too much of a bother?"

"No, not really. Mr. Jacobs would never be insulting, ever. Sergeant Devlin wouldn't allow such a thing."

I sipped more water. Apparently, there were those within St. Clair's camp assigned to watch over Mistress Green. She was, most probably, the daughter of an officer of high rank with his family in tow, and as such, her safety would warrant the detailing of uniformed guards. Which also meant that it was only while answering the call of nature in private and not being guarded that she could have been taken captive. That quirk of fate and how it had eventually resulted in Hardy's death brought my mind back to our present predicament. Much as I was enjoying our early-morning repast, my newly acquired charge was possibly in peril every minute till we drew up before the gates of Fort Hamilton.

"What's ahead of us upriver?"

She picked her words carefully. "Dunlap Station is three miles from here. The station's deserted, has been since last January when the settlers withdrew to North Bend on the Ohio. Beyond the station, there's nothing but empty river bottom till we gain the fort."

"How far is Fort Hamilton?" I asked, wanting to confirm the distances Hardy and I had obtained in Kentucky were accurate.

Again, Mistress Green pondered before speaking. "Our boat captain counted off nine miles from the station to the fort. But that was by water. He talked endlessly of an Injun path bordering the river along the eastern bank, where we stand, that shortened those nine miles considerably."

The question leapt from my mouth like an unanticipated spit. "Captain was a mighty friendly sort, I take it?"

My nosiness perturbed her. A puffing of her cheeks preceded a lengthy sigh. "It was very hot while we were ascending the river. Sharing the cabin roof with Amos Stoddard was decidedly cooler." Her head shook slowly. "As if I have to explain myself to you."

I had me a calming sigh of my own. She had tolerated my poor manners from the beginning, and I didn't need to foster trouble for Paw with any of General St. Clair's officers, regardless of their rank. I vowed I would henceforth abide by my mother's teaching: It cost nothing to be a gentleman in the company of ladies, and to act otherwise diminished not only the man but also his upbringing.

Mistress Green didn't appear put out that no apology was forthcoming on my part. The corners of her ripe lips did twitch, howsomever, hinting at a grin, as I suggested in a quieter, more respectful tone, "If you're through dining, I believe we best be under way."

She came to her feet and peered in the direction of the horses, obviously appraising the bunch of them. "If we must flee, I want as much animal as possible beneath me. Would you please switch the dun mare's saddle to the sorrel?"

Admiring her knack for taking advantage of what was available to her, it was a chore I did gladly. When I led the freshly saddled sorrel forward, she was standing with the blanket she had commandeered tied 'round her shoulders. "I filled the canteen at the river and split the victuals equally twixt the cloth and leather bags in the event we are separated for any reason," she announced, gifting me with the heavier leather pouch. "I'll tote the canteen. You're not armed; it's not wise to kneel over water anywheres."

My only wonderment at her actions regarded the blanket wrapping her upper body, but I came to appreciate that as we started north along the Miami. Thickening cloud blotted out the sun, and the breeze possessed the sharp bite common to early autumn. The day would grow no warmer, and rain was surely in the offing, rendering horseback travel pure misery if your garments became wet and the wind blew cold and constant.

The first few drops of rain commenced falling as we drew cautiously upon the scene of the ambush the previous night . . . and Hardy's remains. I spent a half hour scouting our surroundings before determining no Injuns were baiting a trap with the body. On my orders, Mistress Green, a flap of her makeshift blanket coat now hooding her fiery hair, retained her seat atop the sorrel and continued the watch all about.

Hardy had been scalped and robbed of weapons and accoutrements. Some might have left him to rot on the dank earth and seen solely to their ownselves. But I wasn't cold enough of heart for that, thank you. I rooted my arms under his limb-flopping frame and carted him to where the willows grew thin, scooped a lean hole in the sandy loam with a flat slab of stone, and covered him with layers of dirt, rock, and driftwood. It was a damn shabby grave for a damn fine friend, and despite my resolve to the contrary, I sobbed through the most of it and particularly during the prayer I mumbled over the shallow mound at the finish. I left a hunk of myself in that grave with Hardy, yet I never believed it was enough to atone for my having triggered his demise.

A somber Erin Green acknowledged neither my blubbering nor my tearstained cheeks. At my simple statement that I would shortly be ready to proceed with our journey, she discovered an undeniable urge to eyeball the horses whose lead rope she fisted, granting me a couple of unwatched minutes. I dried my face with a sleeve, primed the pan of my rifle with fresh powder, tied a cow-knee cover over the lock, plugged the weapon's barrel with a carved round of cork, mounted Blue, and off we went.

It proved a wet, gray, miserable morning. The rain started and stopped, matching the fitful breeze. We forded the Blue Rock and stuck to the bank of the Miami the three miles to Dunlap Station. The river circled westward in a giant horseshoe bend, and we cut across the shoe's open end, a course that brought us close by the abandoned settlement's main gate. Weeds swayed in the empty entryway.

The stockade itself, a partial square of cabins anchored by three blockhouses, had garnered criticism from troops assigned to garrison duty there. After observing hounds leap from stumps to the outward-sloping roofs of the individual cabins, claw upward, and jump down inside the picketed walls, alarmed officers had raised the specter of painted Shawnee doing the same. The gaps left in the picketed walls connecting the cabins and blockhouses by sloppy erection had worried officer and soldier alike.

But for all the military protests, these supposed weaknesses hadn't fostered the station's abandonment. The heavily maligned stockade had withstood a full-scale Injun attack 10 January 17 and 91. It was the loss of seventy-five cattle and fifteen hundred bushels of corn outside the pickets that had forced the settlers to concede they couldn't survive so far above the Ohio till the redstick threat was thwarted forever.

We regained the Miami on the opposite point of the horseshoe bend. Rain soaked my hat brim and shoulders. I ignored the discomfort and forged northward at a brisk, unrelenting pace. We could offer so little defense if attacked, I risked an ambush to make the most of the daylight.

We forded what Mistress Green said was Banklick Creek, and the river angled to the northwest. At her insistence, we angled northeast and located without undue delay the Injun trail Amos Stoddard had boasted about during her earlier boat trip. The pathway was no wider than the width of my stirrups but easy to follow since moccasin-clad feet and the hooves of reined as well as wild animals, all marching single file, had beaten its surface bare of growth.

It was well into the afternoon before I heard another peep from my female companion. "Mr. Downer," she called. "I must dismount and stretch my legs, and we must talk."

That wasn't unreasonable, what with the horses needing a blow, too. I chose to halt when the pathway dipped through an oval glade overshot with tall grasses. Once their lead ropes were lengthened, the horses lipped at the rain-moistened shoots with vigor. The mistress walked back and forth till the stiffness from hours in the saddle no longer cramped her lower body. Then she was ready to palaver with me.

"We should swing to the east now, soon as we see the Miami," she proclaimed with conviction.

"And why would that be?" I inquired, sipping water from the canteen she shared with me.

"Captain Stoddard said his Injun trail ran afoul of bogs and thick vines hanging from trees when it met the Miami again a few miles from the fort. He claimed the fastest way there was to turn east and travel the military road the general's army built on their march from the Ohio."

There wasn't any refuting what she proposed. She had so far remembered correctly everything the captain had told her, and I wanted to gain Fort Hamilton as quickly as she did. Beyond the Injuns, in the absence of hard frosts to date, Hardy and I had spent the previous night trying to sleep while we swatted mosquitoes like mad. I shook my head and blew air, recalling Hardy's tall complaint that the skeeters along the Miami had wings big as hawks and could bite damn near as fierce. It would be right fine to spend the evening where it was safe enough from the redsticks to let the smoke of a fire keep winged night creatures at bay.

My headshaking misled the mistress. "You doubt my word?"

"No, not at all," I answered, then drew a laugh from her, repeating the story of Hardy and the mosquitoes. "And if we don't want to be carried off in the dark by those bloody buggers," I continued, "it's time to hurry along. If you need to visit the woods, do so, and we'll go hunt up General St. Clair's road."

Two miles to the east we popped from the trees onto the general's road. Fifty feet in width, the rough track had been cleared by hand axes, and tree stumps, shortened just enough to allow wagon axles to pass over them, littered the brown mud of its bed. Cut timber bridged minor watercourses and the occasional spot of low, marshy ground. For the faster travel it permitted, the whole of the road was more dangerous to a horse's legs than Captain Stoddard's Injun trail.

Picking a path through and around the lurking stumps, we pushed north without exchanging words. Mistress Green, riding beside me now, stood in her stirrups occasionally, anxiously scanning the horizon. I could sense her excitement at how near she was to her home fire and the company of those who loved her, a far turnabout from a few hours ago.

It struck me then how much I would miss her company. But we were, in truth, an unlikely pairing thrown together for a brief while by pure chance. Erin Green was the daughter of an officer and I the son of a trader supplying the army. We belonged at opposite ends of the general's camp, and I couldn't imagine her not having numerous suitors of greater standing and means than Ethan Downer. And even if I could screw up the necessary courage to call on her, I wasn't in the habit of courting disappointment.

Though the breeze held steady, the rain had fizzled out, not that it mattered much, for we were soaked through to the skin. The afternoon light was growing dull when we spied black smoke against the gray sky. The mistress thumped the sorrel's flanks with her heels and coaxed the riding stock into a faster walk. She surged ahead of Blue and topped the swelling rise separating us from our destination.

I knew from her sudden backward tug on the sorrel's reins that all was not as she expected. Blue drew abreast of her, and I had no difficulty discerning what was wrong. A prairie meadow of flattened grass hundreds of acres in length and width extended from the base of the rise below us to the Miami. On the closest bank of the river squatted the massive Fort Hamilton, an irregular stockade sporting four bastions and enclosing within its log walls a barracks for a hundred soldiers and numerous storehouses.

The meadow and the fort were as Mistress Green had anticipated. It was the emptiness of the vast meadow that caught her by surprise. Rowed tents, parked wagons, picketed horses, herded cattle, countless cooking fires, and perimeter guard details should have filled it end to end. That was, if St. Clair's army had still been encamped in and about the fort.

The mistress slumped in her saddle.

"Damn it, they're gone," she cried. "They're gone!"

Chapter 3

Early Evening, 4 October

Tossing me the lead rope of the horse string, the mistress kicked the sorrel into a gallop, descended the slope of the rise, and raced for Fort Hamilton's main gate, which was at the moment hard shut. I followed at a walk, marveling at the sheer size of what St. Clair's soldiers had built. The structure before me dwarfed Dunlap Station, even Kenton's below Limestone. Without a precise count, I guessed the doubled row of pickets forming the five walls of the irregular square, each exceeding fifteen feet in height, numbered two thousand. The sweat and toil expended to fell, trim, and drag the thick posts into position with oxen, then stand them in place in freshly dug trenches in just two weeks, numbed the mind. And all the while, still others were fetching additional logs in the same manner and laying the walls of the bastions, the barracks, and the storehouses. It seemed likely the general's forces, exhausted as they surely had to be, were glad to return to the less arduous chore of going on the march in hopes of finding some redsticks to fight. Carrying a musket beat the wielding of an ax every day of the week.

The gate of the fort cracked open with me still thirty yards away. Loud voices perked my ears, and I rode upon a most unusual scene. A pimply-jawed guard wearing the unadorned uniform of an infantry private was arguing with the mistress. "Don't give me any of yer sass, Erin Green. The whole army marched this morning an' yer maw was right behind 'em liken she an' the rest of her kind always be."

The red spreading on the mistress's cheeks matched that of her hair. "Rupert Lawson, you mind your tongue or Sergeant Devlin will cut it plumb from your miserable mouth, I swear!"

"Not anytime soon, he won't, an' maybe he'll be back an' maybe he won't," the private countered. "So I'll say again, thar ain't no need to bring any officer runnin' to answer the fool questions of Molly Green's daughter."

Gate guard and female stared like fighting bull elk preparing their next lunge at each other. There was much here I didn't know, an antagonism twixt the two of them lingering from some past disagreement. Rupert Lawson's neck was stiff as that of a spurned lover, and the mistress would never forgive his public sullying of her mother, whatever the cause or reason. Believing it a dispute they couldn't settle by themselves, I intervened, but carefully. I didn't intend to interfere with a soldier doing his duty and perhaps spend the night under arrest.

A light jab of my heels, and Blue stepped alongside the sorrel. "Good evening, Private Lawson."

For the first time, he acknowledged my presence. He pivoted on his heel and squared his shoulders in my direction, musket slanted across his chest. "And who might yuh be? Kentucky militia?"

It was a solid guess on his part. The boys from south of the Ohio joining St. Clair's campaign were prone to dress similar to mine—flop-brimmed hat, walnut-dyed hunting frock, full-length woolen breeches, leather leggins, and center-seam moccasins, as well as weapons—either long-barreled rifle or musket. And every solitary Kentuckian despised walking if any animal with four legs was available.

"No, I'm not militia," I responded. "I'm Ethan Downer, and these horses are for General St. Clair's staff."

The private's lips curled in a smug grin. "Yuh wouldn't be kin to Caleb Downer, the trader who supplied us them axes that bent up like dumplings, would yuh now?"

I bit my tongue enough it hurt. Rupert Lawson was pushing the bounds of discourtesy to the edge of the cliff. I shifted my weight in the saddle, waiting while my flaring temper winked out. Once I had as tight a grip on it as I did on Blue's reins, I spoke in a firm, even voice. "Private, till late last night, this young lady was held captive by the Injuns. In freeing her, I lost my best friend and six horses. I've already said these remaining horses are for General St. Clair's staff, and since we've ridden all day in the rain to get here, perhaps you'd better summon your commanding officer."

The cocky surliness slowly drained from Rupert Lawson's features. He licked his lips, debating if he dared risk delaying the delivery of riding stock intended for officers traveling in person with General St. Clair. The threat of discipline came to the fore, overshadowing his row with the mistress. With a nod of the head, he spun about and sang out, "Riders at the gate. Inform Ensign Young, please. Hurry now!"

Beside me, my traveling companion whispered, "That's grand. Andy will tell us what we want to know straight out."

While we waited for the corporal, I watched her out of the corner of my eye and thought back on how Rupert Lawson had besmirched a certain Molly Green. He had said the mistress's mother was traveling behind the army "liken she and the rest of her kind always be." The private's statement hadn't exactly portrayed Molly Green as wife to any commissioned officer, for they never allowed their wives and offspring to traipse upcountry beyond the last secure outpost on the frontier, which was most assuredly Fort Hamilton. I noted again the fraying shirt and oversized breeches of the mistress. Her clothing wasn't that of an officer's daughter, either. Who was Erin Green? Better yet, who was her father? And why had she not mentioned his name and rank as a means of putting Private Lawson in his place from the very beginning?

My rumination ceased with the rap of leather soles inside the stockade. A new infantryman, the single silver epaulette of an ensign sewn on his left shoulder, stepped through the gate, and Rupert Lawson snapped to attention.

The private was forgotten the instant the newcomer spied Erin Green. He removed his tricorn hat and bowed from the waist. He was almost breathless with excitement. "Erin, thank God you're alive and safe. Your mother and Sergeant Devlin feared you were dead . . . or worse off."

I had but once before seen a man truly and totally enamored with a female, that being my father and his love for my mother, so I was no stranger to the sincere warmth of

Ensign Andy Young's smile. He wasn't much older than I, but he would without question gladly lay down his own life for Erin Green. "Good gosh, is that your teeth I hear chattering? You must come inside and warm yourself at our fire!"

The mistress, wrapping her arms about herself against the late-afternoon chill, returned his smile. "That's most kind, Andy. But I must rejoin my mother. Did the army march yesterday or today?"

Andy Young sighed, his disappointment most obvious. "General Butler led them off just this morning. They won't have gotten far the other side of the Miami, but it was take up the march or watch the horses and cattle die from lack of forage."

"Then perhaps if you can spare me a dry blanket for a wrap, Mr. Downer here," the mistress said, waving a hand at me, "who saved me from the Injuns, will escort me home yet tonight."

Ensign Young's curious brown eyes locked onto mine. "I'm most grateful for your rescue of Erin. Do you have business with the army, sir?"

"Yes, sir, I do," I answered, glancing at Rupert Lawson. "My paw is Caleb Downer, the trader, and as I told your guard, I purchased these animals in Kentucky for General St. Clair's staff. I lost six to the redsticks, but I'm fetching these four to Paw anyways."

"Private, please obtain a fresh blanket from the quartermaster. Tell him I will settle accounts with him later," Ensign Young ordered crisply. "Be quick before the lady freezes."

Rupert Lawson saluted and hustled through the gate, shoes slipping and sliding in the muddy opening in his haste. Erin Green slid from the sorrel's saddle in a graceful dismount, stepped before the corporal, raised on her toes, and kissed his cheek. "Thank you, Andy. You are a generous and faithful friend."

The ensign's blush was genuine. If I wasn't mistaken, a frown of disappointment, lasting only a finger snap, marred his features. Andy Young wanted to be much more than a friend to the mistress. Hell's damnation, I was feeling the same urges my ownself, and I hadn't known her long enough for us to call each other by first name. I leaned and spat quiet as I could. Less'n you kept her at arm's length, Molly Green's lovely daughter could be as unnerving as a rash too embarrassing to itch.

His grip lingering on Erin Green's elbow, the ensign said, "You'll have no trouble locating the column. The cattle bringing up the rear didn't pass from our sight till just two hours ago."

I then asked a question of utmost importance to me, a query spawned by Rupert Lawson's earlier pronouncement that trader Caleb Downer had supplied the army with shoddy equipment. "Did my father also march this morning?"

The ensign spoke in return without hesitation. "No, he did not. But neither is he within the stockade. He went south with General St. Clair five days ago. We are in dire need of axes that are properly tempered and powder honestly dry in the keg for the cannon."

The ensign did hesitate now and cleared his throat noisily. "I'm not one to speak ill of any man, but my fellow officers are plumb furious with your father and his superior, William Duer, the contractor. Supposedly, a gentleman named Court Starnes, Duer's partner from Fort Pitt, is meeting your father at Fort Washington with additional packhorses and replacement supplies for those we found defective. I'm giving you fair warning that your name may spark trouble for you across the Miami."

I took no exception to Andy Young's accusations regarding Paw, for it is the errant fool who argues without bothering to learn the whole story. On my mind, too, was the realization that if Paw was ensnared in personal difficulties, trying to successfully explain to him how I had gotten Hardy killed and lost costly riding stock had about as much appeal as enduring a Shawnee scalping. Paw's tongue could cut deep as any Injun knife, even when he was in fine spirits. And though maybe you couldn't see them on my skin, I had the scars on my heart to prove it.

I dipped my hat at the ensign. "I thank you for the warning. I'll not be taken unawares."

The mistress's gaze centered solely on me. I believe she expected me to vehemently defend Paw then and there as she would have her kin, and was at a loss how I could calmly allow the ensign's charges to go uncontested. But much as I wanted to speak out on Paw's behalf, my hair not being fiery red, I stuck to my decision. Tap Jacobs, who I would soon join, would tell me the truth of the situation regarding Paw and contractor Duer.

Private Lawson slipped and slid into view once more. The ensign waited while Erin Green mounted the sorrel before handing her the clean, dry blanket fetched by the private. Then he offered some counsel about our upcoming ride. "Take care treating with the sentries. They greatly fear the redsticks and, excuse my language, shoot at everything from the hoot of an owl to their own farts. Sing out well in advance, and make them respond so there are no misunderstandings. With any luck you should reach them before full dark sets in."

Tap Jacobs having taught me hunters that trusted to luck were often buried first, I nodded at Ensign Andy Young and guided Blue around the upriver corner of the fort, the mistress and the sorrel trailing behind the horse string.

The Miami was a river known for its long stretches of treacherous, sandy bottom, and it was the presence of a rare and extensive layer of stone on its bed that had decided the location of Fort Hamilton. The swift water flowed waist high on a walking man, short of the knee if you were mounted. Blue disliked the fetlock-deep mud beaten and pounded into clinging goo by the cattle that had crossed after the infantry, but he answered a slap of the reins on his haunch and forged ahead into the current. At the middle of the river, I peeked over my shoulder in the dwindling daylight and chuckled at the nimbleness of the mistress. She was far up in the saddle, legs practically around the sorrel's neck, her entire body safe from another wetting.

Blue struggled through another morass of goo on the far bank. There was no problem trailing after St. Clair's regiments. A raw gouge twenty feet wide newly cleared of trees and brush by the general's ax men, and littered with runny dollops of cow dung, straggled northeast along the base of the hills flanking the river. At the first significant break in those flanking hills, the gouge twisted to the northwest like a tortured snake. At that juncture, splotches of dancing flame pinpointed the night fires of the army in the growing darkness.

I slowed Blue, and heeding Ensign Young's warning, pried the plug from the barrel of my rifle, untied the lock cover, and thrust the both of them into the center fold or wallet of my frock. Besides their jumpiness, if I had to give my name and Paw's supposed failures fostered resentment among the sentries, I wanted to be ready for whatever might befall me.

The smell of rain-soaked cow hair and manure was assailing our noses when the challenge rang from the trees bordering the roadway. "Stop! Who rides there?"

I halted Blue, and right thumb on the dog's head of my rifle, answered, "Ethan Downer!"

"State your business an' be damn quick about it!"

"I'm delivering horses to General St. Clair's personal staff."

"Hold tight to yer reins till we close on yuh, yuh don't want to be shot off 'n that animal," the hidden sentry bawled.

Two privates, muskets fully cocked, marched from the woods, trailed by a sergeant, the yellow epaulettes decorating each of his shoulders bright as new gold. I sat rigidly still in the saddle, taking pains to do nothing unusual or threatening.

The privates braced Blue's shoulders. "He did say his name was Downer, didn't he, Sergeant Croft?" the lanky one queried.

"That he did, Eyler, that he did," confirmed the stubby sergeant, giant black mustache bobbing on his upper lip.

"S'pose he's kin to Caleb Downer, the son of a bitch who bought these worthless goddamn shoes an' foisted them on us Maryland levies?" persisted the lanky private.

Butting his musket in the mud of the roadway, the private balanced on his left foot, raised the other level with his knee, and pointed downward with his free hand. The sole of his shoe had parted with its leather uppers and was prevented from flopping about by rawhide thongs that wrapped the entire foot. I suspected the filthy gray object the size and shape of my thumb sticking from twixt shoe bottom and shoe top was a sock-covered toe.

The lanky private's fellow sentry then demanded, "Well, are you kin to Caleb Downer? Speak up!"

I didn't want a confrontation with either the sentries or their sergeant any more than I had with Rupert Lawson earlier, but my patience was ebbing. My father wasn't a cheat. To my knowledge, he had never taken unfair advantage in any exchange of monies or goods, no matter how rough the bargaining. My hackles were on the verge of bristling up right handsomely. On any given evening, a son could forbear only so many of what he knew to be lies about his paw.

There came a rough push against my knee as the sorrel carrying the mistress crowded against Blue. I started but held tongue and hand, for the mistress would now be in the thick of any dispute with those accosting me. "Sergeant Croft, it's me, Erin, Molly Green's daughter!"

Behind the sentries, the sergeant's brow shot upward and his huge mustache quivered. "My God, girl, it's all over our camp that the Injuns got you, and then here you be. Stand at ease, gentlemen, stand at ease," he commanded, pushing his stubby frame to the forefront.

I could only silently shake my head in wonder. In an army that numbered nigh onto two thousand, was there no officer that Erin Green and her mother didn't know?

With her appearance, Paw's alleged transgressions suddenly amounted to no more than a spit into the wind. The privates, grins bright and wide despite broken and missing teeth, stepped aside for the sergeant, who doffed his tricorn and did everything but salute the mistress. "And how were you freed, lass?"

"Mr. Downer snatched me from the saddle in the middle of the Injuns in the dead of night," she explained. "His friend was killed, but Mr. Downer and I escaped unhurt. I owe him my very life."

Sergeant Croft's head bobbed repeatedly, and his underlings stared at me in openmouthed awe. These two Maryland lads had nervously cocked their muskets before they knew whether I was friend or foe, and given how they couldn't quit gaping at me, I had a notion they had never once to date even seen a painted Injun in the flesh. Paw's last letter had mentioned the utter inexperience of General St. Clair's six-month levies, how they were so raw their brief bouts of target practice were a danger not only to themselves but to anyone else within shooting range. The blunt truth was an unintentional bullet from your own killed as thoroughly as a deliberate one from the enemy.

The prospect that additional sentries no better trained or experienced than the Maryland levies were stationed about prompted me to overlook what had been insinuated about Paw. "It will be dark soon, Sergeant Croft. Can you direct us to Mistress Green's family?"

The eager-to-serve sergeant pointed ahead and to the right. "Those not in uniform are beyond the cattle herd, in the woods separating our two roads."

"Two roads?" asked a puzzled Erin Green.

"Yes, young lady, we're building two roads. The men hate it, but General St. Clair insists," the sergeant informed her. "The general says a spread advance allows us to avert an ambush and form into line of battle on short notice. And if that don't rile the men enough, we're throwing up breastworks for defense at the end of each day. It promises to be a nasty drudge of a march, lass."

"I can only keep the tea hot for you, Sergeant. Do find your way to our fire whenever you can," she offered, glancing my way. "If you're ready, Mr. Downer."

At my nod, she took the lead as the sentries stepped to the edge of the forest, granting us a clear path of departure. Grazing bullocks occupied the roadway and its immediate borders, and we proceeded at a slow walk. Deep shadows pooled at the fringe of the forest, and though we saw drovers, no new challenges greeted us. We aimed for the nearest flames to our right and encountered a squad of artillery soldiers and their captain resting about an unhitched field piece. The mistress, of course, was acquainted with the officer, and after the now-obligatory explanation of her rescue, the captain directed us into the trees behind the cannon.

With a jaunty wave of thanks, Erin Green skirted the artillery campsite, me following with the horse string. I had no real obligation to guard her till she was lodged in her mother's very arms, yet I reckoned someone at the Green fire was privy to the whereabouts of Tap Jacobs, and if not

Tap, then another in Paw's pay, Bear Watkins. Equally important was how a particular redheaded female constantly roused my curiosity and kept my blood churning. I couldn't forgo the opportunity to meet her kin, nosiree.

But one must never forget that rampant curiosity makes for a treacherous ally: It can uncover the favorable as well as what you might later wish you hadn't learned.

Chapter 4

Late Evening, 4 October

A passel of cooking fires burned brightly within hailing distance of each other, casting streaks of flickering orange onto tall trunks and clumps of low brush. Beyond the fires, it was black as pitch in every direction. The mistress halted the sorrel and called out her mother's name, then her own. A second calling garnered a lusty response of, "Here, girl! Here we be!"

A hatted figure greatly bowed in the legs advanced from the largest of the night fires. Well, so much for my having to worry about locating Tap Jacobs. The mistress, squealing with joy, dismounted and scampered deeper into the trees. Anxious as I was to meet her folks, I stayed put and saw to the stock according to Paw and Tap's teaching.

The gurgling sweep of running water drifted from upwind. Tiredness cramping my legs soon as I stepped down, I led my string thataway, circling left of the sudden yelling and shouting occasioned by the safe return of Molly Green's missing daughter. I watered each horse in turn, unsaddled Blue and the sorrel, then hobbled all but Blue, who I picketed on a length of rope tied about his off foreleg. If the others started to wander overly far in search of forage, the fussy Blue would resist being left behind and protest enough to awaken me.

Standing on the creek bank, I could discern a large number of glowing fires to the north and the west. The army had halted astride the stream, providing water for men and animals. The air was cold and damp, the harsh chill of it promising light frost within a few days, if not by dawn. I shivered and hefted my rifle and sleeping gear. The long, hard ride was finished, and it was time to warm my bones and fill my belly. I figured Molly Green owed me at least one good sitting for my troubles.

A sizable crowd ringed the fire of the Green family. As I came closer, it was evident the attention of everyone was centered on the mistress, who appeared to be holding court, Andy Young's blanket still wrapped 'round her shoulders. Her listeners constituted as wide a selection of human folk as I had ever witnessed except for my sparse visits to the wharf at Limestone. Uniformed officers of the volunteer levies and the Second American Regiment, buckskin-clad wagoners and ox team handlers, and public men in cloth and linsey-woolsey and high boots listened raptly to what Erin Green was saying. Scattered among them were the women— young, fully grown, middling tall, short, skinny, plump, fair, and bedraggled, most dressed in calico skirts and woven shawls, a few in full-length pants and coarse-hewn shirts. Least obvious but present were twenty-odd children, one so young it was suckling its mother's breast.

An older woman of similar red hair and stature stood slightly behind the mistress. Except for the difference in age, the likeness was so great it could only be her mother. A stout sergeant of the Second American Regiment with a trimmed black beard and oft-broken nose flanked Molly Green's left shoulder. On her right, standing at ease and listening with cocked head, was a clean-shaven captain of dragoons.

Even from a distance, the crispness and flair of the captain's uniform arrested the eye of the beholder. His waist-length, skirted coat of dark blue wool faced with red covered a white linen vest. Neither coat nor undergarment showed nary a spot of dirt or the first wrinkle. The same was true of the white pantaloons that stretched downward to black dragoon boots whose silver spurs sparkled in the light of the fire. The metal buttons of his black neck stock glistened just as brightly. And atop his head rested a billed helmet adorned with a most sensational cockade. Unlike the cockades of plain round leather I had seen on officers in the past at Limestone, the captain's displayed a white core surrounded by circles of light blue, then dark blue. I would later learn the

entire insignia had been sewn from individual loops of dyed
silk. If one hadn't known the contrary, you would have sworn
the captain was but a step removed from the shop of the
finest military tailor east of the Alleghenies.

The hard rap on my arm nearly broke that limb above the
elbow. The rumbling voice that sounded following the blow
was as familiar as that of Tap Jacobs. "That red hair, high
cheekbones, an' fine shape has every jackanapes for a hundred miles in the rut, they truly do, Ethan."

Bear Watkins's blunt remark bore the mistress no malice
or personal rebuke. He was, as usual, describing exactly what
he saw with neither frills nor omissions. He wrapped a
thickly muscled arm about me and squeezed heartily by way
of greeting as he had since my oldest memory. "An' from
what she's telling, lad, you're quite the hero."

I looked amid overhanging brows, flattened nose, and
abundant beard and found not the tiniest glint of humor in
Bear's eyes. He winked and gave me a second hug. "Tap's
gonna be damn jealous, don't yuh know."

The last thing I wanted was for my chance rescue of Erin
Green to cause discord twixt the scout and me. But before I
could express that sentiment to Bear Watkins, Tap spotted
me from where he knelt beside the mistress. He rose and
pointed me out, shouting, "By all that's holy, here be our
hero, come for to receive the glory due him. Step forward,
Ethan, step forward!"

There was no running or hiding. There was nothing I
could do except hang onto my rifle and gear and march
through the cheering crowd. I guessed some might not be so
delighted once they learned I was Caleb Downer's son. I
could only hope that might somehow happen later.

Tap's moon-shaped countenance, with its cleanly shaven
upper lip and whiskered jaws, creased into a grin. He
pounded my shoulder, the fringe on the sleeve of his doeskin
frock bouncing and jumping. "I'm godawful proud of you,
an' Erin's mother surely desires to thank you."

New cheers erupted when the mistress motioned me
closer. Not certain what to expect, and nervous as a convert
who hadn't yet learned his prayers, I found enough of my
manners to remove my hat without dropping my flintlock.

The mistress smelled out my hesitation, clasped my forearm, and pulled me alongside her. "Mother doesn't bite," she murmured.

Molly Green's smile would have warmed a heart of stone, for even the deep lines at the corners of her eyes and mouth, lines like those of my mother's face, softened. Though her calico dress was faded and much worn, and her woolen shawl snagged here and there, she gave the impression she was greeting you at the entryway of a grand public hall rather than before an open fire in the middle of the Ohio wilderness. "Young man, I'm in your debt," she said, extending a callused hand. "I will be eternally grateful for your bravery."

I squeezed her fingers gently and managed a stiff bow that amounted to a quick dipping of head and shoulders. Despite the fluttery feeling of my innards and the big crowd watching and waiting, I somehow spoke without tripping over my tongue. "I was headed thisaway anyhow . . . ma'am."

My response, honestly and humbly wrought, tickled the fancy of all those listening, and the resulting uproar lasted a full minute. If anyone missed what I had said, his neighbor was most happy to repeat it at the top of his lungs. I had no way of knowing it that night, but my five words would be repeated around campfires and in front of tavern hearths for years to come. I would thank the Lord more than once that he hadn't allowed me to act the blithering fool and spout something I had to live down the rest of my days.

None laughed and carried on any harder or longer than the broken-nosed, black-bearded soldier at Molly Green's left elbow. He now offered his hand. "Well enough lad, and will you accept the thanks of me ownself, Sergeant Torrance Devlin, Second American Regulars?"

I walked the safer path this go-round, returning the sergeant's firm grasp with a polite nod and venturing nothing with my tongue. I was grateful the mistress then interceded, for I was at a loss as to what was expected of me in the ensuing silence. She looked sharply at the soldier flanking Molly Green opposite Sergeant Devlin. "And will you not put forth your hand also, Miles?"

The dragoon officer in the nearly spotless and wrinkle-

free uniform drew to his full height and knuckled his forehead instead. "Captain Miles Starkweather at your service,
sir," he announced. "I congratulate you on your rescue of
Erin. Many, including me, are envious of the feat."

A cackling giggle shot from behind Miles Starkweather.
"You bet you be, captain. You want the bold vixen for your
own. Every soul here, if'n they ain't blind, knows that for
chrissake."

Tap Jacobs spun and confronted the speaker. "Careful
what you say, Annie Bower, or you'll sleep in the woods
without a blanket."

"Don't fuss with me, you runt of a woodser. One kiss an'
you'll snuggle up an' keep me warm, no matter where I be!"

A wave of hooting and derisive laughter descended upon
Tap Jacobs. He could only wave a dismissing arm as if he
wasn't the least disturbed at having been bested by a quick-
witted female. Captain Miles Starkweather lacked both Tap's
patience and his tolerance. "It's a sad day when a washer-
woman insults her betters with no fear."

With that, the mistress became riled. "Annie means no
harm, Miles. And remember, if not for Sergeant Devlin,
mother and I would be washing uniforms with her at the
creek every dawn."

I edged backward. I had suffered the attention of strangers
long enough for one evening and wanted no part of any disagreement twixt Erin Green and her supposed suitor. The
savory meal from the mistress's mother I was craving didn't
seem as tempting as it had a short quarter hour ago. Which
just proves that a man can lose his taste for victuals even
though his belly be growling.

But if Erin Green had other designs, escaping her wasn't
easy. She tugged on my sleeve, halting my backward movement. "Stay a while longer, Mr. Downer. You must sup with
us. Please don't refuse."

She laid a neat trap, the mistress did. A refusal of her
offer would be an outright rebuff, and she was trusting I was
mannerly enough not to spurn her openly. I didn't doubt
either that she was counting on her attractiveness to win me
over. And it did, for looking at her across a plate of the
poorest victuals beat jerk and parched corn with Tap and

Bear Watkins every time. Not surprisingly, I was suddenly beset by a ravishing hunger.

"It will be my pleasure, Mistress Green," I said with a firm nod of the head.

With a smile dazzling as sunshine reflecting from a mirror, she wound her arm through mine and led me toward the fire. "Come, I'll serve you myself, and please call me Erin. Will you be staying, Miles?"

The captain hitched the silver-plated sheath of his cavalry sword higher on his hip and touched the curved bill of his helmet. "Not tonight. Jared will have my plate set and my reports for General St. Clair can not wait." He bowed in the direction of Molly Green. "Till tomorrow."

If others watched the departure of Miles Starkweather, I did not, for I was totally distracted by the warm female flesh pressing against me as the mistress guided me to a seat on bare ground on the opposite side of the fire. My ears were working, howsomever, and I didn't miss hearing Tap, walking behind us, mutter, "That Miles can't abide a meal less'n he's sittin' at the table in front of his private tent."

Sergeant Tor Devlin also excused himself. "I must see that my men are properly settled, Molly," he said, kissing her cheek. "Then I shall return."

The excitement having waned sufficiently, the crowd slowly dispersed, trailing off in every direction. I never regretted my decision to remain and partake of Molly Green's culinary skills, for dining of any quality—or quantity— would later become damnably scarce more days than not.

The mistress's mother was well schooled in cooking out of doors. A deep bed of glowing coals topped by dry oak branches nestled twixt two logs. A metal pot hung by its handle from a tripod over half of the fire. Lazy-wife beans soaked in the pot for one night, seasoned with salt pork and molasses and boiled and baked the second night, then reheated the third, teased the nose. In another metal vessel long of pan and resting on clay bricks, a beef roast dotted with quartered onions steamed in its own juices. And the last portion of the evening's fare smelled best of all. The bread browning in the reflector oven squatting at the rim of the coals was a far cry from common johnnycake prepared by heating rounds of flour dough on a flat rock within a fire's ashes. The whole spread left little wonder why, female company aside, wise men continually sought the invite of Molly Green and her daughter.

Joined by Bear Watkins, we dined with the hurry of ill-trained louts, eating more with fingers than spoon and swiping at our tin trenchers with slabs of bread for the leavings. The cups of cold cider served by the mistress from an earthen jug were an added treat. With a gigantic belch, Tap leaned against an unburned log and groaned with happiness. "You may not own pewter dishes like Miles, but you're the best, Molly," he proclaimed, "the very best. Never a scorched bean, ever."

"Well, my dear Mr. Jacobs, since you never ever find the wherewithal to skim or turn while the cooking is under way," our female host related, "you may scour the plates at the creek. And I'll suffer no dragging of the heels, thank you."

Tap could do nothing else, of course, but gather trenchers and spoons and march for the creek. Whatever disgruntled comments followed, and given Tap's distaste for what he considered woman's work some were surely tendered, he mumbled them behind a jaw tightly clamped. A moocher like Tap never wore out his welcome at any fire or any table. Which was why and how, as Bear Watkins frequently reminded him, the irascible scout had grown a large, rounded, beginning-to-droop belly, a mound of fat that shortened his wind on the trail. Which, Bear conceded, was no real cause for alarm long as there was never an occasion when the redsticks were hot on your heels and you might be thinking of asking your fellow runners to carry you out of danger. It was then Bear swore that Tap would satisfy the piper from his own purse.

Three women approached Molly Green from the woods nearby, garishly rouged cheeks red beacons in the firelight. Dirt encrusted the collars and wrists of their dresses and the once-white stockings that flashed with the rise and fall of their skirts. Their laughter was overly loud and rivaled the squawks of startled hens. The middle member of the trio I recognized as Annie Bower, who had silenced Tap prior to our evening meal.

"Is there anything left for hungry doxies from afar?" Annie blurted. "A crumb will suffice."

While the mistress's mother greeted the new arrivals without hesitation and offered them what little could be scraped from pot, pan, and oven, I saw stern disapproval narrow her daughter's eyes before she caught herself and reached for the cider jug. "I'll fetch cups all around."

"No need to fuss with such," Annie crowed. "We drink from the spout liken our men!"

"Not at my fire you won't," Molly Green admonished. "You don't need a roof to act the lady in front of my guests."

"Bring on the tins, Erin. I'll not have the cook insulted an' sleep with pain back of my belly hole tonight," Annie chimed.

Eating like wild dogs without benefit of trenchers, the latecomers attacked the cooking vessels with the spoons Molly Green provided them. Honest truth was, they supped more on cider than anything else. It was mighty lean fare for three grown folks.

The jug was dry by the time Tap reappeared. "Oh, Ethan, me lad," the scout near shouted, "ain't it the Lord's blessing to learn that the tart mouth must beg for the nourishment provided the sweet!"

"Don't you slander me, you randy old goat," Annie Bower countered, cocking her head defiantly. "My skirt's been prim enough for you to lift many a night, hasn't it?"

Tap's accuser allowed him no response. She was on her feet and at my side before the scout's jaw could so much as open. "And what's the liking of your well-knitted hero here? Perhaps he has a pocket full of oblongs to pay for his pleasure." Annie preened, rubbing a breast suggestively against my elbow, then leaning to kiss a neck I was too surprised to move.

The clang of pan and pot banging together snapped the bold harlot's chin sharply about. Annie Bower's rouged cheeks paled in comparison to the deep crimson darkening the skin of Molly Green from forehead to lower throat. But despite our irate host's unbounded anger, her voice when she spoke was level and controlled. "One more word, just one more, and you will never sleep under my cart or tarp again, nor will you ever again taste a morsel of food at my fire. I will not be embarrassed by lewdness in the presence of a stranger who has this very day done me the greatest of favors. Do you understand me?"

"Say yes, Annie, by all that's holy, say yes," pleaded the taller of the harlot's two companions. "We don't want to starve within the fortnight, for good God!"

Had she wiped her features clean of paint and donned a silk gown, Annie Bower could not have been any more the lady born suddenly and completely of necessity. She stepped away from me and lowered her carriage in a perfectly wrought curtsy, and I freely admit my mother had seldom equaled her grace and balance greeting guests before our Kentucky hearth. "Monsieur, you have my sincere and heart-felt apology. I will not have you think poorly of Molly or her child on my account."

All present looked to me. Without undue thought, I reached downward and clasped a hand broken of nail and rough of palm. As I lifted, Annie Bower rose to her feet, and with flair I didn't know I possessed, I kissed her fingers not once, but twice. "Your apology is accepted, madam. Tap and I have suffered no lasting hurt from your funning."

A brief blush rimmed the garish paint decorating Annie Bower's plump cheeks, the same rouge through which a single tear tracked an instant later. She blotted that wet line with her thumb quick as she could, whispered, "I'll owe you forever," and turned to offer her apologies to Molly Green. Though I knew not what would come of it, if anything, I had a hunch I had just participated in the launching of a friendship that would never falter.

Molly Green, her previously flaming face by now mostly reduced to its natural hue, graciously forgave Annie's misdeeds. Her mellowing mood put a lilt in her tone as she next addressed Tap. "And so you will sleep peacefully, Mr. Jacobs, I hope you won't begrudge any slight paid you this evening and avoid my cooking in the future."

"Ain't no danger of that when a man is wedded to his own belly," the delighted scout boasted.

"Till later then," Molly Green said, granting Tap a conspiratorial wink. "Annie, you and the others fetch your blankets. It promises to be a cold night."

I gathered my gear and, joined by Bear and the still grinning Tap, circled the fire. As was our habit, we would sleep near the animals in our charge.

In the hubbub of evening's end, Erin Green unfortunately disappeared among the women gathering around the cart belonging to her mother. Built with a cargo box four feet in width, six feet in length, and two feet high at the sideboards, the cart was supported by carriage wheels and could be hauled either by hand or drayage horse. I watched the women grab the cart's long poles and maneuver it closer to the fire. My curiosity prompted a question I directed at Tap. "All those women sleep under that thing at once, together?"

"Yep, they does. Ain't nothin' like hot flesh to keep a body warm on cold nights. And the colder it gets, the less concerned they be about who's in the mix. Sort of awesome, ain't it, so much of what a man desires day and night piled 'neath that wee cart. Makes you ponder what a treat it would be to sneak into the middle of 'em in the dark of night, don't it, me buckos?"

"Even if'n you snuck in there without an invite, come mornin' or sooner, what'd be left of yuh for them to throw out wouldn't be enough to draw life's breath," Bear opined. "An' that Erin, the youngest of the lot, would be downright unwilling and do you harm, believe you me. Ain't no man gonna touch her 'thout her say-so."

"You won't get any argument from me about that," I affirmed. "Molly Green's daughter walks her own path, regardless."

What I said was indisputably true. What it didn't change was another truth: Erin Green was the offspring of a common camp follower, an unmarried female whose survival was dependent upon scampering from dawn to dusk hoping not to fall behind an army seeking its enemy. She had no father, perhaps didn't know who that individual might be—now or ever. She slept in the open with her mother and females of such loose virtue they would sell themselves to the devil or his henchmen for any cut of coin or federal note with no fear of the consequences.

And being bluntly honest with myself, the mistress, beautiful as she was, would not be welcome at my mother's table. The Downers of Kentucky, late of Pennsylvania, were not so overcome with themselves they snubbed those of lesser station. But neither would the lady of the house accept a stain on its lineage that couldn't be washed away, no matter how strong the soap.

None of these understandings and admissions made for an easy night's sleep. Burning hair and sky-blue eyes and swelling bosoms and wasp waist and tapering legs are what they are—stunning and distracting.

The dream was as powerful as the wondrously strange scent of her.

"Mother, this is . . ."

Part II
The March Upcountry

Chapter 5

Daybreak, 5 October

Come first light, fair young damsels and their mothers were quickly the farthest things from my mind. Paw was suddenly back with us, and he was mighty skillful at capturing the attention of those about him, including certain sons.

It was Bear, God love him, who gave me fair warning. He got a grip on the muscles of my lower leg and squeezed till he wrung a grunt from me. Erin Green and my mother faded abruptly, and I came awake under the oaks where our blankets lay tight about a fire whose ashes still glowed with burning embers. I vaguely remembered Bear telling Tap to add wood to our fire when he rose to pee in the middle of the night.

It was a crisp dawn with traces of white frost speckling the grasses in the small clearing by the creek that held Blue, the horse string, and the mounts of Tap and Bear. Though full daylight was considerable minutes away, drums rolled and the commands of officers echoed to our front as they rousted sleeping soldiers. Behind us, drovers snapped their whips bunching cattle on the military roads constructed just yesterday. Whistles and yips from farther up the creek to our left signaled that the horse master and his charges were about the same task. Every direction I could see at all through the woods, smoke mingled with foggy mist. An army on the rise was a right noisy affair, I decided. No chore for the Injuns to locate by smell and sound, that was for certain.

"Your paw just rode from the trees," Bear confirmed. "He's dismounting next to your roan, and he's not alone."

My father was no less imposing than on other occasions.

He stood a full six feet in height, and his wide shoulders ran parallel to the ground without any slope, making him appear even larger yet. His hair was black like mine and his eyes a deep brown and more piercing, according to Bear, than my own. Since he had forsworn the deerskin garments and moccasins adorning Tap and Bear, he was dressed as usual in ruffled shirt, broadcloth coat, whipcord breeches, and tall black riding boots. His flat-crowned hat was stiff of brim and fawn colored. A flintlock pistol rested in his satin waist sash, and he toted a long rifle with bright brass furniture, a weapon he had given the nickname Kill Dead. The shot pouch and powder horn hanging from straps looped over his left shoulder seemed out of place with Paw's town clothes but indicated how seldom he was caught without the rifle and its necessary accoutrements. My mother, again according to Bear, could pray till kingdom come, but Caleb Downer would never shed the odor of wood smoke and molding leaves, for once a woodser, always a woodser.

The shorter stranger with Paw also made a lasting impression at first encounter. He wore canvas trousers, jackboots, linen shirt without collar, a blanket coat, and tricorn hat. His long weapon was a smoothbore musket, its metal fittings dull and unremarkable. What stood out at a distance was the outlandish size of his upper skull, hands, and feet. Atop his expansive forehead, the tricorn appeared merely a small cap. His booted feet approximated the bulk of flatboats. And the knuckles of his huge hands could be likened to rows of walnuts. For all the coarseness of his end parts, the stranger's face possessed several highly redeeming features. I'd heard my sisters exclaim countless times over Roman jaws, Grecian noses, and dimples, and didn't doubt many in skirts would yearn to meet the swaggering newcomer.

Without ever having been introduced to him, I sensed Paw's companion could, if he were so inclined, prove a formidable and dangerous enemy with either mind or fists. And so did Bear. "We won't dare be careless with that one," he said with Paw and the stranger still out of earshot. "Less'n I'm wrong, that'll be Court Starnes, Duer's partner from Fort Pitt."

I enjoyed Bear's friendship because I could ask him questions about anything, a situation I desired with Paw. "You know of him?"

"Just from rumors at Fort Pitt. It's said he killed a fellow his own size with his bare hands and his teeth in a brawl."

Much as Court Starnes fascinated me, it was Paw I didn't dare ignore as he drew abreast of the fire Tap had rekindled into a leaping flame. Dark circles undershot his eyes, and weariness slowed his legs, and Paw was never easy to treat with when a bleak mood gripped him. He introduced Court Starnes to everyone, then his gaze homed in on me. "I hear you're the hero of the camp followers for sparing a girl named Erin. I allow that's the first respectful utterance of the Downer name in some days, but more importantly, am I to understand Hardy Booth is dead, lost in your heroic rescue?"

I was too growed to stammer and stutter addressing Paw. I had learned to lower my voice and talk slowly so as not to reveal how I was spinning inside like a top just loosed from its string. Neither did I ever try to sweeten bad news. "Yes, sir. The Injuns overrun us and he fell with the first shot."

"That where you lost your knife, too?"

My fingers strayed to the empty scabbard hanging from my belt. Tap always claimed Caleb Downer missed nothing wherever he deigned to look. "Yes, sir. I left it in an Injun's belly."

Paw accepted that bold declaration as if it were of no more import than my saying each of my feet had five toes. He glanced briefly at Blue and the other horses in the clearing behind us. "We lose anything else to the redsticks?"

A horse being somewhat larger than a knife, I was expecting such a query from him. "Yes, sir. Hardy and I bought the ten horses liken you wanted. As you can count, the Injuns made off with half of them."

The successful purchase counted for naught, but I had to spout something in my favor. Paw naturally discounted it. "Son, I'm out a man, gold coin, and valuable horseflesh. Though I don't like it," he said, seeming to stare into my very soul, "I'll swallow it. Long as it never happens again."

Relief shot through me like a bolt of lightning. Maybe he wasn't going to ask in front of the others if I thought, in hindsight, I should have followed his orders to the hilt and stayed with Hardy and the lost horses regardless of what else confronted me. Maybe he wasn't on the verge of sending me quick-footin' for home with my chin hanging low as that of a hound on the scent. Lord, Lord, if I escaped his wrath this time, I vowed there would be no next time.

Paw lifted his fawn hat and smoothed his black hair. "Well, by damned, St. Clair's officers can fight amongst themselves as to who gets what horse, can't they now?"

Paw's following grin and short laugh were glorious to behold, for my recent shortcomings were now considered old news; not forgotten, but shoved to the back of his mind to be trotted forth later if he needed them. Paw remembered past failures in all their insufferable detail as easily as I recalled Blue's name, which made being around him a constant challenge. You had to measure up every hour of every day. I had a notion I was being allowed to remain with his horse crew at the moment solely because he needed another rider, not because he condoned in the least the decisions I had made on the bank of the Miami the previous night. With Paw, blood could get so thin you couldn't tell what was red from clear water.

"Tea be ready an' we wouldn't want her to get cold," Tap announced with a congratulatory wink only I could see with his head slanted toward me like it was.

The scout passed tin cups around and poured a portion of the steaming green liquid into each from an iron noggin. On a cold morning, the warmth was as welcome as the taste, and it was hard not to court a burnt lip drinking too soon.

Court Starnes's question, calmly asked, interrupted our meal of cold johnnycake and jerked venison. "Could you tell in the dark it was a woman the Injuns held captive?"

A smile that at first seemed warm and friendly eased his handsome features. But I couldn't fathom much if any warmth in his pale blue eyes. I remembered a Harrodsburg horse trader whose cold eyes had betrayed a similarly charming smile and how he had appraised Paw through the guise of harmless inquiries so he could cheat him. As Tap opined now and again, "Even a snake can smile if'n you give him good enough reason."

"No, sir, I couldn't. She was dressed in manly clothes."

"None of her choice parts could be seen then?" Starnes persisted.

Wary as to why he was pestering me with foolish queries of no significance, I nevertheless answered, "She wore a floppy-brimmed hat that drooped to her brow, a leather gag covered her mouth, and her arms were tied together in front of her. She looked like a brown lump in the moonlight. Hadn't been for the gag and her bound hands, I would've taken her for an Injun in a white man's hat and let her ride on by."

Starnes's smile broadened. "Glad to hear that, Ethan Downer. Ain't no female, Injun captive or not, worth a white man's life. Nor good horseflesh, neither."

I could hear the dawn breeze above the hissing of the fire. That's how still it was of a sudden. I watched Paw in earnest. While he might have disliked my doing as I had given the results, the fact I rescued a woman had played no part in his judgment of me, for Paw never laid the sour mouth on a woman regardless of her circumstances. Oh, he might jest with them as Tap had with Annie Bower, but he and those about him shared the belief all women were rightfully owed the breath they drew. And horses were what their name implied—beasts of burden whose importance and value never exceeded that of humans, either male or female.

Though lasting less than a dozen beats of the heart, the brief span of silence said more than countless words of rebuttal. Court Starnes with a single arrogant remark had separated himself from Paw, Bear, and Tap Jacobs. They would follow his orders since he was the absent Duer's partner, but never would they befriend Starnes or trust him completely. I would bet on that anytime, anywhere and win handily, the odds be damned.

It was Bear who shattered the quiet. "And what are we about this bloody morning, Caleb?" he asked of Paw.

Paw's answer was blunt and without rancor. "We'll look to Court for our orders from here out. That's as the boss, Mr. Duer, wants."

Court Starnes's huge hands dwarfed his tin cup. He sipped green tea before speaking. "Given General St. Clair's concern that we don't have animals strayin' off during the daily march or at night, young Ethan, Bear, an' Tap will join up with Dodd, Duer's horse master. Caleb an' me will report to General Butler, who's in command till St. Clair returns from Fort Washington. We can deliver the horses Ethan brung when we find Butler. After that, it's the Ohio again for Caleb an' me. We don't poke the boatmen and the packhorsemen with a sharp stick every chance we get, this army will be starving within a fortnight."

"We ate fine last evening," Tap commented with a re-membering sigh of pleasure and a rub of his protruding belly.

"Yes, vittles are plentiful just now. But with twenty-three hundred rations boltin' down throats every day, the flour sacks empty mighty fast," Starnes observed. "An' fresh beef is poor fare by its lonesome."

"That it be," Paw agreed, drinking his cup dry. "Bear, you take charge of Ethan and Tap. The three of you are to stay with Dodd till you next see my face, understood?"

I thought Starnes's cheek twitched a hair at Paw's precise instructions, like he felt Paw was edging in on his authority. But maybe it was just that his skin itched, for he said nothing contrariwise. He simply tipped his hat to those of us not accompanying him, tossed his tin cup to Tap, and made for the horses.

When Starnes was beyond our hearing, Paw nailed me with those piercing eyes of his. "You mind Bear, and keep that rifle loaded an' ready wherever you find yourself. I ain't planning on making excuses to your maw was I to reach home without you." That said, he followed in Starnes's foot-steps to the meadow.

I watched the two of them ride into the trees, General St. Clair's horses and Hardy's mare in tow. Paw was a fellow accustomed to shouting the gees and the haws and having others obey his lead. It figured then that some time in the not-too-distant future, he and Court Starnes would come up against it and clash openly, and deep down I feared for Paw, which shocked me.

Paw's renowned skill with his wits and his weapons, cou-pled with his physical strength, had always been a source of great comfort to those who dwelled beneath his roof. Every member of the Downer family fervently believed he would always be there to protect us whenever the need arose. But lest my imagination was running free of its halter, and I didn't think it was, Court Starnes was capable of matching Paw at his very best.

And the thought of that was mighty unsettling and worrisome, for I couldn't remember when I had doubted Paw before, ever.

Chapter 6

We broke camp, Tap and Bear packing gear and dousing
the fire and me saddling the horses. Blue, his belly full from
his grazing the previous night before frost speckled the
meadow, was in fine fettle and tried his best to accomplish
his usual morning stunt of stepping on my foot if my mind
wandered while tightening the cinch under his belly. Blue
was no different than any other four-legged creature, be it
horse or hound. Let him start something without correcting
him immediately, and it became a habit you endured long as
you owned him. Though he didn't exactly own them and
they were graced with only two feet, Paw always claimed
the same was true of sons.

I endured another daily ritual as we rode west along the
creek bank fronting our camp. It was Tap's want to carp and
complain once Paw was out of sight, and he didn't disappoint
Bear and me. Scratching at his whiskers every whipstitch, he
went on and on. "Besides my one knee throbbin' like a damn
Injun war drum, my backbone's bent crooked from sleepin'
on hard ground night after night. I could bear all that, if'n it
wasn't for the blunt truth I ain't shat for a month of Tues-
days, neither."

Bear, who prized a closed mouth less'n you had something worthwhile to say, sought as usual to silence Tap's
meaningless tirade, and as luck would have it, chance favored
him this morning. He jabbed at the far creek bank with the
barrel of his rifle. "Too bad for Ethan and me you ain't like
that bounder yonder."

Tap and I couldn't miss what he pointed out to us, for a

large pair of white blobs jutted from the brown trunks bordering the current, and twixt the opposing buttocks, a gush of activity was occurring. "You don't stifle yourself, I'm gonna hand you over to that gent. An' by the size of those moons, he's big enough and mean enough to make you grunt till you're as empty as he'll soon be."

Tap knew from Bear's stern tone it was time to cease his morning lament, so he now tried humor to ingratiate himself again with his best friend. "It's our sad luck he won't be with us the next dark night. His arse skin's brighter'n any lanthorn I've ever toted to the necessary."

Though Tap and I rode behind him and couldn't hear his chuckle, the shake of Bear's shoulders gave him away, for it was nigh onto impossible to stay peeved with the bowlegged scout. Still, Bear had gained his beloved quiet, and I was left thinking how glad I was that Erin Green wasn't with us. The scene we had just witnessed did little to disprove Mother's conviction that no female of proper breeding ever willingly sacrificed her privacy to travel with an army of men.

Crisply rendered orders and the whinnies of horses sprang from the trees ahead. We halted at the fringe of the westernmost military road and waited for a wheeled cannon pulled by matching grays to lumber past. Behind it came a company of Virginia levies. Those marching in the double file cast bold, hostile glances our way. "They act like we're the enemy, not the redsticks," I said in a low voice.

"Don't they though," Bear agreed. "You don't know, you best. We ain't wearin' uniforms, an' the levies along with the regulars detest all militia. They been told, and believe, rightly or wrongly, that it was Kentucky militia broke and run on General Harmar a year ago, causing his defeat."

"They better not stick their noses too high. They're raisin' plenty of their own stink, have been since they marched from Fort Washington weeks ago," Tap offered.

New as I was to events north of the Ohio, I asked, "How's that?"

"They're whinin' like cur dogs they signed up for six months and not a half day more. They're arguin' the clock started ticking when they marked the paper, not when they arrived at Fort Pitt," Tap explained. "If 'n they win out, there won't be a levy north of Fort Hamilton come the first week of November, an' that ain't long from now."

"General St. Clair won't stand for their leaving, will he?"

"The general's in a bind, Ethan. He can't convince them to stay, they might start deserting on him an' unravel his whole command," Bear predicted.

"The regulars don't side with the levies, do they?"

"Naw, but they're madder'n hell they haven't been paid forever, an' they don't think any more of the levies than the six-month louts do the militia. How's that fire your wick?"

"Not the least," I judged. "I'm just plumb thankful I'm not wearing General St. Clair's boots."

A sorrel gelding approached from the north on the western edge of the road. Atop him sat Captain Miles Starkweather. Upon sighting us, he halted his mount and crossed the road as the final file of levies tromped beyond our position. "I can't say he don't know horseflesh. That sorrel was the best horse I brought from Kentucky," I conceded to Bear and Tap.

The blue and white silk cockade decorating the captain's helmet was a brilliant splash of color in the gray light. And damned if the sun didn't pop forth as he drew rein. In addition to the sword at his hip, he carried a rifle curled in the crook of his left arm. I didn't feel good about it, for it made me feel I was turning my back on my companions, but I envied Miles Starkweather the cockade, the spanking uniform, and the long blade. He was a picture of the perfectly dressed dragoon officer pursuing his duty, and much as I resented it, he would always grab the attention of the prettiest of the girls ahead of me.

"I saw Court Starnes earlier, Mr. Watkins, and I'm delighted the three of you have been assigned to Dodd and his horse tenders. Dodd desperately needs the advice and counsel of those with experience controlling animals in the wilds. We can't wait each morning for him to find his charges, particularly now that General Butler has changed our means of advancement."

Bear rose in his iron stirrups. "He changed St. Clair's orders?"

I watched the captain like a circling hawk. I couldn't

count the times Paw had written that no one defied Arthur St. Clair, who not only commanded the army but was also governor of the Northwest Territory.

Starkweather's smile was brief. "We will henceforth cut a single road instead of two. Yesterday, not even an extra ration of rum excited the chopping crews. We are naming the streams north of the Miami by distance from Fort Hamilton, and General Butler was not pleased that at the end of the first day we halted at Two Mile Creek. We don't move faster than that, we'll not reach the Saint Mary's River and the Shawnee towns till midwinter."

The captain stood in his stirrups and aimed a gloved hand across the road to the southwest. "Dodd and his men are still chasing down loose stock. I'm sure you will be most welcome," he concluded, dropping back into the saddle. "Mr. Downer, you know your horses. And before you take your leave, I have something for you."

Reaching into a leather saddlebag at his hip, Starkweather extracted a rosewood-handled knife, complete with black leather scabbard. He kneed the sorrel closer and extended his arm. "This will replace the weapon you lost recovering Mistress Green. I would be most proud to have someone of your courage carry it. It's been in my family for many years."

My mouth didn't drop open as far as those of Tap and Bear, though I would have topped them easy had Starkweather's gesture not taken me so aback. It was an expensive gift I couldn't refuse. The twinge of hesitation I forcibly swallowed stemmed from the realization a rival you envied was doubly difficult to dislike if he was generous to boot.

I slid the knife free of the scabbard, admiring the slightly curved handle, small brass guard, and brass end pommel. I ran the cutting edge of the twelve-inch blade along the top of my wrist. Hair parted from skin. The blade was razor sharp. My delighted grin pleased the lieutenant. "It will have the best of care, and I thank you."

Starkweather saluted, reined the sorrel about, and headed north again toward Butler's headquarters. We watched his departure, then Tap suggested we better seek out Dodd on the quick. "With gifts fallin' from the sky, it's got to be a great day awaitin' us."

At the start, Tap's uplifting outlook showed great promise. The bright sunshine was a welcome break from the recent rain, and a light breeze, warming by the minute, skittered early leaves at the feet of our horses. It was a true Injun summer morning, the favorite season of both the raiding Shawnee as well as the Kentucky squirrel hunter.

Unfortunately, we soon arrived at the Dodd horse camp of the previous evening where events soured with the stink of spoiled milk. Packhorses milled in an enclosure built by stringing rope from tree to tree. A larger bunch of unfettered pack animals roamed the surrounding woods. Hoof cuts and bites that had drawn blood told they had been fighting among themselves, most probably over scant forage. Taller riding stock, a dozen in number, stood hitched to a picket line at the center of the campsite.

Despite the hour, nearly eight by the clock, sleeping tarps and blankets lay scattered helter-skelter about a fire not yet doused. The only jasper in sight, a smallish character with narrow shoulders wearing a bearskin hat with a jutting leather bill, sat on a log writing in a bound ledger book, inkwell balanced beside him on the rough bark. His upward peek from beneath the jutting hat bill exposed a pumpkin countenance divided above the lips by the thinnest of mustaches. Spurning even the slightest nod of greeting, the narrow jasper resumed his entries, the quill of his pen dancing merrily.

Bear Watkins was by inclination a mannerly soul, schooled by a mother who taught him, so he said, that neighborliness cost nothing more than a smile and a kind word, which the Lord provided all his subjects free. Bear trusted his mother's teachings without question and, therefore, had no patience with those who were rude without provocation. The sharp clicking of metal against metal, the unmistakable sound of a rifle cocking, overwhelmed the scratching of the quill pen. "Valentine Dodd, ain't yuh?"

The bearskin hat tilted, and small, widening eyes stared flush into the yawning muzzle of Bear's long gun. Hell and damnation, I would've found the gumption to smile real friendly and sincere, too, had I been sitting on that log. And I'll vouchsafe for him, Valentine Dodd made right proper work of it. Stone would've melted in his mouth.

"Yes, sir. I'm Monsieur Dodd," said the rifle's would-be target, bearskin hat suddenly off his mostly hairless head. "And who might you be?"

"I'm Bear Watkins. This is Ethan Downer an' Tap Jacobs," Bear answered, easing the hammer of his long gun to half cock and singling us out one at a time. "Court Starnes sent us to help with the horse stock."

Dodd shot to his feet, nearly upsetting his inkwell. "That is grand news. I'm lacking men, and the redsticks are everywhere. They steal from us every night."

Bear hawked and spat. "You actually seen the Injuns stealing your ownself?"

"No," Dodd admitted. "But Gabe Hookfin reports such, and he knows the Indians true as any Kentucky scout."

"And where would we find your wise Mr. Hookfin?" an openly skeptical Tap inquired.

"He's hunting stray animals with Ira Fellows and Henry Cross. They shouldn't be much longer," Valentine assured us.

Bear stood his rifle on his thigh. "Not to pry, mind yuh, but you or your hires ever been around horses much outside of the stable?"

The horse master answered instantly and completely. "No, we haven't. We were mucking stalls at Fort Pitt when we met Court Starnes. He put coins in our palms and dreams in our heads, and here we be."

"Just as I figured," Bear concluded. "I listen close at night an' I have yet to hear the first bell. You can't keep track of horses you don't hobble or picket at night without bells. Starnes ever mention bells before you sailed from Pittsburgh?"

Perhaps afraid Bear would bring his rifle into play again, Valentine hid nothing. "No, sir, he said we'd have soldiers detailed to help us, so there wasn't any sense paying for gear we didn't need."

Bear's head shook slowly. "Well, let's hope General St. Clair doesn't learn his horses have been allowed to drift free after dark. There'll be the devil to pay if'n he does."

Dodd's ledger book snapped shut, his smile a memory. "I've done the best I could with what Court Starnes gave me.

I can only pray it doesn't prove my ruination. I'm not partial to the stock or a public whipping."

"Neither are we, Dodd, neither are we," Tap said with a sigh.

Hooves knocked beyond the rope pen of the packhorses. Three riders hazed an additional dozen animals behind those already tied to the picket line. The foremost rider booted his mount around the line to within a few rods of us. He was beanpole tall and knife-blade thin in every limb. The flesh of his forehead, cheekbones, and jaws clung to the bones beneath them. His chapped mouth was a mere slit in skin dry and shrunken as drawn leather.

"These gents flailin' your rope, Dodd?" the lean horseman challenged defiantly.

While I wasn't widely experienced in the dealings of hostile men, I had the wherewithal to suspect you never crowded any rider with his rifle standing on his thigh, less'n your own weapon was leveled and cocked. Bear's long gun tilted downward, and Gabe Hookfin's slit of a mouth puckered shut. He had stuck both boots in the manure and knew it, for like Valentine Dodd before him, he had unexpectedly gained the privilege of staring down the barrel of Bear's rifle. The musket resting across his lap, the major source of his bluster, was suddenly of no consequence whatsoever.

It was Dodd who spared the fuming Hookfin a possible ball through the innards. "Gabe," Valentine called in a rising voice, "this be Bear Watkins and friends, come to help with the herding on the orders of Court Starnes."

The change in Hookfin's demeanor was pronounced. His body slackened in the saddle. "Sorry, my friend. I wasn't aware you're one of us."

Bear's rifle never wavered. "We're not one of you. We're here on the orders of Caleb Downer. We work for Caleb, not Court Starnes. Everybody understands that, we can be plumb helpful till Caleb sends for us. When he does, we're gone, be it day or night. That suit you, young'un?"

The beanpole's lengthy stare was ample evidence he detested the comeuppance Bear had laid on him, but pointed weapons are plumb persuasive, and the nodding of Gabe

Hookfin's head, though slow and reluctant, was nonetheless witnessed by all present.

Tap and I had no objection to what Bear had done. Yet there was no denying we now had an enemy within our own camp, and maybe more than one if Hookfin's companions watching from the picket line felt as he did. My own head shook with resignation. Odd it was, that men bearing arms together could be downright touchy with one another despite the fact they shared the same danger and a common enemy.

Peace reigned the balance of the daylight hours, for Miles Starkweather returned, accompanied by other mounted dragoons anxious to bring the baggage horses forward. Once the column lined out, the surveyor with his shielding party of riflemen, the road cutters with their protecting troops, and five horse-drawn cannon led off in that order on General Butler's single highway twelve feet wide. The ammunition wagons and the baggage horses carrying the supplies rolled next, followed by five more pieces of artillery under the protection of a rear guard. The First and Second Americans and their counterparts, the levy regiments, marched to the left and right of the road by single files at a distance of one hundred yards. Mounted dragoons then flanked those marching on foot.

Though tending to fall to the extreme rear and mix with the ragtag collection of camp followers trailing the column, the bullock herd was mostly contained twixt the outside columns and the road. We Dodd men spent the day on the heels of the rear guard where the officers' servants traveled, always well in advance of the camp followers. Our duty was to see after the spare horses of the officers and those pack animals too infirm for hauling that particular morning.

The weather stayed fair and sunny and the going, while faster than the previous day, was nothing to brag upon. At noon, we lurched across Four Mile Creek. Twice during the afternoon, General Butler himself, portly in figure and mounted on a sizable brown mare, inspected the entire column, his visits eliciting cheers from the women camp followers so lusty and sustained we heard them over the lumbering bullocks surrounding us. In late afternoon, the column bore westward up the meandering bed of Seven Mile

Creek, and we halted for the night within the gorge of that shallow stream.

We watered the riding stock and baggage horses, bunching them along the banks of the creek to take advantage of the grasses that had survived the early frost. Sufficient forage was available in the bottoms to keep the herd fairly close about till dawn. At dusk, I was beyond the far bank checking for any additional open ground with good graze when the camp followers continued upstream as would become their habit. The women preferred to spend the dark hours next to the wagoners, locating themselves hard abreast of the fires closest to the rear elements of Butler's command. Missing an opportunity to snatch at least a peek at Erin Green proved powerfully disappointing.

The situation at Dodd's fire didn't brighten my mood, either. Tap and Bear were standing the early watch, leaving me free to sup first with the others. Our campsite was a barren pocket in a beech grove twenty yards from the water's edge. Blazing flames greeted me. Dodd was there, writing in his ledger by firelight, along with Henry Cross and Ira Fellows. Both Henry and Ira were nearly thirty in years and dressed in hide clothing as ancient and patched as that of Gabe Hookfin. Their caps had been fashioned from coon fur complete with ringed tails. They were seated and sharing a jug of rum, waiting for the fire to burn down to coals so serious cooking could begin. I dropped my gear alongside theirs and plopped atop my saddle.

"Where's Gabe?" Henry Cross asked Dodd, stuffing a wedge of leather into a boot to plug a break in its sole.

His quill never stopping, Dodd said, "Off gabbing with his spirit-swilling friends, the Pennsylvania levies. One of them brought word the levies are demanding their discharge end of the month."

"And Gabe loves to stick his nose in wherever there's a dispute, don't he now?"

"Aye," Dodd confirmed. "To the ears, head foremost."

"Well, if'n he weren't there, he'd be tryin' to sniff out Erin Green's scent, though I can't rightly blame him none," Ira Fellows alleged with a rattling chuckle. "I surely did enjoy my gander at her an hour ago."

The mention of Erin's name naturally caught my attention, and with head lowered, I studied Ira from the corner of an eye, not wanting to show too much interest straight off. Maybe he and Henry hadn't heard of my rescue of her. Then again, maybe they had.

Henry Cross stood the boot he was repairing next to the fire. "For a female hardly growed, she's surely strung together something fine."

"Yesiree, she must taste sweet as combed honey," Ira proclaimed with sudden enthusiasm before touching a lighted twig to the tobacco in his clay pipe. He blew smoke, then looked my way. "You spent time in the woods with her. What say you, Downer?"

I peered past the rum jug Ira fisted my direction. Surprisingly, my quick temper stayed to home, for Ira was most assuredly moonstruck just thinking of Erin Green, and neither he nor Henry Cross intended to befoul her name when describing the appeal of her body or pondering what it would be like to be alone with her. That was the way of it with honest men everywhere once they sighted a truly beautiful woman.

"Well, Downer, yuh gonna make us wait a week afore you bother to answer Ira there?"

Gabe Hookfin's outburst gave me a genuine start. Damned if the beanpole, for all his bluster, didn't move about with less noise than a bird on the wing.

"Come on, Downer, let's hear it. She as wild as that red hair?"

I didn't budge a lick. He was behind me, and I feared my temper would betray me. I'd succumbed to blind anger in the past and taken a severe beating when my opponent landed a telling first blow. Gabe's temper was bad as mine. He surely was remembering how Bear had taken him to task. It was entirely possible he was using Erin to rile me into a fight he believed he could win rather than tackle the larger and stronger Bear. Revenge of any kind just now would tickle the beanpole.

I reached and lifted the rum jug from Ira's lingering hand. "I wouldn't have any notion how wild she might be. With all them Injuns lurking about, I was more interested in keep-in' my hair than anything she had to offer."

Hookfin snorted loudly. "Too bad I wasn't there. I would have gotten that silk shirt of hers undone, Injuns or no Injuns, and I'm bettin' she'd have thanked me afterward."

Tilting the jug, I sipped slowly, then downed the liquor in a long swallow. I had to make a decision, a decision that, if wrongly made, could lead to much trouble and perhaps the spilling of blood. And that blood might prove to be mine.

I was in no position to challenge Gabe Hookfin with mus-cle or weapons. He was still behind me, and I was seated with my rifle leaning across my gear and my belt weapons, Starkweather's knife and my hatchet, useless till I stood up-right and freed them. He would have the first play, no ques-tion.

I glanced at Valentine Dodd, who sat directly before me on the other side of the fire, his pen momentarily at rest. He watched me with hardly a blink. Seeing he had my attention, he wagged his bearskin hat ever so slightly. At the wrinkling of my brows, his bearskin hat wagged "no" a second time. Maybe he didn't dare intercede on my behalf, but the horse master surmised as I did that Gabe Hookfin's primary pur-pose in boasting how he would have taken advantage of Erin Green had he been in my place was to goad me into attacking him.

Even knowing that, I was still inclined to turn low and fast and risk being whipped at the get-go rather than knuckle under to the slandering beanpole. But much as it hurt, I swal-lowed my pride, and it was because of Paw that I refrained. My orders were to work with the Dodd men, not brawl with them. Whether I emerged the victor or not, Paw would likely send me packing once he heard the whole story. He didn't need men about him who couldn't overlook a few incendiary remarks about a camp girl for the sake of keeping the peace within their own camp. You engaged the enemy, not your own.

By Christ, I hated the doing of it, but there was only one response that I thought might safely defuse the beanpole be-hind me. I came to my feet like a snake uncoiling, rifle clasped loosely by the barrel. "Ira, the woods are calling, and since I'm not partial to sleepin' in wet breeches, I'm afraid I'll have to let you and Gabe argue the charms of Erin Green."

Deliberately avoiding even a peek at the beanpole, I skirted the fire, the quickest way to put space twixt the two of us, and took for the woods. It was the longest short walk I ever made.

A stride or two into the trees, a string of curses erupted back at the fire, Gabe blowing off his frustration at being outfoxed. He would brand me a coward or at least try to, and some would listen. I could bear up under that, knowing Dodd would tell Paw the truth at my request. I had a hunch Valentine Dodd was neither a weakling nor a liar. He did the best with what the Lord had given him.

I angled toward the creek, the last of the anger that had nearly overcome me draining away. The moon was out and shining through every open seam of tree branch and leaf. Beech trunks shone as if painted silvery gray. The frost had silenced most of the singing, clacking night critters of summer, and dead leaves crumbled beneath my moccasins in dry squeaks. It was a singular repeating of that dry squeaking off to my left that caught my ear. Had it been a horse, a following noise would have confirmed the movement of something with more than two legs.

It was probably a sentry belonging to the army. But I quickly dismissed that, for I was practically stepping on his toes, and he should be calling out his challenge. With everything to lose and nothing to suffer other than a mouthful of leaves and a new fit of wounded pride, I tripped a-purpose and squawked like an alarmed rooster, imitating a clumsy, accidental fall. Soon as I was flat on my back, I rolled and aimed my rifle where I sensed the danger. Then I waited, motionless as a man severely hurt and unable to stir.

My simple ruse put me in better position to locate the stalking enemy. The advancing redstick would count on the thick brush amid the tree butts to hide him. But lying flat to the ground, I hoped to detect the movement of his legs and feet through the lower, spindlier portions of that same concealing brush, a favorite trick of Bear's.

I watched and listened . . . and for all my trouble and play-acting, saw and heard absolutely nothing. I was beginning to feel like a child afraid of the harmless noises natural to the night hours.

Leaf dust tickled my nose, and I reared upward to avoid sneezing. The flying arrow flashed by my throat at such speed the threat to my life wasn't apparent till its flint point, powered by the launching bow, thwacked into the beech trunk next to my ear. The chunking impact stopped my heart no less suddenly than a giant fist smashing into my chest, for the quivering arrow was so tight to my neck I could have laid my chin on its yellow-painted shaft with no strain whatsoever. Had I not raised my head at just the right moment, I would have been pierced from temple to temple.

The arrow had approached from my right, not the left where I had been watching, and with frantic haste, I rolled and squirmed and quit doing so only when I had the protective trunk of that handy beech perfectly centered twixt me and the new position of the enemy. Whoever the Injun was out there, he was damnably clever. Giving himself away with a misstep hadn't discouraged him or deterred him. He had ignored my ruse, circled silently, and missed killing me by the thinnest of margins.

It didn't take much anxious pondering for me to reckon what was required lest I wanted to die then and there. Where I might have been a match for Gabe Hookfin, I was against a superior foe now, and I wasn't shamed by such an admission.

Sooner beating later, I had me a deep gulp of wind, and unlike my slow walk leaving the Dodd fire, departed the sheltering beech trunk in a bobbing, weaving crouch of a run. I prayed at every footfall I was a flitting, difficult, impossible target in the moonlit, brush-choked, heavily treed bottom of Seven Mile Creek. And for what reason I knew not, the Lord in this instance chose to favor me over my enemy.

It was a well from which a man didn't dare draw water too often.

Chapter 7

Nighttime, 5 October

The shimmering waters of the creek loomed before me, and I bore upstream, running fast as I could till I was among the grazing horses. A soft whistle brought me to a halt, and there stood Bear, wide and thick in the moonlight. Damn, but he was a most welcome sight.

"Shadows spookin' yuh, lad?" he asked calmly.

"No, an Injun," I squeezed out, gasping for air.

With that simple statement on my part, Bear Watkins was suddenly serious as a hangman with the gallows rope in his fist. "Was he alone?"

"Don't know. He sent an arrow at me, but I never got the first glimpse of him or any others."

A few pointed questions and Bear had the whole story from me, excepting, of course, why I had been barging about in the woods. That I kept to myself. My squabble with Gabe Hookfin was a private affair.

"Well enough," Bear decided. "We raise the alarm an' bolt after your Injun, we'd likely get one of us killed, maybe more. Come along. We'll fetch Tap and have us a parley. I don't allow that brash pup Hookfin will place much faith in anything I say, but perhaps the other Dodd men will. They deserve fair warning. The Injuns would provide the same for their own."

At our camp, Val Dodd, Ira Fellows, and Gabe Hookfin were roasting strips of freshly butchered beef strung on iron rods over open flames, meat drippings sizzling and popping. A kneeling Henry Cross tended a skillet of johnnycakes lumpier than the head of a frog with the point of his knife.

Brackish tea boiled in a battered tin pot hanging by its handle from an iron tripod. It surely was a far journey backward from the sights and smells I had experienced at Molly Green's fire. Elegant fare being easy to recognize and appreciate, not surprisingly, Tap's nose wrinkled in disgust at what he branded marching victuals, those cooked with few seasonings and little flair.

Bear halted at Val Dodd's shoulder and gazed across the flames at Gabe Hookfin. "Dodd here says you suspect the redsticks are stealing our horses. Ever seen any of your thieves?"

The beanpole's slit of a mouth stopped chewing. "Naw, but they're out there. How else can we be losin' animals?"

"I'm not doubting your word," Bear asserted. "The Shawnee are lurkin' nearby as we speak."

Four pairs of eyes moved as one, first surveying the surrounding woods, then centering on Bear. "How you know this?" a nervous Val Dodd inquired.

"Ethan nearly lost his life to a Shawnee arrow a few minutes ago, that's how," Bear said, settling the butt of his rifle on the ground.

"You wouldn't be tryin' to tree us, would you?" Hookfin asked, his tone both hostile and suspicious.

Bear leaned forward, insuring each of the Dodd men a clear gander at his rough-hewn, fully bearded face. "No, I ain't tellin' nothin' but the truth, and so's Ethan. Ethan ain't no stranger to the wiles of the Shawnee. He wasn't but ten and four when they waited till his paw and the rest of us Downer men, all except the smithy, went off on the fall hunt. Then they burst into the Downer cabin. If'n Ethan hadn't killed two of the red heathen with his hatchet soon as their heads showed at the top of the loft ladder, and Jehrico done for two more and barred the door against the rest, Caleb Downer would be without heirs. Even then, the redsticks still carried off Ethan's brother, never to be seen again."

I'd been watching Hookfin, and he was, in turn, studying me. If Gabe believed what he had just heard, he had to be wondering if I really feared a fight with him. Maybe I wasn't a coward after all. Either way, his dislike for me was obvious and unmistakable, for his close-set eyes glowed hot and bright as the coals of the cooking fire.

Bear peered left and right, head moving slowly. "I ain't blowin' Ethan's horn for the joy of it. We searched the woods after we returned from our hunt an' learned a heap. Them Injuns scouted that cabin for a full week till the time was ripe in their favor. An' they'll be skulkin' thataway along every mile we march into their country, waitin' for the slightest chance to lift our hair. So we want to live to spend Duer's gold, we best not stack our weapons like St. Clair's soldiers. We best keep our long guns at the ready wherever we be an' not venture off alone. The Shawnee and their friends, the Miami, crave a quick, quiet scalpin' with little danger to themselves well as anything."

"You make me wish for the stables at Fort Pitt," blurted Val Dodd. "Once I was asleep there, I had only to worry about the rats gnawing on my toes. How can we best guard the animals until dawn, Monsieur Watkins?"

"Now whoa up, Goddamn it," Hookfin protested. "You're in charge, Dodd, an' we ain't takin' orders from no man of Caleb Downer's."

Henry Cross swallowed a mouthful of johnnycake and pointed his knife at the beanpole. "Don't fret so, Gabe. Ira and me followed Dodd out here from Fort Pitt to store up coin for the coming winter, not to do battle with any damn redsticks. So you speak for your ownself. We'll do our own jawin'."

The beanpole snapped the iron rod in his hand downward, dashing his uneaten meat into the fire. Snorting angrily, he retrieved his musket from the upright stack of weapons behind Ira Cross, snatched his rolled blankets from the ground, and paused at the outer edge of the firelight, a step from the blackness masking the creek. His anger stretched the dry, leathery skin ever tighter over the sharp bones of his lean features. At that moment, Gabe Hookfin appeared more dead than alive.

"I'll take my next orders from Court Starnes an' nobody else!" the beanpole vowed before brandishing his musket and striding into the night.

Ira Cross sighed and stared where Hookfin had disap-

peared. "We told Starnes that skinny snot would be trouble
he hired him. Maybe he gets himself killed, Court'll start
listenin' to us."

"The cold air will cool his temper," Val Dodd concluded
with a shrug, reaching into a canvas bag and passing iron
rods to Bear, Tap, and me. "Meantime, you gentlemen need
not starve. The beef hangs from that limb behind Ira, and
Henry's johnnycakes may be coarse as a dime whore's heart,
but they won't break your teeth."

Not a soul ringing the fire gave the departed beanpole
another thought. Val Dodd granted us time to roast and eat
our fair portion of the available victuals. It was while pouring
scalded tea into our drinking vessels that he repeated his
earlier question. "Monsieur Watkins, how can we stand
watch over the animals until dawn?"

"We can't," Bear answered bluntly.

A startled Val Dodd was at a loss for words. "But, but
we—"

Dense hair covered the top side of the hand Bear raised
to quiet Dodd, and one of the gray eyes almost hidden by
his heavy, overhanging brows winked reassuringly at the
confused horse master. "There's an Injun roundabouts, an'
we ain't sacrificin' any of us to him. We'll move into the
trees and sleep in twos, backside to backside. As for the
animals, we've got the riding stock strung on a picket line.
The creek bottom should keep the packhorses bunched together. Come first light, the riding stock can graze on longer
ropes while we gather the packhorses. Tomorrow, we'll talk
Starkweather into assigning some of his dragoons to help us.
Then we'll be strong enough to post guards on the entire
herd through the night."

Val Dodd's lips curled in a smile so wide it all but buried
his thin mustache. "I believe you and me will become the
best of friends, Monsieur Watkins. I have always trusted you
men from the woods. Let me pour you more tea."

Despite its rank flavor, we spiked the tea with dollops of
rum and finished it, every last drop, then set about retiring
for the night. When Ira, Henry, and Val Dodd saw us Downer
men piling layers of branches to separate our blankets from
the bare ground, they hastily did likewise. Tap didn't say

anything aloud, but he muttered to himself and shook his head at how a body could live years and not know enough to avoid a cold bed.

It was some later that a careful shaking awakened me from sound, dreamless sleep. Tap, his backside pressed against mine, turned his shoulders and whispered, "Take a peek at the fire." I did, and beside what had become a pile of gray ashes and a few glowing embers squatted Gabe Hookfin, blankets wrapped 'round his narrow frame. Tap wiggled closer. "That's a right fine lesson for yuh, sprout. Stubbornness is big a sin as ignorance. It's made Walking Stick there a prime target for your Injun if'n he's still on the prowl. Shame to think a fellow, even a turd like him, might die for just wantin' to be warm a spell, ain't it now?"

Tap, of course, expecting no answer, rolled over and was immediately asleep and snoring. I, on the other hand, lay awake no little time. And when I did drop off again, I slept fitfully, drifting from one disturbing dream of new acquaintances to another. First came a scowling Court Starnes, walnut-knuckled fists poised to strike. Then Miles Starkweather seated on the Kentucky sorrel, examining a long-bladed knife with a rosewood handle. Then Tap's newly named Walking Stick, Gabe Hookfin, dressed like a cornfield scarecrow, yelling orders I couldn't hear. Then a bejeweled Erin Green, clothed in a silk gown, dancing in the middle of a ballroom filled with uniformed officers, a dazzling Erin Green who ignored my beseeching calls from the edge of the crowd. And, lastly, a painted Shawnee with his bow fully drawn, the feathered arrow aimed at my chest.

For all the true rest I gained, I might as well have stayed awake till dawn.

Chapter 8

First Light, 6 October till Retreat, 7 October

My dreams vanished when I came awake at the first hint of day. Wood smoke stained the faint light seeping through the trees as it had yesterday, and leaves pattered the ground, shed from branches by a whisper of chill breeze. Drums rolled upcountry, indicating St. Clair's army, two thousand four hundred bodies strong, was on the rise, as were the shapes lumped in pairs shy of the Dodd fire.

Ira Cross shook free of his blankets, the barrel of his long gun rapping the curve of his skull. "Ain't natural sleepin' with no rifle. Proper man sleeps with a woman, not somethin' cold and hard and likely to gouge him where it's tender."

"Trust me," said Tap. "In a few nights that old gun will seem like a third arm, an' you won't be able to sleep without it no more'n a baby can doze off without his spell at the teat."

Henry Fellows stood and stomped feeling into his booted feet. "Yeah, but no rifle's ever gonna surprise you with a wet kiss in the middle of the night neither, is it now?"

Tap laughed uproariously and swatted Henry on the shoulder. "You'll do to stone the deck with, my friend. You'll do just fine."

Bear then introduced the Dodd men to another dawn ritual, the checking of powder and pan and lock and flint, all of which preceded even the morning call of nature. A genial gathering at a rekindled fire followed, for Gabe Hookfin was nowhere to be found. At the finish of rather scanty fixings, Val Dodd announced, "We must secure new rations from the quartermaster. It is my hope that your father, Monsieur

Downer, has a shipment arriving today. If he doesn't, Captain Starkweather says the general will be forced to reduce us to half rations, perhaps as early as tomorrow. And many in the ranks have threatened desertion if they don't receive what their recruiting officers promised them."

"The silly fools. You ain't nothin' but if'n you believe the army can provide a pound an' a half of flour, a pound of meat, and a half-pint of whiskey every day of the year," reasoned Ira. "So far, they've failed on everythin' at least once but the whiskey, an' that'll dry up sooner or later, mark my words."

We shortly went off on our morning horse gather, and nothing else was said about the critical shortages threatening St. Clair's regiments. For that, I was thankful. After Ira's blaming of the army itself, I had nothing valid to offer as to why paid civilian contractors like Duer, Starnes, and my father had failed to deliver not only the daily rations in a timely fashion but also necessary equipment and dry powder. More and more evidence indicated Paw was in mighty big trouble with General St. Clair, and it bothered me I wasn't at his side. I felt helpless as a blind calf.

Our morning gather revealed we were missing two head of riding stock and an equal number of packhorses, not a large number given the fact that we were responsible for seventy animals of Duer's along with the army's five hundred baggage horses. Miles Starkweather, moving the baggage horses forward with his mounted dragoons, took a different slant on our latest losses. "I must inform General Butler personally. Those are my orders. He's extremely upset that you have neither hobbles nor bells to prevent such occurrences."

"Captain, we need to arrive at an understanding," Bear suggested smoothly.

"And what would that be?"

"Six men can't look after these horses by themselves. We need a guard detailed to help us."

"How large a detail would you need, Mr. Watkins?"

Bear didn't slight the opportunity Starkweather laid before him. "No less than forty men. Combined with what we have, we can split into two squads, one for each half of the night hours."

Starkweather thought a few moments, then his billed helmet bobbed up and down. "I shall discuss the matter with General Butler. Perhaps I can persuade him to listen. Till this evening, Mr. Watkins."

The army jerked into motion at ten o'clock beneath fair skies, and for the next two days clawed a path to the northwest, its objective the upper reaches of Seven Mile Creek, the rim of the valley of the Great Miami River. Tightly growing tree butts and hardy brush impeded our advance every rod. The ground dipped and climbed, and the ring of felling and clearing axes echoed all about us, constant as the beat of regimental drums. Countless streams and shallow ravines required bridging timbers, and the long column, stretching three-quarters of a mile from advance to rear guards, lurched and stopped, lurched and stopped, till the curses of the marchers rivaled the ring of axes and the beating of drums. In forty-eight hours, we marched a grand distance of nine whole miles.

A tired and worn Miles Starkweather joined us in line behind the officer's servants late the second afternoon, 7 October. A smile eased his square, clean-shaven jaws. "Mr. Watkins, I have finally arranged a meeting with General Butler. I shall tell him we lost additional animals last night. You may count on my utmost support in mounting a military guard over the horse herd."

That said, he hefted two fifty-pound cloth bags of flour tied across the pommel of his saddle, one in each hand. "Mr. Downer, I have an errand to ask of you. Please deliver these rations to Molly Green. Sergeant Devlin cannot be spared anytime soon, General St. Clair may arrive within the hour, and those who depend upon Mistress Green are in need. Can I trust you to do so?"

I vowed then and there to pray more frequently. I had spent every waking minute trying to conjure up a means of seeking out Erin Green without leaving Bear in the lurch when it came to my share of our daily duties. And now Starkweather had requested I visit her family on official army business. Blessed be the meek and the faithful.

Bear didn't speak till Starkweather rode beyond earshot. "Deliver the flour and feast your eyes on that sweet gal, if'n you must." He removed his hat and swiped sweat from his nose. "I expect you back by sundown. Can't say I wouldn't race you to the Green camp was I a tad younger," he said with a sly grin. "Be off with you, lad!"

I wove Blue through the three hundred cattle close upon our back trail. The sun was unusually warm for an autumn afternoon, and I couldn't sign wind with even a wet finger. The camp followers brought up the extreme rear, their carts and wagons clogging the narrow stem of raw roadway a distance behind the lowing bullocks. Footsore washerwomen, harlots, and wives, along with their panting children, plodded together in rude masses twixt the carts, at that hour cursing the heat and the uneven ground instead of bickering with each other. The few male travelers present struggled to keep the carts and wagons from falling so far behind the column they lost sight of the cattle drovers to their fore.

I rode in the fringe of the trees crowding the road to get past the clutter and drew abreast of the Green cart. The order to halt for the day swept the length of the column, and Annie Bower, walking beside the swaybacked drayage horse pulling the Green cart, praised the command with a rousing cheer. Blue slipped from the cloaking woods, and she cheered again. "By damn, it's that gentleman who saves ladies 'thout bein' asked, Mr. Ethan Downer hisself. Come to visit me, have yuh, darlin'?"

Blushing like crazy, I lifted the bulging flour sacks straddling Blue's withers and drew yet another bellowing cheer from her. "Lord, I'm glad that's for us'ns. It was a shabby and discouraging meal the last two evenings, which is maybe why Molly took sick," she surmised, pointing toward the cart.

A rigged tarp arched across the cart's wooden bed. Beneath it, Molly Green lay atop rolled blankets and a folded tent. From Blue's saddle, I could see her face glistened with fever. "The army doctor been to visit her?"

Annie Bower sat the flour sacks against the near wheel of the cart, straightened, and swept straggling hair behind her ears. "Yeah, but Erin run him off when he talked of bleeding and purges. Said she'd a cure of her own for her mother.

An' Erin ain't easy to talk out of anythin' once she sets her mind a certain way."

"Don't I know," I agreed. "She about?"

Annie stepped sideways to obtain an unobstructed view of the span of empty road extending southward behind the cart. "Well, damn that child, she was there but a minute ago, I swear."

Hearing Annie's loud exclamation, Molly Green called weakly from her makeshift bed. The harlot, hips rocking under swishing skirts, approached the cart. The women spoke faintly, and I caught only a word or two. Annie returned, a deep frown shaping ruts in the skin of her forehead. "I fear she's been gone longer than a minute, much longer. Molly says she dropped off at the bottom of the last rise to cool herself in the brook that crossed the road there. Molly wants you should go fetch her in."

There was nothing for it except do the fetching, and I had no objection to that, not the slightest. Given my jumpy nerves, I had been mulling over how I might approach Erin Green in front of others without aping the tongue-tied lout, and luckily, the Lord had chosen to favor me again. I matched Annie Bower's wink, tipped my hat to her, and thumped Blue's ribs with my heels.

Tired of slow walking all day, the gelding happily pranced back down St. Clair's road, fresh stumps or no. It was a piece to the rise Annie had mentioned, and we went up its near flank. We topped the crest of the rise and started our descent of the opposing incline, expecting to shortly encounter the object of our quest. I scanned the brook at the bottom of the rise as we approached and still no Erin. My concern mounted. It seemed she'd been tarrying behind a mighty long while just to wash away the sweat of the day. Where the hell could she be?

Fully aware I had asked myself that question before, I drew rein, and rifle seated on my left thigh with the barrel at attention, looked all about. The shallow expanse of the brook was a plat of brown sludge, churned into syrupy mud by the pounding of thousands of feet and hoofs. I didn't bother scouting downstream. The brook would run brown there for a fortnight. A girl wanting to wash her person would seek the clear, undisturbed waters available upstream.

I kneed Blue forward into the muddy sludge and had me a gander the direction I believed I would find her. Beech and walnut branches overhung both banks of the brook. Pockets of brush overwhelmed the northern bank at those spots touched directly by the sun. The way was narrow and lacking in headroom, and I was inclined to leave Blue tied at the crossing, but didn't when I recalled Paw's admonition that the soldier who risked his mount in enemy territory placed himself in jeopardy as well.

Swearing at the prospect of cold, wet feet, I dismounted, and Blue's reins held lightly in right hand, rifle in left, barrel slanted downward, lock buried twixt elbow and waist to protect cock and frizzen from scraping branches, took to wading. A few strides beyond the crossing I located sign of her. Gouges cut into the brook's mossy bed by the footfalls of a recent traveler were fresh enough the current still flushed tiny plumes of dirt from them. I was on the right track. That proverbial question rang in my head again: Where the bloody hell was she?

Forty yards of wading later, I had a glimmering where I would eventually come upon her. She would be enticed ever onward in hopes of locating a clearing providing a little open ground, bright sun, and maybe deeper water for easier bathing. I had myself sought such quiet, restful places too often to count while hunting the Kentucky forest. I put some zip in my step. Autumn daylight had a habit of petering out with a man shy of camp.

The brook bent a hair to the right and gradually widened. Open sky loomed to the south upstream, and I suspected Erin had indeed found her clearing. Heavily wooded, rising ground continued to push hard against the north bank. The trees on the south bank began to thin, and I led Blue onto its level surface. The clearing was now dead ahead, and not wanting to startle Erin unnecessarily, I crept along, alert and watchful.

It was her slim feet and shins that gave her away. They stuck bare and white from the runty grasses blanketing the edge of the brook. She had without meaning to fallen asleep, warmed and lulled by the quiet and peace of the sun-splashed clearing, separated for a blissful hour from the unwanted company of hundreds of strangers foul both of smell and mouth. Heaven itself could have been no more appealing.

Reluctant to awaken her, I lingered where I was. Birds cawed far to the east. The only other sound was the bubbling rush of the brook. I was thinking of lurking redsticks and the necessity of returning to camp before dark, reasons why I should move ahead, when Erin woke of her own accord.

She sat upright, shook her unbound, flame-red hair back and forth, and glanced 'round the clearing. Satisfied she was still secluded and alone, Erin opened a canvas haversack atop the grass, pulled forth a wedge of cloth, rose to her feet, and waded into the water. Her silk shirt sparkled in the sunlight. With her breeches legs rolled higher than her knees, she seemed every bit the girl child at play till she stretched, sweeping her arms above her head and pulling the silk of her shirt tight over breasts fully grown. Instantly, the girl child became a woman, a woman of a rare and ripe beauty that stayed a man's breath and urged him to whinny aloud and paw dirt with his toes.

She rolled the sleeves of her shirt to near the elbow, then bent, dipped the cloth in the brook, and slowly washed her face, neck, and arms, savoring every stroke of the cloth. Absolutely spellbound, I froze, unable to take my eyes from her.

I would have stared endlessly, all other concerns completely forgotten, had she not slipped the dampened cloth behind the waistband of her breeches and started undoing that silk shirt one pewter button at a time. My heart thudded like a hammer. A fanciful and elusive dream was coming to life. She snapped the last button free, regained the damp cloth from her waistband, and inserted its moist coolness inside the open front of the silk shirt.

Prickly heat engulfed my throat and neck. It was a most private moment, one so utterly hers and hers alone, that I expected the slap of my mother's hand against my cheek any second. I tore my prying eyes from Erin Green and fixed them on the hillside beyond the brook, only to encounter an equally stunning sight, the leering visage of none other than the beanpole, Gabe Hookfin.

He was directly above her, hidden except for his hat and face. He was so awed by what he was witnessing his slit of a mouth hung open. I was sure drool dripped from his chin.

Anger, so sudden and so complete it nearly blinded me, jolted my legs into motion. I was astride Blue in a leaping vault, determined to expose Gabe Hookfin for what I was regrettably myself, a shameful son of a bitch taking advantage of a beautiful woman.

But the beanpole, much as I detested him, was no blundering townsman. Even though preoccupied with Erin's bath, he was woodsman enough that any untoward movement where all had hitherto been still and unthreatening caught his attention immediately. He proved a cunning bastard to boot. He spied who I was before Erin was aware of either of us and turned things against me faster than the strike of lightning. He jabbed at me with a bony finger and his booming voice filled the entire clearing:

"Look, Miss Erin, look! You're bein' watched!"

Erin's head spun toward me. Her eyes swelled big as apples, and she lunged from the water, one gorgeous, rose-nippled breast sliding free of her gaping shirt. God, but I was glad she faced me right then and not Hookfin. She swept her doeskin frock from the runty grass and slipped her arms into the sleeves, her sobs tearing at my very soul.

I came down out of the saddle within ten feet of her. She pulled the frock shut over her open shirt, and the fury replacing her initial tears colored her cheeks a deep purple. Her blue eyes were suddenly chill and hostile. "Damn you, Ethan Downer! How could you?" she raged. "How could you, of all men, stoop to sneaking up on me like this?"

I stood speechless, fearful whatever I might say would only add to her fury. Gabe Hookfin appeared behind her shoulder, grinning like a jackanapes who'd just outwitted a rival he despised, which he had, slick as anything. By yelling out first, he had created the impression he had only just stumbled upon the scene and without the least hesitation warned Erin Green that someone was observing her bath from hiding.

He was a crafty turd. I had to grant him that. Where I was afraid to speak, he held his tongue a-purpose. With the field won, there was no need to provoke me into thrashing him within an inch of his life. And his never-ending grin told me he understood exactly what I was thinking.

It was Erin's presence that spared him my temper. Her opinion of me was already low enough without my sinking it deeper by playing the brute and whipping her skinny protector. But I did wipe the grin from the beanpole's lips with a withering glare that would have given a snarling catamount pause. Then I made the best of an impossible situation.

There was no acceptable excuse I could tender the fuming woman standing before me for what I was guilty of, so the only thing to do was get somewhere else, and the faster the better. I did, for the sake of whatever slim hope there was, if any, that she might someday forgive me, first apologize as best I could. And I daresay I managed it without tripping over my own tongue, which wasn't easy with her being twice as ravishing when she was mad.

"I'll not lie to you. I will never say I didn't enjoy watching you in the brook. But it was wrong, and I'm sorry. You need to know though, I wouldn't have bothered if you were fat and ugly."

I could've been mistaken, yet the biting of her lip seemed necessary to keep her from smiling, and with that tiny opening, I kept talking. "Your mother asked me to come and fetch you, and since you've been gone a goodly while, perhaps we should escort you home without delay," I suggested, nodding with great reluctance in the direction of the gloating Hookfin.

A change of mood washed over her like ice thawing. "Oh, my yes, Mother will be frightfully worried. We must go, and right now."

She seized Blue's reins, and leading him to the bank of the brook, aligned the roan's flank with us two men. "Eyes on the clearing, if you please," she requested, prompting Hookfin and me to divert our gaze elsewhere.

The afternoon was well along, the air cooling rapidly, and the beginning hint of evening shadows forming along the eastern brow of wooded heights. Darkness fell swiftly in autumn, and the redsticks were known to prowl in the last hour of daylight, hoping to catch elements of the hated white army unawares while they were busy settling in for the night. And any body of men unfortunate enough to be traveling in small numbers apart from the protection of the larger force during that same hour was particularly vulnerable to the Injuns' most beloved tactic, the surprise attack. We needed to ply the whip hard and right soon.

Following a cheery, "I'm ready," the now properly fastened and covered Erin Green, haversack beneath her arm, popped from behind Blue. Her formerly tearstained cheeks were dry, her chin was up, and the bounce in her step proclaimed she had, at least for the time being, put the ordeal of her interrupted bath out of her mind much as she could. Whatever she felt where I was concerned, she had no qualms about my giving the orders. In fact, she left no doubt as to that. "Mr. Downer, how are we to proceed?"

I took the bit strong and firm. "Hookfin, where's your horse?"

Though the beanpole didn't like answering to me, he was too clever to defy Erin's wishes, a move that might cost him whatever standing he had already gained with her. "He's tied top of that rise. I was hunting for deer when I spied you an' your roan."

It was an outright lie. He couldn't have spied me in the cover of the trees along the brook without my giving away my position. But since it was my word against his, I let his fib go unchallenged. I fisted Blue's reins. "We'll climb the hill, get your horse, and follow the high ground till we gain the army road. There'll be no halting. I'm not aimin' to be caught short of camp at nightfall. Step aboard, Mistress Green. I'll not deliver you to your mother any wetter'n necessary."

We quick timed up the hill, recovered Hookfin's mare, and lit a shuck for the army road. Once there, a hurried trek to the Green cart followed. Erin and the beanpole rode while I trotted afoot in the lead. On my orders, Hookfin trailed behind the entire distance, a decision he enjoyed akin to boils on the arse. Heroes hate to guard the rear, don't you know.

Well before we sighted our destination, I looked over my shoulder and caught Erin swiping at tears with the sleeve of her frock. Farther along the road, I looked again, and the same was true. Why was she crying now?

She wasn't hurt or suffering from any bodily harm inflicted upon her, and she was near to being safely home. I hated the notion she might be crying because of what I'd done, but it seemed the next best possibility. After all, she believed me guilty of deliberately violating her privacy, and her accusing words at the brook sounded in my head: "How could you, of all men, sneak up on me like this?"

The disappointment in her tone had hurt worse than a knife wound in the belly, still did, and might forever lest I could somehow quickly make amends.

But after being so helpful twice in a single day, the Lord was on the verge of extending a cold shoulder to the sinner named Ethan Downer.

Chapter 9

Evening, 7 October

The Green cart sat before an oak grove east of the army road, the tarp arching across its bed starkly white in the fading twilight. Annie Bower and her two harlot friends were cooking and baking at the fire. The absence of Molly Green brought Erin down from Blue, and she ran straight for the cart. I was mighty glad Sergeant Tor Devlin was elsewhere. I had no desire to explain to her protector how I fetched Erin home safe and sound, but at the same time, in tears. Tall explanations that skirted the truth, fell confidently on the ear of the listener, and got the speaker clear of trouble were Tap's bent, not mine.

Erin climbed into the cart out of sight. Annie Bower came sauntering around the fire, beckoning with an outstretched arm. "You must be hungry, hero. Will you dine with us?"

The smaller of Annie's rouged companions looked the newly dismounted beanpole up and down, her calculated grin an invitation to much more than dinner. "I've a fondness for men of long parts. Haven't I seen you hangin' about afore? You're called Gabriel Hookfin, ain't yuh?" she purred like a cat licking cream.

I decided to take my leave. Erin would spend the bulk of the evening caring for her mother, rendering next to none my chances of talking with her alone. And the thought of waiting in a hopeless cause in the presence of Gabe Hookfin had no appeal whatsoever. I forced myself to ignore the warm, doughy, glorious aroma of baking bread and stepped aboard Blue. "Perhaps another night, Annie. I must report as ordered."

Annie knuckled her forehead twice in an exaggerated military salute, trying to hide the sadness dulling her purple eyes. "I understand. That's the way it be with you knights errant. Duty pulls the bung on everythin' else."

I rode away feeling smaller than a tick buried in the belly hair of a hound. I had no idea what the hell a knight errant was. But there was no doubting one thing: Ethan Downer was so ignorant when treating with women, he had no trouble bringing them to tears.

I moseyed past sentries and drovers and cattle and located the Dodd camp where I expected, smack in the middle of the horse herd. Bear, Tap, and Val Dodd tended the fire. Tap's moon face beamed when he spotted me riding up. "Lookee here, Mr. Bear Watkins. It's the roaming lover come home to fill his innards with another meal of fresh beef and little else," Tap chimed around a mouthful. He chewed and swallowed. "We don't shoot us a buck soon, we'll be yonder grazin' an' shittin' with what we're eatin'."

"Light, Ethan. Don't mind ol' slack jaw there," Bear cautioned. "If'n yuh gave him a barrow of free gold, he'd grump about how heavy it was while he wheeled it away."

Unsaddling Blue in the small meadow east of the fire, I let him have his roll, then hobbled him. I placed my gear with that of the others at the edge of the surrounding trees but kept hold of my rifle. True to Bear's counsel of the previous evening, both his and Tap's long guns were propped across logs close beside them within easy reach. Val Dodd's lay across his very lap.

Bear passed me a metal rod. I sliced meat from the tree-strung beef haunch with Miles Starkweather's gift knife, filled the rod with long, narrow fillets, and took to roasting. Bear waited till I was situated before doing his asking. "You see all you wanted of that pretty Erin today?"

I snorted and stared at the fire. I couldn't tell what had really happened, for that would compromise Erin publicly. So I avoided telling any of the details. "Maybe I saw too much of her. Maybe I poisoned the well for myself."

I offered nothing more by way of explanation, and Bear thankfully didn't press. Tap cranked his mouth open to speak, but Bear closed it again with a stern shake of the head.

That same stern head shaking kept Val Dodd quiet, too.

We ate in silence till the beat of hooves drew our attention elsewhere. The approaching horse and rider came not from the headquarters end of the column, but the rear, back toward the Green cart. Miles Starkweather reined his sorrel to a halt in the meadow, stepped down, and walked purposely through the growing darkness to our fire. His stride was that of an officer with orders to be carried out . . . or a bone to pick with someone. I was hoping for the former.

"Mr. Dodd, I bear orders from General Butler himself."

Val Dodd climbed to his feet. "I am listening, Captain. What does your general wish of us?"

"General Butler has consented to the placing of a heavy guard over the horses at night with both mounted dragoons and infantry. But a messenger is to be dispatched at dawn to Fort Washington. He is to inform Court Starnes that hobbles and bells must be provided for the animals immediately, as many of each as can be had, regardless of the cost. Failure by either the messenger or Mr. Starnes is not acceptable to the general. You understand?"

"Yes, Captain," Val Dodd answered with a slow nod, "very clearly. Did General Butler name his would-be messenger?"

Starkweather slapped his left palm with his gloves. "No, he did not. The choice was left to me."

"And who might your choice be?" Bear asked in that smooth manner of his that never offended.

Starkweather's gaze fell on me. "Mr. Downer is the best mounted of you Duer men. I would prefer he make the ride, if you and Mr. Dodd concur."

It was two days to the Ohio, a fifty-mile journey across wooded terrain where savages might wait in ambush behind any tree or just 'round the next bend. The danger of such a journey for a lone rider dried my throat. I never realized till that moment how much I had depended upon the deceased Hardy Booth, how much, funning aside, I had leaned on his steady strength and gumption. Nor how much I truly missed him.

"I have no quarrel with your choice of riders, Captain," Bear said. "It's just that two riders travelin' together an' watchin' opposite sides of the road have a better chance of getting through to Court Starnes."

Bear's proposal perked my interest like the hound hearing the fox bark. Would he himself accompany me? Perhaps one of the Dodd men, either Ira, Henry or, God forbid, Gabe Hookfin, though the latter seemed the least likely choice given his continuing absence from our camp. The only person I didn't consider was Tap, he of the overblown belly and ancient mare for a mount.

And the old border scout, naturally, was Bear's choice from the get-go. "Mr. Jacobs will ride along with Ethan," Bear said straightforward as if announcing it was dark in the woods at night.

Starkweather didn't share Bear's confidence. "It is an arduous trek, and I fear Mr. Jacobs's age and that of his horse will delay the journey and disappoint the general."

No matter the truth of the captain's opinion, Tap's moon-shaped face turned rooster-comb red at what he considered a personal insult from an officer with no experience fighting the redsticks. The old scout reached for his belted knife. "Why, damn your snobbish hide, I'll—"

"Quiet, Tap," Bear interrupted. "This is my decision, an' it will stand," he said, squaring his wide shoulders with those of Starkweather.

"Mr. Jacobs rides in my stead, Captain. You can overlook the fact he's a mite hefty an' his hair's gone. He's still feisty enough to bite the head off'n a woods rattler with his hands tied behind him. He knows the Shawnee well as Kenton an' Tice Wentsell, the best border spies to ever draw a hawk. An' he'll be aboard that brown gelding of mine, animal enough to carry him to kingdom come twice over. Meantime, you an' me will see the army still has horses to bell and hobble when Tap and Ethan bring such to us. That's how Caleb Downer would want it done, and that's how we'll do 'er."

Bear Watkins was a persuasive fellow. Behind his hirsute countenance lurked a mind second only to that of Paw. Like Paw, he wasted few words and never drifted from the business at hand. Most times, arguing with either of them over men, long guns, Injun fighting, or horses was tantamount to shooting your ownself first in one foot, then the other, a mighty useless sort of habit when you thought on it.

Miles Starkweather thought on it and saw that disputing the sense of what Bear proposed would only make him appear unduly stubborn. He smiled politely, slapped his gloves against his thigh, and said, "Too bad you don't command a regiment, Mr. Watkins. I would feel much better about the days ahead if you did. Please dispatch our messengers at first light or shortly thereafter."

His gaze settled on me again. "If he would step to the horses, I would like a minute alone with Mr. Downer before I depart."

Bear nodded. "Go along, Ethan."

Puzzled as well as concerned, I followed the captain into the meadow. I had not forgotten my impression on his arrival that he might have a bone to pick with someone within our camp, namely me, depending on what he might have learned at the Green cart.

"Mr. Downer, understand me when I say I will not judge you based on the reckless contentions of one Gabe Hookfin."

His gloved hand lifted as he saw me stiffen. "Stand easy, Mr. Downer. I repeat. I will not stand in judgment. I simply want to warn you that the same accusations were made to Sergeant Devlin. Unfortunately, Erin was with her mother, so the truth went wanting. It would be wise for you to avoid any meeting with Sergeant Devlin till his ire cools. He is frightfully touchy about Erin and her mother."

Though I clenched my fists hard enough my fingernails threatened to break the skin of my palms, I fought to remain calm and not let my anger set me to shaking. In my worry about how I could make things right with Erin, it hadn't dawned on me how easily Hookfin could arouse Tor Devlin against me. The wheel was spinning backward faster and faster on me.

Miles Starkweather watched me closely, patiently waiting for me to speak, and after a gulping breath, I told him the straight of it. For some reason I didn't yet understand, I didn't want this particular captain thinking poorly of me. "I was searching for Erin at her mother's request, and no matter what Hookfin claims, I stumbled upon her bath without

meaning to." I dug at the ground with a toe and hoped the
dimness of the meadow masked the red on my face. "She
was so beautiful, I couldn't take my eyes off her, and neither
could Hookfin. He yelled to her like he had caught me deliberately hiding just to watch her, and I couldn't do anything
except apologize to her."

It sounded embarrassingly lame after I got it out, and I
hastily asked an obvious question. "Did you pick me to be
the general's messenger to keep me away from Erin and the
sergeant?"

"No, you are the best-mounted rider for the task," Starkweather insisted. "It's just fortunate for all concerned that
you'll be away from the column a few days. Even then, I
suggest you consult with me upon your return before making
any attempt to visit with Erin. Tor Devlin's temper is legend
and can try the patience of a saint. He is a very unforgiving
soul."

I held my tongue then and waited expectantly for any
indication the captain believed my explanation as to what
had really happened at the brook. But Starkweather abided
by his earlier statement that, not having talked with Erin
Green, he had no intention of passing judgment on Ethan
Downer. He adjusted the sword hanging at his hip and tugged
his gloves tighter over long fingers. "I trust you will be ready
to take your leave at dawn. I bid you good evening."

A quick salute, and Starkweather was mounted and disappearing from sight. It was a real chore to keep my head
from hanging when I stepped alongside Bear at the fire. He
shot me a concerned look but didn't pry. And his previous
admonishment kept Tap glumly silent. I had a hunch the old
snake biter would be spouting questions tomorrow plumb
down to the Ohio.

New hoofbeats and the tramp of marching feet heralded
the arrival of the mounted dragoons and infantry levies assigned to help guard the horses. Commanding those afoot
was Daniel Croft, the stubby sergeant with the huge black
mustache Erin and I had encountered after fording the Great
Miami. Bear assigned me to Croft's squad for the first half
of the night, and much to my chagrin, the sergeant proceeded
to ask me so many questions about Erin a lengthy pestering

by the effusive Tap would have proved a welcome relief.
Through it all, I marveled at how men of every stripe never
forgot a solitary detail regarding Erin Green, no matter how
little they had enjoyed her company. A word and a smile
from her and they were smitten. As I could damn well testify.

I spent the balance of the night with my backside flush to
Tap's spine. It didn't bother me a lick the old scout was by
then too exhausted for anything but sleep. I tossed fitfully,
and my dreams ran sour on me before dawn. The prospect
of hurrying forever through the forest in pursuit of an Erin
who refused to stop and face me, regardless of how loudly
I yelled after her, was so disturbing I came awake in a sweat,
quaking and moaning. I grasped the rifle twixt my thighs with
both hands, listened without moving, and was relieved to
hear nothing except rasping snores and smacking lips.

Bad enough to be hopelessly in love, worse yet to confirm
it by acting the fool in front of friends and strangers. Even
the smitten have their pride.

Chapter 10

8 October

Whether Bear Watkins observed my fitful night, I was never to learn. But he had figured what was upsetting me, and prior to my departure for the Ohio, he led me into the trees where the two of us were in no danger of being overheard. The squaring of his thick shoulders and the butting of his rifle told me he was speaking as the man Paw had left in charge, and I came alert accordingly. While seen less often, Bear's wrath equaled that of my absent father.

"Lad, I'll not have you be the death of Tap," he stated vehemently. "Was we back at the Downer place, I'd not fault you for mooning over Erin Green. But your attention needs to be on your duty an' nothin' else."

He was flush on the mark. Till he spoke, achieving even a minute alone with her had been foremost on my mind. "Ethan, lovesickness can get you killed fast as anything in enemy country. You listenin' to what I say?"

I forced myself to meet his intent gaze, not an easy feat given my embarrassment that he had had to single me out and yank my chain good and proper. I fought the urge to look at his feet and nodded. Weakness gained you naught with Bear Watkins.

Still watching me with nary a blink, Bear lifted his rifle and cradled it in the crook of his elbow. "I'll take you at your word, Ethan. Mayhap a time apart from her will set your thinking to rights. Now, you an' Tap ride straight through the day an' rest your animals overnight. You should sight Fort Washington late tomorrow evenin'. Find your Paw soon as you can, an' tell him, not Court Starnes, what needs to be done."

Bear hawked, turned at the waist, leaned forward, and spat, affording me a chance to suck some wind. His voice and his gaze were just as firm as before when he continued. "You set the pace for Tap. He'll carp his arse hurts, and he can't feel his feet his legs are so cramped. Ignore him. His complaints get tiresome on the ear, threaten to tie him in the saddle. That always stifles him for me. You followin' me here?"

He waited for my nod. "Sleep without a fire tonight. Expect the Shawnee anytime, day or night. Never doubt they're scoutin' the military road, every last mile of it. They spy on all we're about, whether we lay eye on them or not. Understood?"

Bear wasn't telling me anything I didn't already know. That he felt compelled to do so deepened my embarrassment. I was losing ground with friends as well as the ladies. I wasn't careful, I'd either be dead or home in Kentucky milking the cow and following the bidding of my house-bound sisters, a fate worse than death. It was time for Ethan Downer to get his thinking in order, and damn fast.

Bear wasn't seeking any lengthy, windy promises maybe I wouldn't keep, and I didn't spout off with any. I simply met his hard gaze best I could and said, "I'll not fail Tap. I'll not let my troubles bring him to harm."

"See to that, lad, for his blood would be on your hands," Bear warned solemnly. He glanced skyward. "The sun's up, the weather shows fair, and messengers should be a-horseback and travelin'. Come along."

Aware Bear had left much more skin on my behind than Paw would have in similar circumstances, I followed him to the morning fire determined to devote my sole attention to the ride ahead. If I didn't, I wasn't acting, but was indeed becoming, the addled fool I loathed. Only an addled fool tortured himself over a woman whose true intentions were unknown to him, a woman who might well never speak to him again. I wasn't a terribly happy fellow as I swung aboard Blue and led Tap from our camp. Sometimes I feared I was as green as new apples, just like Paw claimed.

We rode south under a sky dotted with high clouds. A moderate wind stiff enough to flutter the brim of my hat and toss Blue's mane blew from the southwest. I won't deny I didn't stand in the stirrups and give the Green cart careful scrutiny as we went past, but no female of red hair, mother or daughter, was out and about. Nor were Hookfin or Sergeant Devlin. Annie Bower and the harlots were easing the old swaybacked horse twixt the poles of the cart. They hooted and hollered, mostly ribbing Tap for not calling on them in recent days. The old scout yelled a ribald retort, and then we were beyond the cart and free of the column.

The brook where I had sought Erin the previous day was still running brown west of the ford as we splashed across. Afraid I was about to relive the scene upstream in all its gory details, I drew a snort of surprise from Blue when I thumped him into a gallop with my heels. A few dodges around protruding stumps, and I hastily slowed him to a trot. It was a small man who endangered a fine mount to assuage his own tormented feelings.

Backtracking on the St. Clair military road at any constant pace was a formidable task. Granted, the way had been cleared to a width of a half-dozen yards in most places. But in addition to the stumps and small brush littering its uneven surface, the open swath twisted left and right at random, the army having sought to avoid huge fallen timbers whenever possible and gain the most level course in traversing the ascending and descending slopes. And while the rider's eyes had to be constantly fixed on the dangers of the open path directly ahead and below his mount's nose, oak and hickory butts frequently wider than the arm span of a giant dominated the uplands, pushing hard on the edge of the road. In bottoms cut by small runs of water and outcroppings of stone white here and brown there, butts smaller but more frequent in number, these of black walnut, maple, and beech, undershot with screening brush, crowded the roadway no less hard. Everything weighed against those traveling in light company and favored those lying in wait, fingers caressing the trigger of a long gun balled and primed. With each mile, women and love seemed ever more distant.

Through the morning, Tap and I hardly spoke. The only

sounds were the beat of hooves beneath us, the sigh of the wind, and the hollow thudding that arose whenever we crossed the wooden army bridges, large and small, that spanned every measurable waterway and abrupt break in the terrain. The echoes of our crossings rippled in every direction, announcing our passage, but walking the animals at each bridge would have lengthened our journey unreasonably, sacrificing too much time for what little extra safety we might have gained. As Tap observed early on, "I'd rather be on the move if'n I'm ambushed. Injuns disappearin' behind a runnin' horse be a mighty attractive sight. You can't enjoy your whiskey, yuh ain't alive to drink her down."

We chewed stringy fingers of roasted beef and sipped water from tin canteens in the saddle. When we did rest the horses, we did so whenever possible on the highest available ground where the trees were thinner and we could maintain a more effective watch to both sides of the road. It was during one of the brief blowing of our mounts in early afternoon, still well above the lower reaches of Seven Mile Creek, that we first heard the pounding approach of other riders from the south in the direction of Fort Hamilton.

Tap came upright, eyes squinting against the sunshine. "Must be our'n. Ain't no Injuns gonna sashay about in the open this hour of the day."

We straddled the road and waited. A military detail totaling six riders hove into view below us. "Well, for the love of God if'n it ain't him!" Tap sang out.

Tap had been around Fort Washington with Paw for weeks, so for him to become all excited about sighting any particular soldier called for some explanation. "Who is it?" I asked, foolishly rising onto my toes in hopes of seeing better when we already held the high ground.

"It's St. Clair his-by-God-ownself with his private minions," Tap answered, his voice lowering. "He's in the middle up front with Major Denny on his left, and Count Malartie, his aide-de-camp, on his right."

Major General Arthur St. Clair was a mighty striking figure astride his muscular white horse, like a diamond among shards of coal. The silver stars on his gold epaulettes sparkled in the sun, and the red turban of his bearskin-crested cap, bathed with the same bright light, seemed afire. As he rode up to us, I made out his blue coat was trimmed and lined with buff. His vest and breeches were of the same tannish brown. His boots were tall and fashioned of soft, black leather. Though his face was stern, it was not ugly, and his shadowed eyes held a man's attention when he looked at you, which he was doing with me just now. He inspected me carefully, then gave Blue a going over, too. Thorough, I decided, very thorough was Major General Arthur St. Clair.

The officer Tap had identified as Major Denny spoke to the general, and the entire detail reined to a halt smack before us. "You are acquainted with these gentlemen, Major Denny?" the general asked, his tone sounding a little aloof if I heard him right.

"Yes, sir, one of them. The bowlegged jasper is Tap Jacobs, a fine scout and tracker."

St. Clair's shoulders shook like he was loosening the muscles of his back. "If I may inquire, Mr. Jacobs, what are you about?"

Not the least awed in the presence of a major general, Tap said bluntly, "We're bound for Fort Washington for hobbles an' bells on the orders of General Butler, sir."

Tap's pronouncement roused interest in St. Clair. He leaned forward in the saddle and inspected the old scout anew. "What is your regiment, sir?"

"None, sir. I'm with the contractors, Caleb Downer and Court Starnes."

The general leaned the opposite direction in the saddle. "Mr. Jacobs, I pray you won't take this as a personal insult, but if you are successful in your mission, it will be the first time anyone associated with William Duer has succeeded at any assignment, and I repeat, any assignment, in recent memory. And with that, I bid you good afternoon. Major, if you please."

The major's arm lifted, and the detail swung into motion, passing over the crest of the rise. My initial excitement at seeing Major General Arthur St. Clair in the flesh faded quickly when I realized my delight that he hadn't learned I was Caleb Downer's son was downright selfish and grossly disloyal to Paw. St. Clair's damning words had put teeth in my fears for Paw. He was on the thinnest of ice with the general and his officers, the whole army in fact, and that would bother and worry Paw day and night. Paw set great store by his reputed honesty in his dealings with others, for he believed only the beat of a man's heart exceeded the importance of his good name.

I stepped into the saddle and kicked Blue southward. Tap frowned at my sudden abruptness but followed without commenting aloud. I think he was getting used to my moodiness.

Our next encounter with military personnel headed the opposite direction from us occurred in late afternoon. Across a bridged ravine the road narrowed and twisted to pass around an outcropping of blue stone higher than a two-story blockhouse. In the bend beyond the blue stone marched the lead ranks of a large force of Kentucky militia, citizen soldiers easily identifiable by their numerous pelt caps, walnut-dyed shirts, patched trousers, shabby footwear, and poor weaponry. No military issue muskets or rifles in decent order graced their shoulders. These sons of the bluegrass toted instead light-caliber flintlocks best suited for hunting squirrels, ancient muskets with stocks pieced together with leather thongs and rope, and even older, rusted blunderbusses with flaring muzzles. And their ages were as varied as their weapons, for I spotted graybeards as well as cheeks too young for the bite of the razor.

The advance ranks, sauntering along haphazardly four abreast, were followed by a covey of mounted officers. "That's Colonel Oldham on the gray with the black mane. I tipped many a jug with William my early years," Tap bragged with a chuckle.

We cleared the road, and the militia went past. Colonel Oldham called out to Tap and saluted the old scout. "Chrissakes but I wish him luck with that bunch of tadpoles and dying fish. One boo in the dark an' they'll be crowdin' behind each other like rats cowering from a lanthorn in the hold of a ship."

The comments of the militia as they filed by did nothing to disprove Tap's poor opinion of them. "Don't you tell me to be quiet, Sergeant Fox. You ain't no more a sergeant than my two-year-old mule."

"Yesiree, Fox, you lift your nose any higher, it'll match St. Clair's, an' he's ridin', an' you're a-walkin'."

"Shut up, all of yuhs. You'll spout a different ditty once we meet up with them redsticks. You'll damn well wish you was home flouncin' your woman's skirt then."

"Shut your own trap, Haffey. You ain't seed a live Injun for twenty goddamn years, an yuh won't be any braver than the rest of us come the fight."

Tap could only shake his head. I counted three hundred and forty-eight pelt caps and hats, and the sentiments I overheard regarding General St. Clair, their own officers, and the folly of attacking the redsticks in their Miami towns on the St. Mary's never once wavered. "It's a damn sad day for Kentucky, is all I have to say," Tap concluded. "I'd rather tend the king's arse than admit I know anyone from that bunch but Oldham."

The winter daylight was waning rapidly, and we hurried onward. A few miles later, Tap posed an important question. "Can we make Fort Hamilton afore the horses fail us?"

I reined Blue to the side of the road and dismounted. We had covered twenty-plus miles since leaving the Dodd camp. By my reckoning, Fort Hamilton was another half-dozen miles. I checked Blue's legs and those of Tap's brown gelding. It was a real push for the animals, but both seemed in good fettle.

"Sure would be special to sleep beneath a roof tonight," Tap opined from atop his mount. "My bones are achin' like they was broke an' never set. I'll not mention my arse."

I couldn't help but grin. "All right, we'll push ahead. It'll be your reward for not griping and carping the whole day. If Ensign Andy Young's about, perhaps we won't be turned away. Besides, you've eaten every scrap of beef in our poke."

The sun was long down and the sunset a dying streak of purple when Fort Hamilton loomed on the far bank of the Great Miami. We forded without difficulty and circled the log pickets to the main gate. The evening sentry barked his challenge from the inside catwalk adjoining the gate.

"Ensign Young, please!" I replied.

"Who be you? Answer my challenge, or burn in hell!" cried the sentry.

The voice possessed a familiar croak. "That you, Private Lawson?"

By the sputtering curses that erupted on the catwalk, my guess was correct. "You don't mind, please inform the ensign a friend of Erin Green's is at the gate. I'd not want you to come to any grief later, Private Lawson."

More sputtering curses rent the air. Rupert Lawson was too doggedly stubborn to go himself, but other boots rattled the ladder providing a means of descent from the catwalk and faded into the interior of the fort. A short, quiet wait, and two pairs of boots returned. A new voice called forth, "Identify yourself, please!"

It was Ensign Andy Young. "Ethan Downer and Tap Jacobs, sir, riding south to the Ohio on General Butler's orders."

"Open the gate," Young ordered.

Hinges creaked, and the right-hand gate slowly opened. Andy Young emerged, tricorn clasped tightly against his chest. "Good evening, gentlemen. How may I be of help, Mr. Downer?" he inquired with a friendly smile and firm handshake.

"Fodder for our horses, hot victuals, and a bed for the night. If that's too much, we'll settle for the feeding of our horses."

"Nothing is too much for those traveling on General Butler's orders," the ensign responded. "I'll not have it said Andy Young doesn't abide by the wishes of his superiors. Corporal Balser and Private Langford, step forward!"

Two uniformed bodies hustled through the gate and came to attention. "Take the mounts of these gentlemen to the picket line on the river. Corporal Balser, you know horses. See that these animals are properly watered and fed from the prairie grass we gathered this morning. I will hold you, and you alone, accountable for their care and protection overnight. Is that understood?"

Corporal Balser's prompt "Yes, sir" confirmed he knew exactly what was expected of him. "Satisfied, Mr. Downer?"

I nodded at the ensign and thanked him. "Then bring your personals and follow me."

Tap and I secured our rolled blankets and gear, and Andy Young led us into the fort. Barracks, departmental quarters, and storage depots surrounded the empty parade ground. Grease paper windows glowed in log walls, and the rising smoke of cooking fires hid blinking stars above clay and wattle chimneys. Much laughter and caterwauling marked the largest and longest of the buildings as the enlisted men's barracks. The ensign headed us toward a smaller structure in the opposite quadrant of the parade.

"There are just three officers on duty, leaving ample room for you two to bunk with us," reported the ensign.

Tap, wary how we civilian contractors would be received within the commissioned officers' barracks, asked from behind me, "We ain't tramplin' on any toes, are we, sir?"

Andy Young paused on the stone stoop of the officers' barracks. "No, only Captain Steddeman will actually sleep here tonight. Lieutenant Garst bunks in the loft of the quartermaster department. Come along, gentlemen."

With a shrug in Tap's direction, I followed the ensign through the plank door. The old scout mumbled a further protest but quieted while astride the threshold. The sizzle of frying meat and the whistle of steeping water has that effect on souls both thirsty and hungry.

A private, the only current occupant of the barracks besides us newcomers, cooked at the hearth centering the rear wall. Rope beds holding what appeared to be tick mattresses and woolen blankets filled each corner and the end walls. Wooden dowels and small shelves hung in rows above the rope beds. To the left of the entryway, opposite the swing of the door, stood an upright wooden rack for long guns. To the right reposed a writing desk, complete with clean sheets of parchment, an inkwell, and a small pottery urn that sprouted quill pens. A rectangular table flanked by benches filled the middle of the room.

Andy Young pointed at the gun rack. "Seat your weapons, gentlemen. This is Private Oakley, who is preparing our dinner. The fare is squirrel shot by Captain Steddeman, beans and dried peas with salt pork and wild onion, bread freshly baked, and black tea freshly steeped. The quality wouldn't satisfy Miles Starkweather's palate, but he's not with us this evening, is he?"

Hanging his tricorn on a wall peg, the ensign now pointed at the rope beds in the end of the room to the left of the table. "Your choice, gentlemen. Captain Starkweather, Major Denny, and Count Malartie are all in the north with General St. Clair."

I was by then feeling unwashed, bewhiskered, and decidedly out of place in such neat and tidy quarters. "Ensign, I would like to look after myself before dinner. May I have a few minutes?"

"Yes, Mr. Downer, you may. The officers' water basin and latrine are to the right out the door."

"Have you a candle and mirror, sir?"

Adequately supplied for the venture, I departed the barracks. Mother had always insisted that, weather permitting, we men bathe daily in the creek prior to her serving the evening meal. And to appear unshaven was asking to be dismissed with an empty belly. I stripped naked above the waist, washed with clean water, then shaved by candlelight with Starkweather's knife. It was sharp as a stropped razor.

Tap came along, splashed water on face and wrists, visited the latrine, and pronounced himself ready to dine. "I love yer maw, but she's a mite demandin' at times, young'un." Too tired and famished to argue with him, I simply patted his shoulder and agreed.

Captain Steddeman was present when Tap and I rejoined Andy Young. He was a stalwart officer with jaws big as a steel wolf trap and a closely cropped black beard shot with gray. He said little, coughed constantly, and ate in large gulping swallows. At the conclusion of the meal, he bolted upright and informed the ensign he would "button" the garrison for the night. Everyone at the table sighed with relief as the door banged shut behind him.

Ensign Young dismissed Private Oakley, and Tap, yawning and shaking his head, refused a final slurp of whiskey, a rare event, and retired to the rope bed of his choice. I took the opportunity to shuck my moccasins and thoroughly dry my feet and footgear in front of the hearth, for while sleeping away from the fire in the open at night protected your scalp, it was an injustice to your lower limbs. I did apologize to Andy Young for the rank smell I unleashed. But the ensign merely smiled and poured more tea into my noggin. "Captain Steddeman won't be offended, either. He constantly preaches that damp feet are more dangerous to the frontier officer than the redsticks."

We talked about Erin and Molly Green, the ensign wondering how they could be spared the rigors of a protracted campaign. Neither of us had a solution to that dilemma for mother or daughter. I made no mention of the incident with Erin and Hookfin. The warmth and longing in Andy Young's eyes as he discussed Erin and her situation said everything. He was more hopelessly in love with her than I.

Once Tap was settled and snoring, the ensign went to the writing desk and fetched a sheaf of rolled parchment from a side drawer. "Mr. Downer, I have something that might be of interest to you."

I set my noggin aside and waited as he unfurled the sheaf and spread two sheets of parchment side by side on the table. "I've not yet shared this with my superiors. What I'm showing you I discovered while reviewing supply vouchers, shipping manifests, and other documents for General St. Clair."

"Why would they be of interest to me?" I asked, honestly perplexed.

"Because you did Erin Green a great service at your own bidding, and you are deserving of something in return. These papers may have much to do with your father's present troubles, namely, the failure of William Duer and his agents to supply adequate equipment, rations, clothing, and powder for General St. Clair's campaign."

"Keep talking, Ensign," I said, suddenly captivated by his every word. I swung my bare feet beneath the table so I was facing him.

"Let me explain. My father, Falkner Kensington Young, the Third, owns the largest shipping and trading house in Philadelphia. Until I talked him into letting me seek a future with the army, I clerked for the family firm, certifying shipping manifests at the company wharves. I spent many months doing precisely what I did with your father at the Fort Washington landing in September. I counted and verified cargo as it was off-loaded from numerous ships. Later, at the company offices, we would review the manifests a final time to insure they were in proper order and that they had been signed by all required parties before payments were extended to ship captains. My father was very exacting and had a passion for accuracy. So, Mr. Downer, I know of what I'm speaking."

I had a sip of whiskey from the table jug. "I'll grant you that, Ensign."

"Good. Now let's look at the shipping manifest to your left for a Kentucky boat captained by Dyson Barch. The boat sailed from Fort Pitt 15 September. It landed at Fort Washington 25 September. The manifest reads sixty saws, sixty broadaxes, sixty adzes, forty dozen files, four hundred pairs of overalls, twelve hundred pairs of stockings, one hundred dozen musket balls, twenty-four kegs of black powder, and so on and so forth. And here, near the bottom, certifying that the quantity of each item listed on the manifest is true and correct, are the mark of Dyson Barch and the signatures of your father, representing Duer, and me, the officer on duty at the Cincinnati landing 25 September. At the very bottom, affixed later, we find the signatures of Court Starnes, chief agent for William Duer, along with that of Army Quartermaster Samuel Hodgdon, these last two required to initiate payment by the army for equipment and supplies received in proper condition.

"The Barch manifest was included in a bundle of documents given to me by Samuel Hodgdon on the orders of General St. Clair during their stay here yesterday evening. Mr. Downer, General St. Clair has no confidence in Samuel Hodgdon, who is very careless with details in all his transactions. And being personally acquainted with my father, the general asked me to check that the documents were in proper order and that each bore the required signatures, then forward them back to him for final signature and eventual payment of the monies owed Starnes and Duer."

The ensign wet his throat with a swallow of tea. "Captain Dyson Barch has a patched eye and a livid scar that runs from the center of his forehead down alongside his nose to the corner of his mouth. I remembered the captain, and hence his boat and its cargo soon as I started reading the manifest. What I didn't recall was that the quantities he off-loaded were so generous. I remember them being no more than half of what is shown here. And the more I dwelled upon it, the more I trusted to my memory."

I couldn't help it, my hackles rose. "Now, hold on here, Ensign. My paw's signature is right there beside yours. He made the count with you, did he not?" I demanded.

Andy Young nodded. "Yes, he did. But that's not what I'm doubting."

I was admittedly confused and getting angrier. "I'm lost, Ensign!"

"That's not my signature," Andy Young stated blunt as a striking ax. "And I believe your father's is fake also."

Hackles sinking fast, I clasped the edge of the table with both hands and gathered the wind he'd knocked from my sails. "Can you prove that?"

"Probably not in a court of law. But I know how I write my name, and the letters are a tad small for my hand. I wouldn't have noticed if I hadn't questioned something else about the manifest."

"What about Paw's name?"

Ensign Young tapped the second document on the table with a finger. "This is a voucher prepared by your father to request payment for packhorses purchased by him at Limestone, Kentucky, last month. Notice anything unusual about his signature here compared to the Barch manifest?"

I studied the voucher, the Barch manifest, then the voucher again. "Not much difference that I can tell except his signature on the voucher for the packhorses isn't nearly as neatly written as that on the manifest."

"A sharp eye for detail, Mr. Downer. That's what led me to finally conclude that I'm correct, that the Barch document is a forgery. Your father and I signed the rightful manifest atop an overturned hogshead that made do for a desk at the landing. These fake signatures, besides the inappropriate size of the letters in my name, are too neat, too precise. They were rendered with great care by the forger, too much care!"

I had me another sip of whiskey and asked the question that needed answering the most. "If somebody went to all this trouble, they're serious about their stealing. Since they forged Paw's name, he must not know what they're about. Then who's behind this?"

Ensign Andy Young's face was sober as a magistrate passing judgment on a prisoner. "It can only be Court Starnes. He was the last civilian to sign before delivery of the manifest to Samuel Hodgdon and the army for payment at set prices for each item listed. And as Duer's chief agent, the monies will be issued directly to Starnes. If he didn't forge the document himself, it was done on his orders. I learned while working for Father's counting house that the captain of the ship is seldom ignorant of anything that happens aboard his vessel."

I thought on that, and it was like a candle suddenly flaming up in a dark room. "Starnes is stealing from the army, and William Duer isn't even aware of it, is he?"

The ensign's eyes brightened, and his head bobbed with vigor. "Exactly," he gushed. "He collects funds against the bloated forgery but forwards only the original manifest and the lesser monies due against it to Duer in Philadelphia. Quite a clever scheme, isn't it?"

"Do you think he's doing this with many of the Duer boats coming downriver?"

The ensign pursed his lips. "No, that would soon be discovered. I haven't located any other obvious forgeries in the bundle Hodgdon gave me. But if Starnes is submitting, say, a forged manifest every other week, there's little risk he'll be discovered, and he'll soon amass a small fortune. It was just a fluke of fate that St. Clair remembered my father and my clerking on the Cincinnati landing. Otherwise, he wouldn't have directed Hodgdon to have me review the quartermaster's paperwork."

I ruminated some more. "Starnes can't know what you've discovered, can he?"

"No, he wasn't present the other evening with Hodgdon and the general. Far as I'm aware, he hadn't yet arrived from Fort Pitt when I was on duty at the landing and checking cargo with your father. Then I was assigned to Fort Hamilton on 1 October."

"Have you ever seen Starnes from even a distance?"

"No, I don't believe so."

The picture of Starnes, his Roman features, his oversized skull, fists, and feet, flashed through my mind. "Trust me, Ensign. You've never laid eye on him. For once you have, you never forget him. He's as powerful as he is ruthless."

It was time for the question that loomed over the both of us like a storm cloud. "What are you intending to do next?" I inquired softly.

"Why, inform General St. Clair of what I've discovered. What else?"

The words seemed to pop from my mouth by themselves. "Ensign Young, could I ask you to wait a few days, maybe a week?"

The ensign's backbone straightened and his head cocked. "Why should I? It is of utmost importance that General St. Clair understands how his army is being swindled. He's anticipating the eventual receipt of supplies from Hodgdon's efforts that don't exist."

"I couldn't agree more. But you yourself admitted you don't believe you can convince a court the manifest on the table is a forgery."

Andy Young sighed heavily. "Not with just my testimony. Not without additional evidence," he admitted.

"Then hear me out, please. I will be at Fort Washington tomorrow evening. I will tell Paw everything and ask him if his memory of the Barch boat matches yours. If it does, and I can damn well swear Paw hardly ever forgets anything he sees, even if it was years ago, let alone a few weeks, you've got another witness. And just maybe Paw, who has no great liking for Court Starnes, knows of other shenanigans by Duer's hires harmful to the army. Paw ain't one to brook dishonesty from anybody, whether he's in their pay or not."

The ensign helped himself to his first drink of whiskey the entire evening. He set the jug down and scratched above his ear. "I suppose a few more days wouldn't ruin the entire campaign. I do need your father's corroboration. It would be best if I can present indisputable evidence to General St. Clair that will allow him to take corrective action immediately thereafter and end Starnes's deception once and for all. But I will wait no longer than a week. If I'm ordered to join

St. Clair's staff to the north, which may happen, I want your promise you or your father will still seek me out without fail."

"One of us most assuredly will. My orders from General Butler and Captain Starkweather are to return with bells and hobbles without delay."

"Fair enough," the ensign said, rising to his feet and extending his hand. "And if anything happens to me, make your findings known to Captain Starkweather. He may be finicky about his victuals and his person, but he can be trusted, no matter the circumstances."

Though warmed through in a bed with woolen blankets and a straw tick mattress, I spent another restless night. Acquiring sufficient evidence to convict Court Starnes of theft from the army would be a formidable task. And that was just the first step. Then would come the real challenge: bringing him to justice. I couldn't imagine a man of Starnes's strength and cunning peacefully surrendering to the army for trial and sentencing, perhaps to the hangman's rope.

I hardly thought of less menacing prospects such as love and the beautiful maiden with the flame-red hair.

Chapter 11

9 October

No one had the opportunity to linger beneath his blankets in the morning at Fort Hamilton, not with Captain Lucas Steddeman on duty. At first light that stalwart officer cleared his perpetually clogged pipes with a hawk that rattled shutters throughout the entire compound, trudged to the door, and launched the contents of his wolf-trap jaws across the stoop with a spit rivaling the blast of a discharging cannon. Maybe it was coincidence, but I swear the drum roll commencing morning parade rat-tatted before his flying wad of spit hit the ground outside.

Tap and I broke our fast with jerked beef, leftover bread, and hot tea served by Private Oakley while Captain Steddeman and Ensign Young oversaw the morning parade. The sun was on the rise when the two officers joined us at the table. The glum captain ate with head lowered over his tin plate, no more inclined to friendly chatter than he had been the previous evening.

"Corporal Balser is bringing your horses in from the picket line," Ensign Young informed us twixt swallows. "They were fed and watered last night and again before dawn. Private Oakley is bagging a ration of jerk for each of you. The weather appears to be as fair as yesterday, and you should have no particular trouble reaching Fort Washington before nightfall."

Clutching a second noggin of steaming tea, the ensign rose and walked to the desk he shared with his fellow officers. Upon his return, he remained standing and handed me a rolled sheet of parchment. "For your father," he said. "Not the signed manifest we examined before retiring, but a complete copy of what that document claimed was aboard Dyson Barch's boat. I will retain the signed manifest until I meet with your father in person." I concurred with the ensign's thinking and nodded.

Tap sat beside me, rapping the table with his knuckles and listening. The old scout's curiosity was so great his brows were threatening to brush the ceiling. He stayed quiet, howsomever, fearful that if he sniffed where his nose didn't belong, I might not share anything with him later either.

Tap and I took our leave after checking the priming and flints of our long guns and collecting our gear. I tied the bags of jerk filled by Private Oakley across Blue's withers and was delighted, upon hefting our canteens, to find they had been replenished by Corporal Balser. Andy Young was mighty thorough. If summoned, he would be a valuable addition to General St. Clair's headquarters staff.

The ensign himself escorted us to the main gate. "Don't forget our agreement, Mr. Downer. One week, and one week only, no longer."

A few miles south of Fort Hamilton, we trotted past the point at which Erin Green and I had come upon the military road on our ride north some days ago. Tap being more familiar with the country from there to the Ohio, I followed his lead as to when and where we could best blow the horses and ease our own legs.

The miles slipped by under Blue's belly with me keeping a sharp vigil to my side of the road, but my thoughts inevitably ran to Paw and what he had endured since his decision last spring to become William Duer's western agent. Disputes regarding the legitimacy of Paw's ownership of more than half of our home place south of Lexington had created a desperate need for cash money and lured Paw into Duer's employ. All Paw had sought was an honest share of the profit for supplying St. Clair's forces. His initial letters had been full of promise. Gradually though, the spirit of the letters had diminished as did their number. Then, with September nearly half over, Paw had requested that Bear Watkins join him and Tap in Cincinnati. The next week, another letter arrived authorizing me and Hardy Booth to draw on family reserves, purchase no fewer than ten personal mounts for St. Clair's officers, and fetch them to Fort Hamilton without delay.

I understood now, after talking with Ensign Young, that something big had started to go amiss on Paw if he suddenly needed extra hands and eyes that wouldn't fail him short of death. Only the direst of situations would have caused him to so drastically reduce the number of men assigned to protect my mother and sisters and complete autumn chores on the Downer plantation. The farther south we pounded on the military road, the more anxious I grew to learn the truth and size of Paw's troubles. It was all I could do to keep from kicking Blue into a gallop, a poor notion what with our still being miles shy of our destination.

A little added pondering, and I decided I'd no choice except to tell Tap the whole story. If anything befell me before we reached Fort Washington, what help Ensign Young could offer Paw might die stillborn. I seized the occasion as we rested the horses before starting the ride across the broken hills that separated us from Mill Creek and the descent into Cincinnati. "You saw the paper the ensign handed me upon our departure?" I started.

Tap lowered his canteen, nodded, and listened with rapt attention as I proceeded to tell him about Dyson Barch's Kentucky boat, the forged manifest, and my commitment that either Paw or I would be in touch with Andy Young within the week. At the finish, the old scout stared at the nearby trees and sipped more water. When his canteen lowered again, he was ready to parley.

"Forged manifest, huh. Well, I can damn sure nail to the hoof of the jasper you want to ask how that came to pass. You need to root out that clerk Court Starnes sent from Fort Pitt ahead of hisself . . . Cyrus Paine, that's his name. He's ugly as a wharf rat, bald as me, an' wears a long black coat, no matter the weather. He took charge of the ledgers an' shipping papers the day he arrived. Had him a letter from Starnes, he did. He keeps every scrap of paper under lock and key."

"How does Paw feel about him?"

"You know your paw. He ain't much for bitchin' over which dogs he has to sleep with when he makes the bed hisself. That is, till he learns you're a thief or you're lyin' to him. Then the devil, clever as he be, can't hide yuh from Caleb Downer."

"Then we best go share what we've learned with him, hadn't we?" I proposed, stepping aboard Blue.

Tap chuckled and mounted Bear's brown gelding. "Yeah, could make for a little excitement down on the river tonight."

The St. Clair road was twisty as a coiled snake in the miles where it forged through the hills above Mill Creek. We moved along at a brisk trot though, for the road was now wider and the stumps fewer, the result of extra labor by the general's regiments during the weeks the army had camped at Ludlow's Station on the creek's west bank for training in the field.

We gained the deserted station at midafternoon and halted in the yard fronting the blockhouse to blow the horses and eat the jerk Private Oakley had bagged for us. Tap had observed St. Clair's forces while they were encamped on Mill Creek and couldn't resist relating the gist of what he'd seen. "It was somethin' to behold, lad. Most of them Philadelphia and Baltimore recruits, bein' fresh from the tavern an' the jail, had never fired off a musket afore. And the bulk of 'em had the shakes, that bein' because they couldn't lay hold of liquor here like they had every whipstitch at Cincinnati. Lordy, but they was a danger to flying birds, clouds, the sun, an' anybody a-watchin'. The safest place to be them days was with the targets they set up over on that stretch of high ground shy of the creek. That was true the last week same as the first. It was a terrible waste of black powder."

We watered the horses at the creek, crossed the knee-deep stream on the solid limestone bottom of McHenry's Ford, and slanted southeast for Cincinnati and the Ohio. The weather remained fair and cool with the faintest of breezes stirring, ideal conditions for riding stock beginning to tire from hours of constant motion and little forage. The country bordering the road had been grazed clean of grasses by the advancing army's cattle, oxen, and horses. Tap, also aware of the scarcity of natural forage, quipped, "Damn rabbit would have to pack his own victuals to travel through here without starvin'."

Paw being a surveyor, he was always searching for ways to describe land and its many settings. In the letters he faithfully wrote to Mother, he called Cincinnati the "giant's eye," the high tier of hills north of the city forming the brow, the city and its surrounding environs the ball, and the Ohio the lower lash. Our approach to Cincinnati being from the north, we enjoyed an awesome sight from the giant's craggy brow, for we could see the whole of the huge eye from Deer Creek in the east to Mill Creek in the west in a single vast sweep. Straight brown streaks, obviously the wide streets of the city Paw had noted in his letters, slashed through yellow-leafed trees on the eyeball's downward curve. Thin stems of smoke, narrow and straight as lines drawn by a quill pen, sifted upward from the area of the lower lash.

"Cincinnati's a mighty peaceful lookin' place from up here, ain't it," Tap commented. "But there ain't a hellhole the equal of it this side of the Alleghenies. Garrison town, she is, the army suckin' the fore teat in everythin' from trade to sin. The dice box, the whiskey keg, an' the card table be the king and the queen for one and all. Come along, lad, the first visit is always the best for you young studs."

Compared to Lexington, Kentucky, with its 800-plus inhabitants, 200 dwellings, numerous trading houses, and well-appointed taverns, Cincinnati resembled a festering sore on a sow's rear. Its permanent population barely exceeded 200. Its building inventory consisted of 60 raw structures huddled mainly in a straggling cluster along the river on the flat below Fort Washington. The wide streets and unproven out lots running back to the base of the northern crescent of surrounding hills composed the bulk of the city. On the plateau extending east and west the width of the city above the river flat, a large pond of water at Fifth and Main Streets necessitated the construction of a causeway to enable travelers to escape its miring clutches. Frogs not yet driven underwater by autumn frosts serenaded Tap and me as we walked our mounts across the timbers of the causeway in the last tinges of daylight.

We turned east at Third Street, and even in the growing darkness Fort Washington dominated the eastern skyline. The fort was an imposing structure 180 feet square with two-story blockhouses at the four angles. Cabins a story and a half high made up the walls and doubled as barracks, those better furnished being assigned to officers. A two-pole alley, the easternmost street of Cincinnati, extended north and south parallel with the fort's main gate and slanted downward to the flat adjoining the river.

We reined south into the alley short of the fort, and the watery expanse of the Ohio came into full view. The hour seeming of little consequence, the farther down the alley we rode, the more human folk we encountered. Every kind of dress, whether of broadcloth, buckskin, linsey-woolsey, linen, or calico as well as every size and shape of hat, whether of furred pelts, leather, knitted cloth, or feathers, adorned the men and women passing by.

Crews unloaded Kentucky boats and smaller craft tied to wooden landings along the riverbank. Bodies big and small hustled from cabin to tavern to shop. Outhouse doors closed with sharp bangs, the clap of wood against wood booming above the loud talk. Weapons, whether rifle, musket, pistol, or bladed, were in evidence everywhere. More than a few armed men and leering women stopped and appraised us with frank stares. Had I any doubts of Tap's assessment of Cincinnati's rude character, our ride along the city's waterfront dispelled them forever.

A two-story log building forty feet square soared above smaller cabins at the water's edge, the massiveness of the structure blotting out the entire expanse of the Ohio once we came abreast of it. The push and rush of inbound and departing occupants was eased by the presence of three main entryways, and given the size of the crowd entering and taking their leave at the same time, a fourth would have been helpful. A female face, coarse and painted beneath a towering black wig, appeared briefly among the crowd jamming the center doorway. The sour, angry expression contorting the painted face vanished as eyes red-veined and bleary spotted Tap riding at my left stirrup.

"Tap Jacobs, yuh ol scamp! Come to lift my skirt agin, have yuh now?" shrilled what was most certainly a tavern wench accustomed to offering up more, much more, than tankards of rum and whiskey.

I glanced at the old scout. No blush of shame or embarrassment darkened the bare skin above his chin whiskers. Instead, an ornery grin surpassing that of the painted harlot knotted the corners of his mouth. "In a while, Sally me darlin'! I'll be back in a while!"

A surge of the inbound crowd swept the harlot from the doorway. When I looked again at the old scout, he was sitting higher in the saddle, his once tired eyes fairly dancing. "Maw's right. You are a seeker of fleshly pleasure at every opportunity," I joshed.

Tap chuckled. "Yeah, I'm doomed to sinning," he shot back. "But don't tell your maw I admitted such. It's better she believes she can save my soul. Then if I ever have to fall on my knees an' beg her forgiveness, it'll be real meaningful for her. She can take great pride in having saved me from eternal damnation."

I chuckled and turned in the saddle for a final gander at the two-story building with three doorways. "What goes on inside there, anyhow?"

"That's the Scarlet Knight, the prime rum parlor of Cincinnati. At the Scarlet Knight, the keg never runs dry an' the dollies are never scarce. Saul Bartlett, the owner, brags it's the onliest tavern on the Ohio big enough to warrant not one, but two three-holers. That's the both of them behind the near corner there. Mighty plush fixin's, wouldn't you agree?"

I could but nod my head and wonder if the rear wall of the Scarlet Knight sported as many doors as did the front. With the river readily available, it seemed like a waste of costly lumber if it didn't.

Toward the western end of the waterfront, a plank cabin sat landward of a double line of tents that extended downriver another fifty yards. Beyond the tents, packhorses milled within a fenced enclosure. The light was by then so poor I could just make out their shapes enough to recognize that the baggage animals were present.

Tap reined up before the cabin and dismounted. A slim, black male with a decided limp emerged at his yell of greeting. "Evenin', Mr. Jacobs. How may I help yuh?"

"Tige, is Caleb Downer about?"

"Naw, he ain't here. Ain't nobody here but me," Tige said

slowly. "Mr. Downer, he went upriver to Columbia yesterday."

Tap sighed. "Where might we find Cyrus Paine?"

Tige's brief smile flashed large white teeth. "He be at that tavern, that Scarlet Knight. He likes the table at the back, Mr. Paine do, sir."

"You got anythin' warmin' over the fire, Tige?"

"No, Mr. Jacobs, I doesn't. I'm right sorry. Wasn't expectin' no one at the table till Mr. Downer returns in the mornin', sir."

I was onto Tap's thinking. Paw was away, and Tige had no victuals ready after a long ride. He had a perfect excuse for seeking sustenance elsewhere, elsewhere being the place we'd most likely encounter Cyrus Paine during the evening hours. And just in case Tige had to vouch for us later with Paw, Tap stated our excuse loud and clear.

"Well, by damned, young Mr. Downer, that presents us with but one solitary choice," the old scout chimed. "We'll have to partake of dinner at the Scarlet Knight, won't we now? Let's care for these animals. I'm hungry enough to eat fresh dung."

Horses unsaddled, watered, and fed what meager forage was available at the stock enclosure, we wended back along the waterfront. We left our saddles and gear with Tige but went armed and ready. Tap issued a blunt warning before we entered the nearest door of the huge tavern. "A man can lose his life easy as his vitals here any night with a mere wag of the head. Stay on my shoulder, Ethan. I knows who greases the hog at the Scarlet Knight an' who don't."

I didn't mind the old scout giving me orders. He had me so anxious and excited to push inside, I would've carried him across the threshold if necessary to hurry things up. It wasn't often a young gent got to look the elephant square in the eye. The trick was to not let the elephant stomp you too badly.

A few grunting shoves, and we slipped inside. Smoke from countless clay pipes pooled in clouds that hung like white fog over a sea of heads in the flickering light of the guttering candles. The room was more crowded than I would ever have imagined without seeing it firsthand. The shifting press of flesh in the space surrounding the dining tables and the square bar fronting the fireplace of the rear wall threatened to knock you from your feet if your legs weren't solidly braced at knee and hip. Drink requests were called out, and tavern wenches responded promptly, threading through the dining tables to pass into the crowd steaming tankards fresh from the insertion of a fire-heated poker. How those painted, sweating females made any sense of the myriad requests being shouted at them, I was never to determine.

For some minutes it was purely a treat to hold your place with outthrust elbows and watch. But before long, you realized you could go thirsty as well as hungry the entire night you didn't assert yourself. Tap's impatience was no less severe than my own. Our saving grace proved his friend and ardent admirer, Sally with the tall, black wig. Somehow she spied the old scout among that shouting horde. Tap yelled for me to follow him, but I did him one better. When the bodies separating us from the dining tables parted slightly in response to Sally's repeated pleadings, I latched onto Tap and forged ahead, his smaller frame riding on my cocked hip. It damn near winded me, but I levered us free of the crowd.

Next we needed to locate an available table. Sally solved that problem by leading us around the corner of the serving bar to empty chairs against the rear wall. I shouldn't have been surprised. The one occupied chair at the table was filled with a bald rat of a creature wrapped in a black coat despite the blazing fireplace scant steps farther along. Tap's greeting was an unnecessary confirmation as to the creature's identity. "Evenin', Cyrus. Considerate of you to let us join yuh."

Paine's laugh was sharp and brittle. His voice was mostly a grating squeak. "I'll extract proper payment from our Sally whore later, never you fear."

I could tell by how Tap squeezed his lips together he resented Paine's public branding of Sally for what she was, but the old scout kept the peace, having bigger game to hunt this night. "What they servin', Cyrus?"

"Many meat stew and bread dry and crusty," squeaked the clerk. "Though that don't tally to nothing, the rum is hot and buttered like always."

Two heaping platters, followed by two steaming tankards, thudded onto the tabletop, and Sally bent to give Tap a big, wet kiss, smearing his cheek with her thick rouge. Tap circled her waist with an arm and hugged Sally close, then released her as the hearty aroma of the stew teased his smeller. "Fill your gullet, yuh old goat, an' we'll make the rope sing later," she promised, returning to her duties at the bar.

We ate while Cyrus Paine sipped steadily on his rum. The clerk, I decided, was flat-out ugly. It was as if a huge hand had grasped his nose, cheeks, and chin and pulled most of the flesh and bone into a long snout undercut by buckteeth that overlaid his lower lip. His amber eyes, cold and inhospitable, were without brows and ceaselessly roved the tavern. He showed so little interest in us we might as well have been made of wood.

Tap Jacobs, howsomever, was not to be ignored. We had finished our second platter of stew and bread and were into our third serving of rum, my ears beginning to ring from the liquor, when his tankard smacked down on the table. "Cyrus, yuh seen anythin' of Dyson Barch the past week or two?"

The clerk's amber eyes stopped roving and focused on the old scout. I knew what Tap intended and was wishing maybe he had waited till we talked to Paw first. A man who rudely awakened a pack of sleeping dogs risked losing a chunk of his leg. And Paw liked to handle his own affairs without any meddling from others, including those in his employ.

The old scout leaned forward, his beard hovering over his empty platter. "Yuh deaf, Cyrus?" he demanded.

I tried kicking Tap out of sight to gain his attention and missed entirely, managing to smash my moccasin-covered toes against the center leg of the table. I winced at the pain setting my foot to throbbing as Cyrus Paine demanded in turn, his voice suddenly less of a squeak, "An' what business would you have with Barch if you did find him?"

The wily clerk had trumped as well as stumped Tap at one and the same time. The old scout should have ceased and desisted then and there. He had failed to learn Barch's whereabouts without raising Paine's suspicions. But the old scout's open dislike of Paine, coupled with his stubbornness, was his undoing. He wasn't about to concede the evening to the individual he believed was the cause of some, if not all, of Paw's troubles.

He proceeded to upset the whole kettle of soup. "I want to chat with Barch about the manifest for the shipment Caleb and Ensign Young inspected last month," Tap blurted, laying his rifle on the table with a loud clatter.

If Paine was roused or upset by the abrupt appearance of Tap's long gun, it showed nowhere on his snout of a face. A small red tongue resembling that of a snake licked the bottom edge of his buckteeth. His amber eyes glittered in the candlelight. The squeak was almost entirely gone when he spoke. "Don't threaten me, you old windbag of a fart. You lay a finger on me, you'll answer to Court Starnes. He'll kill you with his bare hands."

Tap wasn't a coward, but he recognized an honest threat to his person when he heard it. Anger colored his cheeks, but he sat still as a tree butt as Cyrus Paine slid his tankard toward us and rose slowly to his feet. He flexed his arms to settle his black coat smoothly about his shoulders and with a glare of defiance, swooped around the table and was gone into the milling throng beyond the bar. I watched him depart, realizing that the clerk's true image was more akin to that of the nocturnal bat as opposed to the wharf rat.

A different realization now flushed the wind from Tap's sails. He groaned and threw himself against the back of his chair. "Oh, for chrissake, Ethan, I don't need to fret about Starnes killing me. Soon as your Paw learns how far I stuck both feet in my mouth, he'll shoot me or hang me. Rum, Sally, bring me rum! Bring 'em two at a time, darlin'! Only a fool can reward his own stupidity."

The midnight hour came and went, the crowd gradually thinning. Tap's thirst never slackened. He resisted my plea that having possibly ruined Paw's day in court, perhaps we should retire so we could at least talk sensibly with him upon his return from Kentucky later in the day. Tap's response was to tug his purse from his frock yet again, dump additional coins on the table, and slobber on Sally's neck. My being drunker than ever before myself, my speech was so slurred I was probably wasting my breath. The urge to pee had me thumping my knees together. I left Sally to watch the old scout and stumbled through the nearest rear door, my objective either one of the Scarlet Knight's three-hole out-houses.

Stars pulsed bright then dim in the black of the night sky, or it seemed they did in my rum-blurred vision. I lurched and swayed. I avoided stepping on a prone body just off the stoop, then saw no one else. The log wall of the outhouse was raw on my palms. I fumbled, found the latchstring, and plunged inside, yanking the door closed.

Thank the Lord, I was alone. I had no idea where the seat holes were in the dark, and the last buttons of my breeches proving too great a chore, I yanked them over my hips, and let fly, spraying merrily I knew not where, but by the rapidly spreading wetness, mostly down my own legs.

Starlight illuminated the seat hole inches from my knees as the door swept open behind me. Cursing that I had been caught peeing on myself, I spun about. There was a slight whisper of air, a cracking thud, and exploding pain. Fast as a candle being snuffed, my eyes snapped shut, and I was out cold face first in my own piss in less time than that.

The black void I fell into was at first without sight and sound. After a while, I sensed I was approaching whorls of fuzzy light. I don't remember if I had to open my eyes. Red flame, hot and searing, leaped and spat. A brown line split the fire. I peered closer, and the line gained detail. It was the rosewood handle of Starkweather's gift knife, and blood not yet dry stained the blade. I tried mightily to move, to stand and run, but my legs were heavy as lead. Then the pain was upon me once more, greater than ever.

I succumbed to it, seeking that wonderful, feathery black-ness, seeking to escape the fire and the heat and the blood, for I could be nowhere but at the rim of the devil's abode.

And if that were true, I was dead.

Chapter 12

The worst part of hell aside from the heat and the pain was the stench: the raw, ripe stink of vomit, dung, and rancid sweat. The stink was so powerful it overwhelmed the nose and threatened to overturn my innards.

Paws rough and clasping lay hold of me from out of the blackness. I struggled to escape them, twisting and turning, fearful that I was about to suffer the sinner's ultimate fate, the headlong toss into the fiery pit of damnation where you roasted forever.

A voice sounded, garbled and distant. I tried to listen, and the voice stopped speaking. I concentrated, praying it would return, and I could yell for help.

The rough shaking popped my eyes open. All was a gray, whirling blur, but at least, by damned, there was no fire, no searing heat, and only the godawful stench. Maybe I was being carried from the devil's clutches to safety. Then I felt myself being lifted and launched. I cringed, not knowing where or how I would land. Straining to see, I thrust my arms in front me, hoping to break my fall.

The cold shock of the water chilled me to the core and chased the breath from my lungs. I kicked and thrashed and gulped, sucking in water instead of vitally needed air. My elbow struck something solid. I felt quickly with my hand and encountered what had to be thick mud—bottom mud. I thrust upward with my head and pulled my legs beneath me. Before it was too late and I blacked out from lack of wind, I pushed downward with all my might as soon as my feet touched the mud. My head broke the surface, and as I spat my mouth empty and filled my lungs, my vision cleared somewhat, and I discovered I was standing in a mere three feet of water.

Protests erupted over my shoulder. "Goddamn it, it ain't fair. Only a son of a bitch dunks a friend!"

I came about, and a large splash drenched my face. The body suddenly in the water with me flailed and sputtered. I peered at what I now knew was the bank of the Ohio, and a murky shape stood at the water's edge. Even in the dark of the night's final hour, one look at what I could make out, the flat crown of a hat and wide shoulders told me it was, of all people, my father.

Tap lunged to his feet and wrung water from his beard. "Goddamn it, Caleb, I catch my death, I'll never forgive you," he cried.

"Be quiet and follow me, the both of you, less'n you want to hang," Paw ordered.

Those words took the zest out of Tap's bitching in one fell swoop. The pain where I'd been struck on the forehead was awesome but not so great I didn't hear precisely what Paw had said. Maybe the hurt was the least of my troubles.

Tap and I waded from the river. Tige waited with dry blankets. "Get those about your shoulders and come along," Paw said. "We've a fire burning at my tent. Hurry now!"

How we had arrived there, I didn't know, but we were well down the river toward the stock pen, a goodly piece from the Scarlet Knight. A fire roared twixt an oversized tent and the water. Two wagoners, heavy of beard, muscle, and boot, lounged by the fire with our rifles. They levered upright upon sighting us.

"Thank you, Thaddeus," Paw said. "You and Timothy have been most helpful. We'll break the fast together later this morning. Rest assured, I won't forget the service you've rendered."

"Our pleasure, Mr. Downer," Thaddeus responded. At a nod from Timothy, the wagoners passed Paw our long guns and walked in the direction of the stock pen.

Paw stowed the weapons in his tent, opened a trunk, and emerged with a pair of full-length woolen breeches and a fringed, buckskin hunting frock. "Here Ethan, you're growed enough to wear these. Best jump into them quick. Come day-break, we wouldn't want the women gawking thisaway."

The frock being a favorite of his, I done as told with no lost time. Tap having no spare clothing, he shucked to the skin, wrapped his blanket tighter about himself, and spread his discards over a log next to mine to dry.

The old scout warmed shaking hands over the fire. "Wondered who was toting me. They could've been a mite more tender with me. How come they didn't bring me all the way here?" The old scout shivered from hairless head to bare feet. "Caleb, you're a danger to the best of friends, damned if'n yuh ain't."

"Not nearly as much as you two are to yourselves," Paw countered.

"Now just a solitary minute—"

"Quiet, Tap," I interrupted, my patience with the old scout ebbing. I stepped closer to the fire to keep my teeth from chattering. "Paw, you said something about our hanging. What'd you mean by that?"

Paw bent at the waist and fished fingers into a tall riding boot. What he slid forth was my knife. He flipped it end to end, something I couldn't accomplish without cutting myself, and presented it to me handle first. "Since the scabbard on your belt is empty, I assume this blade belongs to you, Ethan. Am I correct?"

I took the knife from him and stammered, "I must have lost it on the floor of the outhouse."

Paw fixed his piercing gaze on me, the one that held you spellbound. "Nope, that's not where I found it."

"Then where?" I asked.

"Sticking in the guts of Cyrus Paine lying next to you," Paw informed me, his tone level and deadly serious.

My jaw sagged nearly to my waist. "Chrissake, I didn't kill him. I swear I didn't!"

Paw's head shook. "Never said you did. You're not a killer, Ethan, not even when you're liquored up. But somebody wanted to make it seem thataway."

I was thoroughly confused and unable to think. "How'd you get involved, Paw?"

"Tige is fascinated with the dice box. He likes to sneak

to the rear window and watch the gaming at the Scarlet Knight. He saw you enter the privy. He looked a few minutes later, and the door was ajar with an arm flopping over the sill. He ran to the privy, saw it was the same young Mr. Downer who'd been with Tap earlier, and Tap being too drunk to help him, he came to get Thaddeus to tote you to my tent. About then I rode up, home early. On our way back to you, a cabin across the street from the Scarlet Knight burst into flames when the mantle log burned through. The whole damn tavern emptied to battle the fire."

Paw scratched his cheek, his gaze never leaving me. "It was a mighty curious situation when we reached the privy. The door wasn't open with your arm flopping through it like Tige described, but closed. I opened it, and there was Cyrus between you and the seat holes, your blade in his belly." Paw's brows arched. "I spied your empty scabbard and figured the blade was yours. So I blocked the doorway, keeping the others behind me, till I hid it in my boot. You know the rest."

He glanced at Tap. "I had Ethan thrown in the river to wash the vomit and the blood off of him and bring him around. I ordered the same for you, figuring you were responsible for his drunkenness."

Tap's chin drooped, and he mumbled to himself, not daring to contest the truth of Paw's accusation.

Paw's recounting explained much for me. The crackling flames, the heat, and the bloody knife hadn't been the work of the devil on a rampage. And by the purest stroke of luck, the late hour and the cabin fire had kept any sober tavern patron from visiting the outhouse and observing the scene of Cyrus Paine's murder with me and my knife present.

Tap could restrain himself no longer. "Well, by damned, if'n Ethan didn't gut the clerk, who did?"

"We may never find out unless a witness comes forth," Paw acknowledged with a sigh. "Tige said he told you two Cyrus was at the Scarlet Knight. Did you see or talk to him?"

The pain of the lump on my forehead was lessening. Someone had to tell Paw what had transpired, and I preferred I be the one rather than Tap. With a big sigh of my own, I started talking, relating everything from my conversation with Ensign Young till I was struck senseless in the privy. I tripped over my tongue some, repeated some things, but in the main did a credible job of it. Paw and Tap, though the old scout toed the ground with a bare toe now and again, heard me out without comment or questions.

Paw stared at the fire. "Well, Cyrus didn't kill himself. He told somebody about your wanting to discuss that manifest with Dyson Barch. Whoever he told either murdered him or was the cause of it being done."

Tap, relieved Paw didn't intend to scold him for confronting Cyrus Paine on his own volition at the Scarlet Knight, at least not at the moment, ventured, "Like Court Starnes?"

"Probably not. Court should be on his way downriver from Limestone with a shipment of flour and more packhorses," Paw informed us. "He's not due till day after tomorrow at the earliest."

"What about Barch?"

"Might could've been Dyson," Paw conceded. "He's been Starnes's lackey ever since Court arrived from Fort Pitt. It seems his sole duty is to guard Court's backside when he's in Cincinnati and spy on my doings when he's not. We'll have to inquire as to his whereabouts tonight." Paw glanced at Tap. "But a little less brashly this go-round, you don't mind, Mr. Jacobs."

It was always a telltale sign that Paw's mood might be changing if he started addressing you as "Mister." Tap was suddenly furiously busy donning his clothes, not overly concerned whether they were dry or not. Aware of Tap's ruse, Paw just smiled and turned to me. "What brings the two of you to Cincinnati, anyways? I gave you specific orders to stay with Bear Watkins, I remember."

My answer was delayed by Tige's arrival. Skin black as midnight in the brightening dawn, he came bearing a copper kettle of tea and an armful of tin cups. He poured from the yawning vessel without spilling a drop. Never before had plain green tea tasted fine as Madeira wine. "Morning victuals are nearly ready at the cabin," Tige announced.

"We'll be right along," Paw assured him. "Thanks much for the tea. Well, Ethan?"

"General Butler wanted a message delivered here that we

must supply him hobbles and bells for the horse herd immediately. Captain Starkweather picked me to make the ride. Bear insisted Tap join me, two rifles being better than one."

"I take it immediately means yesterday to General Butler?"

"Yes, sir. The captain says he's at the end of his tether with contractors. And General St. Clair is of the same opinion."

It wasn't a pleasant chore, but I revealed to Paw St. Clair's biting condemnation of Duer's supply efforts to date during our chance meeting of the general's entourage north of Fort Hamilton. Paw's hat brim dipped, and he rubbed his cheekbones with thumb and forefinger. His jaw lifted, and I noticed in the increasing daylight how severely fatigue had deepened and bunched the lines at the corners of his eyes and mouth. To my dismay, he appeared much older than when he had recently visited us upcountry.

It hurt me inside to admit Paw was aging. Like every son who revered his sire, I boyishly believed he would remain handsome and young and bull-strong forever. I loved him, so I wanted nothing whatsoever to harm him or make him less of a hero. God, standing there sipping tea, how I wished we were home in Kentucky with the whole Duer mess behind us. I would even tolerate the silly dizziness of my sisters, were that required.

I drained my tin cup with a final swallow and plopped on the log that held my drying clothes to don my moccasins. Wishful thinking, I reminded myself, amounted to less than a quick spit. Paw would never renege on his commitments and leave St. Clair's forces in the lurch. Every ounce of energy he possessed would be expended to rectify what had gone awry, whether the blame fell to him or not. That was the way of a man totally dedicated to what was right and proper. He wore mighty big boots, my Paw did, and I doubted I would ever wear that large a size. My most fervent hope was that I could be more of a help than a hindrance to him.

"Gentlemen, here's our plan for the day," Paw said, finishing his own tea. "First we eat. Then, while you sleep off your drunk, Tap, and Ethan rests that knot on his skull, I'll scavenge up every scrap of leather in Cincinnati. This afternoon, the two of you can start making those hobbles for General Butler."

"What about Dyson Barch?" Tap put in. "Ain't we gonna scout around for him?"

"Naw, he'll show of his own accord," Paw contended. "Meantime, before Court Starnes lands from Limestone, I intend to search Paine's office for the original manifest. I doubt it's there. Lest Cyrus was a fool, he destroyed it soon as he sanded his forgery. But I've got to have a look. Without the original manifest, it's our word against that of Starnes."

Tap grimaced and disgustedly tossed the balance of his tea into the fire. "I'm the fool, Caleb. My loose mouth has taken our bobber under."

As was his habit, Paw removed his flat-crowned hat and ran fingers through his black hair. "Don't condemn yourself just yet, my friend. Thievery and murder often beget punishments befitting the crime, punishments harsher than anything we might imagine."

It was a point Paw didn't need to repeat. The fate of Cyrus Paine—a knife in the belly—seemed plenty harsh to me. What could be harsher than that?

Chapter 13

The dizziness beset me following the morning meal. I stepped from the stoop of the Duer company cabin, and my legs buckled. Confused by my sudden helplessness, I lay on my backside in the dusty street, trying to decide which of the twin Paws frowning down at me was real and which the imagined. Though he was but inches from my nose, Paw's words echoed like he was shouting in a rock gorge. "Must be that blow to his skull. Let's carry him inside. Tige will look after him for us."

Five nightmarish days followed. I slept mostly, time being of no importance. My lucid minutes were limited and difficult to remember. I did later recall hearing Paw at the table opposite my rope bed claim rumor abounded on the waterfront that the powder kegs intended for General St. Clair's artillery had been dropped into the Ohio below Marietta the previous summer. Unfazed, the boat crew had recovered the kegs and not reported the incident upon docking at Cincinnati. Paw had reminded his companions of General St. Clair's oft-stated conviction that his army could defeat any force of redsticks it encountered due to its possession of cannon and its superior numbers. But what would happen, Paw wondered, if those heavy guns proved ineffective because of powder fouled months earlier.

If I tried to move my head the slightest, eye-watering pain rippled through my brain. The good thing was that during my few lucid minutes, Tige was always present with a noggin of meat broth and a spoon. The fact that more broth rolled out the corner of my mouth than I swallowed bothered the black cook and roustabout not at all.

By noon of the fifth day, 14 October, I managed to touch the knot on my forehead without suffering undue agony. By early afternoon, I was sitting up with my legs draped over the railing of the bed. Nature called shortly thereafter, and the resourceful Tige held the slop jar for me. Lured by the aromas of his cooking, I was already seated at the table and partaking of his evening victuals when Paw, Tap, and the two wagoners, Thaddeus and Timothy, entered the cabin at dusk.

"Well, lookee by God here," Tap intoned. "Now that all the damn hobbles are made, our young bucko's emptyin' a plate like a starved hound."

"I'm pleased you're upright, Ethan," Paw said, pulling a chair from under the table. He waited for the others to fill chairs also. "Gentlemen, an army messenger just dismounted at Fort Washington. He rode one horse to death and wind-broke a second reaching here. St. Clair's situation is desperate. He had but a two-day supply of flour remaining yesterday morning. Nothing breeds discontent and inspires soldiers to mutiny and desertion like short rations. If we don't replenish the army's stores jack quick, the whole campaign may well collapse."

I laid my spoon on the table. "Has Court Starnes landed yet?"

"No, but he could any hour. He probably had trouble purchasing pack animals. We've acquired about all the available horseflesh in northern Kentucky as it is, have we not, Tap?" With the old scout's vigorous nod, Paw continued. "We need another ten animals to complete a decent pack string. We've two thousand pounds of flour in our warehouse on the high ground above the stock pen. Court must fetch another two tons if we're to alleviate St. Clair's shortages for just half a week. We'll depart for the north within a few hours after Court lands, be it day or night. Understood?"

Given the danger of what Paw was proposing, General St. Clair had to truly be in desperate straits. I had been awake before dawn and heard heavy rain falling, and the air was damp and raw whenever the cabin door opened and closed.

The weather was changing and not for the better. Additional rain would turn the military road accessing the army into a muddy slough. Traveling that slippery surface in the dark of night would imperil the legs of the horses every step. And then there was always the redsticks and their constant way-laying of travelers to worry about. Yet not a soul at the table voiced an objection. Such was their loyalty to my father.

The meal went quickly, Tige refilling plates till each diner held up a hand signaling he was full. "Tige, you're a wonder, an honest-to-God wonder," Tap praised with the usual strok-ing of his belly.

"He's a liar, Tige," Thaddeus interjected with a rumbling laugh. "The last cook who feeds him is always an honest-to-God wonder, same as the last woman who doesn't run off when he unbuttons his breeches afore her."

"Damn you, Thaddeus, it's sad the Lord gifted you with all that heft, or I'd whip you to a fare-thee-well," the not-so-insulted Tap crowed.

Even Paw laughed at Tap's empty brag. "Gentlemen, I believe we have unfinished business. I trust the hobbles are sacked and ready, the packsaddles lined out at the warehouse, each packhorse checked for sores or lameness, and our per-sonal gear, including the field tents, packed. Am I correct?"

"Yes, sir, you are," Timothy responded. "We let Tap tire his jaw the whole day, an' he didn't hinder our work nary a bit."

After another good laugh at Tap's expense, Paw dismissed the old scout and the wagoners, bluntly stating he was dis-missing them to the river tent to sleep and not the Scarlet Knight to imbibe. That restriction set Tap to carping how seldom sincere toil was fairly rewarded as he went out the door on the heels of Thaddeus and Timothy.

Paw's staying behind was deliberate. I rose from the table and strode to the rope bed in the room's far corner, striding carefully but purposefully. The pain had diminished to a dull throb across my forehead, and the dizziness was finally gone. All in all, I was in much better shape than the year before when I'd stupidly allowed Cass Talbot the first punch and been thrashed within an inch of death. Then I'd hurt everywhere imaginable from his punching and kicking and seen double for a week.

"Ethan, how do you feel?" Paw asked, dragging his chair to the side of the bed.

I settled on the lumpy straw-tick mattress. "I'll be ready to ride with you and the others. I won't be left behind."

Maybe Paw wasn't in the mood to argue. Maybe he was beginning to abide by my judgment at least once in a great while. More likely, he remembered the Talbot fight and how quickly I'd recovered, for Paw was short of men he could rely upon, men in whom he had absolute confidence, men whose first allegiance was tied to him and not Court Starnes. Anyway and anyhow, he avoided any argument over whether or not I was able enough to mount a horse and stay in the saddle for hours on end with a closed-eyed nod.

That agreement secured, I broached another subject quick as could be by asking a question that nagged me unmercifully during my wakeful periods. "Did you find the manifest in the clerk's office?"

Paw sighed. "I didn't expect it to be there. Tap forewarned Cyrus Paine, and Cyrus was thorough with his transactions. He may have destroyed the original soon as he finished the forgery."

"Then why kill him or have him killed?"

"If he had already destroyed the evidence, it was to keep him out of our grasp. I read every manifest and receipt of purchase in his office. None of them looked like forgeries, but I don't doubt other manifests and receipts were bloated a-purpose, just not as blatantly as with the Barch shipment. Remember, if not for Ensign Young's sharp eyes, we wouldn't be any the wiser."

"So it's our word against that of Court Starnes?"

Paw nodded. "Lest we can find other written evidence or witnesses who will testify before the army," he concluded.

"Didn't anybody see what really happened at the privy?"

"No one's stepped forward yet. And maybe that's not all bad. No one saw Cyrus with your knife in him, either."

"What about Dyson Barch? Was he in Cincinnati that night?" I persisted.

"Yeah, he was. He was in the Scarlet Knight that evening."

I rose excitedly onto an elbow, but Paw raised a placating palm. "His being about proves nothing, though I can't fathom who else Cyrus had reason to warn with Court upriver at the time. Barch may have murdered Cyrus on a whim if he thought the blame might be laid at his stoop. Dyson Barch is as ruthless as Court."

I dared a question next that could easily rile Paw, who never revealed more of his personal thinking than he thought necessary, even to blood kin. "Did you suspect they were stealing from the army?"

Paw's sigh now was deep and heartfelt. "I suspected something was amiss. Officers from General St. Clair to the lesser ranks have complained of shortages of equipment like axes as much as they have of how poorly the axes were tempered. With what we've discovered, no one can say with any certainty how many axes or quantities of other items were actually purchased and shipped downriver. And Hodgdon and his quartermaster department are no help. They can't add or plan ahead, and are found wanting every week. The army would never have marched from here if St. Clair hadn't established his own manufactory and armory inside Fort Washington. His artificers turned out everything from musket cartridges to leather splints for the wounded."

Paw lifted wearily from his chair. "We can't allow St. Clair's soldiers to suffer short rations, not as long as we can do something about it. For the moment, the success of his campaign is more important than proving Court Starnes and his henchmen are cheating the army."

I couldn't let Paw retire without assuaging my own guilt. "I'm sorry I fouled the nest for you. I shouldn't have gotten drunk with Tap."

"Ethan, we can't undo the past. It pays to remember, though, that we can't outrun its consequences. Get your rest. There may not be much warning before we push north."

Paw bade Tige good night from the door and was gone into the dark outside. It was as much forgiveness as I was to receive from him. But injury or no injury, I wasn't being left behind. Through the five days of dizziness and pain, always there in the back of my mind, pretty as a polished gemstone reposing in a pool of clear water, had been the face of Erin Green. And sorry as I was for Paw, the prospect of not seeing her again was as devastating as having to confess I had failed him as well as Ensign Young. Perhaps more so. That disturbing realization only strengthened a final, nagging, unanswered question, the one that had plagued me since Tap and I departed for the Ohio:

Would she ever even speak to me again?

Chapter 14

15 October

The rain resumed the latter half of the night. The steady
drumming on the cabin roof put me in such deep sleep it
required much shaking by Tige to awaken me. The slim
roustabout scalded the grogginess from me with a noggin of
piping hot tea laced with whiskey. "Your father stuck his
head in the door. He says Mr. Starnes has landed many Kentucky boats. You're to report to Mr. Downer without delay."

Not desiring to foster any doubts as to my strength and
vigor on Paw's part, I donned my moccasins and blanket coat
with haste and departed with a wad of Tige's cured jerk
filling one pocket. When Paw laid into a chore, his bent was
so serious, victuals were unimportant till the work was done.
A wise man under his direction, therefore, protected himself
from the natural onset of hunger every chance he could.

It was a gray, miserable dawn. Drizzling rain fell, and the
dirt of the street separating the company cabin from the line
of tents and the river across the way was slippery and pitted
with shallow puddles. Drifting mist hung over the surface of
the Ohio, thin and wispy as bodice lace on a sack gown.
Stalled clouds obscured the hills lining the river's far bank.

Wetness shone in the feeble light on the haunches of the
packhorse string being led before the four Kentucky boats
moored beyond the tent line. The boats were tied well up the
bank, the rise of the river having covered the low-water mud
flat that had imperiled shipments of men and materials the
whole of the preceding summer. Paw was there in the middle
of the action, shorn of his usual town clothes except for his
flat-crowned hat and tall black riding boots. He wore linsey-

woolsey trousers and a knee-length canvas coat that shed moisture like duck feathers, a concession to the weather that indicated he was traveling far today.

Paw was conversing with a shorter individual in a similar canvas coat whose huge skull and equally large feet, though he presented but his backside my direction, told me it was Court Starnes. I realized as I drew up to them that while they weren't being loud about it, they were arguing rather than merely talking. "Court, I'll say it a last time; it don't count for squat ten more boatloads of flour and horses are a day's sail or two behind you. We must move forward this morning with what tonnage we have or risk so enraging St. Clair he'll surely cancel Duer's contract and take control from us. That happens, he'll fight over every farthing due us for months. We may never receive all that's owed us."

Starnes's big skull shook. "All right, if you believe the whole contract's at stake, I'll concede to your wishes," he stated tersely. "I just know if we delay a bit longer, that haughty bastard of a general will get desperate enough he'll give us armed escorts to protect our men and animals from ambush like we asked earlier."

"I'll take Tap, Thaddeus, Timothy, and my Ethan," Paw affirmed. "Hopefully, we'll have forty-eight horses to cart six tons of flour, a fair load for each animal. We should raise St. Clair's camp the fourth day if not sooner. You need to follow straightaway with every ounce of provisions that land in the meantime. Even at that, the army will be on short rations again for a period before you arrive. We cripple St. Clair's campaign for lack of trying, we'll be chased out of the country."

"All right, all right, I don't need to be reminded more'n once our arses are hanging naked in the wind," Starnes growled.

Paw was aware I was waiting behind Starnes and motioned for me to follow him as he turned toward the Ohio. Starnes had no way of knowing who I was till I stepped past his shoulder, and I saw his disliking for Paw on his Roman face before he recognized me and smiled hastily. I nodded without speaking and kept moving, wondering if I suddenly spun about would I discover he had no great love for Caleb Downer's son, either.

A chain of boatmen hefted flour sacks ashore, and Thaddeus and Timothy, both expert packers, lashed them to the saddletrees of the horses Tap led forward. I followed Paw to the farthest boat where the last of the pack animals newly purchased in Kentucky were being off-loaded by others of the boat crew.

"Christ, what a sorry lot," Paw judged.

What constituted an ideal horse for packing was debated constantly among those who relied upon the creature for their survival and livelihood. Most wagoners agreed the upper portions should feature a short, muscular neck, prominent withers, powerful front- and hindquarters, well-developed back, and rounded barrel with well-sprung ribs. The ideal lower extremities exhibited strong, straight legs with short, wide cannons, short pasterns with moderate slope, and tough feet proportioned to support the overall size and weight of the animal. Spirit wise, the most dependable load-bearers possessed a gentle, friendly nature, had no fear of their handlers, and embarked willingly under pack. The final and ultimate test, though, came on the trail where the animal needed to demonstrate the even temperament, grit, sure feet, and minimum of rock and roll required for what always lay ahead, a long pull upcountry.

The fifteen newly purchased horses could at their very best be deemed the slimmest of pickings. Certain minor shortcomings could be overlooked, but low, rounded withers, overly flat backs, weak pasterns or tender feet invited trouble the first stretch of rough terrain. Paw went over the animals with a critical eye and exploring hands, me right alongside him. There being no sense in asking any beast to do what would only injure or lame him, we eliminated four animals outright. Five more, we determined, would require constant watching. "I wouldn't risk taking these five," Paw admitted, "if every pound of flour wasn't vital. We'll count on their having stout hearts. Ethan, you'll bring up the rear and watch for any sign they're breaking down. We gain enough distance with them, mayhap we can spread the additional load through the rest of the train the last miles."

Paw nearly lost his temper anyway after the boatmen threw packsaddles onto the bank that initially appeared to have been condemned by their former owners in the distant past. But we sorted through the pile of dry, cracked leather strapping, frayed pads, and rotting trees and produced enough acceptable saddles. "Must have been some gleeful laughter in the Limestone taverns when the locals spent Starnes's money," Paw speculated. "Damn gleeful!"

A gloomy future loomed that I knew Paw also appreciated. "If there aren't enough good horses on future boats," I suggested, "we'll never deliver the balance of the flour to General St. Clair fast enough to save his campaign. He's doomed to fail, no matter if we get through or not."

"Not necessarily," Paw countered. "The Ohio's finally on the rise, and tons more flour are en route. The general will have no choice but to loan us horses from his baggage train. He can't sustain his northern march without adequate rations. I intend to apprise him of the situation by calling upon him with Starkweather soon as we catch up with his regiments."

The transfer of the flour from the boats to the backs of the unloaded horses consumed an hour of early daylight. Upon completion of the tying and lashing at water's edge, combining the horses brought by Starnes with those already saddled and loaded at the company stock pen and warehouse, forty-seven animals lined the riverbank. Each animal carried 130 pounds, meaning we were setting out with a total flour shipment of 6,110 pounds. A final animal, the sturdiest and most dependable of the lot, toted the hobbles fashioned by Tap and the wagoners, our field tents, camp gear, evening victuals, and stocks of tea, whiskey, animal fat, and salt.

Paw was mighty anxious to be away. He gave us scant minutes to secure our long guns from his tent, during which time Tige provided each of us travelers leather pouches containing jerked beef and nocake, along with freshly filled canteens, trail victuals to be eaten on the move. The forty-eight pack animals were then divided into four strings of twelve tied head to tail, one each for Paw, Tap, Thaddeus, and Timothy, and off we went, me bringing up the rear on Blue.

We headed east and reined left onto Main Street, those folks out and about despite the rain stopping to watch us pass. The red- and yellow-leafed maples of the river flat surrendered to the stark brown beech and oak covering the higher plateau extending northward to the brow of Paw's imaginary giant's eye. We boomed across the causeway spanning the frog pond at Fifth and Main, drawing a curious few from Avery's Tavern, who graced our effort on behalf of St. Clair's forces with sincere cheers, their vocal support momentarily brightening the soggy morning.

We weren't yet beyond the giant's brow when Erin Green popped to mind, and I started debating what kind of reception I would receive upon sighting her again. My feelings toward her were so unsettling, the mere likelihood Gabe Hookfin was hanging about in my absence gnawed my nerves raw and testy. It was a helpful thing that morning that I was separated from the others, for my company would have been even less thrilling than the weather.

Our pace on level ground was a fast walk, steady and measured. We slowed on the upward inclines and approached a near trot on the downward slopes, Paw knowing from long experience in the lead how to husband the strength of pack animals and draw the maximum miles per day from them without breaking them down.

The rain fell in an incessant patter, thick drops bouncing from hat brim and rein hand and rifle barrel. We rode with those barrels plugged and lock covers tied snugly in place. Through the descending veil of water, I could see steam rising from the shoulders of Timothy directly ahead of me. Despite whatever outer garment covered a man, the dampness eventually penetrated to the skin everywhere on the body. It was akin to riding with your arse in a puddle.

We made one brief halt during our initial six-mile trek to Ludlow's Station, and that solely to check each animal for shifting loads and loose cinches or lashings. The train was loose of muscle and into their work by then, and Paw, anxious to establish what would be expected of them the next several days, cut them no slack. We were under way again without our feet seeming to touch the muddy roadbed more than a minute or two.

Ludlow's squat gathering of cabins and blockhouse hove into view at noon. Paw's arm shot upward and swept in a wide circle with the last horse string still crossing McHenry's Ford. No shouted command was needed, for true to Paw's training, down the line behind that suddenly upthrust and signaling limb, we halted our mounts on the instant, came alert, and hastily shucked barrel plugs and lock covers from our long guns.

From the slightly elevated terrain at the very rear I could make out that gray smoke huddled about the chimney of the blockhouse. Though the structure had supposedly been abandoned after the army marched for the St. Mary's and the Shawnee towns, why was Paw cocked in the saddle like a hound on point? Injuns didn't hang about in daylight, and any army personnel enjoying a repast in their travels to wherever would pose no real danger to us.

Paw, head frozen and gaze never leaving the blockhouse, motioned Tap forward and issued orders that didn't carry to my straining ears. The old scout reined his brown gelding in a circle and dismounted at the far corner of the blockhouse. Thaddeus and Timothy were also out of the saddle. They eased left and right away from the horse train so as to have a clear field of fire past Paw to our front.

Me, I done what I'd been taught was proper for the situation. I stayed put atop Blue and maintained a look-see roundabout to the flanks and behind us to prevent our being surprised from those quarters, a formidable task what with the blockhouse and its mysterious occupants being the source of all the excitement.

Tap slid along the front wall of the blockhouse, rifle barrel poking ahead of him like a pointing finger. He moved slow and careful, listening close all the while for any noise above his head that would indicate someone watched him through the gun ports cut into the floor of the structure's overhanging second story. At the entryway, the old scout, exposing only that poking rifle barrel to anyone inside, pushed the door inward with its muzzle.

My wind caught a breath or two. But no flash of exploding powder or flying ball sprang from the wedge of black interior exposed by the swinging door. One foot on the stoop, Tap peeked around the jamb an inch at a time, hesitated, then, belying his sagging paunch, leaped across the threshold.

My breath caught a bunch longer, finally easing when the old scout bellowed, "No one to home, Caleb! She's empty!"

With whoever Paw thought might threaten us having departed, his immediate concern was avoiding further delays. He ordered the horse strings turned about for a fast watering at the creek, activity that naturally left my curiosity aflame. I held my position on the opposite bank of the stream anyway, fully aware I would rouse his temper if I didn't maintain the expected watch roundabout.

Tap emerged from the blockhouse and conversed with Paw while he and the wagoners proceeded with the watering. I knew soon as the old scout mounted his gelding and rode toward me that we weren't entirely free of whatever danger Paw had put to flight. Paw wouldn't bother sending Tap through the rain to relate what he'd found inside the blockhouse lest it was imperative I know straight off rather than hearing it later over the evening fire.

"They was deserters," Tap revealed, "two all told. They was burnin' table legs an' shutters to dry out. By the drippings next to the hearth, they leaned their weapons agin the wall while they built their fire. They sighted your Paw and us'ns an' lit a shuck out the back entry. Length of them strides in the mud yonder, they'd no interest in greetin' visitors with more'n their backsides."

"Must be hell to be that frightened," I reasoned, shuddering.

"Yeah, probably be. But desertion's a hangin' crime with the army, an' I wouldn't trust St. Clair to spare me the rope was I guilty of such, no way, no how. I'd die afore I let myself be captured."

I nodded that I understood Tap's sentiments, sloshing water from my hat brim. "Paw feel they might linger about?"

Tap nodded now. "They could decide a horse would be plumb helpful gettin' to the Ohio. An' bringin' up the rear, you might appear the best pickin's."

I wagged my head. "Won't be long till there's as many enemies within our camp as there are Injuns outside of it."

"Yeah, ain't no doubt it's a tangled mess of a campaign. But you keep your barrel unplugged an' tie that lock cover with but a slipknot, case you need to defend yourself sudden like. Don't fret any cause they're white skinned liken you an' me. Your Paw says we'll bury 'em where we kill 'em."

Warnings presented per Paw's instructions, the old scout kept watch so I could dismount and water Blue. He then wheeled the gelding and splashed across the ford one kick of that animal's flank ahead of Paw's yell for us to pull out. With the rain pelting down constant as ever, on backward glance, the open door of the blockhouse was mighty inviting as we departed Ludlow's Station, mighty inviting.

The hour being but early afternoon, it was apparent our destination was Fort Hamilton, sixteen miles to the northwest. We would arrive there well after dark, but Paw was likely figuring forage in the form of collected prairie grass might be available, and a night in the presence of soldiers offered protection from at least the red enemy.

The rain ceased at nightfall. Its ending inspired no lift in my spirits, for by then my thighs and calves, trapped twixt wet cloth and wet skin and sawed back and forth with Blue's every stride, were chafed raw. My hat brim drooped to my nose, and water trickled in runnels round my belly hole. My tender skull thumped and throbbed. And though my lock cover was securely in place, I doubted my priming was dry enough to accept sparks from my rifle's flint. We rode the final few miles humped in the saddle like broken old men, too exhausted to fear attack from the surrounding darkness, dwelling solely on Fort Hamilton with its warming fire and hope of something hot and drinkable.

Paw's booming "Hello the fort" jerked me awake in the saddle. The sentry's answering challenge rang from the black mass suddenly blocking the roadway. A wedge of faint light bloomed before Paw and widened as gates cleaving the black mass swung open. Uniformed infantrymen ran forth and led the pack strings westward along the fort's picketed curtain toward the Great Miami. I waited till the road cleared and clucked Blue forward.

At the gate I recognized Captain Lucas Steddeman not by his wolf-trap jaws or officer's epaulettes but by his familiar hawking spit. "Well, by damned, young Mr. Downer has returned as promised. Too bad Ensign Young ain't about to greet yuh."

I halted Blue. "He's gone?" I stammered dully.

"Yes, sir. Orders come yesterday directly from St. Clair's own quill no less. The ensign was in the saddle and gone in less'n twenty minutes. Wants to be part of a fight the worst way, that boy does." The captain chuckled, the first lightening of his normally sour demeanor I'd ever witnessed, and from how the sentries stared at him, perhaps the first occasion for everybody else acquainted with him. "He's so anxious to engage the redsticks, he lays into wavin' that sword of his about, he might accidentally scalp hisself. Follow me, Mr. Downer, you'll find me downright hospitable to men who've ridden all day in the rain to feed a hungry army."

Captain Steddeman's claim proved no idle boast. In a controlled rush, he assigned our horses to their previous hostler, Corporal Balser, dispatched the wagoners to the enlisted men's barracks, sent a messenger to roust Oakley, the cook, from his bunk, then personally stoked the hearth fire of the commissioned officers' quarters into a roaring blaze. He next brusquely ordered Paw, Tap, and me from our clothes, stripping blankets from his own bed as well as those belonging to his absent fellow officers to hide our nakedness. We hadn't any more gathered before the fire when our robustly smiling host offered a tin of bear's grease to soothe our raw thighs and set a jug of whiskey on the table to slacken our thirst. Three long swallows later, a beaming Tap Jacobs solemnly and most reverently nominated Captain Lucas Steddeman for sainthood in the church of his choice.

We cheered Private Oakley's entry, for he bore our dinner with him in a large kettle. The kettle contained a dish new to us, a concoction of hard biscuit and molasses called burgoo the captain explained Oakley had learned to prepare during his years as a pressed seaman aboard British naval ships. Taste was lacking, but served hot, the concoction slid down the gullet slick as greased butter and seemed to warm your innards for hours afterward.

All things considered, it was a highly enjoyable repast that overshadowed my disappointment that we had missed Ensign

Andy Young. It was good we made the most of it, for Paw, Tap, and I were not to be together again, warm, entirely dry, and pleasantly full of belly at one and the same time for many, many moons to come.

Chapter 15

Paw's unrelenting approach to the business at hand was fully evident before first light. His call to be up and about sounded ahead of Captain Steddeman's morning spit, which meant we went to bed in the dark and rose in the dark. "Ain't fair when a man can't sleep till daylight," Tap groused. "Pity some men givin' orders trust others are liken them, young forever."

Paw was no more tolerant of Tap's early morning carping than Bear Watkins. "Yeah, but the arses on you old goats are worn the same shape as the saddle. You can sleep for miles without losing your seat. Stifle your tongue and shuck into them breeches before you miss the breakfast victuals."

Captain Steddeman went to retrieve the pack trains and our horses. Private Oakley passed him at the stoop, inbound with a fresh kettle of burgoo. Served two meals in a row, hard biscuit and molasses rapidly lost its appeal. Black tea replaced the whiskey of the previous evening, sparking much comment by Tap who, one eye always on Paw, confined his displeasure to a series of rambling mumbles, the content of which not a soul could decipher. For all his complaining, the old scout, nonetheless like us, ate his plate empty.

Paw knowing it to be the Sabbath, he led us in prayers of thanks before we rose from the table. Then dressed, fed, and proper with our Maker, we wormed the balls from our flintlocks and reloaded with fresh powder charges in barrel and pan, a necessary precaution since the rain had resumed after midnight and continued unabated. We sallied forth into the downpour, fully resigned to the discomforts of the long, wet ride awaiting us.

Our order on the trail was the same, Paw in the van with the lead train, followed by Tap, Thaddeus, and Timothy with the balance of the horse strings, yours truly bringing up the rear on Blue. The Great Miami was running full twixt its banks, and our crossing was fraught with close calls and near accidents, but in the end we gained the far bank without losing a single packhorse. Our collective sigh of relief as the last animal fought free of the current could be heard over the moderate wind blowing from the southwest.

We pursued the westernmost road of the two opened by the army before General Butler had switched strategies on his own volition and built just a single track. The rain tapered to intermittent drizzle late in the morning, too late to matter, as all of us except Paw in his canvas coat were soaked through the first few miles. Early afternoon found us in the gorge of Seven Mile Creek. We watered the strings there and nibbled on the nocake and jerk remaining in Tige's pouches.

Paw gathered us for a parley once the horses were watered. "If the last express from the north Captain Steddeman received was accurate, the army's encamped thirty-eight miles ahead, erecting another fort of deposit. It's anticipated the construction will take a week. We better plan right now how we can best reach their fort without our animals breaking down."

Paw rolled his eyes at the gray clouds flitting past overhead. "More rain's likely, and loaded horses can't go but fifteen miles a day in bad weather less'n they're well rested and well fed. Fording the river tired these animals somethin' fierce, and they can't handle but eight additional miles today. And from here forward, the country's pretty much grazed over, so we'll halt and camp with some daylight still available to assist our forage hunting. That'll leave us thirty miles from the fort, two days of travel. Mount up, gentlemen. If it isn't too much bother, I wouldn't hold prayers for dry weather against any man."

We must have prayed with Paw's fervor and caught the Lord's ear, for the rain halted shortly thereafter. We spent the balance of the afternoon traversing the broken country leading to the upper reaches of Seven Mile Creek in weather mild enough we shed our wet coats and dried out somewhat underneath in the warming southwestern breeze. Twice more we passed through sites of past army encampments, locations where the stench of discarded slops and slit trenches visited by hundreds of soldiers fouled our nostrils and urged us onward to escape the rank smell. By mere chance we crossed what I now called Erin's Run and halted for the night along another small stream approximately two miles beyond the army camp at which I'd last seen her.

Once memories started me thinking about her again, I couldn't stop. I went through the evening chores—the dispersal of the pack trains within the small meadow adjoining our fire, the off-loading and hobbling of the animals, the gathering of firewood, the erection of our tents—in a numbing daze that inspired knowing winks and snickers among Tap and the wagoners. Busy inspecting the backs, limbs, and feet of his four-legged charges, Paw missed out on my bumbling, scatterbrained antics. That was most fortunate for me, as I would never have been able to adequately explain to him how his oldest son had managed to bounce off a tree butt with his arms full of firewood.

The redstick threat notwithstanding, Paw risked a sizable fire to dry clothing and skin on the outside as much as possible and fill the belly on the inside with something warm. Tige had packed tins of salt pork and small leather bags of ground meal. The first boiled in a small kettle, and the second, mixed with water and salt, kneaded into johnnycake, and baked in hot ashes, tasted grand. Course, I allow the hot tea laced with whiskey may have heightened our appreciation considerably.

Victuals bolted with dispatch and clothing warmed through if not dry, Paw assigned the first round of night guards, then insisted the rest of us dampen the fire and seek our tents. Rain, a steady downpour that showered our tents with falling leaves as well as water, commenced after midnight, and with that event, wild dreams of Erin Green that made no sense then or later disrupted my sleep. I tossed and turned like an empty keg trapped atop a churning sea. I came awake at Paw's morning call feeling I hadn't rested a wink.

"Lad, we catch up to St. Clair's miserable excuse for an army," Tap said from alongside me, "visit that gal straight off an' settle things with her one way or the other. Much as I prize our friendship, I'm too old to be pounded to death in my sleep."

I went sheepishly forth into a dawn bereft of rain but weak of light and choked with fog. If Tap knew of whom I dreamed, I wondered what craziness I had spouted aloud during the night. By the finish of a cold, hasty breakfast, the morning tent striking, and the reloading of the packhorses, I was for my own safety as well as those about me vowing that I somehow had to buck up the strength to keep Erin Green from haunting my every hour. The necessity of my doing just that became more urgent with Paw's terse instructions for the day. "Tap, take the rear in place of Ethan. Ethan, you lead the second string behind me. Let's move out, gentlemen."

The others accepted the change in our order of travel without comment. But it left me pondering a serious question: Had I been mistaken? Had Paw observed my ridiculously stupid encounter with the tree butt the previous evening? That possibility weighed heavily on me the next two days. Paw discerned much from little, and the last thing I wanted on God's earth was for him to decide I couldn't be trusted to share his company. I had no desire to forever be a boy in the eyes of Caleb Downer.

We rode St. Clair's military trace northwest the whole of the rainless, cheerlessly gray morning. The ground leveled each mile into gentle swells defined fore and aft by small streams. The underbrush within the timber flanking the road disappeared, and the southwest wind sheared leaves from towering oak, ash, walnut, sugar tree, and beech of a seemingly boundless number. The rich soil of the open woods drew approving comments from Paw seconded roundly by the wagoners. Even the chore-hating Tap crowed during a blowing of the horses how "country like this could lead a man into settling on one porch with the same woman in his bed till kingdom come." Such an out-of-character sentiment from the skirt-hungriest scout west of Fort Pitt so astounded his listeners we simply walked away with brows arched and heads shaking.

The clouds thickened, and the rain and the wind, strong

as in the night, resumed in the afternoon, pelting us with swirling leaves. The leaves already covering the muddy road, deepened by the fresh overlay, slid beneath the weight of striking hooves on uneven ground, adding to the burden of the pack animals and slowing our pace. Wet and soggy everywhere once more, it was extremely difficult not to at least shout curses at the elements with raw abandon. But the sheer will of Paw discouraged such useless outbursts. Backside ramrod straight and never glancing backward, he led us upcountry like the sun was shining. And damned if any of us in his wake were about to suggest we stop for any reason less'n a horse dropped dead in his tracks, and maybe not even then.

Late in the afternoon we crossed a stream of fifteen feet. On the far bank a pole and bark lean-to, the roof in a state of tattered collapse, stretched twixt two beech trees. Paw pointed with a jabbing arm as he passed. Understanding its significance, we each in turn took a long gander as we came abreast of what was obviously the first Injun camp sighted by St. Clair's forces, enough of a rarity in itself that the rotting structure had been left undisturbed by all concerned.

The sighting kept us on the alert the last miles we traveled 17 October, for several additional Injun campsites, complete with stone fire rings, sided the roadway, clearly establishing that the St. Clair trace paralleled a redstick path of some history. With the rain and wind finally abating, near dusk we crossed another fairly wide stream, and Paw halted for the night beside the largest Injun camp we'd seen yet. Facing back down the line of horses, he announced, "We're between army encampments with good water. We'll have to scavenge for forage, but there must be a prairie nearby for the redsticks to camp here so often. Stand down and let's look about in pairs. Ethan, you stay with the animals."

Whether assigning me the least dangerous task of overseeing the horses was another example of Paw not trusting me or simply a figment of my imagination, I didn't while away the time lolling about. I had one horse string watered when Paw and Timothy appeared from upstream. A sharp whistle from Paw summoned Tap and Thaddeus from downstream.

"Goodly meadow sixty yards upstream with enough grass to halfway feed the horses," Paw stated. "We'll camp there and chance a fire for a couple of hours. You haven't noticed, the air has a bite now and smells of rain soon. We best not waste a minute."

It was as mean an evening as we'd experienced since departing the Ohio. A horse string spooked during their hobbling, Tap guessing it was bear stink that set them off, and it was well after dark before we had all the animals offloaded and hobbled, a fire ignited, and our tents staked. The evening meal came off without incident, but at midnight a northern wind bared its teeth and spat rain that changed swiftly into hail. Having just relinquished the guard to Timothy, I ran through a shower of frozen pellets the size of buckshot and dove into the tent I shared with Tap.

My sudden entry awakened the old scout. He listened to the hail peppering the canvas above his prone body, shivered, and burrowed deeper beneath his blankets. "Jumpin' Jesus, wet I can stand. But I can't bear freezin' my arse day and night, too."

I slipped down next to him and snuggled up to my flintlock, wondering if Erin Green was warm and dry this particular night. Steady rain replaced the hail, and I lay awake, remembering the beauty of her as she lunged from the run to escape the prying Hookfin and me. We would arrive at the army's new fort of deposit tomorrow, and my longing to see her again was greater than ever, forcing to the fore the old nagging worry she would refuse to even speak to me. Or perhaps Sergeant Tor Devlin would dictate I wasn't permitted anywhere near her. I fell asleep cursing Gabe Hookfin with renewed vigor. Damn the skinny beanpole and his interfering, anyway.

By dawn the heavy wind and rain had blown eastward, leaving high clouds and a dying breeze out of the northwest. Our fourth consecutive meal of boiled pork and johnnycake, whether hot or cold, lost its appeal as had Private Oakley's burgoo. Tap's and the wagoners' solution to the growing dullness of fare was to nibble at the leftover pork and johnnycake while gulping large slugs of whiskey. According to Thaddeus, such manly slurping required innards of iron. Ignoring his blustering challenge, I stuck with water from my canteen. Paw did likewise.

We were under way shortly after daybreak, and it pleased me that Paw, without any explanation, assigned me to the rear for the final day of our northern trek. "Stay alert. These animals are footsore and underfed. We aren't patient with them, the weaker ones will falter on us."

The miles passed without incident till we spied the first of the bloated horse carcasses that suddenly littered the edges of the roadway. Toting animals perished rapidly if worked day in and day out without adequate nourishment, and a paucity of sufficient forage exacted a terrible toll. A few of the dead beasts bore the brand U.S. Army on their hindquarters; a greater number did not, which identified them as contractor horses in the care of Valentine Dodd.

Of greater import to the finishing of our trek was the huge swamp that blocked our path in the afternoon. Weak sunlight reflected from standing pools of brackish water that soured the air, and dying trees listed in all directions. Had autumn frosts not killed the skeeters and deerflies that swarmed such sunken prairies during warmer months, we would have been eaten alive in broad daylight. Hoofprints in the glistening black muck leading to a water-filled hole formed by the belly of a mired horse showed the folly of trying to cross the swamp by a direct route.

Our initial fear we might have to travel extra miles skirting the sunken prairie was dispelled by the discovery the army had located dry ground but a quarter mile to our right. Once we had the train strung out along that safe passageway, we rested and inspected our strings before continuing. Tap stood watch while Paw and the wagoners helped me halve the loads of six animals that were beginning to tire and stumble, sure signs of sore shoulders and lameness. We split the additional burden equally among the strongest of the other horses. Then, after downing the last of our whiskey, we set off on the final leg of our trek, my mind already far ahead of the plodding pack train.

Five miles later, we gained the upper perimeter of the swamp. The St. Clair trace ran true north a mile from that point before disappearing over a gentle ridge of high ground.

A hovering cloud of rising smoke, bright gray in the shine of the setting sun, signified the precise location of the general and his army beyond the ridge. Our trek was nearly at an end.

It was all I could do not to race past the plodding horse strings. But I gripped Blue's mane with both hands and held my place at the rear. Patience was what was needed, not brashness. I had no solid feeling as to Paw's true sentiments regarding Erin Green. He recognized her by name as the camp girl whose rescue resulted in the death of Hardy Booth. I couldn't fathom how he might react if he learned I intended to call on her seriously. Perhaps he would have no objection. Perhaps he would heat up like a blazing stack of hay. So it seemed the safest bet to bide my time and wait till the flour was delivered and the horses tended. Maybe after that I could somehow finagle a way to visit the Green camp without rousing his suspicions.

Past the bloated bodies of still more dead pack animals Paw halted our strings on the crest of the ridge separating us from St. Clair's forces to study the army's current encampment. The general's newly constructed fort of deposit centered a swell of ground that descended in a series of small knolls to open prairie on the east and west. Bastions protected three angles of the fort's horizontally laid walls. A two-story blockhouse occupied the northeastern corner. Smack in the middle of the whole shebang sat a squat powder magazine complete with an underground entryway shielded at top, bottom, and side by thick logs.

Precise rows of regimental tents lined the general's trace plumb to the fort's main gate. Cavalry flanked the tent lines, and beyond the cavalry, horse and bullock herds filled the eastern and western prairies. Parked supply wagons and irregularly placed tents belonging to Kentucky militia occupied the immediate ground directly below us. My heart hammered with excitement, but try as I might in the dwindling daylight, and I tried desperately hard, I couldn't pinpoint the whereabouts of Molly Green's cart amid the confusing welter of supply wagons, militia tents, and cooking fires at our feet.

We went down the far slope of the ridge at a steady walk. Members of the militia saw us before we reached the nearest of their tents, and the news a pack train was arriving spread ahead of us like a breaking wave of seawater. Kentuckians in varying states of dress flooded from tent and fire to watch us pass by.

More than a few cheers rang forth. Howsomever, a greater number of the militiamen made no attempt to hide their dislike for contractors whose tardiness had allowed the entire army to be shorted of the daily flour ration.

"You ninnies deserve the noose, by damned!"

"Bloody buggers! Yuh shouldn't be paid for nothin'!"

"Yuh bastards ought to bake bread for us fightin' men!"

Anger stirred my blood and clogged my throat, the heat of it hot on my cheeks. But much as I wanted to lash back with tongue and fist, I ceased searching left and right for the Green cart and kept my eyes where Paw did—directly forward, and my jaws in the same position as his—tightly clamped. I learned an honest, bitter lesson that October evening. Failing to meet your responsibilities in a timely fashion courted the disdain and rancor of those you served, and those you failed were mighty unforgiving.

The thousand-yard ride seemed miles long. We fared little better coursing twixt the rowed tents of the regulars and the levy regiments. It was full dark when we thankfully drew up before the open gates of the fort. Paw exchanged greetings with a sergeant, and we were waved inside. The gates closed behind us, and soldiers detailed to guard duty helped off-load and stack the flour in a log hutment east of the powder magazine. Paw rode alongside the emptied strings and rose in his stirrups. "The sergeant says Val Dodd's camped on the western prairie along the creek. We'll unsaddle the horses there. After me, and quickly. The disgruntled will be storming the gates."

The gates opened, and sure enough, officers and their angry charges were massing outside the main entryway. We kicked and goaded liveliness into animals dead tired and took leave of the gathering mob close onto the south wall, enduring a parting round of jeers and insulting gestures. The darkness of the western prairie was most inviting.

Paired sentries both afoot and on horseback guarded the army's baggage horses and the pack animals remaining in

Val Dodd's train. Under a feeble moon, we identified ourselves to the commanding officer of the sentries and presented him with the hobbles fashioned days ago in Cincinnati. We received in return enough gathered grass to passably feed our unsaddled packhorses. Exhausted as they were, we had no worry our strings would stray far before daylight and let them drift unhampered. Our personal mounts we hobbled.

Personal gear and long guns in tow, we trudged to the Dodd fire. Seeing how I was worn through and bone weary, I figured it would prove my ill luck to find Gabe Hookfin lolling about with a satisfied smirk on his leathery features. Thus, it was a relief to find not the beanpole, but Captain Miles Starkweather ringing the fire along with Val Dodd, Henry Cross, and Ira Fellows.

Upon spying Paw, the captain walked our direction. "Evening, Mr. Downer. I hate to impose an additional burden, but General St. Clair would like you to report to his tent immediately The general was disappointed with the limited size of your shipment. He wants to discuss precisely when future supplies will arrive."

Paw had no valid excuse with which he could refuse the general's request. "Keep the fire hot, Valentine. I'll return within the hour. Bear, soon as he's through eating, send Ethan to watch over the riding stock. I don't trust the army sentries to stay alert."

Paw went off with Captain Starkweather, and we were finishing a meal of roasted beef and watered whiskey when a muscular figure strolled from the direction of the fort. I was about to welcome Paw back, but the words died in my throat. It wasn't Paw who stepped into the firelight. It was Sergeant Torrance Devlin, Second United States Regiment, who stepped from the darkness.

The sergeant's flushed, troubled countenance signaled his blood was up, threatening to erupt into boiling, uncontrollable rage. Was he seeking me out? Was he here to extract satisfaction for my intruding on Erin Green's bath? I froze in place and stayed my ground, glad the fire separated us for the moment.

The sergeant planted his feet, butted his musket beside

them, and snapped to attention. Without any sort of hello, he blurted, "We Devlins handle our own troubles, Jacobs. But much as it shames me, I've no choice except to request the help of you and Watkins."

Tap frowned. "What's chawin' on yer knee, Sergeant?"

"My child's been taken!" Devlin roared. "Taken, do you hear!"

Had I heard correctly? His child? What child? Who did he mean?

A cold, numbing chill speared my innards. God's bones, he was speaking of Erin. And taken? Taken by whom? Hell and damnation, he could only mean the Injuns! The redsticks had taken Erin Green captive a second time!

Chapter 16

Nighttime, 18 October

I swear my tongue worked of its own accord. "The Injuns have Erin? How did they capture her?"

The sergeant ignored me and spoke to Bear. "It wasn't the red enemy who carried her off. White men they be!" Devlin managed, barely restraining his fury. "Deserters from the Kentucky militia, by damned!"

Our encounter with the deserters at Ludlow's Station was still vivid in my mind. Thus, the sergeant's admission the redsticks weren't responsible for Erin's captivity did nothing to ease the coldness gripping my belly. Regardless of their origin or the color of their skin, desperate men were the most dangerous to deal with, and those having abandoned their sworn duty and fearing the hangman's noose would be doubly so.

Bear waved a placating spread of fingers before Tor Devlin. "Pour the Sergeant a cup of whiskey straight from the jug, Tap. He calms himself a mite, mayhap we can make sense of what he's sayin'."

Tor Devlin gulped the fiery liquor in three huge swallows, never so much as blinking, and swiped his lips. "Now, tell us exactly what happened, Sergeant," Bear said soothingly. "Where from was your child taken?"

"The spring at the northern edge of the eastern prairie. Her mother's cart was nearby, and she went for water, the child did."

"Did you yourself see her carried off?"

"No, not I. It was Marabee. Private Horace Marabee of me own company."

"An' he's sure of what he saw? No chance of his bein' mistaken?"

"None, none whatsoever," the sergeant answered impatiently. "Marabee trips over his own shoes at drill, but he's a keen eye for anything out of the ordinary."

Bear sipped tea from his noggin. "All right then, how many deserters took Mistress Green, and when?"

"Four of the bastards there was. Marabee saw them marching to the spring, piggins in their grasp, the corporal amongst them giving the orders."

"Was they bearin' arms?" Tap put in.

"Yes, muskets, pistols, and knives, each and every one. That's why Marabee noticed them, all those weapons just to fetch four piggins of drinking water. Marabee was at the fringe of the bullock herd an' saw Erin join them. The child, unfortunately for her mother and me, knows no fear of strangers. On Marabee's next round, they were gone, the child and every last one of the bloody buggers. Marabee rushed forward for a closer look but couldn't see them anywheres. Had they walked toward the fort, he'd of spotted them straightaway."

"And when did they take her captive, Devlin? What time was this?" Tap persisted.

"While you were bringing your pack train down from the ridge past our tents. Two hours back, it was now. Marabee reported her taking to me an hour ago."

"An' you didn't chase after them?" an incredulous Tap wondered.

Tor Devlin's features grew stormier than they'd been when he strolled to our fire. "I was refused permission to do so by our major. Four of our own showed their heels last week, and the major fears anyone venturing beyond our pickets will prove themselves of the same stripe. He won't risk me or a detail to rescue what he deems a camp girl of little consequence to the campaign."

"An' you figure our bein' unattached, we could track down your missin' child?" Tap speculated.

"Yes, there's no one else I can call upon," Tor Devlin admitted with a reluctance that had to hurt him deeply. "There's no one else free to go in search of her."

Bear and Tap studied each other under the expectant gaze of everyone ringing the fire. It was those two Devlin specifically sought to trail the militia deserters and retake Erin. The sergeant apparently didn't want Ethan Downer anywhere near his beloved child, not this go-round, anywise.

It was Bear who broke the silence. "But not tonight, Sergeant. Not tonight."

Tor Devlin's impatience rose to new heights. "Why not tonight? Why must you delay?"

Bear sipped more tea. "Findin' her an' her captors will be nigh onto impossible in the dark. An' that's if'n we can get outside our own sentries without their detainin' us or shootin' us by mistake. Those muskets firin' every whipstitch at night every time some dimwit believes a flicker of moonlight be an Injun are loosin' real balls that can kill yuh plumb dead forever. Come mornin', we'll locate their tracks and light a shuck after their miserable arses."

Devlin's next contention mirrored my own thinking. "But they might harm the child in the meantime!"

Bear stared at the woods north of our fire. "Not likely. They'll keep movin' fast as their legs will allow all night. She don't fall behind or slow their pace too much, she'll be alive at daylight. Even scum such as deserters might find murderin' a white girl hard to stomach. An' we can gain every hour on 'em tomorrow with us ridin' an' them afoot. Agreed?"

Tor Devlin hated the idea of postponing the pursuit, but he had no recourse lest he wanted to desert himself. He bobbed his head, conceding the field to Bear.

"Then it's best you rejoin your company before that major sends a squad to arrest you for not manning your post," Bear reminded him. "You'll be the first to learn what comes of our search in the mornin', that I promise."

Tor Devlin braced his shoulders, extended his hand to both Bear and Tap, pivoted about, and faded into the surrounding blackness. "That man swallowed a heap of pride tonight," Bear observed solemnly to no one in particular. "A heap of pride."

Tap was now staring into the northern trees. "They

scooted off in the direction of the Shawnee towns. Suppose they're plannin' on joinin' the redcoats?"

Bear finished his tea. "Naw, they'll feint north just long enough to divert our attention, then swing 'round to the west. I scouted thataway with the Kentuckians when we were huntin' a route clear of that big swamp. There's an Injun path runnin' north and south five miles west of the swamp that lends itself to fast travel afoot right smartly. Them Kentucky boys will seek it out. They's bound for the Ohio an' home."

I went about preparing for my upcoming stint guarding the horses as if nothing extraordinary had occurred. Keeping my hands steady so neither Bear nor Tap would suspect how fiercely my heart pounded, I fastened the belt securing the Starkweather knife and my hatchet around my waist, slipped the carrying strap of my powder horn over my head, and checked the flint and priming of my rifle. I filled not one, but both of my coat pockets with strips of roasted beef, the same as any night guard would on the chance his relief was delayed. I was sly enough not to appear totally unmoved by the excitement of the evening. "I trust I will be allowed to help search for Erin?" I inquired of Tap and Bear.

Tap's smile was full of devilish understanding. "Thought you'd never ask, lad," he chirped. "And how's Devlin to know, huh?" But a second later his smile vanished. "Though it'll be for your Paw to make the final decision, won't it now?"

That was my main worry. What if Paw decided the Downer men needed to head south with the Dodd packhorses on the morrow to speed up delivery of additional flour and other vital supplies? Given his penchant for seeing to essential business first and incidentals later, Paw could easily determine we had no time to spare searching for a missing girl whether we were subject to the command of the army or not. And wasn't it rumored that St. Clair viewed all camp followers, men, women, and children, as chronic nuisances he'd sooner be shed of at the earliest possible date? There was much against even a cursory look for the mistress, even more against a full-scale, serious hunt.

Repeating the password supplied by their lieutenant earlier, I identified myself to the outlying sentries fronting the creek and sought our riding animals. They were scattered along the near bank, pawing and scrounging for what few nibbles of grass remained on ground grazed over for days by horse and bullock alike. The extreme shortage of forage convinced me more then ever that Paw would return south at daylight. He would at least move the animals in his charge where he could provide them sustenance.

I located Blue and rubbed his neck while pondering how best to proceed. I gave no thought to the danger involved in a lone pursuit of the four, armed deserters holding Erin. Nor did I dwell on the repercussions that would result from openly and willfully defying Paw's authority. If I did either for a single, solitary minute, I feared my nerve would falter.

Well, damn, if I was hell-bent on risking my neck for a slap of the face, first I had to get clear of the army sentries posted along the creek around their herd of baggage horses as well as our packhorses. Much as I wanted Blue with me for ease of travel and a quick ride home once I had freed Erin, too many sentries patrolled the dark night for me to sneak beyond their watchful eyes leading a horse. So, it was make the trek afoot or wait till dawn. I was too anxious to be away from the army camp and Paw's authority for the latter.

The moon peeked through a break in the clouds, and continuing to stroke Blue's neck, I inspected the expanse of prairie bordering the creek. A copse of trees on my left flank, twenty yards off, offered cover on the near bank. Across the creek, trees crowded the waterway east and west to the stream's nearest bend in either direction. Thick tangles of brush, too dense for any four-legged animal, blanketed the far bank beneath the crowding trees. Deeper into the woods, a solid mass marked the presence of higher ground. Once beyond that rise, a night marcher would be shielded from the sentries patrolling the prairie.

Wind-drifted cloud masked the moon. I dropped into a crouch, seized a fistful of Blue's mane, and coaxed him toward the creek. Despite his hobbled front legs, he took a notion we were playing a new game and advanced in steady, measured hops. Not for an instant did my hat crown lift above his shoulder. I flattened on my belly short of the creek amid scattered piles of ripe horse dung and wriggled the last few yards required to gain the protecting copse of trees.

Assuming a low crouch again, I inched to the water's edge and positioned myself where tree shadows extending from both banks meshed together above the surface of the creek. Much as I hated wet, cold feet, I fashioned a sling for my rifle with a length of leather thong from my coat pocket and slung that weapon on my backside. Then, strap of my powder horn looped about itself and clasped twixt my teeth, I crossed the knee-deep, thirty-foot stream on all fours. No yell of alarm rang out, and but the tiniest splash of water and crackle of brush revealed my passage as I slithered ashore on the far bank.

A pair of sentries circled behind the copse of trees next to Blue. The pair exchanged "All's well" with their counterparts bound the opposite direction on the perimeter of the horse and bullock herds. I grinned in the night. My disappearance had gone undetected.

Immensely pleased with what I considered a clever duping of St. Clair's sentries, I crawled a safe distance into the northern forest, stood, and began climbing to higher ground with long, purposeful strides. Everything was suddenly fine and dandy with Ethan Downer, who was off to rescue his true love—or the woman he hoped would be his undying love.

God forgive my shock and surprise when I topped the rise and discovered to my dismay Tap Jacobs leaning nonchalantly against a tree butt, hatless dome of his bald head shining ghostly white in the moonlight. I stood before him, cursing my sodden feet and the energy I'd needlessly wasted escaping from the prairie. "How did you get here ahead of me?"

Tap giggled, further infuriating me. "Wasn't anything worthy of a bell ringing. I told them peach-bearded sentries I was traipsing across the creek to unbutton my breeches in private, and if they didn't approve of my goin' alone, they could trail along and smell my scat for themselves. Way their mouths drawed up tighter'n the skins on regimental drums, I knowed they weren't about to stop me. They wouldn't of cared if'n I'd stumbled into a passel of Shawnee on the other bank."

"I'm not about to be stopped either!" I declared vehemently.

Tap settled his hat on his bare head. "I'm not here to drag on your coattails, an' I'm too old to fight with young buckos liken you. I'll just mosey along an' keep yuh from losin' yer scalp or yer lifeblood savin' that Green gal."

"Does Bear know you're here?"

"Naw, he thinks I'm visitin' the Green wagon, an' he's gonna be mad as Hades when he finds out otherwise. But not nearly as upset as yer Paw will be. Now, I ain't tryin' to change yer plans, mind yuh, but are you sure you don't want to talk this over with yer Paw?"

I lunged past the old scout and bolted down the slope of the rise. "Well, hell's bells, I guess not," Tap yelled, scrambling after me. "Sweet Jesus, my maw must be wailin' for joy in her grave. Her onliest son is about to attempt somethin' noble, even if'n it gets him killed. Ain't nothin' more pitiful than an old dead fool . . . well, less'n it would be a young one!"

Chapter 17

Daytime, 19 October

Once on level terrain again, I darted westward beneath the shielding shoulder of the rise. It was after midnight, and thickening cloud blinded the moon again. The leaf cover of open spots of ground was inches thick under my moccasins and slippery as grease. Briars and brambles rimmed the open places and clawed at my coat sleeves and the skin of my hands and neck. I plunged ahead, wending left and right among the tree butts, taking no heed as to the noise I made.

When Tap started gasping and wheezing and falling behind, I halted briefly at a small brook for a spelling drink. The old scout sucked water greedily on hand and knee, then scooted his backside against the nearest of the towering tree butts. "You are prayin' every step, ain't yuh, Ethan?" he inquired.

"What the hell you blubberin' about?" I snapped.

The old scout sighed. "If'n yuh ain't prayin' for the Lord's help, yuh best get at it mightily an' sincerely, 'cause the ruckus we's makin', any Injuns out an' about will hear us miles off. Chrissake, we'd be easier to ambush than a newborn squalling in its crib."

I gulped wind and calmed myself. I was glad to have Tap along. He was a tracker the equal of Tice Wentsell, Kenton, or Boone and had survived many a brush with the redsticks. But I feared his legs and his wind would give out on him. "We've got to risk bumpin' into the Shawnee tonight. We can't allow those deserters too much of a head start. The farther they get from the army, the greater the chance they'll kill Erin."

Tap wasn't cross with me, though I was telling him what he already knew. "What's your thinkin'?" he asked.

"We must reach that western Injun path Bear described close onto daylight as possible. Our only hope is that we can locate some sign of them there. We don't, Erin's the same as dead."

Tap hitched his feet under him. "Leastways your foul temper ain't clogged your head none. Lead off. I believe these old limbs will last me till dawn."

Ancient legs or not, I soon came to rely on Tap's wisdom and experience. In the middle of the night, with my own considerable strength flagging, he barked, "Put a bung in yer hole a while, lad. You're driftin' off course a mite."

He fumbled in his haversack and produced a small, flat box made of tin and another the same size of wood. "Grab me a few dry leaves," he ordered. Opening the tin box, he extracted bits of charred cloth, a piece of flint, and a steel dowel three inches in length. He knelt so a deadfall screened him from the chill night wind, laid the charred cloth on the leaves I fetched, and striking flint against steel, showered the blackened cloth with sparks. The cloth began to smoke. Tap immediately bent at the waist, blew downward with gentle breaths, and nursed the flickering embers into flames that spread quickly to the leaves underneath.

He then hurriedly removed the lid of the wooden box. Inside was a brass-dialed compass. Holding the instrument beside his tiny fire, he peered intently at the dials and giggled. "Damned if'n I ain't near skillful as yer Paw. We're traveling northwest, not due west like we should be. We angle too far north, we'll delay gainin' that Injun path an' mayhap miss our quarry altogether."

He rose and stomped out his tiny fire. Though I couldn't be certain, he had to be grinning in the dark. "Old goats with weak limbs can still be of some help, lad. Turn halfway about where you stand, follow your nose, an' by the by, we'll find Mr. Bear Watkins's Injun road."

Tap enjoyed funning me, which I deserved, and I bore him no ill will. Long before first light, he again proved indispensable. His soft whistle sounded while I was resting, waiting for him to catch up to me. I backtracked and found him standing in an opening not a dozen feet wide. "We're there, lad."

I hesitated, peering at the shadowy shape of him, and he beckoned me forward. "I toed the ruts of traveling horses. Your stride's longer'n mine, and you stepped plumb over them. We've found our pathway."

I thumped Tap's upper arm. "Then let's settle somewhere till there's enough light to hunt for sign."

The old scout grunted. "Spell of sleep wouldn't insult me none, neither."

We retreated from the Injun road and hunkered down. I closed my coat collar. Was the mistress clad warmly? She'd be hard pressed to stay warm in nothing but her thin shirt. And where was she? Was she still drawing breath? Had her captors abused her?

I shrank deeper into my coat and strained to clear my head. I'd been awake a day and most of a night, and sheer tiredness dulled my senses, lulling me asleep. No matter how often I shook myself, the tiredness won out, and within minutes I dozed off.

I flamed red from embarrassment when the old scout, seeming frisky as a spring colt, kicked me awake. Though the sky was overcast, the dawn light was stunningly bright. I jumped to my feet, and Tap laid hold of my coat sleeve. "Hang still, young'un, ain't no point gettin' all riled up for nothin'," he advised.

"What you mean by that? You find sign or didn't you?" I demanded.

"Yeah, that I did. Step over to the pathway, an' I'll show yuh."

The old scout, grinning with the utmost satisfaction, positioned me shy of the hoof-carved ruts he'd located in the dark of night and knelt between them. "Four pairs of shoes, soles holed and flopping, it appears." His bony finger touched the dirt of the path. "And here, part of a much smaller print, made by a moccasined foot. That'd be yer mistress, most likely."

I fought against sinking spirits as I had sleep. We'd missed intercepting them, but at least Erin was still drawing breath. "How far behind are we? Can you tell?"

"I'd guess from the crust on these prints 'bout half a day. These boys planned ahead. They went north only far enough to lose sight of the army encampment, then bee-lined for this here pathway."

Tap stood and gazed southward. The slim pathway meandered to the left and disappeared from sight within twenty yards. Injun roads weren't like those the army hacked out of the forest on a constant compass heading. They followed the contour of the land, seeking the most natural, open course of travel. In low, flat country, they favored waterways leading to ever-larger streams while at the same time never neglecting the sites of the closest springs and salt licks. The deserting Kentuckians owed the redsticks much. Even if green to the woods, they needn't fear getting lost. Stick to the Injun pathways crisscrossing the Ohio wilderness, always bearing in the desired direction, and they would eventually emerge from the otherwise trackless forest smack on the bank of the Ohio.

Tap turned his attention to me. "Give a listen, lad. If'n we're to overtake this bunch, we've got to husband our strength. We wind-break ourselves, yer gal be good as dead. It don't wound yer pride too awfully much, I'll set the pace an' pick our course. Mayhap we can shortcut now an' again an' save some steps. Yuh want to hurry along any faster, remember, they ain't slept at all, and sooner or later, their legs will give out. That's when we'll gain the most on them. Once we lay eye on them, we can get down to the serious part of our business."

"Which is to rescue Erin," I interrupted.

"Yeah, but be warned, we'll have to snatch yer gal away from them. They ain't gonna free her willingly with a smile on their ugly faces just 'cause we ask. She's the person whose story, once told, guarantees them a dangle at the end of a noose. We better be prepared for a helluva fight."

It was Tap's sincerity about recovering Erin that won me over to his approach. He would ensure my impatience didn't get the best of me on the trail, then be there at my side when we confronted her captors. In a tight situation, with a man being outnumbered, a supporting rifle might not even the odds, but the added weapon could give him some chance of success.

Tap smiled at my nod and passed me his haversack. Then, moccasins hardly lifting from the pathway, he set off in a ground-devouring half trot that he sustained without tiring. He sipped water from his canteen on the move, gently chiding me for having left mine at the Dodd fire, but still sharing. As the miles mounted, he showed me the legs of his youth when his belly was small and riding stock was scarce. He showed me the endurance of the early hide hunters like himself who had dared to kill and skin game in the bluegrass Shawnee country and outrun the redstick foe to save their scalps. And he showed me the valiant heart of a true friend willing to risk his own life to spare a slip of a girl unfairly taken by her own kind.

A northerly wind pushed at our backs. The sun shone weakly the hour before and after high noon. Tap's eyes never ventured from the tracks we followed except on those occasions when we would veer into the woods for a spell. Despite his claim he had never before so much as sashayed north of Fort Washington, we always regained the Injun pathway with unerring ease. It was as if at one glance he grasped the lay of the land. His frequent brags were suddenly the truth of the moment.

The old scout's half trot never slackened till near dusk. His halting was so abrupt it scared me, and I dropped to a knee, rifle poised and ready. Tap's hand leapt upward, and his head turned slightly. I stayed silent, for I could see his jaw was hanging open. He was listening.

A dull boom like the faint rumble of thunder beyond faraway hills teased my ear. The booming noise was faint enough, had I been on the move, I would not have heard it over the tread of my feet and the working of my lungs. But how had Tap known to stop and listen for it before it happened? Amazing fellow, Tap Jacobs, damn amazing.

His explanation tarnished the feat not a whit. "That was a second musket firing. They must have missed the first try."

"Redstick ambush?" I asked in a whisper.

"Naw, there'd be more shooting. Our boys be awfully hungry. Probably startled a deer and let fly. Hell's bells, the milk ain't even dry on some of those militia boys' lips. They'd shoot game inside St. Clair's tent and gut it in his lap, the devil with the consequences." Tap's smile was wicked and cunning. "Makes them easy to hunt, don't it though?"

Tap dropped to a knee and sipped water, then tossed me the canteen. "What do we do now?" I inquired.

"Well, they're gonna eat their bellies full, all the while talking themselves into believing it's no big risk was they to sleep the night through beside a nice warm fire."

I started to stand, and the old scout glared at me. "Settle back there, lad. We need be in no great rush." He grinned to lessen the sting of his rebuke. "Trust me, we ain't shy on time. We're gonna sleep our own bones fresh while the day ends itself. Once them boys yonder is sawin' the log, we'll lay a right proper sneak on them in the dark. Might help get yer gal loose if'n they was to think we was Injuns, mightn't it now?"

The prospect of gaining the advantage by scaring the deserters out of their wits plastered a huge grin on my own face. Reaching them across wooded terrain buried in leaves in the black of night without raising the alarm gave me pause, but I would depend on Tap's experience to avoid such a disaster.

"Too bad we're shy victuals our ownselves," Tap opined.

I yanked the sacks of roasted beef I had stashed for guard duty from my coat and shared one with the old scout. "Young bellies may not be the wisest, but they never travel with empty pockets, they can help it."

Tap beamed. "Damned if'n you ain't yer Paw all over again, lad."

I enjoyed the compliment but fell asleep in the nearby brush doubting Paw would second Tap's enthusiastic endorsement of his oldest son just now. Trouble, big trouble, loomed for Ethan Downer at both ends of the journey. I decided a few earnest prayers were in order. A young man about to undertake a dangerous venture needed all the support he could muster.

Chapter 18

Midnight, 19 October

Wily Tap located the deserters' camp by the simple expedient of following his nose. He circled around southeast of where he guessed we would find them, then quartered northwesterly into the wind till he sniffed the smoke of their fire. We fetched up to a creek fifteen feet across and turned due north hard along its bank, treading earth swept clean of leaves by the freshets of recent rains. On the sneak, Tap employed a crouching, wide-kneed gait that resembled the walk of a waddling duck but produced less noise than a stalking ghost. Try as I might, I was sweating inside my coat and still not matching his stealth.

A shaft of moonlight pierced the spotty clouds. The creek bent away to our left, and Tap motioned for me to squat and wait. I couldn't spot the deserters' fire, but we had to be drawing close, careful as Tap inched straight ahead into the trees. Though I was alone for mere minutes, the waiting played havoc with my nerves. Clouds shrouded the moon, and Tap's unexpected whisper from arm's length gave me a genuine start. "Found 'em."

"Erin there?" I whispered anxiously.

Tap's breath was damp on my ear. "Seems to be five lumps 'round the fire. Seein' as how I can't tell which one she be, might be wise we surprise them at first light when we can sort things out."

My overwhelming devotion to Erin's ultimate safety negated that strategy. "Ain't nothing guaranteeing they'll all be asleep then. They spy us, they mightn't kill her, but they hold a musket to her head, we'll have to let them go free and take her along."

"What yuh plannin', lad?"

"What you said earlier. You cover me with both our rifles. I'll sneak in and bring her clear. Anything goes amiss, I'll take her to ground with me while you let loose an Injun war whoop and shoot over their heads. That should create enough confusion I can tug her into the trees."

"Dangerous, lad, powerful dangerous. But I agree they'll hide behind her we give them the chance, an' I can't think of anythin' better." Tap's sigh tickled my ear. "All right, we'll do 'er. I hate to admit it, but you bein' younger and stronger, yer a better choice to sneak in amongst 'em. Just remember one thing, by God."

"What's that?"

"Worse comes to worst, it means nothin' they're white like us'ns. Don't hesitate to draw blood. They kidnapped that gal to save their hides. They'll kill you an' her in a wink 'thout a twitch of regret. They ain't no better'n the Injuns took yer brother Aaron. Yuh don't believe that, you hold the rifle an' leave the knife work to ol' Tap."

"I promise. No quarter for any of them."

"Good lad," Tap commended with a rap of my shoulder. "Now, shuck yer belt, coat, an' that frock of yer Paw's. Less they can grab onto, the better. Move low and quick, they discover yuh. Strike down with yer 'hawk an' up with that Starkweather knife. An' don't forget to whoop yer ownself. Scare the nerve from a man, yuh muddle his thinkin'."

The night wind was shivery cold on my bare chest and raised gooseflesh on my forearms and shoulders. I hefted my hatchet in my right hand, knife in my left, and followed on Tap's heels as the old scout retraced his earlier steps. The ground lifted slowly beneath my moccasins. We topped the swell and waited for a break in the clouds. When it came, I made out the creek and then beyond it the deserters' camp, which occupied a treeless spit of sand bounded by the creek and a smaller stream flowing from the west. I estimated the glowing embers of their fire to be no more than twenty yards from Tap and me.

Tap stretched and removed my flop-brimmed hat. His arm

pointed below us. Leaves piled deep by past winds lay in heaps at the base of the swell. Tap's arm swung to our right and jabbed at a lengthy deadfall on the slope of the swell whose trunk slanted into the water of the creek like a thin, black bridge. Tap's first and second fingers switched to and fro, aping the legs of a marching man. I gulped. Lord Jesus, he expected me to climb down the slanting trunk of the deadfall and drop into the creek.

I didn't hesitate. It was the quietest route leading into the water. I eased next to the deadfall and levered myself up onto its trunk. I turned sideways and spread my arms for balance. Traversing the smooth bark of the dead beech was akin to sliding from the neck to the tailbone of a greased hog with the hog standing on his hind feet. The roots at the bottom of the trunk rose in front of me. I wedged the blade of my knife twixt my teeth and wrapped my right arm 'round a root to arrest my forward progress. I hung there a minute till I was reassured my clumsy descent hadn't alerted the deserters, then slipped into the creek with no more ripple than a diving muskrat.

The water was knee deep, and exploring the bottom for rocks or holes with my toes, I waded without lifting my feet above the surface. I ignored the shocking chill as my moccasins filled with water. Better wet footgear than to risk a sneak in bare, unprotected feet.

The weather wasn't helpful. The clouds had thinned to wisps, and the moonlight appeared brighter than full sunshine as I placed a foot on the sandy bank fronting the sleeping deserters and their prisoner. Lowered in a crouch, I crept ahead two steps, then another. The wind suddenly bore the sound of heavy snoring. In the woods beyond the fire, an owl hooted. Leastwise I hoped it was an owl and not real Injuns lurking about.

I advanced a long stride, straightened up a tad, and studied the bodies surrounding the fire. The smallest of the sleepers, whom I took to be Erin, lay closest to the dying fire. Beside her, almost touching her, sprawled the largest of the deserters, his bulk equal to that of Bear Watkins. I crouched again and crept onward, taking pains that I didn't cast a shadow on the outlying sleepers. The big body next to Erin stirred.

I sank onto my haunches, shrinking small as I could. The burly bastard lifted Erin's arms and felt her wrists, apparently checking that her bonds were secure. I heard his short, snorting laugh as he wriggled against her. His companions snored wildly as ever.

I hung still and calmed my nerves. If the burly bastard was mistreating Erin, I'd no intentions of betraying my presence till the last second. No quarter, I'd said. And I'd meant it.

The moon was a white ball in the nearly cloudless sky. The wind rustled my hair. I rose into a crouch and tiptoed toward the two of them. Erin was twixt the glowing embers and the big Kentuckian. I was appreciative his backside faced my approach. A discarded musket angled along his spine.

At my last creeping step, my moccasins brushed the stock of the musket. "Ain't yuh a sweet thing, my missy," the big deserter muttered hoarsely. Erin squirmed, pulling apart from him, and I saw his left hand squeezed her neck while the right was inside her silk shirt, caressing her breast. Anger overwhelmed me as Erin struggled harder, her strangled "No" barely escaping past the fingers clutching her windpipe.

I swept the hatchet above my head, drawing back for a lethal blow to the deserter's shaggy skull. But at the top of my reach, with every muscle flexed and poised for that cleaving, fatal blow, I failed myself. I broke my vow. I froze for the slightest instant, paralyzed by the awareness it was not an Injun I was about to kill without warning but a fellow white man.

Whether Erin saw me and her widening eyes alerted him or the big Kentuckian saw my hatchet lift out of the corner of his own eye, he reacted with astonishing speed. In one swift movement whose pieces knitted together in a single blur, he freed Erin, flipped from right hip to left, and lashed out with a booted foot while his hands streaked for the discarded musket. The lashing boot smashed into my left thigh and staggered me. Even with my balance in peril, I leaned into him, trying to keep my descending hatchet on target.

The rising stock of the deserter's recovered musket met the blade of my hatchet in a thudding impact that tore the weapon from my grasp. The deserter slanted the musket across his chest as I landed atop him. The weight of my body made no more impression than the bump of a floating feather. He didn't so much as grunt. Braced against the ground, he pushed upward with both arms. I grabbed the barrel of the musket with my now empty right hand and jabbed at him with the knife in my left. But the jabbing blade found only the bony back of his shoulder instead of soft, yielding flesh.

The deserter sucked wind and gathered himself. Desperate to stop his throwing me aside, I loosed the knife and thrust my left arm between us. My palm slid along his forearm. I felt the hairs on the back of his hand, then the finger curled about the trigger of the musket. I grabbed and yanked backward. Excited as I was, I still had the wherewithal to shut my eyes against the flash of the muzzle blast. Flint struck metal. Hot flecks of exploding priming seared my bare ribs. The roaring boom of the musket set my ears ringing something awful.

A mighty heave of steely muscles, and I, no small man, went flying, the musket barrel ripped from my fingers. Sandy loam broke my fall, but I was prone and unarmed with the excited shouts of the awakening deserters filling the creek bottom. I opened my eyes, and the big Kentucky deserter, stock of his smoking musket raised to bash in my skull, loomed above me. I was a goner!

The Shawnee war whoop and sharp bang of a rifle firing sounded one after the other. An unseen blow knocked the big Kentuckian backward. He pivoted on legs suddenly unable to bear the smallest of burdens and toppled.

I rolled onto my hands and knees and scrambled toward Erin. The awakened deserters were looking frantically about, confused and unsure as to just where their enemy was and how many there were. Panic cracking his voice, one wailed shrilly, "Corporal Deeds? Corporal?"

Erin had drawn into a ball, making of herself the smallest possible target. The blade of my missing hatchet shone in the moonlight. I seized the smooth wooden handle. A diving body smashed into my ribs and spun me around. I hit the ground on cheek and shoulder, the breath whooshing from my lungs.

Stunned to the quick, I tried to roll and separate myself

from my attacker. A knee caught me in the middle of the back, pinning me flat. Metal rapped my forehead, slid downward over my nose, split my lip, and passed under my chin. The musket barrel lodged against my throat, shutting off my wind. I tried to move, to escape, but I was helpless, my arms trapped beneath me. My lungs screamed for air and my senses reeled. Holy Jesus, this time I truly was a goner!

My attacker grunted, stiffened, and a quaking tremor coursed through his entire frame. The press of the musket against my throat eased. Someone yelled, "Yuh little bitch!" I drew breath, hitched my hips, and bucked sideways, sliding from beneath my attacker. I rolled into a sitting position and took a quick gander about.

My attacker lay belly down next to me, the handle of the Starkweather knife protruding from just below his ribs. Another deserter held a flailing, kicking Erin by her long, red pigtail. A flintlock pistol occupied his other fist. I pulled the Starkweather knife from dead flesh and bolted upright.

A rifle cracked! Erin's captor jerked, rose onto his toes, and collapsed at her feet. And there, behind her, was the final deserter, lifting his musket to his shoulder. With no more pondering than that required to swipe snot from a nostril, I lunged forward into the line of fire, tensed for the coming bullet.

The upward sweep of the deserter's musket halted abruptly. His eyes bugged, his fingers opened, and he pitched onto his face. Sticking from the center of his shoulders, curved blade buried nearly to the handle, was a tomahawk that could belong only to Tap. The old scout walked calmly from the direction of the creek. "Might touchy there for a flash, huh, mistress?"

Next thing I knew, she was in Tap's embrace, crying and snuffling and thanking him again and again. Me, the would-be hero, I was quickly and totally forgotten, exactly what I didn't expect nor want to happen. So I huffed across the creek and recovered my hat, hunting frock, and coat.

Damned if I was going to freeze to death, too.

Chapter 19

Past Midnight till Noon, 20 October

It was a childish fit of anger and disappointment, the kind a grown man usually regretted sooner than later. And for sure, the regretting came mighty quick on this occasion.

I returned from my brief sojourn fully dressed. I bore Tap's haversack and canteen, along with my reloaded rifle, the weapon recovered from where Tap had deposited it atop the swell after his first shot. The old scout was feverishly busy scalping the deserters. Scalping was gruesome to behold, no matter who wielded the blade, and her gaze averted, the mistress knelt well beyond the faint embers of the fire slicing haunch meat from the deer the deserters had slain earlier.

The sight of pink scalp flesh and dripping blood cooled me down sudden as a bucket of icy water. It wasn't necessary to ask Tap why he was lifting the hair of white men. He told me straight out. "We ain't wastin' time buryin' these rascals, an' anybody was to stumble upon them, it'd be best they believe the redsticks caught them by surprise. We don't want ourselves crosswise with Colonel William Oldham. He watches over those in his militia ranks somethin' fierce, deserters or no."

Tap wiped his knife clean with a handful of sand and washed the blood and gore from his four scalps much as he could in the creek. He then wrapped them in a shirt stripped from one of the dead. "We'll bury these later."

We walked together to where Erin knelt. She was stacking the deer meat on a section of the hide. "Tie that off, Mistress Green. We must get along right smartly."

Erin gathered the edges of the hide and tied them together. She stood and came about. She wore a woolen coat too large for her that smelled of blood. Though my outright anger had faded, I was still perturbed enough with her for having run into Tap's arms instead of mine. I waited for her to speak first. "Mr. Downer, I thank you once more for risking yourself on my behalf. But I do wish you'd moved faster."

I couldn't help myself. My fuse caught fire again. "Faster? What the hell you mean by faster?"

Tired and overwrought as she had to be, she wasn't short on spunk and sass. "I let that big oaf paw me to hold his attention. I didn't figure on you letting him enjoy it so."

"You knew I was there all along?" I sputtered.

"From the moment you stepped from the creek. That's why I didn't knee him or bite him when he reached inside my shirt."

My temper boiled over, threatening to blind me. I had snuck into a camp of four armed men solely on her account, come close to being killed twice, and here she was criticizing me for being too slow about it. "Why you ungrateful little wench," I blurted, stepping toward her. "I ought to turn you over a knee and blister you good!"

She held her ground without flinching. Her head tilted back, and moonlight silvered her forehead and high cheekbones. "You wouldn't dare lay a finger on me," she challenged.

Then Tap was in the middle of us. "We've no time for these shenanigans. Quiet, the both of you."

I stayed my feet. Mad as I was, I'd no cause to disobey Tap and involve him in a personal dispute. Not trusting my tongue, I backed away and went in search of the 'hawk I'd lost in the scuffle with the Kentuckians.

She let me hunt till I kicked sand in frustration. "I have your hatchet, Mr. Downer," she chimed sweetly.

Peacemaker Tap quelled another fiery outburst on my part. He extended his hand, and she immediately relinquished the tomahawk. He crossed the half-dozen paces separating us. He spoke in a bare whisper. "Wouldn't want you to give her cause to do you harm with it. Now, get a grip on that temper. Yuh listenin', Ethan?"

At my nod, he spun and faced Erin. "We need to get upcountry, an' we don't dare follow the Injun trace on our return. We barged after you like scared rabbits. We don't start showin' a little caution, the Shawnee will be liftin' our scalps. Mistress, fill our canteens. Ethan, gather the Kentuckians' horns, pistols, an' muskets. The Injuns wouldn't leave them behind."

While I roamed among the dead, Tap removed a rolled blanket from his haversack, replaced it with the deer meat, and smothered the coals of the fire with sand. Chores completed, we rejoined the old scout, Erin occupying his opposite shoulder. "Mistress, you fetch my blanket and canteen. Ethan, you tote the deer meat an' two of the muskets an' pistols. I'll fetch the rest. We won't be burdened with them for long, I promise."

I positioned the haversack on my backside and a musket on each shoulder, thankful the militia, poor as they were equipped, had been supplied leather slings for their long guns. The pistols I slipped behind my belt.

"We'll head west, then work gradually to the north. At dawn, we'll hole up till dark," Tap informed us. "I know it'll be hard on your mother for you to be missin' another whole day, but thisaway the odds are more favorable she'll see you alive again. Yuh understand, girl?"

Erin sighed and nodded. "At least I have only Injuns to fear now," she said, peeking 'round Tap's chest. Damn, but how she loved to tease me.

"Well and good then. Ethan, you bring up the rear. Mistress, on my heels, yuh don't mind. Any alarm, we drop where we stand and hold tight till we sniff things out."

Erin fell in behind the old scout, and he led us along the run that joined the creek from the west. He stuck to the bank of the run for a mile before angling upward soon as higher ground presented itself. Bearing two heavy-caliber muskets, two pistols, and my own rifle, I was a walking arsenal, but ponderous and strained in motion as a pregnant plow horse. At the top of the low ridge I was huffing and puffing, the powder burns on my chest were afire, and my split lip was swelling and throbbing nicely. I had no objection when Tap halted beside a huge, hollow deadfall and shed the deserters' muskets, pistols, and powder horns. I did likewise pronto.

"Mistress, I believe you have a blade an' a coat not your own," Tap mentioned. "If'n you please. We want no unnecessary questions when we reach St. Clair's camp."

Erin cast the knife into the dark hollow of the deadfall and slid from her bloodied coat. The old scout threw the garment after the discarded knife. Then, leaning his rifle against the trunk of the fallen oak, he unfastened his belt and laid it over the curve of the trunk, enabling him to remove his hooded capote. "Try this, mistress."

Erin hesitated to take the proffered coat. "What about you?"

"Never worry about us old cusses, my child. Hand me my blanket." She did, and with a few slashes of his knife Tap cut openings for his head and arms and fashioned a makeshift outer garment for himself. "Will you be warm enough?" Erin fretted.

The old scout laughed deep in the belly. "Young woman, I ran twenty miles in the dead of winter wearin' nothin', and I mean nothin' else, anywheres, but a blanket. That's the fate of a man caught kettle bathin' by the Shawnee with the Licking frozen an' snow flyin'."

"You must have been a sight," Erin said, giggling.

"Yeah, an' a heap colder than I will be on this little jaunt." The old scout wrapped his belt about his waist and fisted his rifle. "Come along. We got tracks need makin' before first light."

Tap wheeled and set off, Erin a stride behind him. As she had when following me after I freed her from the Shawnee, she was like a fly on the old scout's shoulder, always in step, never hindering his pace or progress. Other than her tart mouth, it was difficult to find fault with Mistress Erin Green.

Once the high ground petered out, Tap shied from the smallest trickle of flowing water and sought the most negotiable path through the deepest forest. While we disturbed the heavy leaf cover there, our tracks were much less obvious than those we would have left in the softer earth bordering the waterways. The moon slid low in the sky. The night was approaching its blackest and coldest hour when the old scout halted. "Two of yuh plunk down here. I'll find us a day camp with cover where we can risk a fire and smoke that venison."

The old scout allowed us a hefty drink, reclaimed his canteen, and disappeared among the tree butts. Without a peep, Erin Green plopped against a handy trunk and scrunched deeper into Tap's coat. She was surprisingly small seated thataway. I put a few paces twixt us and kept watch roundabout from a knee. After a spell, I heard low sniffles and her shoulders began to shake. I laid my gaze elsewhere. I wouldn't have wanted sympathy from a stranger just then, either. I knew from experience there was nothing wrong with a good cry: It cleansed the hurt from your heart so you could gather the courage you needed to carry on. I think she slept once she finished wiping her tears on the arms crossed over her knees, for though the air grew ever colder and had me stamping my feet to stay warm, she didn't stir again.

The first glimmer of dawn light brightened the tall trunks surrounding us. To avoid spooking me unnecessarily, Tap spoke before stepping forth into my line of sight. "Hold still, lad. It's me, the bellied one," he said gently, easing into view.

Frost sprinkling the shoulders of the old scout's knife-fashioned garment sparkled in the growing light. His breath froze in small, white clouds. "Found us a likely den in the middle of a briar thicket half a mile ahead."

The mistress rose and stretched. "Can we have a fire?"

Tap wet a finger and stuck it above his head. "Sure enough. Ain't hardly no wind, an' there's plenty of wood that'll burn with but little smoke. Follow me."

The old scout's den was well chosen. A high wind of some bygone storm had felled an expanse of oak trees. A wide swath of sprouting trees and briars thick as a man's thumb circled the mass of fallen timber. Tap never said what led him to brave those slashing thorns and stick his nose into the middle of that towering pile. But he had, and he had discovered the rotting trunks lay atop each other in such a way they formed a pocket in their center not unlike a cave whose roof was partially open to the sky.

Tap pushed briars aside with his forearm. "In here, mistress. Walk sideways an' watch yer eyes." We slithered forward, wincing as thorns tugged at our clothing. One long stalk raked my knuckles, another my throat, both drawing blood. The mix of briars and sprouting growth closed behind us.

Fallen trees blocked our path. Large roots supported the nether end of the nearest oak, creating a natural opening beneath the slanting trunk. Loose dirt thrown by sizable claws indicated either a bear or a wolf had recently been at work enlarging the opening. "You first, mistress," said Tap.

Erin, no stranger to the woods, hesitated and seemed to grow taller. "You've been inside, Mr. Jacobs?"

Tap chuckled. "Yep, an' there ain't no four-leggeds about this mornin'," he assured her.

So great was Erin's trust of the old scout, she dropped to her knees and crawled under the slanting trunk without further protest. Tap, fisting a branch adorned with brown leaves, waited for me to crawl after her. I managed to wriggle through on my belly. I heard Tap's oak branch sweeping loose dirt behind me, smoothing what tracks we had left at the opening.

Dust floated in shafts of sunlight. The ceiling of our makeshift cave was high enough Erin could stand erect. It was wide enough across to comfortably hold twice our number. Stacked wood varying in length and thickness, obviously gathered by Tap, filled its center. Shed hair, coarse and gray colored, littered the bottom of the far wall. Except for the lack of a spring, it was a fine den in which to spend the day hidden from the pesky Injuns.

"Right clever spot, huh, mistress," Tap commented, chest puffing. "What little smoke we make will draw through the roof holes nice an' thin. An' I refilled the canteen a mile from here. Dig out my tinderbox an' that deer meat, Ethan, for I shrink to nothin' but bone."

Erin then took charge. She shooed us to far walls, ignited a small, bright fire with Tap's flint and steel, strung strips of venison on our ramrods, and heated them over her flame. Meat drippings sizzled and popped. Tap gave his empty belly that loving rub familiar to all acquainted with him. "You're a treasure, lass. A real, genuine treasure."

Even in the sun-dappled gloom of the deadfall cave, Erin Green was a most stunning creature. I watched her hand Tap a bark slab of roasted venison and decided there wasn't a single part of her, be it sunset-red hair, sky-blue eyes, high cheekbones, lush mouth, or full breasts pushing against the front of Tap's coat, that didn't fit together to her advantage. It was impossible to imagine any woman matching her beauty. The trick was to keep her beauty from dazzling you to the point you couldn't think straight. Rescuing her from danger either time hadn't been easy or without peril. But us Downer men being far more formidable with fist than tongue, convincing her I was something other than a prying, leering dolt ready to argue with her every word was shaping up to be a much more demanding task.

I expected the three of us would sleep the day through after we finished our meal of venison and water. While Tap did doze off and take to snoring soon as he filled his belly, my scorched ribs throbbed just enough to keep me from sleeping for now. Though I couldn't tell she was hurt any-place, an equally alert Erin sat opposite the fire, weaving slender branches into a smoking rack for the balance of the venison. She sensed me watching, and her gaze lifted to meet mine. "That chest wound bothering you much?"

Not wanting to fuss over what I believed was a minor hurt, I hesitated to answer, but she was having none of that. "I saw you jerk when the musket went off between the two of you. There's probably burnt powder trapped under your skin. We best look at it," she said, walking 'round the fire on her knees.

I still thought we were making a fuss over nothing, but at least she was talking to me. I remained seated, untied my belt, and drew open Paw's hunting frock. Showing not the slightest embarrassment, she hovered before my bared chest, red pigtail dangling in front of her shoulder. Her breath and her touch were surprisingly warm and excited every part of me. How I couldn't fathom, but she smelled of rosewater, a scent common to my mother and sisters. Maybe being wounded wasn't such a bother after all.

She rested on her heels. "There are two holes, both deep and fouled with powder. They must be cleaned," she decided. "I'll need your knife."

I slid the Starkweather blade from its scabbard and passed

it to her, handle first. "Best stretch out on your back. I don't want to dig too deep."

I did as she requested, demonstrating more confidence than I felt. She positioned herself beside me and leaned close. Deft fingers tugged at my flesh, the tip of the blade descended, and pain shot everywhere. She felt me flinch and squirm. "Grab onto my leg you need to," she instructed. "The next hole is the deepest."

She started scraping again, and I quickly forswore the much-ballyhooed hiding of the greatest pain no matter the size of the hurt I'd heard older backwooders brag about and grabbed hold of her thigh. Hell's bells, for a few seconds I was convinced she was doing more damage to me than the original wounds. I swear the point of the knife struck bone before she was satisfied she had removed every last speck of black powder of any size. She tilted back on her heels and smiled. Blood dripped from the Starkweather blade. "Well, those holes won't fester on you now. Too bad we don't have some whiskey or brandy to pour over the openings. Guess I'll have to sear them closed once I heat the knife."

Waiting for neither a yea nor nay from me, she pulled free of my clutching fingers and knee-walked to the fire, where she inserted the knife blade directly into the flames. She held it thus for what seemed forever, then scurried to my side once more. It wasn't really so, but the hot blade appeared to glow cherry red. Without comment, she grasped my hand and placed it on her thigh. I tensed, and the stench of burning skin assailed my nostrils. From behind eyes tightly shut I heard her say, "That'll heal nicely you don't scratch or poke at it."

I kept my eyes closed. Showing pain was acceptable. Showing tears wasn't if I could avoid it. Gentle fingers pressed against my split and swollen lip. I pulled away and she laughed. "Not to worry. I'm through doctoring."

I opened my eyes and she had returned to her smoking rack. The scent of rosewater still sweetened the air. The warmth of her thigh lingered on my palm. Her nimble fingers bent and wove the branches together, and I wondered if she had found it as exciting to be near me as I had her. Reluctant to surrender her attention, I rolled upright at the waist and covered my bare chest. "Your mother teach you to doctor?"

"No, I learned listening to Annie Bower."

My mouth dropped open. "You'd never tended to anyone before this?"

Erin laughed. "No, but Annie's very clever about it. She was bound out to a surgeon during the Redcoat War. Believe it or not, she carries a tin of maggots she lets eat their fill if wounds turn proud on her."

"Well, least I was spared that," I acknowledged. "I guess I have the both of you to thank."

Erin placed her smoking rack over the fire and began slicing the remaining venison into long, thin strips on a bark slab with my knife. "I'll remind you of that when we next see Annie. Men are seldom interested in what she's smart about if it doesn't involve satisfying their other desires."

"She does encourage boldness in a man," I suggested, realizing immediately I had no call to insult Annie Bower. I spoke again as Erin grimaced. "But she's got little choice in her present circumstances. No one likes sleeping on an empty belly."

Erin sighed and lined thin slices of venison in a neat row atop her smoking rack. "Sometimes men conspire against a woman, and it takes great courage and cunning if she's to avoid having to sell herself. It's why I so love my mother. She's never let that happen to either of us."

I was treading private, perhaps dangerous ground, but I couldn't keep from asking. "Is the selling worse than being captive of the Injuns or the deserters?"

"It would be for me," she claimed, chin jutting forth. "So you know, the Injuns never touched me that way, and the Kentuckians argued forever about which one was to have me." She fed new branches to her fire. "You know, there are worse fates than shaming yourself to eat. And I don't mean death."

That assertion puzzled me thoroughly, and I made no response whatsoever. Her blue eyes settled on me. "Aren't you curious enough to ask what's worse than shame and death?"

I nodded. "But I've no right to pry into your affairs."

She smiled briefly. "And though I don't know you hardly at all, I believe you," she said, face sobering. "So I'll tell you. Nothing is worse than when your own stepfather betrays you. That's what unraveled life for Mama and me, when she caught Moses Bean with me pinned between him and the stable door, his big paw tearing at my buttons. She threatened him with the tines of the hay fork till we were outside, and then we ran, straight into the night." Her head lowered and shook. "It was miserably cold, and Mama cried and cried, blaming herself for trusting Moses wouldn't molest her girl child."

She had me bent forward and listening. She slowly turned the strips of deer meat. I couldn't wait any longer. "Where did you head? Did you have victuals? Warm clothing? Kin that would help?"

She sat and drew her knees beneath her chin. She was silent for a long period, long enough I began to think she wouldn't share the rest of her ordeal with me. Slim fingers rubbed her forehead. "We had no food, no clothes but those covering us, and no friendly door waiting with the latchstring out. Mama supposed Moses wouldn't waste his breath chasing us. She guessed he'd wait for us to come home with our tails dragging, begging his forgiveness and panting for a rightful whipping. But my mama wasn't dressing that hog, not that night nor any other."

Erin stared at the fire. "Lord, but it was as frightful as when the Shawnee had me. Wolves were howling, the wind moaning, and there wasn't a star in the sky to guide us. We followed the Forbes Road toward Fort Pitt, two days away." Erin shuddered. "We might have given in to the fright if Mama hadn't noticed the tiny red smudge far ahead along the road. The farther we walked, the bigger the smudge of light became. The Lord watched over us that night, for it was the campfire of the Devlin brothers, Torrance, and the younger, Brendan. They were hauling a load of salt and whiskey for the army, and God never created two men more respectful of women. They asked no questions and took no advantage. They fed us and gave us blankets, and come dawn, we rode their wagon seat the two days to Pittsburgh."

She paused, and I frantically fished for an inquiry that would keep her talking. "Was it winter when you arrived?"

"Yes, it was a year ago come December. Brendan Devlin

coughed horribly from the moment we met him. We slept in a damp, drafty warehouse along the Allegheny, and Brendan's cough worsened with the weather. In less than a week, his lungs filled, and he died. Mama was with him every second till he was gone. Tor Devlin was by then hopelessly in love with Mama, but Mama refused to let him spend his monies feeding us. She served the crowd at a roadway inn for food. I helped scrub the floor, haul water, and wax candles, and the owner allowed me to sit at the table once a day with Mama and share from her plate. We slept on the floor before the hearth and managed till the weather warmed."

Tap stirred and rolled onto his opposite side, interrupting Erin's story. She waited till the old scout was again snoring loud as a rooting hog, then continued. "In the spring, an acquaintance of Moses Bean stopped at the inn. He never admitted it to anyone, but he surely recognized Mama. That encounter seemed to sour what meager fortune we had enjoyed since meeting Torrance Devlin. The next day, the innkeeper's wife accused Mama of lusting after her husband. It was an outright lie, but nonetheless, Jonas Grant dismissed us from his employ that same morning."

Erin fell silent, as if choosing her next words with great care, a habit I'd noticed during our sojourn up the Miami to Fort Hamilton. "Mama and I were now without table or bed a second time, and it was Tor Devlin who spared us, same as he had that cold night along the Forbes Road. He heard we'd been cast adrift, and having enlisted in the Second American Regiment with the rank of sergeant, he was entitled to extra rations. Mama agreed we would accept shelter from him till she could find work that put a roof over our heads. God love Tor Devlin, he gave us his tent and slept in the open," Erin praised, suddenly drying her eyes with a sleeve. "We were with him three weeks while Mama inquired at every Pittsburgh tavern and business where the owner had a wife and children, thinking I would be the safest in such a situation. But no owner wanted the both of us . . . or so they claimed. I really believe Mama's beauty scared their women." *Or more likely, that of her daughter had,* I thought to myself.

"About then, Sergeant Devlin announced his company

had been ordered to Fort Washington," Erin revealed, "and Mama began hunting even harder for a place for us. I think she had come to love Tor Devlin, but no matter how much we both despised Moses Bean, she was his legal wife. We were near desperate when the innkeeper who cast us out did us a great favor. Tor had visited us at the inn in his uniform, and Jonas Grant remembered him. In the hope he might reach us through the sergeant, he sent a note warning us Moses Bean was lodged at his establishment, asking after his run-away wife and daughter."

Erin sipped water from Tap's canteen. "Moses Bean would force us to return to his farm, and the law would do nothing to prevent it. We had to leave Pittsburgh before he located us. Tor Devlin bought us passage on a flatboat whose captain had his own family aboard, and we floated down the Ohio behind the barge of the sergeant's army company. Once we landed at Cincinnati, Mama quickly determined there was nothing decent for us to do in the city to earn our keep." Her blue eyes stared at me now, not the fire. "That's how we came to traipse after St. Clair's troops. Mama began cooking for the sergeant's men and the wagoners. They turned their rations over to her, and we would prepare their meals. That way, we had plenty to eat and a safe haven for sleeping." Erin's sigh was the heaviest yet. "As God is my witness, Mama doesn't prefer harlots and loose women for friends, but they don't lie or cheat or demand you be other than yourself. And they don't ask for anything but the same in return."

She was daring me to find fault with her mother, and it required no pondering for me to shy clear of that. Others might contend you couldn't tell the women apart sleeping beneath the Green cart, but I had learned firsthand that wasn't true. Fear and threat of starvation linked folks together otherwise unlikely to speak to each other. And no mother worried about propriety and appearance to the detriment of her children. I had seen my own mother the maddest when she felt her offspring were being denied the protection and sustenance due them from their elders. A sow bear protecting her cubs with fang and claw was no less a fearsome sight.

"Your mother has kept you from both harm and disgrace.

What the loose-jawed and narrow-minded spout off about doesn't bother me any," I stated bluntly.

"Thank you," Erin said softly. "It gladdens me that fairness holds sway in a few hearts." Her hands closed into a single fist that shook with determination. "We Greens won't always be beholden to others."

My questioning frown firmed the angle of her jaw. Her blue eyes glittered in the firelight. "I'll be properly married and become a woman of property," she vowed. "We'll own acres of rich land. Our cabin will rest on high ground so it can't be flooded. The cabin will be so big inside we won't have to make a table of the front door in the yard when serving company. Its walls will be so thick the hearth fire will lick the cold from the room on the worst night of winter. Hunger and fear will be strangers to me and mine. That's what I'll have, and nothing less for me and my children."

It was a fanciful dream for a penniless young woman whose current home was a cart pulled by a nag whose innards were best friends with his backbone. But the earnestness and passion with which she spoke indicated this was no spur-of-the-moment rendering of her innermost longings. Erin Green had convinced herself she would have her day in the sun where all things would shine as she desired. She fully expected to marry a man of great wealth who could provide for her on a grand scale, a mighty grand scale you asked me, grandest I could imagine.

Those glittering blue eyes never left mine. She took my silence to mean I doubted her dream. "Think I'm addled in the brain, don't you? Can't believe I crave so much, can you?" she challenged.

I flopped on my backside, cursing myself for stirring the wound on my chest. I couldn't halt what flew from my mouth. "If that's the way it has to be, you better be prepared to spend a long time huntin' your future husband, 'cause damn few free men on either bank of the Ohio eat from silver plates. And that includes all of Pittsburgh, from what I hear."

Erin Green snorted angrily. "I'll find him, never you fear. You may not believe me, but he'll be looking for me, too."

"Well, I hope it's daylight when you meet up with him.

It'd be something awful was the two of you to pass each other in the dark of night."

It was a raw, spiteful thing, and I shouldn't have said it. I was really upset with myself, not her. I had somehow been foolish enough to suppose that if I was around her a while, she would simply jump into my arms and we would be together forever. I had never considered that she might not possess similar yearnings.

This should not have been a great surprise to me. In all honesty, I wasn't a handsome and uniformed man like Miles Starkweather, and what earthly possessions I could call my own amounted to my weapons and the clothes on my body, less Paw's frock. I had no title to land of my own, and despite Paw's success, with five sisters sharing an equal claim, there was no inheritance of any size looming in my future. Even the roan gelding Blue, along with his bridle and saddle, belonged rightfully to Paw. Thus, being neither rich nor handsome, it seemed to me the chance of Ethan Downer winning the hand of the ravishingly beautiful Erin Green was about as likely as the mighty Ohio suddenly reversing its course overnight.

My wry comment about missing her intended in the dark had the result I anticipated. It earned me a view of Erin Green's red pigtail that lasted the morning. Eventually, I bored of the silence and drifted off to sleep thoroughly discouraged that my ultimate reward for helping save her from captors both red and white would be to see her wed another man. A nastier turn of events was beyond my grasp.

Chapter 20

Evening Hours, 20 October till Dawn, 21 October

I awakened from a most unpleasant dream, that of Erin Green's wedding to an officer resembling Captain Miles Starkweather, he of the handsome countenance, the spotless uniform, and moneyed family. I was disrupting the ceremony with the help of a balled and cocked rifle when someone began shaking my arm none too gently for real. I came from sleep kicking and flailing. "It's not the Shawnee, lad. It's me, Tap!"

I quieted at the sound of the old scout's voice. The fire was out, and cold wind whistled through the openings in the logs stretching overhead. "Pass him meat and water, lass," Tap ordered. "We'll let him eat, then take our leave. I've scouted about, and there's no hostile company anywheres around."

I was stiff and damnably sore from my wrestling bout with the deserters and climbing into a sitting position was downright painful in places. Erin was a blurry shadow, and I smelled her more than I saw her. She laid a bark slab of smoked venison and a canteen in my lap and retreated. I ate in huge gulps as if starvation had a death grip on my throat.

With his excellent night eyes, Tap spied my finishing swallow of water. "I checked your rifle before dark, an' you're ready to travel. We'll get shy of this hole an' allow the mistress a few minutes alone. After you, lad."

The wind was colder outside, the moon peeking over the horizon. Tap pulled his covering blanket tighter about his shoulders. "Gonna be colder'n a frozen Injun's arse," he lamented. "The ground will be white as snow come dawn."

I shrank deeper into my own coat. "Yeah, Miles Starkweather fears a killing frost more'n anything. With all the woods forage gone, the packhorses will be lucky they can stay upright with their saddles empty." I hawked and spat. "Tap, you think General St. Clair can hold his army together long enough to whip the Shawnee and the Miami?"

"I'm growin' damn doubtful. If'n it ain't missing equipment, short rations, or desertions, it seems the weather's agin him. But he's a stubborn son of a bitch. I'll grant him that. If'n he wasn't, he wouldn't have launched his campaign late as he done. I just hope his ambition doesn't ruin his judgment. He wants a victory over the redsticks much as you want the mistress for your ownself."

My jaw was opening to counter Tap's assertion when Erin Green slithered from within our hideout. Peeved as I was with him, I ignored Tap's smug grin of triumph and stood mute as she joined us. "What's our plan of travel, Mr. Jacobs?"

"We'll move fast and steady, sticking to the best cover. Any movement in any direction, we hunker down till we figure who's out and about. Bear in mind you're as dead shot by your own as the red enemy. We keep a goodly pace, we should reach St. Clair's fort short of daylight. Any questions?"

I was on the verge of inquiring where the Starkweather knife might be when a last check of my weapons revealed it was in its scabbard on my waist belt. A certain female had to have returned it while I was asleep. It grated on my nerves how she made it so damnably difficult to stay mad at her.

We marched in our usual line, Tap in the van, me in the rear, our female charge between us. The wind swayed tree branches and swirled leaves underfoot. The moon hung high and bright in a black sky brilliant with stars. Tap wove left and right to avoid the heaviest timber, thickets of brush, and rocky, uneven terrain. His course, howsomever, never wavered from roughly north by northwest. Twice Tap detected movement over the wind and the scurry of leaves and we halted, crouched, and listened till he determined whatever moved beyond our range of vision had more than two legs and didn't threaten us. He later calmly ignored the nearby scream of a panther that raised a small yelp of alarm from the mistress and lifted hair on the nape of my neck.

We had our first blow early after the midnight hour. Tap conferred briefly with the mistress in whispers. She then relinquished the canteen, slipped past me, and walked back the way we'd come.

Tap knelt down, dampened his thirst, and fisted his canteen my direction. "Nature called again. Wonder it didn't happen sooner what all she's been through."

I fell to a knee beside him and drank without comment. Tap watched me with an unsettling intentness. His query still caught me off guard. "Them moccasins fun to chew on, are they?"

"What the hell you mean?" I demanded brusquely, lowering the canteen.

Tap's grin, easily seen in the moonlight, was mischievous as that of a taunting child. "Oh, slick as you put your feet in your mouth whenever you gab with the mistress, it must rightly pleasure you."

I hoped the embarrassment I felt didn't show on my face. "It ain't none of your affair what I say to her, you old fart," I fumed.

Tap's grin faded as rapidly as it had appeared. "No, it ain't," he agreed. "But it pains me that you young buckos have no patience with women. You barged about thataway huntin' game, you'd waste away within the month."

Curiosity cooled my temper. "What you mean now?" I inquired.

Tap's sigh was only slightly less powerful than the wind. "Dreamers like the mistress ain't to be hurried. They don't rush into a man's arms. They pick and choose their lovers with deliberate care. Around her kind, you go nice an' easy like the last thing you want is even the smallest kiss. You don't frighten them off before they can warm up to you. But you best remember, you win her over, you better be prepared to have her in front of your fire forever. She'll stick to you like a woods tick."

"She's after someone rich enough to build her a mansion," I pointed out. "She ain't gonna share her blanket with any man whose horse belongs to his Paw."

"For chrissake, Ethan, have a little faith in my judgment of women. Dreams are just wishful longings that hardly ever bear a full tree of fruit for anybody. Your shoulders are plenty wide, you ain't downright ugly, and twice you risked yourself for her of your own choosin'." Tap grinned knowingly and winked. "You stop snortin' an' pawin' like a rogue bull 'round her, she might discover she's in love with you. Ain't no man gonna get close to a woman who's fearful of him, not a beautiful one, that's for damn certain." Tap's expression grew serious. "Here she be, lad."

"Sorry I was so long, Mr. Jacobs. But I'm rested and ready to follow along," Erin informed the old scout. She did nod my direction as she stepped twixt the two of us.

"We'll take another blow middle of the night, somewhere near water," Tap announced. "Sharp lookout now, Ethan. We're more likely to encounter Shawnee on the fringe of St. Clair's fortifications than here in the deep woods."

Our course remained north by northwest, the pace fast and steady. Tap's counsel was foremost in my mind every stride those many hours. I didn't doubt what he told me, but it was ridiculous for him to expect I could suddenly be meek and mild and gentlemanly in the presence of Erin Green. The beauty of the woman plain and simple set my blood racing so lightning fast I was afraid my heart might explode from my chest. And her sass and spunk and cleverness, instead of tainting her appeal, only added to her allure. It was all I could do at that very moment to keep myself from sweeping Mistress Erin Green into my arms and having my way with her. My frustration was such I wanted to yell ahead to Tap that patience and rectitude was expected of saints, not young men on the scent.

I might have dwelled upon that seemingly impossible situation the balance of our night march had not Tap turned my attention elsewhere, a feat he accomplished with a single, probing question: "What you gonna tell your paw when we see him next?"

At his asking, we were resting beneath the wall of a cut bank that bordered a north-south-running stream. The lip of the cut bank rose no higher than my waist, but once I squatted on my heels, the wind, flowing from the west, blew above my flop-brimmed hat. The mistress, chewing deer jerk and sipping water from the canteen, shivered repeatedly. The moonlit night was as cold as Tap had predicted. "Well, how are you gonna explain yourself to your paw, Ethan?" the old scout asked again.

"Ain't much I can say. I was to guard the riding stock. Those were Paw's exact orders. I'd no permission to do otherwise," I conceded, "and Paw won't be inclined to forgive my abandoning my post, whatever the excuse."

Erin Green swallowed hastily to clear her windpipe. "You disobeyed your father to rescue me, didn't you? You're in trouble because of me, aren't you?" Her head spun toward Tap. "And what about you, Mr. Jacobs? Are you in trouble with his father?"

Tap nodded. "Afraid I am. Caleb was countin' on us returnin' south with him jack quick to fetch more supplies. He don't hold with strayin' from your intended business."

"Particularly if it involves helping the daughter of a worthless camp follower," Erin insinuated.

"Now wait here, by God," I blurted. "That's unfair. Paw wasn't aware you'd been taken, and the army refused to send out a search party."

"Easy, Ethan," Tap said smoothly, lifting a placating hand. "He's right, mistress. Let's not condemn Caleb Downer too quickly. He wasn't at our fire when Tor Devlin sought us out, an' Ethan an' me lit a shuck before he returned from his confab with General St. Clair. It ain't helpin' you that has us in trouble. It's Ethan sneakin' off agin his paw's orders an' me followin' after him the same way. The reason we done it ain't important."

Erin eyed me with concern. "It was my own fault I was taken. It wouldn't matter if I apologized to your father for upsetting his plans?"

"No," I answered promptly. "It's better Tap and I report to him alone. Paw's mighty forceful and strict, but he ain't cruel. I'll get what I deserve."

Tap's head shook. "So will I. He won't be any easier on me 'cause I'm older an' sided him for years, neither." The old scout stood upright. "Too bad your paw ain't swayed by beauty liken us, Ethan. The upcoming mornin' would appear a tad brighter if'n he was. I'm just thankful he ain't prone to the whip. Follow me, children. We've a distance to mosey yet."

Tap quartered toward the northeast now and slowed our pace after pushing hard for an hour. Though we were on the move constantly, the cold made you want to rub hands and stomp feet. The wind finally died to a bumbling rush of air. The moon fell, and it was black and silent all about as prowling creatures sought lair and nest. Our footfalls on the dry leaves sounded thunderously loud, the scrape of dry branch on cloth almost a screech. At the top of a small hillock, Tap stopped to listen and perhaps judge our direction. We plunged onward, the mistress remarking more to herself than anybody how small and insignificant and alone a mere three travelers seemed in the vast Ohio wilderness.

The harrowing suddenness of that vast wilderness struck a pulse beat later. I was churning inside as to what punishment Paw might proscribe for me. I'm sure the mistress was lost in her own thoughts. Tap's attention, thank all that's holy, was where it belonged. The old scout's fist shot skyward, the signal accompanied by a blunt, hastily whispered, "Down an' be quiet."

My eye caught the rise of his arm, my ear the hissed warning, and I paused in midstride. The distracted mistress for once suffered a misstep. Tap's abrupt halt startled her, and she stumbled, toppling toward his crouching backside. I lunged forward, planted a foot, and hooked my right arm around her upper body, arresting her fall. In the flurry of the moment, I was acutely aware of the press of my arm against her bosom. She had at least heard Tap's whispered command, for she offered no resistance. She settled against my solidly braced chest and we sank slowly downward. I came to rest on my left knee, my grip securing her all the while.

Tap's spine was rigid as a fence post. The flat of his palm, fingers spread wide, appeared inches from our noses. His alarm was unmistakable. Danger, great danger was upon us. Erin gathered breath without noise but made no attempt to alter or escape my grasp. Me, I tried to focus on what threatened us and not what I held. Be damned, be damned, but I would forever be a heathen sinner.

Shadows fluttered and joined and separated scant yards from where we knelt. I counted silently as ten tallish figures at first indistinct but for the bulk of chest and thigh crossed our path. Each shadowy form then passed an opening in the trees. I swore I saw the sharp crest of feathered topknots and the thin, straight line of rifle barrels, and I sniffed the rank odor of bear-greased skin over my own stink and that of the mistress's rosewater. The unmoving stillness of Erin Green's every muscle confirmed what I saw and smelled was not a figment of rampant imagination.

Time crawled. My leg began to cramp. I held out till Tap, palm still raised for quiet, eased back on his haunches. I did likewise, and the mistress came to rest in my lap. She made no effort to escape my embrace, and we sat thataway till Tap lowered his cautioning hand, something that occurred before my rising nether parts, roused by her weight and warmth, alarmed her. I loosened my arm, and the mistress, with no great hurry, rolled from my lap. On hand and knee, her lips at my ear, she purred, "For a strong man, Mr. Downer, you can be quite gentle."

The touching of my ear lobe, coupled with her compliment, absolutely inflamed me, probably more than anything else she could have done except appear in front of me without her clothing. My bodily excitement growing by leaps and bounds, I stammered an excuse about nature's mysteries to a puzzled Tap and hustled out of sight. Once hidden by the forest, I sucked wind into my lungs, pumping my chest like a blacksmith's bellows. I couldn't get enough fresh air fast enough.

In a while my head stopped whirling and my heart thudded less severely. For chrissake, I told myself, get a grip on your halter, or you'll have yourself barging into trees again. Tap's not lying. Keep stomping and snorting like a stud horse and bolting into the night, and you will turn her against you. I delayed my return long as I dared, dallying about and gathering nerve. Then, with the deepest, most forceful breath yet, followed by a prayerful vow to deport myself in a manner more closely befitting my age, I crossed my fingers and rejoined the mistress and Tap.

Neither of them acted out of the ordinary. Tap frowned and asked, "Yuh ain't sickly, lad?"

I couldn't help but lower my head and inspect the toes of my moccasins as I said, "Naw, I'm hale as ever. What's next for us?"

Tap butted his rifle and sipped from his canteen. "We'll travel west a half mile, then circle to the north to put a little space twixt us an' them Injuns. Redsticks don't often come and go on the same path, but we don't want to chance overtakin' them. They're plannin' on scourin' St. Clair's perimeter for the careless an' the stupid, what we ain't."

I dallied not at all now. Head still lowered, I said, "Lead off. I'm right behind you," at the same time sneaking a peek at Erin Green. Catching her unawares, I discovered her studying me, lips curled in a whimsical smile.

That smile, before it disappeared, told me a heap. She knew. The woman knew. She knew precisely the effect she had had on me with her body and her words. And she was enjoying it, perhaps savoring it. Or so I wanted to believe. Maybe the winning of Erin Green wasn't such an impossible task. Maybe a poor man could succeed with Molly Green's daughter. Just maybe.

That thought put a near strut in my gait. Tap led us west, then north, then northeastward. The old scout was doubly cautious after our initial sighting of prowling Shawnee. Our pace slowed to a crawl of a walk, and he never ceased to peer 'round about. He didn't need tell us we were approaching the Injun trace bordering the St. Clair camp on the west. There was no upraised fist, he simply motioned for us to kneel, which we did quietly for long minutes while he listened and sniffed the breeze bumbling now from our rear quarter.

The first faint smidgen of dawn light brightened the open spaces among the tree butts. Frost lay white wherever the ground was open to the sky. When we rose to our feet, my joints were stiff and bunched from cold. A musket boomed to the east, followed by the random firing of other long guns. Tap looked at the mistress and me, his breath freezing in icy puffs. "What a waste of powder an' ball," he said, head shaking sadly. "We'll wait an' cross the trace in full daylight.

Ain't no way we want to be confused for anything other than white folks by them idjit sentries."

We waited without further words. Erin Green sipped water from the canteen and passed the vessel to me without meeting my gaze. Soon as Tap judged the light was sufficient, we advanced to the edge of the trace, where he again peered about and listened with great patience. When he was satisfied we were in no immediate danger, he led us across the worn pathway in rapid strides.

We regained the trees and continued eastward. Though the breeze blew from behind us, we shortly heard the roll of drums, the lowing of cattle, and the cracking of whips. The wind direction did delay our first whiff of perimeter slit trenches and poorly buried cattle carcasses. I knew from minuscule experience that a large army encamped in the same location for only a few days poisoned the air about itself most foully.

The first sentry we encountered was leaning in the crook of a forked tree, chin resting on his chest. The snores emanating from beneath his tricorn hat equaled those of a sleeping Tap. The regimental coat of dark blue wool faced with red and lined with white, black-painted cartridge box, linen overalls, and most particularly, the bearskin-covered knapsack flanking his brass-buttoned shoes, identified the sleeper as a private of the First American Regiment. A musket, broken wrist clamped with sheet brass and bound with strong cord, slanted casually against the trunk of the forked tree beside his left hip.

Taking no chances, Tap crept up, laid hold of the slanting musket, and backed off a step before jabbing the private's belly with its muzzle. He jerked upright, and watery brown eyes ripe with alarm fixed on us. He felt frantically at his side till he realized it was his musket Tap held.

"You sentries always stand watch in pairs. Who's with you?" Tap demanded, head turning left and right.

The private's chin quivered. "I'm ... I'm ... I'm stationed here alone," he managed.

Tap cocked the stolen musket. The private's eyes tried to leap from their sockets. "That's the truth," he stammered, suddenly bending at the waist as a series of harsh coughs wracked his thin frame, coughs so deep and phlegm-ridden they threatened to expel a lung. The sentry straightened and wiped a gob of snot from his nostrils and upper lip, both of which were red and raw from undue rubbing. "My whole company's ailin'. Ain't but half of us able to answer the drum at dawn."

It wasn't lost on me that if the bulk of the private's company, a unit of the First American Regiment, the best-clothed soldiers in the army, was sickly and confined to their tents, circumstances continued to weigh against General St. Clair without relief. Shoddy equipment, forged shipping manifests, depleted rations, dying pack animals, desertions, the weather, and now illness: What else could hamper, perhaps ruin the general's expedition before he sighted the red enemy? And what would happen if his faltering, weakening ranks met the red enemy in great force? It gave a man reason, honest cause, to seriously ponder his future safety and that of his companions.

The private swallowed, his Adam's apple bobbing. "Yuh gonna report me to Sergeant Harwell?"

Tap lowered the cock of the musket, gripped the weapon by the barrel, and presented it to the private. "No, lad, I'll not make trouble for you, an' I've a cure for your heavy eyes. We saw ten Shawnee two hours before daylight, bound thisaway. Come along, Ethan, we've got business needs tendin'."

Frost crackled beneath our feet. Beyond the private's forked tree we began to encounter elements of St. Clair's encampment. A dragoon detail rode past. Its captain, lacking the gaudy neatness of Miles Starkweather, touched the bill of his leather helmet upon sighting the mistress. A body of levies numbering between a squad and a company crossed before us, one profane officer lamenting the necessity of gathering forage for the nocturnal feeding of the bullock herd. Next came the cattle themselves, guarded by infantrymen, then the bank of the creek bordering the west pasture. Smoke from countless fires rose in straggly lines in the crisp air. The log walls of the general's fort of deposit loomed in the distance. Tap paused at the creek bank and glanced over his shoulder. "Almost home, girl. Ethan, you best tote her across."

Before she could object to Tap's suggestion if she was of such a mind, I had my rifle slung on a shoulder and was lifting Erin Green off the ground. My, but was it fine to smell that rosewater up close again. And the shine of bright gold had nothing on the tiny freckles dusting the side of her neck where it emerged from the collar of her shirt.

She didn't squirm even when I held onto her and kept walking once free of the creek. Her face turned, and bright blue eyes looked into mine. She smiled, tilted her head, wound an arm around my neck, filled her lungs with a deep breath, and kissed me flush on the mouth. It was no quick peck on the lips. The woman laid into it with solid purpose, tearing the scab covering my split lip. Roused by her boldness, I ignored the taste of my own blood and was beginning to match her fervor despite a growing shortage of wind when she abruptly withdrew her lips and said politely, "Please put me down, Mr. Downer."

As surprised by this request as I had been by her sudden, ardent embrace, I promptly stood her on the ground. Her eyes had lost their sparkle. "I can never thank you properly," she said softly. "I owe more that I can repay."

Then she was gone, scurrying after Tap. Unsure how— or if—I could call her back, I stood rigid as the lawbreaker strapped in the village stock and watched her catch the old scout and continue with him toward the Dodd fire. Though Paw might be waiting there for me, ready to administer the punishment he believed I justly deserved, at that moment I could think of but one thing: What man had taught Erin Green how to kiss so hard and long and deep?

Part III

Fort Jefferson

Chapter 21

By dawdling behind, I missed the opportunity to escort Erin Green to her family cart. Tap rushed her off without delay soon as Bear Watkins informed them the Mistress Molly Green, after showing signs of improvement, had fallen gravely ill once more. Bear repeated this distressing news to me in the presence of Valentine Dodd, the only other person gracing the Dodd fire. The keenly observant Bear also took note of my rapid eyeballing of the area in all directions.

"You can relax, Ethan. Your paw ain't here," he informed me, tendering a tin cup whose contents steamed in the dawn air.

It was something, had I not been distracted by romantic daydreams, I should have surmised immediately, for just our personal riding stock along with a few horses bearing the brand of mounted dragoons and numerous ox teams remained in the west meadow. The Dodd pack animals as well as the sizable herd of military baggage animals that had grazed there earlier were missing.

"Paw head south again?"

"Yep," Bear said, "two days ago. He took Ira, Henry, Thaddeus, Timothy, and Hookfin with him. St. Clair sent nearly three hundred army horses with them. He wants three hundred horse-loads of flour delivered pronto, then one hundred and fifty horse-loads every seven days thereafter, and no excuse is acceptable to him."

It wasn't hard for me to imagine Hookfin chafing and huffing under the strict control Paw exercised on the trail. I kept from smiling out of respect for my bleeding lip. "How come you're not with Paw?" I asked, sipping tea so weak it could hardly be called such.

Bear poured the dregs of his own cup into the fire. "He left me to locate you and have you here when he returns."

I licked my bleeding lip, made more painful by the hot tea. "Maybe the ride will soothe his temper," I suggested halfheartedly.

"Not likely," Bear predicted. "He had him a real fright of a mad up from the moment he learned you'd snuck off to chase after Erin Green."

I felt as if I was standing in a huge hole, and the hole was getting steadily deeper. Bear thankfully changed the subject. "How'd Tap an' you convince them deserters to let hold of the Green gal?"

Val Dodd leaned ever closer from his perch on the log flanking our fire. Tap and I hadn't discussed what story we would tell in the presence of outsiders once we rejoined St. Clair's army, and not intending to dig that huge hole any deeper than it already was, I answered blandly as possible. "Better Tap tells you. It was mostly his doing."

Skin pinched together in the narrow cleft separating Bear's hairy brows, but he took no exception to my evading his question. He nodded slowly from behind the seated Valentine Dodd and asked, "Be yuh hungry, lad?"

My quick response that I was starved prompted Val Dodd, his pumpkin face sad and forlorn, to speak. "The fare is plain and dull this morning, Monsieur! Boiled beef and tea must suffice. The soldiers received a half ration of flour each. Our meager quarter ration is gone, and I fear there will be no more till your father returns."

Without rising from the log, the horse master speared chunks of boiled beef from a blackened kettle hanging over the fire with a thin-bladed knife, slopped them onto a metal trencher, and fisted the meat my direction. After the piddling few slices of venison jerk the previous night, plain boiled bullock, though stringy and tough, was damn near heavenly where smell and taste were concerned. Besides, the lack of bread shouldn't fluster a truly hungry soul privileged to fill his belly, a sentiment I shared with Dodd twixt gulps.

"No Kentucky militiaman agrees with you, Monsieur. Despite the remaining bullock herd, they whine and carp without end lest they have their flour and whiskey, most assuredly the liquor. Never before have I heard those not hungry complain so bitterly. They threaten desertion if their demands are not met. I believe they fear the Shawnee and seek an excuse to flee like the rabbit," the horse master concluded.

Bear drew upright. "Val, that's an opinion best left unsaid away from our fire, an' I wouldn't repeat it even here. Some of your supposedly gutless Kentuckians can get right hostile if'n another white eye challenges their courage. They've been known to shoot quick an' apologize later, and an apology's worthless to a dead man."

Dodd's thin mustache twitched as his mouth pursed in thought. "I accept your warning with no offense, Monsieur Watkins. It is the fool who ignores one wiser than himself."

I finished my beef and tea, which by then had cooled. The welcome victuals helped ward off the morning chill that sifted through the blanket coat protecting my backside. The wind, persistent as ever, had begun wafting from the north forceful enough to stir leaves and brighten the coals of the fire. Clouds hid the sun, promising a day shy of warmth and likely to grow colder by the hour past noon. I was tired from the long night march but not inclined to sleep, and passing time in my blankets, fretting over a future confrontation with Paw while waiting to doze off, held no attraction. It was a dilemma solved shortly by the appearance of a highly unexpected guest, none other than Ensign Andy Young.

The ensign came from the direction of the fort astride a gray mare prone to toss her head at every step. The sighting of him brought to the fore all that had transpired at Fort Washington, and preceding that, my promise at Fort Hamilton that either Paw or I would be in touch within the week regarding the alleged crimes of Court Starnes. I hadn't kept that promise and had no way of knowing if Paw had, following our arrival with the pack train three days ago. The blankets waiting in the tent I shared with Tap suddenly had a certain appeal after all.

Smile sincere and friendly as always, Andy Young stepped down, ground reined the mare, and walked forward with hand outstretched. "Mr. Downer, what a delight to see you again. I have just departed the Green cart and bear a message from Captain Starkweather."

I couldn't help thinking as my palm met that of Andy Young how Miles Starkweather always seemed to position himself and others in his charge so he was informed as to whatever took place at the Green cart nearly 'round the clock.

"It's seldom anyone gets to shake the hand of the man who's rescued the same beautiful woman not once but twice over," the ensign proclaimed with the utmost sincerity.

I felt the heat of scarlet ears and prayed the drooping brim of my hat hid them from Bear and Val Dodd. "Ensign Young, you've met Bear Watkins and Valentine Dodd, have you not," I ventured hurriedly, nodding toward my two companions.

Sweeping his tricorn from his head, Andy Young bowed from the waist with a genuine flourish. "A pleasure to make your acquaintance, gentlemen. My business involves you also, Mr. Watkins."

Bear grunted and walked about the fire. "What is your captain wanting, Ensign?" he inquired.

"General St. Clair wants the country scouted to the northwest, and the captain desires to hire the two of you as paid trackers. Mr. Jacobs declined the same proposition, claiming tiredness."

Bear chuckled. "Tap's had himself sweatin' proper the past two nights, and for once, probably ain't stretchin' the truth a lick." Bear's eyes narrowed. "If'n we accept, what's the captain's pay?"

"An oblong and full rations for every day spent afield. A most generous offer, if I say so myself," related Andy Young. "But he'll want to leave within the half hour."

Bear laid a hard, steady gaze on me. "It's fair and generous, Ethan. Yuh too tuckered for a long scout?"

I thought on that and decided being in the saddle outweighed tossing and worrying in my blankets, sleeping fitfully every other hour, for I was truly most anxious to learn away from the ears of Val Dodd where the ensign stood regarding Court Starnes and the forged manifests. Maybe I would learn something useful to Paw. A condemned soul had to cling to the slimmest of hopes, did he not? And maybe

I'd learn more about the situation at the Green cart, which wasn't a bad thing, either.

"I'm game," I assured Bear.

"The captain will be most pleased," Ensign Young announced with a wide grin. "Be at his quarters within the next thirty minutes, gentlemen," he ordered, spinning on his heel and mounting his gray mare with a quick hop off left foot and graceful swing of right leg.

I fetched Blue and Bear's brown gelding from the meadow and saddled both animals. Bear by then had gathered our blankets and rolled them for tying behind our saddles. The taking of blankets was only a precautionary measure, for Bear's parting words left no doubt as to my lowly circumstances. "Val, if'n Caleb shows, you can tell him I have his son in tow an' that we'll return before the evening is out."

We rode east around the west wall of St. Clair's as yet unnamed fort. The levy regiments had completed the morning parade, and those enlistees moving about their tents were mostly hauling firewood or tending company fires. Many were abed or huddled in skimpy blankets or ragged coats close upon the same fires. Though the tents and fires of the regular army units we coursed past exhibited fewer ill and infirm personnel, the number was still significant, confirming what the sleeping sentry had told Tap earlier.

"Never seen such sickness," Bear commented. "Course, holed shoes an' misbegotten shirts an' breeches like those issued the short-timers can be your death in foul weather. Damn shame yer paw fell in league with those sons of bitches Duer and Court Starnes, lad. An outright, damnable shame he may never overcome."

Allowing as how Bear might inwardly consider me yet another burden weighing on Paw, I rode silently at his off stirrup. We crossed the road accessing the main gate of St. Clair's fort, and Bear pointed to a dozen oversized tents bordering the eastern meadow. Bear reined his brown gelding confidently among the wind-billowed tents, and trusting Blue not to grow nervy, I followed in his wake. A striped marquee sporting a poled canvas overhang squatted at the very edge of the meadow, and Bear drew up before it. Through the wide entry beneath the poled overhang, I made out a rectangular table draped with green velvet. Beyond the table, a pair of leather traveling trunks with brass trappings sat at the head of a field cot. The corner posts of the cot, carved from the wood of the cherry tree, supported a canopy of sheer netting designed to thwart winged critters that whirred in the night. A turned-back coverlet fashioned of wolf pelts overlaid the cotton ticking of the mattress. At the foot of the cot rested a brass chamber pot with a hinged lid. The furnishings of Miles Starkweather's personal marquee exceeded those of the rooms maintained for paying guests at Monet's, Limestone's most extravagant roadhouse. Starkweather was indeed a fabulously wealthy officer, one quite capable of satisfying Erin Green's most fanciful dreams.

"Sirs, are you calling for Captain Starkweather?"

The polite query came from a solidly limbed black male of short stature adorned in green livery trimmed with gold braid, the same green as that of the velvet draping the table within the striped marquee. The dark-skinned servant, bearing a silver tray and teapot, had halted at the nearest corner of the tent.

"Jared, belay your chores and help me with my sword, please," an unseen Starkweather requested from within the marquee. "We must be off immediately."

The servant obediently placed the pot and tray upon the green velvet table and joined his master. Metal rattled against metal, and Starkweather, scabbard and sword belted about his trim waist, stepped forward under the canvas overhang. "Gentlemen, I'm most happy you have entered my employ," he said brusquely, tugging at the visor of the cockaded helmet. "Follow me!"

Starkweather quick-footed into the eastern meadow where a detail of mounted dragoons that included Ensign Andy Young waited. I seized the chance for a gander all around in hopes of pinpointing the exact whereabouts of the Green cart, which I knew to be near or within the eastern meadow, but to no avail. I suspected it was hidden by the tall freight wagons rimming the open ground to the south.

The captain stepped aboard his sorrel gelding and reined him about to face the single line of mounted dragoons.

"We'll travel in standard formation, no larking or talking. Keep an eye peeled left and right. We have reports the enemy lurks on our perimeter day and night." Then, with Bear siding him, followed directly by Ensign Young and me, Starkweather led the detail in columns of two across the shallow creek flanking the upper curve of the meadow and turned to the west. At the Injun trail down which Erin's captors had fled, we swung northward along its narrow confines, the forest undergrowth brushing our iron stirrups. We were now paralleling St. Clair's purported future line of advancement.

Though their basic garb was hardly distinguishable from the dress of the Kentucky militia who served on foot—blanket coat, hunting frock, and woolen breeches—Starkweather's detail did wear matching leather helmets with bearskin crests and riding boots with spurs in lieu of flop-brimmed hats, leggins, and moccasins. And to the man they were armed with swords as well as flintlock long guns. It intrigued me that none of the other dragoons I had seen to date, except our morning detail and the balance of Starkweather's company encamped adjacent to his marquee, were so outfitted. Nor did any other dragoon officer to my knowledge match the captain's resplendent personal uniform. Had his own purse borne the cost of his company's helmets, boots, and swords? During a dismounted pause to blow the horses, I couldn't resist questioning Andy Young, who being dressed from hair to heel in the standard uniform of the First American Regiment and who did not carry a sword, was obviously on detached duty with Starkweather's dragoons. His smile told all.

"You've guessed correctly. Captain Starkweather's father commanded a cavalry regiment in the Redcoat War. He believes mounted infantry essential to the defeat of the Shawnee and Miami. He argued mightily with General St. Clair when the general decided mounted troops were too expensive for his treasury and too difficult to discipline. That didn't deter the captain any. He raised his volunteer company with his own monies, and they answer to him, with the general's permission, of course."

"Is that why you're attached to his person? To watch his doings for St. Clair?"

Andy Young looked to our front to ensure the captain's attention was occupied elsewhere and he could speak without being overheard. "The general thinks him overly zealous to validate his contentions. But I will make a poor spy, for I admire Captain Starkweather's verve and fortitude. And others in the general's own tent agree with him regarding the need for mounted infantrymen."

While at some point in time he might prove an insurmountable rival for the affections of Erin Green, I couldn't disagree with what the ensign had said about Starkweather's character. He seemed to possess the stubborn will and exactitude I admired in Paw. And though I had heard him chided for his spotless uniform, peculiar habits, and taste for fancy victuals, I harbored no misgivings that Miles Starkweather would reveal himself a coward under fire. He was an officer one could well consider emulating. He appeared the perfect mate for a beautiful daughter, an opinion with which Molly Green would undoubtedly take no exception.

I wanted to question the ensign further, to inquire about Molly Green's health and whether or not he and Paw had ever succeeded in broaching the misdeeds of Court Starnes to General St. Clair. But Miles Starkweather was astride his sorrel once more, his slanting right arm swept forward, and the detail was in motion again.

We held to the Injun path, a true northern route over rich, level terrain thick with stands of fine young white oak, walnut, hickory, and ash timber broken at intervals by flat expanses of sandstone. At what I judged just shy of six miles, we encountered and forded the first water, a handsome stream forty feet wide running to the east and shallower than our stirrups. We rode onward without halting to water our animals, a decision that provoked low mutters from the dragoons to my rear. Within a hundred rods, howsomever, we skirted an abandoned Injun camp with the now-familiar fire rings and pitch-roofed lean-tos, and Bear's discovery of warm ashes silenced the disgruntled dragoons. Amazing how a single stark reminder we were in the country of an enemy out and on the move stilled the loosest of tongues. Stiffened tired muscles, too.

The sky darkened and the wind picked up, bringing air

raw with cold and damp down upon us, threatening snow despite the calendar, and sure enough, the first small flakes whipped about as we dismounted to noon along the near bank of an easy-flowing stream of twelve feet. We watered the horses in pairs while the entire detail stood guard, then Bear, having fetched pouches of boiled beef and filled canteens for the both of us, presented me with one of each. Soon as he rejoined the captain, I wasted no breath resuming my inquiries of Ensign Young. "Is Molly Green desperately ill?"

"Yes, she suffers from a persistent, worsening fever. Sergeant Devlin finally wilted before the persistent pleas of Annie Bower. With Erin's consent, the Bower woman began treating her this very morning with black powder diluted in water."

I nearly choked on the beef I was chewing. "Black powder, for chrissake! I've never heard of anyone swallowing gunpowder a-purpose!"

The ensign's tricorn bobbed in agreement. "Me neither, but Annie Bower swears the surgeon she accompanied in the Redcoat War had nothing else during a prolonged siege, and it helped more of the wounded with terrible fevers than it killed."

"More than it killed? Erin must have thought her mother's situation was truly desperate."

"She did. She feels her mother must get better quickly, or she will simply waste away. The wagoners think Molly Green a saint and are building a cabin to protect her from the wind and damp. They were felling logs for the walls in the woods beneath the eastern meadow when I left to bring the captain's message to you and Mr. Watkins. Even soldiers sick and coughing themselves have offered to help the wagoners. Erin's mother is in the prayers of many serving the army. General Butler confesses he has never seen its equal for a camp woman."

We ate quietly for a few minutes, mulling over the plight of Molly Green. It wasn't lost on me that if the mother overcame her fever, the newly built cabin would negate the need for her and her daughter to traipse after the army for the balance of the campaign. And it didn't slight me the least bit that while Miles Starkweather would march north with the army, I would periodically pass the Green cabin with future pack trains. The morning suddenly seemed brighter than it had since Erin Green's surprise kiss.

The ensign sighed, as if he had resolved something his own self, and said, "You are aware, are you not, that your father and I conferred privately with General St. Clair concerning Court Starnes and his henchmen. I trust he made you privy to the results of that meeting."

I lowered my canteen. "No, I've not talked to Paw since our arrival with the pack train. He went off to meet the general, and I chased after Mistress Green. He was gone when Tap and I returned with her. Did he hear you out?"

"Yes, General St. Clair listened from his bed. His gout was such he couldn't lift his shoulders from the mattress without great effort. I told him about the forged manifests, how we believe Starnes and his henchmen have been stealing regularly from the army."

"Did he believe you?" I asked anxiously.

Ensign Young shivered and shrank deeper into the collar of the greatcoat he had donned upon dismounting. "It's difficult to say. We had to stand over his bed to hear him speak. He didn't dispute what we were charging. But he refused to order Starnes's arrest unless we have the original manifests or witnesses to their forgery. He will not act without corroboration. Thus we left the general's tent disappointed but not defeated."

I studied the green water of the creek. "Cyrus Paine, the forger, is in the grave, and the original papers are nowhere to be found, and St. Clair won't act without one or the other. Sounds like maybe we're trying to ride a dead horse."

"No, not necessarily," the ensign countered.

I stared at him now. "And how's that?"

"Your father reminded me that our cause isn't lost so long as Dyson Barch is alive," Ensign Young answered. "He's convinced Barch murdered Paine to protect Starnes, and if that's true, Barch had to be aware of the forgeries or the killing makes no sense whatsoever."

Captain Starkweather mounted his sorrel, and I rose to my feet, sliding the carrying strap of my canteen over my shoulder. "I'm not certain even Paw, strong as he be, can force Dyson Barch into betraying Court Starnes. Barch knows Starnes will cut his throat in the wink of an eye if he speaks against him."

The ensign's face grew serious. "Your father warned me Starnes has no compunction about killing his fellows at the slightest provocation. He instructed me quite pointedly not to discuss our visit to General St. Clair's tent with anyone but you."

I stepped into the near stirrup and swung astride Blue. I waited till Andy Young was aboard his mane-tossing gray mare. "It'd be wise to heed his counsel. Paw believes the good of heart will always win out, no matter what. We best pray he's right, or maybe we'll all come to grief at the hands of our own rather than those of the enemy."

The detail continued northwest on the Injun pathway, our order still columns of two. An hour later, the captain motioned Ensign Young to the head of the line with Bear and fell back beside me and Blue. "I want to thank you for returning Erin Green to her mother once more. She may be seriously ill, but she's aware of everything that happens to her daughter. Again, Molly Green thanks you, and I thank you."

"It was the least Tap and I could do."

Starkweather's brow lifted. "If I'm not prying unduly, just how difficult was it to convince those four deserters to free Erin?"

I took my time responding. It was obvious that neither Tap nor Erin had told the captain much, if anything, upon reaching the Green cart. "I'll let Tap tell you the whole story over the evening fire. I wouldn't want to cheat him of his chance to brag."

The captain smiled wryly. "My, but we can be as close-mouthed as our father, can't we? I won't pursue the matter further. I bear no sympathy for those who desert their comrades, none whatsoever."

We then rode a full mile without exchanging a solitary word. The small flight of snow vanished quickly as it had appeared, but the wind and cold continued without relief. I had now been awake some twenty hours, and the tiredness was telling on me. My leg muscles ached and twitched from hip to ankles, and my arse was as Tap often complained during a prolonged stretch in the saddle, numb as dead meat. Only Miles Starkweather's renewed chatter kept my head from drooping.

"Right attractive country," he observed. "Hogs would fat of themselves in these woods. Once the redsticks are gone from here, boundless opportunities await those bold of nerve. Has your father considered moving north of the Ohio?"

I straightened and squared my shoulders, warding off the drowsiness. "No, sir, he's struggling to obtain undisputed title to our Kentucky plantation. He admires the bluegrass prairie above all else. Says it's home to him, and he won't be forced out or swindled of what belongs to him."

The bill of the captain's leather helmet pointed my direction. "What about you? Ready to seek your own plantation in this fair country and settle with the woman of your dreams?"

It was a mighty leap from Paw and Ohio land to Ethan Downer and the woman of his dreams, and I came to full attention, my nose scenting like a hound on the point. Was Starkweather just being friendly, or was he playing sly with me, ferreting out what leanings I might possibly harbor of seeking acreage of my own, acreage that I might try to occupy with Erin Green, the beauty he perhaps wanted for himself?

I confess, though, more than just the potential rivalry of Miles Starkweather had my nose up and sniffing. Amid my all-fired, frenzied rush to win the love of Erin Green, I had never stopped to ponder what would happen after I gained her hand. Where would we settle? Closer to the wick, not only where, but with what monies would we put down roots? Seeing how the mistress likely wouldn't be welcome at the Downer plantation, a burdensome situation compounded enormously by my empty purse, it was a question that couldn't go begging.

The bill of Starkweather's helmet was still pointing at me, and I swallowed my pride and trusted to what I hoped was a budding friendship. "To be honest, Captain, Ohio always seemed as far upcountry as Canada, and I've never thought much of claiming land anywhere lest it be near Paw," I ad-

mitted with surprising candor and no reddening of neck or
ears. "If I may ask, what are you planning after the campaign?"

"Since I do not wish to maintain the family estate across
the eastern mountains, I intend to acquire considerable Ohio
land. Judge Symmes at Cincinnati has title to thousands of
acres he is surveying for sale. If it doesn't sound overly
boastful, I may found a town in my family name."

It was a stunningly ambitious dream for so young an officer, a dream that exceeded my imagination. "What is there
for those with empty purses?"

"The Congress may well issue land warrants in lieu of
pay to the federal officers and enlistees serving with General
St. Clair. They did for General Washington's troops. Bounty
lands are not to be scoffed at. They've been tantamount to
salvation for countless veterans with nothing else on their
table."

Not expecting to inherit great wealth or become a regular
soldier anytime soon, I took a different fork in the road. "I've
been told surveyors can obtain title to goodly acres as their
pay, it being such a dangerous undertaking."

Starkweather nodded. "Judge Symmes is in dire need of
chain bearers at this very time. He refuses to allow our campaign to interfere with his line running and is insisting St.
Clair guard his crews with soldiers. I believe he's desperate
enough to exchange parcels for services rendered."

The captain rearranged his grip on the sorrel's reins.
"Course, there's a simpler means by which a desiring man
might accumulate his stash for the future."

I tilted sideways in the saddle and spat, not wanting to
appear too eager, too much the fish swimming straight for
the hook. "And what would that be, Captain?" I inquired,
my voice level and easy.

"Mr. Downer, I speak solely for your ears. I'm not at all
pleased with the progress of this campaign. We are proceed-
ing ever deeper into the Indian's hunting grounds in deteri-
orating weather while depending in the main on dismounted,
untrustworthy forces. I'm tiring of an army in which barrow
men, drunkards, and felons swept from the gaols, the taverns,
and the alleyways masquerade as soldiers. No matter the uni-

form, they've proven themselves bad of leg and heart and lack even a smidgen of courage. In a crisis they will undoubtedly fail the army and themselves. To avert that miserable prospect, I chose my dragoon company with great care, being determined to prove that mounted infantry properly trained and disciplined can best defeat the red savages. I will not allow my fine men to fall prey either to shallow strategy or surprise. The former I will treat with personally. For protection against the latter, I need trackers and scouts, borderers like you, Bear Watkins, and Tap Jacobs, men who understand and don't fear the forest. And I will pay damnably well, Mr. Downer, three oblongs and a full ration for each day spent in camp or afield. What say you?"

In my rising excitement I clung tightly to Blue's mane. The captain's offer was generous to the extreme, thrice what Ensign Young proposed at the Dodd fire. In a month or two I could amass enough oblongs to acquire sufficient acreage via Judge Symmes's land sales to start a plantation of my own. Maybe my dream of Erin in front of the evening hearth, her attentions devoted completely to me, was more likely to occur than rain at high noon with a full sun shining, after all. I savored that possibility with the joy of the condemned man suddenly freed with the hanging rope tightening about his neck.

But alas, in the next rap of hooves my joy soured and ebbed, for nothing devastates the male offspring who worships his father as rapidly and thoroughly as the guilt of betrayal. What about my obligations to Paw, the sire who had fed, clothed, and sheltered me since birth? How could I entertain the notion I would—or could—abandon him in the days of his greatest need so as to indulge my infatuation for a female yet to give the slightest indication beyond a passionate and unexpected kiss she might ever return my love? Lord, if the woods skunk was deemed the lowliest and most useless of woods animals, Ethan Downer was crawling beneath its belly, down where the dirt stank of your own piss.

It nonetheless took all the will and gumption I could gather to forgo my cravings for the mistress and utter what next came from my mouth. "I can't speak for Bear and Tap, Captain, but I can't scout for you. I thank you for the offer, but with Paw short of packhorsemen, I can't shirk my duty to him."

The captain's head slowly nodded. "If your affairs assume the opposite tack, the offer still stands. Too many men today are faithful only to their own greed, and I prize loyalty above all else in my dragoons."

Proud as I was of myself for sticking by Paw, I was miserable as a sinner burning at the devil's post the whole of our return trip to General St. Clair's encampment. Fatigue and saddle soreness set my legs and thighs afire, and I suffered equally hard from a heart heavy and dispirited. I rode glum and morose beside the ensign through the fading light of waning afternoon into the darkness of early evening, rudely spurning his attempts at conversation. Try as I might, I could discern no course by which I could do right by Paw and serve the captain simultaneously. The unfairness of that galled my feelings raw as an open wound dashed with salt water, and my mood blackened every mile. By the time Bear and I approached the Dodd fire, I was a bomb waiting to explode, and who was there to light my fuse but Walking Stick himself, brash and boastful Gabe Hookfin.

The beanpole, every skinny inch of him, was seated beside Val Dodd on the horse master's customary camp log. Upon sighting us, Hookfin stood and lifted the iron brewing noggin from the tripod suspending it above the fire. Bread browned and meat boiled in separate vessels beneath the tripod. "Don't be shy, buckos. We've bread an' fresh tea, courtesy of Court Starnes," the beanpole sang out shrilly, pouring tea into his tin cup.

When Bear and I merely nodded without speaking, Hookfin's thin slit of a mouth twisted into his excuse for a grin. "Yesiree, won't never be no poor pickin's on our plates from here out, not with Court the boss. He sent me ahead with two weeks' rations an' a new jug of whiskey. Said we ain't goin' without ever again, he did," the beanpole rattled on, "not even if'n the by God army starves."

I placed my saddle next to Bear's, and both of us took the cups Val Dodd offered. Our continuing silence didn't deter the beanpole. "Yep, Court's ridin' the lead horse now and says we ain't suckin' the hind teat for nobody. Says he'll

bury that fat General St. Clair in flour an' whiskey if'n he
has to kill every horse in Ohio doin' it."

Was Starnes en route with the incoming pack train? And
where was Paw? I desperately wanted to ask after Paw's
whereabouts but hated to show the slightest interest in Hookfin's shrill gloating. He was so full of himself he spared me
the bother.

"Yep, your paw wanted to travel less miles each day an'
rest the horses more, but nosiree, Court wasn't havin' none
of that. He said St. Clair finally showed a lick of smarts, an'
now that we gots the army's horses at our beck an' call, we
can line our pockets with federal gold easy as wipin' snot
off'n a baby's nose. Said we'll all be by God rich, Court did,
rich as kings and princes."

I glanced at Bear, who was studying Hookfin with the
intentness of a diving hawk. "Court sent you on ahead, did
he?" Bear asked, his tone smooth and unruffled as always
while I grappled with a surge of dislike for the beanpole that
threatened to gag me.

Hookfin helped himself to more tea and hung the noggin
back on its tripod, leaving Bear and me standing with empty
cups. His lack of manners wrung a grimace from the normally unflappable Bear Watkins that the beanpole either
didn't notice or overlooked. I hastily filled our cups.

"Yep, Court made me his personal emissary to St. Clair,
he did," Hookfin boasted. "Told me to tell that gouty old fart
of a general eyeball-to-eyeball there'll be more'n ten thousand pounds of flour comin' over yonder ridge on the morrow with him at the fore. Told me to tell the general, he did,
that with him in charge now, ain't no need to worry about
short rations if'n the army's still out here huntin' Injuns when
snow covers the ground."

Hookfin paused to gulp tea. His cup lowered, and that
poor excuse of a grin returned. "I swear there ain't no one
can hold a candle to Court Starnes when it comes to bold,"
he claimed bluntly, striding within arm's length of me.
"Know what he went an' said 'bout that snooty Green girl,
Downer?"

I trusted myself to only a shake of the head. Hookfin
edged closer. "Court said anytime the notion strikes him,

he'll have hisself a peek at what's under that white shirt of her'n, an' dare any man to stop him, includin' Sergeant Tor Devlin. What say you to that?"

Hookfin had to be counting on the backing and authority of his new mentor, the absent Court Starnes, to hold me at bay. Otherwise he wouldn't have been confronting me at close range, relaxed and loose-kneed, with both hands wrapping his tin cup. Maybe he believed I wouldn't fight him like before. Either way, it was a grievous error in judgment on the part of the beanpole. I slid my left foot forward, rolled my shoulders, and without spilling a drop of the tea in my left fist, drove my right straight for the middle of his nettlesome, sorry-arse smile before he could so much as blink. My weight settled on my left foot and flying knuckles met flesh and bone, every ounce of disappointment and frustration I'd experienced the entire day adding force to my punch. Teeth flew in accompaniment with Hookfin's cup. His jaw snapped upward, his arms dropped to his sides, and he staggered toward Dodd's log. His heels encountered the log, and he toppled backward, fortunately for him away from the flames of the fire. So great was my anger at that instant, I was never to decide whether I would have bothered trying to catch him if he had fallen in the opposite direction.

The loudest noise in the hush that followed was the hiss of the fire and my sudden gasp, for unbeknownst to myself, I'd been holding my breath all the while. The next noise reaching our ears was Hookfin's bubbling moan. Bear walked past me and stepped over Dodd's log. Dodd remained where he was, and I did the same, rubbing my bruised knuckles. Sucker punch or not, it had been one fine blow, delivered dead on target at maximum strength. And there would be no apology, now or ever. The beanpole had begged for it, and I'd been most happy to oblige him.

Bear held Hookfin upright till his legs steadied. Blood poured from his mangled mouth, and his eyes were dull. The beanpole swiped at his dripping chin and shook free of Bear's grasp. He stumbled around the end of the log and laid hold of his ratty saddle and lone gun. He stared at me with a look of pure hate. Mashed lips and broken teeth garbled his words, but I understood him well enough to make out what he said. "Wait till you answer to Starnes for this," he spat, wincing with pain.

The beanpole departed, saddle stirrups and rifle butt dragging the ground. I'd no sympathy for him whatsoever. I sipped tea from my cup. "Well, leastwise we won't have to share the bread with the son of a bitch."

Val Dodd chuckled, and the usually solemn Bear smiled. After that brief spate of humor, a quiet meal ensued. Not a soul said so aloud, but we each knew there would indeed be a reckoning with the arrival of Paw and Court Starnes, both about my defying Paw's orders to retrieve Erin Green and my sucker-punching Starnes's personal, hand-picked messenger. Bear and Dodd didn't share their thinking with me during the evening meal. But squaring things with Paw scared me the most.

Later, I lay in my blankets, unable to sleep.

Damn it to hell, how could the loving of a beautiful woman thrill a man so grandly yet complicate the whole of his being?

Chapter 22

22 October

I finally slept fully in the hours prior to dawn. During those hours, another body settled next to mine, probably Tap Jacobs, with whom I was to share the tent. But I couldn't force my eyes open to greet him for the tiredness consuming me, and much later I awoke alone in scanty daylight under the canvas sheeting. I rolled from my blankets stiff and heavy of limb and, being immediately alarmed that an outraged Paw might catch me abed with the day under way, I ignored the protest of sore muscle and sinew and bolted to my feet.

I relaxed somewhat when I could spy no one about our campfire except the ever-present Val Dodd. Rifle in hand, I stepped from the tent, gladdened that despite the soreness besetting me everywhere, my actual wounds were minor and tolerable. The powder burns on my chest ached but little, and with deep female kisses again scarce as perfectly square rocks, the split in my lip was knitting together nicely. As for my knuckles, while they were black and blue from the punching of Hookfin, I detected no swelling, and my fingers moved freely.

It was a pleasant enough morning, cold and chill with fair skies and a light, steady breeze from the common source of the wind in recent days, the northwest. Yesterday's brief snow seemed of a different autumn, but that was what one came to expect from the weather north of the Ohio, for it truly was as Tap described, fickle as the maiden pursued by a dozen lovers.

"Good morning, Monsieur Downer," greeted Val Dodd.

I fisted the cup of green tea he held forth and sipped

carefully, guarding my healing lip against the liquid's fiery touch. I gazed into the meadow where we'd hobbled our horses the previous evening and asked of Dodd, "Bear and Tap off scouting already?"

"There is apparently some confusion as to what General St. Clair expects of his mounted dragoons this morning, and Monsieur Watkins awaits your orders at Captain Starkweather's tent. It appears the two of you will scout for the captain till your father arrives with the pack train. Monsieur Jacobs declined to accompany Monsieur Watkins. He ate most heartily of the Hookfin rations and went to help with the cabin the soldiers are throwing up for the Molly Green woman."

That was Tap, all right, anything to shuck the saddle. Val Dodd passed me a plate of what had become our standard fare morning, noon, and night, bullock and bread, and I sat on the camp log with him to eat. I would've preferred cabin building my ownself, and the resulting opportunity to inquire firsthand as to Molly Green's health, and in so doing perhaps gain a chance to talk with the mistress personally, though about what I knew not. But I was in Bear's charge and would hence avoid any action that worsened my troubles with Paw. I'd enough to account for as it was.

Not wanting to add to that already sizable ledger, I didn't loll about waiting for Bear to return. I saw to the cleaning and reloading of my long gun, fetched Blue from the meadow and saddled him, then filled two pouches with beef and bread and two canteens from the supply of water Dodd had boiled clear over the fire. When half an hour frittered by with no sign of Bear, my patience evaporated, and I swung into the saddle, thanked Dodd for the supplies, and went in search of him.

Thinly numbered companies of levy and American regiments formed in front of General St. Clair's as yet unnamed fort, assigned to either guard the perimeter or to continue scouring forest and meadow to the north, east, and west for grasses to sustain the oxen teams and artillery horses. Other companies prepared to guard the remaining bullock herd and its drovers during their daily graze southward along the military road. Numerous levy and regular soldiers obviously still too ill for duty languished about their tents. Through the open gates of the fort I counted a fatigue of approximately sixty additional uniformed men laboring to finish the final yards of a log-buttressed tunnel accessing the underground powder magazine at the center of the parade.

Past the gates of the fort, I halted while a motley collection of Kentucky militia bearing piggins brimming with water crossed my path. They were arguing loudly with their officer, a fuzz-cheeked corporal, protesting the need to scout woods they had already traversed countless times. Their complaints had some validity. Bear had made known to me Starkweather's concurrence with General St. Clair's decision that the Kentucky militia companies were too undisciplined to be trusted with any assignment except routine scouting patrols and the guarding of road builders once the army was on the march again, which should be soon. With his fort nearly completed, the surrounding meadows grazed out, and the country scouted in all directions, only illness among his forces and the belated arrival of the pack train from Fort Hamilton with fresh provisions prevented the resumption of General St. Clair's northern advance.

The confusion regarding the general's orders of the day that had forestalled the departure of Starkweather's dragoons had been clarified, for when I rode alongside his striped marquee, the captain was seated on his sorrel before his entire troop, shouting instructions for the morning. "Our horses are in need of sustenance. Therefore, our destination is a large meadow five to six miles to the northeast. We will graze the horses there and return before dusk. We will travel in columns of two, on the alert and watching all the while. Dragoons, form column!"

As Starkweather's troop wheeled into proper formation, Ensign Andy Young, flanking the captain atop his own gray mare, pointed in my direction. Starkweather lifted an arm and beckoned me forward. I clapped heels to Blue and he fast-stepped into the meadow. "You will accompany Mr. Watkins in the lead, please. I want no surprises, no ambushes, Mr. Downer, am I understood?"

Delighted that he hadn't held my tardiness against me, I gave him a forceful and forthright, "Yes, sir," knuckled my forehead, and hustled Blue into motion with another thud of the heels.

Bear sat his powerful brown gelding at the head of the column. He didn't act the least surprised to see me and accepted the pouch of victuals and iron canteen I passed him with a slight nod and soft smile, like I was doing exactly what was expected of me. It always amazed me how he often taught more with his quiet, unspoken responses than other men did with a hundred words.

Bear led the troop across the creek into the untracked, northeastern woods. There were no Injun paths there to chart our course for us. But that didn't faze Bear. Where Tap Jacobs was most comfortable traveling hostile country afoot, Bear Watkins preferred the saddle. With the gentle pressure of his knees and an occasional flick of reins, he guided the brown gelding through and around trees, boulders, thickets, and other obstacles with an enviable skill, head always level and still, never leaning left or right in the saddle. Never did his decisions or bodily signals cause his animal to hesitate or shy. It was as if he became one with his mount.

The woods thinned along the base of uplifted terrain short on height and bulk, and the brown gelding slowed. I drew even with Bear's stirrup. "We're not hunting squirrels now. We're hunting a cunning enemy where cover is plentiful, so learn to look wide as you can from the corners of your eyes. With practice you can look behind the points of your shoulders. No, not like that. Don't turn your head any at all. Be a little sly your ownself. The redstick loves to let you come abreast of him, then loose his ball or arrow. But at the last second, he must take aim with his rifle or draw his bow, and to do that, he has to use his hands and arms, and that's what will give him away. You see the leveling of a rifle barrel, the glide of tawny flesh, don't hesitate. Shoot for the body, below whatever moves. You understand?"

"Yes, sir, look wide, shoot below whatever moves," I affirmed.

"Good lad. It's always better to waste a little powder than chance your last breath," Bear advised. "Another thing, after you shoot, charge straight at the bugger an' give him what for with the butt of your rifle before he can reload. That or dismount behind your horse an' reload your ownself. Don't never sit the saddle gawkin' after your ball, wonderin' if'n you shot true, 'cause if'n you miss or the red devil ain't alone, you'll likely be a dead man damn quick. Understand me, lad?"

The trees thickened, and I was forced to rein Blue behind Bear's gelding once more. I wasn't certain he saw my honest and sincere nod that I had indeed understood him. But let me tell you, such was my respect for whatever training Bear deigned to offer, he had me peering first past one shoulder, then the other throughout the morning with no loss of interest, even when I didn't sight anything of consequence or danger.

Bear's unerring sense of direction and ability to sense the lay of the land outside his direct line of vision didn't fail him, and he brought the troop plumb into the large meadow Starkweather mentioned at the outset of our scout as if he'd visited the site just yesterday. Starkweather complimented Bear openly, then, with sentries posted about the rim of the meadow, the remaining dragoons nibbled at their rations inside the circle of our girth-loosened, grazing horses.

Ensign Young sought me out of his own accord. Embarrassed at the wealth of beef and bread I carried compared to the scanty fixings borne by the individual dragoons, I attempted to share equally with the ensign, but he declined. "I dined with Captain Starkweather last evening, and his table is seldom found lacking. In fact, we supped on tinned sardines and, of all rarities, pickled oysters from the Maryland shore. And the wine was delectable as always.

"But enough of what's old news. I came to inform you that Molly Green is some better. Her fever seems less severe and, according to Erin, she slept through part of the night. Annie Bower has been with Molly practically every minute, bathing her patient with cool water and administering her potion of gunpowder, whiskey, and water. While it won't happen anytime soon, Erin believes her mother will recover completely once she's warm and snug in her new cabin, the logs of which are being chinked this very morning."

I drank from my canteen. I envied the ensign his contact with the mistress and wondered if she ever mentioned my name or inquired as to how I might be. But my pride kept me from broaching those subjects with him. "Glad to hear Molly Green is on the mend. Sergeant Devlin must be the happiest soldier in St. Clair's army."

The ensign laughed. "Lord yes, he is. Annie Bower reported he promised Molly on his knees that if she got well, she would never know another day of want or danger, neither she nor her daughter. Then he made Annie vow she would never leave Erin's side. The sergeant's not risking Erin's safety ever again. He even procured Annie a pistol and a long, wickedly keen knife. And as the Lord is my witness, Annie's taking her new duties mighty seriously. She has her friends caring for Molly and shadows Erin's every step, whether Erin approves or not."

I smiled at the picture of Annie Bower stepping smartly on the heels of the mistress, who was accustomed to marching any direction she pleased whenever the mood hit her. It was a significant change for a young woman who prized her independence and moments of privacy. But from Tor Devlin's viewpoint and mine also, she was much safer under the constantly watching eyes of Annie Bower, a female whose moral character might be questioned but one I suspected was quite capable of shooting or stabbing any man, red or white, in defense of her charge. I smiled again. Given her obvious liking for me, I doubted Annie Bower would object to my calling on Erin and her mother when I ventured past the newly built Green cabin with future pack trains. I wouldn't allow the same would be true for other potential suitors except possibly Starkweather and Ensign Andy Young, both of whom would be occupied in the north with the army. I smiled full bore now. The competition would be elsewhere along with the indomitable Sergeant Tor Devlin. The days ahead might prove brighter than I had supposed except for one small hitch: Could I smooth things over with a certain father of mine?

Ensign Young observed my series of smiles and sudden

sobering with a puzzled frown but didn't pry. "Do we know with certainty that Court Starnes will be with the incoming pack train?"

"Yes, Gabe Hookfin bragged at the Dodd fire last evening that he would be leading it," I informed him.

It was the ensign's turn to display a most sober countenance. "I'm extremely concerned about trouble twixt your father and Starnes. Your father doesn't seem a man who would suffer a wrong for any length of time without seeking redress of some nature. He will, I predict, try to find Dyson Barch and somehow make him talk. If that fails, do you think he will confront Starnes directly?"

My answer was quick in the coming. "Yeah, God forbid, he likely will. Paw's patience can shrink down next to nothing on him, he's made to fret in the halter too long. He doesn't fear Starnes in a fight. But I'm afraid for Paw. If'n they get to brawling, the fight won't stop till one of them is dead."

The ensign's nod was slow and deliberate. "I fear that, too. Perhaps the army will move soon, and the campaign will take precedence over all other matters. Leastwise, we can pray for that eventuality."

There was a question I had to ask, even though it might challenge the ensign's loyalties. "Why does General St. Clair believe he can defeat the redsticks come what may?"

The ensign plucked and chewed on a stem of grass. "General St. Clair is convinced the red enemy cannot muster a force as large as ours. Even if they do so, he believes we possess the deciding military arm in any battle with them, namely, Major Ferguson's artillery."

"Captain Starkweather doesn't agree with that, does he?" I countered.

"He doesn't criticize General St. Clair's strategy publicly," Ensign Young confessed. "He has, though, attributed the general's zeal to engage the enemy to the expresses forwarded almost weekly by President Washington and Secretary of War Knox. The president himself is personally demanding a victory afield before the snow flies, mainly to stifle the complaints of the Marietta and Kentucky settlements. Some enjoying close proximity to the general complain he would sacrifice this entire army to satisfy the president's wishes."

I pondered on that. While I was a mere packhorseman and scout, it surely seemed understandable to even a young man of meager stature that a general in the field wouldn't hardly dare thwart the desires of President Washington, not without courting the ruination of himself and his career. From where I was seated, General St. Clair's burdens and responsibilities piled up higher than the Alleghenies. Which meant just as surely there would be a fight with the Shawnee and their red cohorts less'n they abandoned their villages and fled, something Tap and Bear didn't feel was about to happen. Wise old Tap was correct. In the dealings of men red and white, blood frequently spilled easy as rain wet the ground.

The ensign and I fell silent, watching Blue and his mare graze. Warm in my blanket coat, I dozed off now and again. When awake, my thinking inevitably centered on my upcoming reunion with Paw to the exclusion of all else, even Erin Green. What would he say? How would he punish me? How long would it take for me to regain his good graces . . . if ever? Would he be merciful, or would he ban me from his sight? It was hard to believe helping another in distress could so foul one's own existence. It smacked of unfairness. Damned if it didn't!

While I rested and dozed, Bear twice circled the meadow afoot, conversing with the sentries. The ever-restless Captain Starkweather passed among the members of his troop, inspecting each dragoon's horse and equipment. He was a stickler for detail, the captain, which made his error upon our departure strikingly out of character.

Bear, you must know, had a standing rule about traveling in Injun country the same as Tap. Simply stated, to diminish the likelihood of surprise or ambush, you never returned to camp via the exact same path. With Bear guiding the Starkweather troop the previous day, we had naturally altered our return route to General St. Clair's fort.

On this early afternoon, the captain, now leading Bear's gelding, paused before the ensign and me and, for whatever reason, suddenly ordered his lounging dragoons into the saddle. The captain's abrupt order came with Bear at the meadow's northern rim, opposite the point from which we had originally entered the meadow, the farthest distance possible from our commanding officer. "Hold here with Mr. Watkins's horse, Ensign. At my stirrup, Mr. Downer, if you please," the captain barked.

Lost mainly in my own problems, I briskly followed orders, and it wasn't till the column had formed and was moving that I realized the captain's intentions. He was riding straight for the shallow notch twixt two opposing hillocks by which we had accessed the meadow. The closely set tree butts bordering the sides of the notch bristled with low branches and tangled brush, affording excellent concealment for those on the stalk. I gave no thought to contesting the captain's intentions. But Bear's speech about how to watch to both flanks at once being fresh in my head, I came fully alert, nearly standing in the stirrups before recalling his admonition that one needed to be a little sly so as not to forewarn the lurking enemy.

I strained my eyes as the captain and I approached the notch, then rode into its narrow mouth. Trees closed about us. But there was nothing out of the ordinary to be seen, nothing but dark trunks, low branches, and tangled brush separated by glimmers of sunlight and shadow.

Relieved no shots or whizzing arrows greeted us, I was easing in the saddle when beyond the head of the captain's sorrel the thin line of a branch shimmied and rose in defiance of the breeze . . . or had it? I stiffened even as I doubted my own eyes. I stared, and new activity at the end of the branch where it should have mated with a tree trunk made the decision for me, for it matched the short, smooth stroke a practiced hand might employ tugging the hammer of a long gun to full cock.

The captain was on my left flank, same as the Injun, if he was really there, and the branch if it was a rifle barrel was pointed dead center on the captain's chest. There being no time to yell a warning, I loosed Blue's reins, turned slightly in the saddle, and snapped the stock of my own rifle tight to cheek and shoulder, cocking the piece as it settled against flesh and bone. I squeezed the trigger without drawing a true bead, shooting for the enemy's body as Bear had instructed. The sharp snap of hammer on frizzen jerked the captain's chin about an instant before the blast of my rifle shocked both him and his sorrel.

"Injuns!" I screamed, "Injuns!"

Starkweather's recovery was nothing short of miraculous. With knees and reins he kept the sorrel from shying and was immediately shouting orders above the echoing report of my shot. "Troop halt! Form line abreast! Form line abreast!"

Behind us, Ensign Young and the sergeants, voices shrill and laced with excitement, repeated the captain's orders. "After me, Mr. Downer," Starkweather called, reining his sorrel to the rear. I spun that Blue horse about and done as ordered, scrunched low in the saddle as I could get.

Though I had never trained under Miles Starkweather, his strategy was simple and unmistakable. If the Shawnee waited in ambush within the restricting confines of the notch, he refused to fight them on terrain of their choice where his mounted dragoons couldn't charge and pursue and thus exploit their dual strengths of flying hoof and flashing steel.

I rode through the dragoon line, halted Blue and, listening for those familiar Shawnee war whoops, the boom of muskets, and the harsher crack of rifles, began reloading my long gun in earnest. But other than the rattle of bridle chains, the creak of saddle leather, and the occasional nervous cough, silence befell my ears. I seated my ball with a solid thrust of ramrod and glanced up to find the bulk of the dragoons watching me, not the surrounding forest in which I had sighted the enemy, and from whence he was most likely to launch his attack.

But silence prevailed, not the noise and clamor of battle. Not a single enemy shot had been fired, and it became as obvious as the derisive stares of the dragoons that the entire troop believed me a cowardly pup of a scout who had sparked a false alarm over nothing. I seated the ramrod in its thimbles beneath the barrel of my rifle and sat Blue at attention, refusing to drop my eyes or cower before them. Judge me they could, but I knew what I had seen.

The captain wasn't as quick with an opinion as was his mounted infantry. "Mr. Watkins, Sergeant Baker, Privates Crane, Langtree, and Sharp, reconnoiter to our front, please," he ordered.

Bear Watkins, still afoot, positioned the mounted sergeant and three privates in the throat of the notch, then glided into the trees. The troop waited, long guns poised and cocked. The minutes crept by, and the low mutterings of the dragoons made it plain they felt the scouting party was a monumental waste of time and effort. When no shout of discovery or alarm was forthcoming from Bear, the dragoons grew more restless. Catcalls and snorts of satisfaction rippled through the dragoon line as Bear emerged calmly from the trees and led the scouting party before Captain Starkweather.

"Your report, Mr. Watkins?"

"All clear now, Captain," Bear said.

"Now? Did you say now, Mr. Watkins?" Starkweather questioned loudly.

The dragoons quieted except for the repeating of the captain's query at the ends of their line. Bear stepped beside Starkweather's sorrel. His right arm extended upward. Dangling from his hand was a large maple leaf. "Blood, sir, wet and fresh. I found a heel print, but no other sign. It was a close thing, sir, mighty close."

The captain reached down and delicately grasped the bloody maple leaf with the tips of two fingers. He studied it, then turned in the saddle. "Congratulations, Mr. Downer. You're the first of my command to successfully engage the enemy. I shall long remember this occasion. I salute you," the captain said, raising his leather helmet high above his head with his free hand. "Gentlemen, a cheer for Mr. Downer!"

Bearskin-crested helmets lifted skyward, and the accompanying cheer like to hurt my ears. My chest bulged more than a tad, I can tell you. It was probably the most recognition any borderer ever received for merely wounding the red enemy. But damn, I was proud that my judgment had held water.

Ensign Andy Young, whose foremost ambition was to

fight the Shawnee in person, could talk of nothing else
throughout our return ride. I repeated the details of the attempted ambush of the captain to him every other mile,
which did me the great favor of mostly keeping my mind off
my situation with Paw. In fact, it took a new burst of cheering from a different source to finally draw the ensign's attention elsewhere.

We were fording the creek on the northern fringe of
General St. Clair's encampment when the shouting and
yelling commenced. Once started, lusty, sustained cheers
rolled over us in waves to echo in the creek bottom. We
rode from the water, and the ensign stood in his stirrups,
hoping for a better view of the commotion. "Other than
General St. Clair aborting the campaign, nothing but the
arrival of the pack train could cause such excitement,"
Andy Young concluded.

The ensign's statement made perfect sense. General St.
Clair had dispatched three hundred baggage horses south to
speed the shipments of flour and supplies, in the process,
provoking considerable talk and speculation. From the loud
and raucous nature of the cheers, which continued unabated
as we entered the eastern meadow, the arriving pack train
had to be much longer and better stocked than the general's
forces had dared anticipate.

I didn't share the joy of the multitude, for it meant I would
shortly find myself standing before Paw. Having promised
Paw I would be present at the Dodd fire upon his return,
Bear wasted not a moment separating us from Starkweather
and his dragoons. We gained the military road dividing the
encampment and waited with the watching soldiers while the
small drove of cattle bringing up the rear of the packhorse
train plodded past.

The cheering had finally died down, and Bear leaned from
the saddle in the gathering dusk to inquire of a levy private,
"Big shipment, my friend?"

The slack-jawed private was only too happy to relate
what he had observed. "Two full brigade of horse. Must be
nigh onto ten tons of flour and plenty of jug whiskey," he
gushed.

"Yep, Tate, that be true," a pipe-smoking levy chimed in.

"An' we gots that big fellow Starnes to thank. He done made double good on his brag to St. Clair."

The levy's unsolicited opinion hit a nerve with me. All of Paw's prior efforts seemed forgotten with the sudden emergence of Court Starnes. I just prayed Paw's rivalry with Starnes hadn't put him in a totally sour mood. God's bones, Paw was difficult enough to deal with if'n he was merely riled up. You couldn't reason at all with him during his black spells. Then, he was as Mother said, "Quite impossible."

Bear and I picketed our horses in the western meadow and lugged saddles and gear to the Dodd fire, which burned bright and cheery in the gray twilight. Val Dodd, Ira Fellows, Henry Cross, and the wagoners, Thaddeus and Timothy, were present. Val Dodd was seated on his log, singing as he tended baking bread and roasting meat. The rosy bloom on his plump cheeks indicated he, like the others, was being generous with the whiskey jug. "Come, come, my bosom friends, a fine evening beckons, does it not?"

Greetings were exchanged, and the jug made a round, then another. I drank heartily both passes, seeking a little liquid courage. I managed to conjure up enough to pose the fatal question: "Is Paw with you?"

"Yep, he be," Ira Fellows said following a mighty slurp from the passing jug. "He's reportin' to St. Clair along with Court Starnes as we drink."

"An' Hookfin, too," Henry Cross slurred. "Starnes took his personal spy with him, broke jaw notwithstandin', mayhap to kiss the general's boots for him."

Lord, it couldn't be worse. No doubt Hookfin had gone running to Starnes, and Court was rubbing Paw's nose in the shit royally. I slugged another dollop of the raw whiskey. Hadn't Paw said on numerous occasions a wild temper could lead to a man's downfall easy as murder, lying, and cheating? Why did I always learn the truth of what he said too late?

I sighed heavily and settled on my haunches with a tin plate of victuals. The others joked and wove tales of incidents on the journey north with the pack train. I chewed and gazed at the fire, there being nothing left for me except to while

the time away till Paw showed hisself. It was near dark when
Ira Fellows tapped my shoulder and said quietly amid the
laughing and joshing, "Horses comin', Ethan."

Gabe Hookfin, hurt jaw swollen the size of a large gourd,
rode into the firelight. Behind him came Court Starnes, then
Paw. Paw's glance as they proceeded past the fire into the
western meadow to picket their mounts was stern and un-
smiling. His solemn nod merely acknowledged the presence
of Bear and me. As I had feared, I faced a truly bleak evening.

Hookfin, Starnes, and Paw returned together, Paw in the
van now. The talk about the fire stilled at the sighting of
Paw's dark visage. Muscle bunched at the hinges of his jaws.
His eyes shone bright with pent-up anger. The greetings of
the Duer crew, including that of Val Dodd, were bland and
cautious.

I expected Paw to take me aside, as was his custom, to
discuss what I believed private business. Instead, his voice
leaped at me soon as his saddle touched earth. "Ethan, you
have much to atone for."

He kept walking, and halted a stride short of me, his
shoulders squared to mine, and I realized I would be frayed
bare in public, though thankfully, it appeared, with just the
tongue, for Paw bore no whip. I could almost feel the heat
of Paw's ire, and his words fell upon me like blows from a
hatchet.

"Ethan, I can no longer trust you. First, you disobeyed
me and we lost Hardy Booth and valuable riding stock.
Next, you traipsed off, again against my orders, to rescue a
camp girl. Then, last evening, at this very fire, over a few
words you apparently didn't like, you broke a man's jaw
without warning. Am I not telling the truth of your failings?"

I wanted to explain myself, to make him understand how
I loved Erin as deeply as he loved Mother and could not let
her come to harm of any kind nor brook anything foul or
slighting said of her. But he wouldn't listen to what he would
consider merely lame excuses. I knew that same as I knew
he was right in what he said. In every incidence, I had directly disobeyed him.

"Well, Ethan, am I telling the truth?" Paw demanded.

Afraid my voice would quake, I resisted the urge to shuffle my feet, and nodded. Paw swallowed, like maybe even he didn't like the punishment he was about to dictate. "Ethan, since I can't trust you, there's but one thing to be done, and that's send you home to your mother and sisters."

Though I didn't take my eyes from Paw, it had to be Hookfin who chortled with glee, the skinny son of a bitch. I wasn't certain later just what I had expected from Paw, but I shouldn't have been surprised in the least. He had previously threatened to send me packing with my tail twixt my legs. But to be dismissed entirely from his service in such a humiliating fashion was worse than suffering a whipping that left scars. And it took but a moment's reflection for me to realize that if I acceded to his wishes, I wasn't likely to lay eyes on Erin Green ever again. Lord God almighty, the speed of my response and the strength behind it shocked even me.

"No, sir, I won't go!"

"You what?" an equally startled Paw shot back.

"I'm not returning home," I repeated, my voice still solid and unwavering. "I'll make my own way from here out."

Paw edged closer, and the raw, naked fierceness of his stare nearly wilted my knees. "Then so be it. You may have the roan gelding you ride and everything you have in your possession I have provided. And since you are now without ties to your family or us Duer men, you will immediately seek sustenance elsewhere. We tolerate only our own at this fire."

Shock rippled through me anew. I was being dismissed from camp plumb into the night. I steadied my nerves and my limbs, cocked my chin defiantly, circled around Paw, retrieved my rifle, saddle, and gear and, without a solitary good-bye or backward glance, walked into the enveloping blackness.

My feelings were so roiled, I don't remember much about the saddling of Blue. But I won't ever forget my departure. My destination was as yet undecided, but as I skirted the Dodd fire, I kicked Blue into a gallop and flashed past with my hat brim pulled low.

Damned if I was going to let any of the watching crowd, especially Hookfin and Court Starnes, see tears in the eyes of Ethan Downer now that he had declared himself his own man.

Nosiree!

Chapter 23

Late Evening, 22 October

Once well away from the Dodd crowd, I slowed Blue to a walk and dried my tears. Some serious thinking was required on my part, and hurriedly to boot. I had been set adrift within a military encampment and had to decide where to cast my lot, for I had no desire to enter the enemy-infested country alone in the night.

Though I would find some friendly faces there, particularly those of Annie Bower and Erin, I quickly discounted the Green cabin as a possibility. The mistress had enough of a burden looking after her mother, and I didn't want her worrying that she had caused the rift twixt Paw and me. Nor did I want her sympathy.

In the whole of the St. Clair encampment, the only other place I might be welcome was Starkweather's marquee. He had offered me the opportunity to scout and track for him. And had I not saved his life earlier this same day? So to the eastern meadow I went.

It wasn't a particularly long ride, but my feelings were together somewhat when Blue answered a gentle tug of the reins alongside the overhang of the captain's marquee. A table lighted by a lanthorn, the candles of which flickered in the light evening breeze, reposed beneath the overhang. A place setting of white china and silver tableware rested on the velvet-covered table, and a small fire straddled by an iron tripod holding a boiling kettle of water burned before the overhang. It appeared the captain was preparing to dine.

No one was about, and a sheet of canvas at the rear of the overhang hid the interior of the tent. My call of greeting

died on my lips as a hand, black and bluntly fingered, gently
lifted the canvas door and Jared, the captain's servant, slid
through an opening not an inch bigger than his liveried
frame.

The servant toted an empty kettle. Blue tossed his head
and snorted, drawing Jared's attention. Not the least perturbed or frightened, the servant halted and asked, "Who be
it, please?"

"Ethan Downer, here to speak with Captain Starkweather
about scoutin' for him," I informed Jared.

Jared smiled and bowed slightly at the waist. "I remem-
bers you. You called with another gentleman yesterday. I tell
Captain Starkweather you be waitin'. But you best step down
an' be patient. Captain, he just started his bath."

With a similar polite bow, Jared hustled to the fire, removed the kettle of hot water, refilled the empty kettle from a
leather piggin, hung it on the straddling tripod, then slipped
back through the canvas doorway with the boiling one, leaving me peering after him openmouthed. Bath, he had said, an
indoor bath in a tent in the middle of the Ohio wilderness. I
was familiar with creek washing of exposed parts and feet on
the trail whenever time and place permitted, and practiced
such, though the opportunities of late had been woefully
scarce. I clucked in admiration. Miles Starkweather had
brought the comforts of home into the field with him on a scale
as grand as that normally enjoyed by colonels and generals.

I loosened the girth of Blue's saddle, added wood to the
fire, and took a seat on a nearby log. By the faint light of
candles within the closed tent, I saw a shadowy, lean figure
lift a leg high, pause, then lower it behind a low wall I assumed was the side of a metal or wooden tub large enough
to engulf an entire body. I can't lie. I wondered just how
luxurious that warm, soapy water felt. Understand now, I
didn't abide that cleanliness was next to godliness from birth
to grave like Mother, but the weekly bath I was missing had
enormous appeal given the state of filth I was experiencing.
As of that evening, being downwind of Ethan Downer was
a threat to the nose of the most unrefined soul, male or female.

Starkweather was in his tub long enough for the water to

turn icy cold before Jared emerged and fetched another kettle of the boiling stuff. "He'll be dressed soon," the scurrying servant announced over a shoulder. And sure enough, within short minutes, Miles Starkweather stepped into view wearing tall boots, pantaloons, and a fringed hunting frock in lieu of his standard uniform coat. He wasted not a second getting to the business at hand. "Evening, Mr. Downer. Jared says you're here to discuss scouting and tracking for my dragoons."

"Yer, sir, I am," I said.

The captain frowned. "You're no longer in the service of your father?"

"No, sir. I'm my own man. I serve where I please."

My respect for Starkweather grew by leaps and bounds, for he didn't pry. Had he demanded an explanation of my sudden change of circumstances, I might have turned blubbery and teary-eyed and perhaps fled into the surrounding darkness. To my utter joy, he simply took me at my word. "You will be a welcome addition to my troop. But are you willing to take the oath, an oath that would obligate you to my employ for the duration of the campaign, however many months that may be?"

I didn't answer straight off. My hesitation stemmed from the realization the taking of Starkweather's oath meant I had truly broken with Paw. There would be no going back, no belated apology and mending of fences. So ingrained was Paw's sense of family and personal loyalty there was a goodly chance I would never again grace the stoop of the Downer plantation house, even as a visitor, if I pledged myself to anyone not blood kin. But, ironically, it was the absolute stubbornness and steadfastness of purpose I'd inherited from the ferociously loyal Paw that gave me the courage, despite the pain and sacrifice of my choosing, to say to Starkweather in a plain, clear, unmistakable voice, "I'll swear your oath, Captain. I will."

My heart fluttered with that momentous decision, and nearly breathless, I accepted Starkweather's invitation to enter his striped marquee. Inside, I swore an oath on his Bible, and he produced from his writing table an enlistment voucher that required my signature. "Your pay will be as I stated yesterday: full rations and three oblongs for each day in the field. Since this is a volunteer troop and not the regular army, I assign the rankings. Hence, you will hold the rank of ensign and serve as my aide-de-camp. You'll sleep in Jared's tent. I trust you find these terms acceptable?"

"Yes, sir, I surely do," I responded with sincere enthusiasm. Nothing like solid victuals, generous daily pay, and dry night quarters to ease a man across the most crucial watershed of his young life.

Starkweather's smile was equally sincere. "Ensign Downer, welcome to the ranks. We must now pursue some additional details," he proclaimed, opening the brass latches of the traveling trunk flanking his sleeping cot. He rummaged about inside the trunk and produced a metal and leather dragoon helmet, an exact duplicate of that he himself wore when on duty except for his signature blue and white silk cockade. Then, opening the second of his traveling trunks, he lifted free a pair of tall riding boots. "I believe we are the same size at the head and feet, Ensign. Try these," he said, sliding the chair from beneath his writing table.

Overwhelmed by his generosity, I laid my flop-brimmed hat on the table and settled the helmet in place. The captain was correct. It fit perfectly with no wobble fore and aft. I sat in his canvas-seated chair and removed my moccasins. As I feared, the odor that flooded the tent was an acute embarrassment. Starkweather's nose wrinkled, and he pursed his lips. "Perhaps we should forgo trying the boots till after I grant you a visit to my tub."

I made to protest that such an offer was too much, but he shushed me with an upraised palm and turned to Jared, who waited patiently at the entryway of the tent. "Fill the tub, please. Our newest recruit won't be ready for dinner without a proper soaking."

Jared departed, and Starkweather crossed to the yawning brass bathing tub opposite his cot. From a small folding table next to the tub he retrieved a looking mirror and razor. Gilt framed the mirror, and the razor bore a carved ivory handle. He pointed to a longish leather strap hanging from the tent pole behind the tub. "Strop a fine edge on her. It's a quality blade from Mahon's of Philadelphia. Shaves without nicking when sharp, she does," he said with great pride, returning the mirror and razor to the folding table. "I'll retire outside while you tend to yourself."

A most delectable hour followed. I stripped to the waist and shaved while Jared fetched steaming kettles till the tub was adequately filled. At his signal, I finished undressing and plunged into the scalding water. Before leaving me, Jared placed bars of scented soap and drying cloths within easy reach.

Mercy, but did the dirt float that evening. My freshly scrubbed skin was white as bleached bone. Danged if this being a dragoon officer didn't have some advantages. Course, once I was clean everywhere and relaxed as a catamount sunning hisself, I overwore my welcome by dozing off. What saved my being found out was the growing coldness of the water. I came awake with a start, checked the entryway for onlookers, and relieved I was still alone, bolted from the tub, dried off quickly, and shucked into my clothes. I plopped in the captain's chair and donned his spare boots. They were tight but would loosen with wear.

Rising from the chair, my gaze drifted to the surface of his writing table. A sheet of parchment lay atop a walnut board resting on the green velvet coverlet. The opening salutation, "My Dearest Mother," caught my eye and, sinful or not, I was suddenly bent over, the flame of the table candle nearly touching my cheek, unable to stop reading.

"I am in receipt of your recent missive concerning Madison Elizabeth. I am most thankful for the care you have provided her in my absence. Hopefully, the current campaign will be concluded within the next month, and I can again assume responsibility for her. You need not fear for your granddaughter's future. It is my intent to again take a wife . . ."

My eyes froze on those last five words: "to again take a wife." Did Starkweather mean Erin Green? Hell's bells, who else could he mean? That explained why he had tracked every happening at the Green cart and continued to do so at the Green cabin. My heart raced crazily. Had he made me his aide-de-camp so he could . . .

Canvas rustled at the entryway. I lunged into Starkweather's leather-seated chair and commenced tugging at the tops of the boots he had loaned me as if demons were chasing me and I had to escape or perish. Lordy, lordy, had my shadow shown on the tent front and revealed me snooping in his private papers my very first hour of service?

But Jared, the servant, not Miles Starkweather, superior officer, slipped past the canvas sheeting. Jared smiled as though he had witnessed nothing out of the ordinary, and I beamed right back at him, my heartbeat no longer raging in my ears like a madly stroked drum. "Dinner be ready," the servant announced.

I followed Jared outside. Starkweather was seated at the overhang table, sipping red wine from a stemmed glass. Another place setting of china lay beside his own, arranged so that his guest would also be oriented to the fire. "Join me, Ensign. You may replace Ensign Young, who is absent for the evening. Mannered company is not abundant in the land of the savages, fair land though it be."

Never mind I had eaten earlier at the Dodd fire. I supped on an array of delicious fare, the tinned sardines and pickled oysters Andy Young had praised as well as others just as mouthwatering: beef braised with brandy and dried peaches, roasted hazelnuts, and fleshy papaws Jared must have gathered while we were off scouting. I made it through the meal without a major catastrophe, not a solitary noisy slurp or wet smacking of the lips or unseemly belch, the common accompaniment of borderers partaking at an open fire, by pretending to be at Mother's table where the rude were neither welcome nor tolerated. Maybe, as she had claimed at every correction the whole of my growing years, her careful scrutiny was actually part of some divine plan to prepare me for a later, higher destiny. I was more willing to embrace that view now than when under the lash of her tongue, a concession less difficult for me with each sumptuous sip of red wine.

"Perhaps coats are in order, given the chill air," the captain observed. Once ensconced in warm outer garments, we moved close to the fire and enjoyed a final glass of wine together while Jared cleared the table. Starkweather was in a mood to talk, and I sipped and listened without interruption.

"Serving in my command, Ensign, you'll visit General St. Clair's tent on occasion and be privy to vital information. You must keep what you hear in the strictest confidence or be summarily dismissed from my dragoons. Do you understand?"

At my nod, the captain resumed talking. "It's my desire that dragoon officers know as much as possible what confronts this army, and the future doesn't bode well. After all the equipment deficiencies and shortages suffered to date, we have discovered the osnaburg end flaps of the tents furnished both the regulars and levies weren't waterproof, and thousands of paper cartridges stored in them have been ruined by the damp. Thus, we could run shy of cartridges in a prolonged battle. Of more pressing concern, at their insistence, an entire company of Virginia levies was discharged the twentieth. The other levies, every company, claim their enlistment expires the last day of the month. Then there's the Kentucky militia. They continually defy the simplest order to do other than scout or stand guard, and suffer desertions what seems nightly. St. Clair's army is falling apart piecemeal on him. Before it's in tatters and total disarray, he must tighten the discipline and march farther north, far enough beyond this fort it would be more frightening for the levies to be discharged or the militia to desert rather than engage the enemy en masse."

Starkweather sipped wine from his glass. "Ensign Young is attending General St. Clair's meeting of field officers in my stead. It will be no surprise if the general plans a Monday march after the Sabbath observance tomorrow. That would leave him the disciplinary problems to solve prior to our departure, though the sated and full-bellied soldier tends to obey orders with an alacrity missing in those hungry and grouching," the captain related with a sweeping wave at the boisterously rowdy evening fires of his own dragoons.

The captain sighed. "The next northern march will be most dangerous for everyone connected with the army, particularly unarmed camp followers." His gaze sought mine. "Fortunately, the illness of Molly Green will result in her remaining behind, along with her daughter. According to Ensign Young, Annie Bower with her pistol and knife will afford a modicum of protection in our absence. If he agrees, I will hire your friend, Mr. Jacobs, to guard the Green cabin till the campaign comes to some conclusion. Would he be amenable to such a proposal, do you suppose?"

I drank the last inch of wine in my glass, certain now that Miles Starkweather was a most serious rival for the affections of Erin Green. He had no other earthly reason to provide for her safety once the army marched. But he wouldn't be alone with her for any length of time that I could foresee, and if I couldn't stand watch over Erin my ownself, Tap was the next best thing. He would say or do nothing that would diminish my stature, howsomever slight that might be, with the woman I loved. I was learning. The underdog had to seize opportunity whenever he could and advance his cause by whatever means available.

"Tap pursues whatever whim strikes him," I said calm as I could. "If Paw will allow it, he might prefer a stretch of guard duty rather than the long traipse back to Fort Hamilton."

"That's most promising," Starkweather responded. "Ensign Young was to deliver my proposal to Mr. Jacobs once the meeting at the general's headquarters concluded." The captain stood, and I did likewise. "The ensign should be joining us within the half hour. In the meantime, you best picket your mount and place your blankets in Jared's tent."

After a proper knuckling of forehead and profuse thanks for the elegant dining, I led Blue along the fringe of the trees to where Starkweather's sorrel and a score of other horses were being guarded by a detail of dragoons. I then carted my saddle and gear to Jared's tent adjoining the captain's marquee. The structure was large enough to sleep four men, a satisfying discovery, as I'd no desire to have my presence create a hardship for the kindly servant.

When I emerged from Jared's tent, Andy Young, dispatch pouch in hand, was dismounting from his gray mare at the fire. The ensign stretched tired legs and saluted the captain. "Reporting as ordered, sir," he announced, catching my approach out of the corner of his eye. He hesitated at that juncture, unsure if he should speak in front of me.

"You may continue, Ensign," Starkweather assured him,

accepting the dispatch pouch. "Mr. Downer is now Ensign Downer, First Volunteer Dragoons. Much to my delight, he will serve as my aide-de-camp the balance of the campaign."

The momentary tightening of Andy Young's features hinted he would have many questions for me later. For now, his reply was most direct. "As you wish, sir."

Without instruction, Jared had fetched Starkweather's writing chair from within the marquee, and we seated ourselves around the fire, the servant seeing to the ensign's mount. At Starkweather's nod, Andy Young proceeded with his report. "As you anticipated, General St. Clair has imposed the death penalty on three soldiers; two artillerymen for attempting to desert to the British and a levy private for shooting a comrade and threatening an officer. They will be hung at dawn before the entire army," the ensign said solemnly. "Capital punishment will henceforth be the reward for any who abandon the colors."

"He has no druthers," Starkweather interjected. "An undisciplined rabble is an army begging for defeat. Let us pray these deaths won't be in vain. Any decision as to when we will resume our northern march?"

"As close after sunrise as possible, day after tomorrow. The fort will be christened Jefferson the same morning in honor of that esteemed Virginian. A fatigue of those too sick or infirm to accompany us will remain behind and garrison the fort."

Starkweather leaned forward in his chair. "And the rest of your business for the evening?"

"I located Mr. Jacobs. He was at the Dodd horse camp in the west meadow. I arrived there and found all was in an uproar," Andy Young said, glancing anxiously in my direction. "Mr. Jacobs informed me Court Starnes and Ensign Downer's father had engaged in a tremendous fight."

Starkweather came upright as did I, my breath running shallow on me. Had Paw been hurt? Killed, God forbid?

"Is Paw all right?" I blurted.

"Yes, it seems Mr. Watkins and Mr. Jacobs, along with two wagoners, interceded and stopped the fight. Your father is alive, but like Starnes, he suffered a frightful beating. Mr. Jacobs told me your father will bear scars forever but will recover fully, though it will take some weeks. I dislike telling you, but Starnes was still on his feet when the fight was halted, and he went berserk, according to Mr. Jacobs. He grabbed up a pistol and ordered your father and all associated with him back to Fort Hamilton without delay."

"But Paw shouldn't travel hurt like he is," I protested.

"He won't," the ensign assured me. "Mr. Jacobs tossed Mr. Watkins a rifle, and he confronted Starnes, ordering him to drop the pistol. Starnes finally did so, and Mr. Watkins then said your father would be removed to a separate camp. That's when I arrived."

"Where's Paw now?"

"Farther into the west meadow near the creek. Mr. Watkins, Mr. Jacobs, and the wagoners are with him."

I was reluctant to ask but couldn't stand not knowing. I braced myself and said, "What provoked the fight? Did Tap say?"

The ensign's eyes lowered, then raised to meet mine. "Yes, Court Starnes accused you of being a coward. He claimed only a coward would break a man's jaw with a sneak punch, and your father took offense. When Starnes refused to retract his allegation, your father went for him."

I looked away quickly and stared into the darkness beyond the roof of the marquee. What an infernal mess I had made of my affairs and those of Paw. It was a hellish long journey for a single day, but I had gone from hero in the morning to disloyal and spurned son in the evening, and I had managed to drag Paw down into the foul dirt and piss beneath the woods skunk with me. If there was a being lower than me, he was already burning in the eternal fires of damnation. Damn love to hell and gone, anyway.

"Do you wish to visit your father, Ensign?" Starkweather inquired.

In spite of Paw's desperate situation, wounded feelings, though far less hurtful, shackled me to my chair. "No, sir, not tonight," I said, voice on the verge of cracking.

Though my decision had to puzzle Starkweather, as usual, he didn't pry. "Well and good, Ensign. Gentlemen, given the lateness of the hour, I suggest we retire."

The captain's suggestion suited me just fine. There being

no hole for me to crawl into and bury myself, a pair of blankets in an unlighted tent was the next best thing. Thank God, Andy Young, who also shared Jared's tent, exhibited the same respect for the privacy of others as the captain, and with a soft "Good night," he crawled into his own makeshift bed.

I was too old to cry myself to sleep, but I was no less miserable. And when I did doze, it was fitfully, for I dreamed over and over I was astride Blue, friendless, loveless, and horribly alone, riding an endless trail that led nowhere.

Chapter 24

23 October

I awakened mean and ill of spirit in the tattered gray of first light. I vaguely heard Andy Young mutter, "Drum call," and a dull thumping as he stomped into his boots. His hand suddenly clasped my shoulder. "Best be coming alive. Captain Starkweather never wastes a sliver of daylight."

I unwound from about my rifle and staggered upright. Footfalls thundered in the meadow, Starkweather's troop forming the morning parade. I roused myself with a thorough shaking of head and limb, slipped into my own boots, tugged my new new helmet in place, and bolted after Andy Young, vowing there would be no oversleeping in the future. Without thinking on it, I knew Starkweather, as my superior officer, would be no less exacting than Paw, and the wise bird didn't foul the only nest available to him.

Luck smiled on me that first parade. I was unschooled as a soldier, and while I held my rifle properly across my chest, the weapon was not presented at half cock with the frizzen open. But the captain's cursory inspection of each dragoon that morning did not extend to a close look at our long guns in the weak light of the overcast dawn. I made myself a second vow then and there: No detail of dragoon duty would ever be too small for my attention.

The captain's haste that early dawn stemmed from the executions that would shortly occur. Starkweather read St. Clair's condemning order aloud, a document he had received in the evening message pouch delivered by Ensign Young. After his strong, deliberate reading, the troop marched afoot from the meadow and aligned itself shoulder to shoulder with the closely ranked companies of the First American Regiment. From that location abutting and well up the military road leading to the front gates of the newly named Fort Jefferson, we enjoyed an unobstructed view of what followed in grimmest detail.

At the final tally, nearly nineteen hundred regulars, levies, militia, artillerymen, and dragoons were present at the grand parade and watched the whole sorry spectacle unfold at sunrise. The limbs of a towering oak, jutting stark and powerful against a backdrop of walled fort and low, gray sky, served as the gallows. Though it was impossible, at the dreaded carrying out of St. Clair's order, it seemed we heard the necks of the three condemned snap in unison as the arm of the executioner fell in a sudden, silent arc to the accompaniment of a tremendous drum roll. The sight of three pairs of legs kicking and stiffening for naught seared itself in my memory to the final breath of my life.

But St. Clair wasn't finished, for next came the punishment of the living. The comrade who had lost his desire to join the British and snitched on the two hanged artillerymen was bound to the whipping post and given one hundred lashes, the whip slicing his bare white backside into a trough of red meat. No less bloody were the three soldiers subsequently given fifty lashes each for falling asleep on sentry duty. The dismissal drum sounded none too soon, for at the last fall of the whip, every member of the watching multitude was thoroughly and completely impressed with the absolute military authority of Major General Arthur St. Clair and his fellow officers.

The sunrise executions and punishments lent a lingering sadness to that entire Sabbath. Gone was the exuberance spawned by the arrival of the pack train the previous evening, for no amount of bread or whiskey or cooked beef could lighten the mood of a subdued army when word was in the air it would march deeper into enemy country on the morrow. And being melancholy about what I had witnessed, I weakened and took to dwelling on Paw and how he was and whether I dared ask permission to visit him. But the captain negated the question by involving the entire troop in a whirl of activity that consumed the daylight hours in rapid succession.

Every horseshoe nail, saddle girth, and bridle, every rifle barrel, lock, and flint, every ball and ounce of powder, every sword hilt, blade, and scabbard, every boot heel, spur, button, and helmet, every blanket roll, victuals pouch, and canteen was examined, cleaned, repaired, oiled, sharpened or replaced as needed and inspected thrice, first by each dragoon, then the sergeants, then the captain himself. With our animals and equipment in proper order, we then scavenged the surrounding woods in pairs the entire afternoon and somehow procured enough meadow grass both to feed our mounts for the day and accumulate a meager stock to be borne with us upon the Monday march. Dusk found us tired and hungry before the evening fires, and here new surprises from the captain awaited me.

Jared was preparing to serve dinner, and I was fit to burst about Paw when Starkweather strode from his marquee in possession of a sword and its shoulder scabbard. "Ensign Downer, I believe we omitted a major accoutrement that distinguishes the dragoon from his fellow combatants. Please accept this with my most earnest apology."

I was taken aback, for I had never before so much as toted a sword, and the wielding of a long knife during a charge on horseback was as foreign to me as Frog curse words, a truth I readily stammered to Starkweather. The captain dismissed my qualms with the wave of a gloved hand and bade I take receipt of his gift, which I did. "I'll teach you proper conduct with the blade," he promised. "And Ensign Young, being an excellent swordsman, will augment my teachings. The essentials will come easy to a man of your determination."

I decided a nod of acceptance instead of an awkward thanks would suffice, and the moment not feeling right to request I take leave of the captain's company on personal matters, I held my tongue altogether. I laid the gift sword carefully aside, and we seated ourselves at the table, Ensign Young and I bracing the captain. We dined in silence, guilt over the neglecting of Paw souring my appetite, till the distant blast of a firing musket lifted our heads. Two additional shots followed on the heels of the first, the echoes rolling flat across the meadow.

Starkweather, never so much as flinching, calmly sat his wineglass on the velvet coverlet of the table. "As the Lord is my witness, nerves are certainly of a tremble. Enough to frighten the venerable owl from his perch, hey, my young men," he ventured.

We laughed with the captain, Andy Young taking particular delight in Starkweather's humor. "General St. Clair remarked just yesterday, sir, that he prefers an attack by the savages to enduring the judgment of our sentries in the dark."

"And since I was not in attendance at St. Clair's tent again today, what was the tone there after the hangings, Ensign?"

Andy Young's face smoothed. "Most solemn, sir. But of greater importance is the vicious rift amongst those reporting to General St. Clair."

"I am aware of certain disagreements and dislikes. Have you heard anything new in that regard?"

"Yes, sir, just this afternoon. Rumor has it General Butler requested privately of General St. Clair two days ago that he be permitted to proceed ahead with a thousand picked men and surprise the Shawnee in their villages before winter sets in. General St. Clair refused to grant his request serious consideration, and General Butler left the headquarters tent angry and insulted. He now hardly speaks to General St. Clair."

Starkweather's lengthy sigh pumped his chest up, then down. "Meaning no disrespect to our commanding officer, given the late date and our myriad problems, Butler's strategy has considerable merit. Never forget, gentlemen, discord at the highest rank is the unwitting ally of dissension in the lowest. It can cripple a campaign as fully as the enemy without." The captain refilled his glass along with ours. "And what of your other business, Ensign?"

"I visited the Dodd camp at noon, sir."

My wineglass stopped short of my mouth, and my ears opened wide. Maybe Andy Young had news of Paw. It was like Starkweather to inquire of his own volition.

The ensign didn't disappoint me. At Starkweather's

prompting, he continued. "Ensign Downer's father departed for Fort Hamilton before dawn, sir. Mr. Watkins and Mr. Jacobs accompanied him."

A great weight fled my body. Paw had proven spry enough to ride, despite his injuries. Now I had only to deal with the guilt of my failure to rush to his side after the fight with Starnes. Funny how happenstance often saved a man from his own shortcomings.

"And the others in Dodd's camp?" Starkweather asked.

"Starnes and the balance of the Duer men are resting their pack animals. They will return south in the morning."

Starkweather bit at his lip, assessing possibilities as I was. "Ensign Downer, I pray for the sake of us soldiers that Starnes and your father fulfill their obligations. Supplies are still the major question once our march resumes."

Distant as I was from Paw now, I wouldn't have him doubted because of our separation. "Never you fear, sir, duty comes before all else with Caleb Downer. To that, I can freely attest."

"I misspoke, Ensign. It's not your father I question but those most closely tied to William Duer, namely Court Starnes and his ilk," the captain responded with utter frankness. "There will be a legal reckoning someday to set right the wrongs done the army these past months. It is my hope your father will bear witness against those at fault."

Andy Young and I exchanged glances. To my knowledge, Andy hadn't shared the facts of Starnes's Fort Washington thievery with the captain. But Starkweather was a clever fellow who, like Paw, missed nothing about him. Maybe Court Starnes would yet face the judge for his misdeeds. My worry in that regard was that Paw would somehow be unfairly painted with the same brush as the guilty.

"Ensign Young, I believe you have other business to report," Starkweather prodded.

"Yes, sir," Andy Young responded instantly, accidentally dribbling wine down his chin. The ensign grinned sheepishly and dried the errant drizzle from skin and clothing with the flat of his palm. "I visited the Green cabin early this afternoon as ordered."

My ears shot straight up as did my frame, and I

couldn't help but lean toward him. I swear Starkweather straightened somewhat also, though I may have imagined it. An old admonition of Mother's flashed to mind: Less'n wisdom prevailed, jealousy bred bad blood twixt the finest of humankind.

"I am pleased to report Molly Green has taken a decided turn for the better," Andy Young said. "Annie Bower observed a smile on her face when she predicted she would soon rise from the sickbed."

Starkweather grimaced at the mere mention of the harlot. "And how are those about her faring?"

Andy Young chose his wording carefully, as if utmost accuracy was expected of him. "Sergeant Devlin is mostly beside himself. He does not relish having to leave his beloved in the care of others, devoted though they are."

"The sergeant should be thankful she will be spared the rigors of the march in commodious quarters," Starkweather snapped. "And the daughter. What of her?"

The captain's avoidance of Erin's name appeared deliberate. Was he trying to sound impersonal to hide an abiding personal interest?

"Erin frets no less than Sergeant Devlin but displays her usual spunk," Andy Young said. "She cannot countenance other than a complete recovery by her mother."

"Yes, the daughter is quite remarkable for her unflagging fortitude as well as her beauty," Starkweather stated admiringly. "The finest gentleman would be proud to have her on his arm."

And was that arm to belong to the handsome Miles Starkweather, who intended to take another wife? I thought it but felt less of myself for doing so. I was beginning to understand the hazards of a totally consuming love. Maybe it required a bigger and wiser man than I to love so profoundly and completely and not have that love prove your ruination.

In a giddy rush, a wild urge to lay eyes on Erin Green the slimmest of minutes beset me, nearly overwhelming my senses. I could barely restrain myself. If I couldn't hold her and kiss her, I at least had to sight her from afar, at least wave good-bye to her. And I was suddenly afraid the morning with all its final preparations to march would be too late.

Her whereabouts were no mystery. Andy Young, it was, had early on pointed out the mud and wattle chimney barely visible within the fringe of trees bordering the south rim of the eastern meadow. I had glanced that direction the entire morning, vainly seeking a glimpse of flame-red hair. But disappointment had ruled the day and was destined to reign through the evening. Before I could ask permission to take leave of the dragoon camp, Starkweather terminated our dinner with a most restrictive command. "To bed with you, gentlemen. All members of the troop, including officers, are confined to camp till our departure. I will hear no requests to the contrary and will punish violations to the full." Starkweather rose from his chair and called, "Jared, you may clear the table."

I suffered another fitful, restless night. Everything touching upon me was in complete turmoil. The father I loved, admired, and respected had disowned me, then suffered serious injuries defending my name. But even if I wanted to achieve some reconciliation with him, he was away and gone, riding south opposite my future line of travel. And the longer we stayed apart, the greater the odds our mutual stubbornness would preclude us ever seeing eye to eye again.

Separation from the girl I loved made every beat of my heart doubly painful and aching. I wasn't certain Erin Green returned my love, and the upcoming march northward with the First Dragoons would forestall any chance to even talk with her for perhaps weeks. Hadn't other men been forgotten or bested during shorter absences?

I moaned in my blankets. An additional torture was my fear for Erin's safety till the army returned. Only the infirm and the unfit would remain behind to garrison Fort Jefferson, and the Injuns could appear anywhere at any time. Starkweather had intended to hire Tap to guard the Green cabin while the army was away. But Paw's brawl with Court Starnes had inadvertently drawn Tap elsewhere.

I tossed and turned and schemed, but every path circled

back upon itself. Starkweather's oath had me snared tight as a steel trap. There would be no peace for me till St. Clair's army did battle with the Shawnee . . . and only then if I survived the fight.

Part IV
The March Resumed

Chapter 25

24 October till 28 October

The dream just prior to dawn was the worst. I relived the ghastly military executions, and in my mind's eye the lifeless middle body, face purple and bloated, was none other than that of Ethan Downer, hung, not for deserting the First Dragoons, but his father. I jerked awake scared and shaking, awash in cold sweat.

I discovered the blubbery groans I heard were my own and, stifling them, glanced frantically at the other occupants of the tent. Andy Young slept soundly beside me, and Jared snored merrily near the front entryway. Grateful I had not awakened them screeching like a child frightened by his own nightmares, I pulled my blanket tighter about me and lay quietly in wait of the morning drum.

Mother had always been wont to warn, cast a stone upon still waters and the ripples from the splash will roll to the bank steady as the sun crosses the sky from morning to night. I had by choice made of myself a dragoon, and there would be no more wayward, willful pursuit of personal whims and feelings for any cause, no matter how just or proper. The punishment now wasn't banishment to Kentucky but the whip or, God forbid, the hanging rope.

On that Monday, 24 October, with me gaining nary a peek at flame-red hair, St. Clair's army, resembling some serpentine monster with bristling head and countless legs, crept forward at nine of the A.M., traveling the northern-bound Injun path the First Dragoons had scouted three days before. Six miles later, at the stream of forty feet where we had located lean-tos recently frequented by the

Shawnee, the army ground to a halt and deposed itself in two lines with the artillery and cavalry upon the right and left, and the militia in the rear. General St. Clair then determined his forces were, despite the recent Starnes shipment, insufficiently supplied with flour and beef for any extended forward movement, and the intended overnight camp stretched to five full days.

It was a goodly thing devotion to duty had come to the fore of my thinking, for Miles Starkweather now proved himself the ultimate taskmaster, more exacting than even Paw. We burst from our blankets before first light, and training and foraging filled most every minute of daylight. No matter the hour, we maintained a constant guard detail whether in camp or afield. The captain's aversion to surprise became the Bible by which we sucked each breath and made the tiniest move.

He scouted out a large meadow to the west and drilled us on horseback, rain or shine. The first morning he presented me with one final, last piece of gear: a chest sling to hold my rifle on my backside with its stock behind my left shoulder and the barrel protruding past my right hip. He then taught me the elements of the mounted attack. I learned how to draw my sword without endangering myself or Blue's ears. I learned how to grip Blue tightly with my knees and slash full force at grass-filled sacks shaped like red enemies and tied upright before buried posts. I learned to disdain the tempting skull of the head and target the soft curve of the neck. I learned with diligent practice how to roll my wrist after impact and free my blade with an upward slice through bone, flesh, and arteries. The sword was a fearsome weapon, and I gained greater respect for it and the horse beneath me with each charge. Blue never once faltered or shied from the would-be enemies, the galloping animals flanking him, or the thudding strike of strange steel. Indeed, he relished the morning dashes to the target, the quick spins, and return passes.

Starkweather took note of Blue's superb performance and inquired as to his breeding lineage and temperament. He was no less serious about the daily tending of our mounts. Dawn and dusk we inspected from teeth to tail and backbone to hoof for sores, swelling, lameness, and loose shoes. After morning drill, we traipsed the meadows every afternoon to secure adequate forage. While other army horses frequently perished due to poor treatment and starvation, the mounts of the First Dragoons, except those lost in battle and to accident, survived the campaign. Starkweather supposedly buried men easier than he did the four-legged, and I for one, believed it.

We escaped the captain's rigorous fervor for constant activity only at the evening meal. Unlike other high-ranking officers who had continued to burden the few remaining pack animals and horse-drawn wagons still available to the army with their personal possessions, Starkweather had stored his marquee tent with its cherry bed and brass bathing tub at Fort Jefferson. We dined nightly, therefore, under a single canvas awning aligned to shun wind and rain. Jared seemed more put out than did his master that we ate now on plates of tin instead of china and drank from cups of the same metal in lieu of stemmed glasses. Somehow the servant had brought forward a few tins of sardines, a small crock of pickled oysters, and select bottles of wine, but his demeanor grew morose as his meager private stores dwindled, and we became increasingly dependent on the army for our rations.

Andy Young visited General St. Clair's headquarters daily at dusk and returned to the Starkweather awning post haste with whatever news he obtained. Not surprisingly, the captain's prime interest each evening centered on any reported sighting of the enemy as well as the current prediction as to when fresh provisions would arrive from Fort Jefferson. It was on 28 October that Andy Young, toting a sizable cloth sack and a clay jug, joined the captain and me in a state of excitement. "Pack train bearing twelve thousand pounds of flour and whiskey showed earlier while we were foraging."

Starkweather, seated at the fire, frowned. "Only twelve thousand pounds. That's but a four-day supply."

The ensign laid his cloth sack in Jared's arms, and the servant hustled with it to kneading board and metal baking oven. "Yes, and Court Starnes, who brought the pack train into camp, wasn't exactly precise about future shipments, which naturally infuriated General St. Clair," Andy Young related, tugging the wooden bung from his clay jug.

Starkweather bleakly eyed the green tea in his tin cup, a brew he drank for its warmth, not its taste. He extended his cup, and the ensign carefully topped its contents with a dollop of raw whiskey. "The lack of wine is a mortal shortcoming," the captain lamented after a hefty drink. "St. Clair put three hundred army horses at Starnes's beck and call, yet he can't meet the general's requirements of one hundred fifty loads of flour every seven days. What's his excuse?"

Andy Young passed me the whiskey jug and poured himself a steaming cup of tea. "Starnes says there was much confusion and stealing at Fort Washington before he arrived from Fort Pitt. He said he couldn't be faulted for the misdeeds and failings of others. He vowed he would return south at daybreak to insure all necessary actions are taken to satisfy the general."

I grasped the whiskey jug tightly so neither the ensign nor Starkweather spied my shaking hands. Damn Court Starnes to hell, anyway. He was not only the true culprit but also a bold and artful liar. Paw had toiled day and night organizing the welter of animals and supplies that flowed haphazardly into Cincinnati from Starnes's yards at Fort Pitt and elsewhere along the Ohio. He had made order out of utter chaos, preserving every item received. Now the person who had stolen what never really existed was falsely portraying Paw's tireless efforts as erratic bungling and thievery. I slugged whiskey in a gulping swallow. It irked me royally how an unscrupulous rogue like Starnes could seemingly turn every trying situation to his advantage with a glib tongue.

There was much I wanted to ask of the ensign, like who had accompanied Starnes into camp and what might they know of those staying behind at Fort Jefferson, but Starkweather's questioning took precedence. "Did Starnes speculate as to when additional provisions might be forthcoming?"

"He claimed a large shipment borne by two hundred horses is plying the road twixt Forts Hamilton and Jefferson, a claim the general's couriers haven't substantiated."

"Then the army is to stand idle?"

"General St. Clair's too crippled with the gout to travel. We will remain encamped for another day, but the deputy surveyor and a fatigue party of one hundred twenty will open a road tomorrow. A detail of twenty friendly Chickasaws will be dispatched to reconnoiter the country ahead in hopes of locating the enemy and perhaps take an Indian prisoner."

Starkweather sighed. "Well, thank God, we're finally demonstrating genuine interest in finding the redsticks. But idleness is the soul mate of shiftlessness. It destroys an army's resolve. What is the mood of the levies?"

"They're threatening mutiny once more. Their enlistments expire on the first day of the month, if not before, and Adjutant General Sargent believes nothing will keep them from showing their heels. He believes the militia will follow them to the man, that is, if the Kentuckians don't bolt first."

Starkweather sipped from his cup and stared at the fire. "The horns of General St. Clair's dilemma are particularly sharp, my young buckos. If he advances with a weakened, hunger-stricken army and suffers defeat, he will be reviled and condemned by his superiors. If he retreats without a fight, he will be equally condemned."

Andy Young couldn't contain himself. "What would you do, Captain?"

"An army gains nothing by retreating. I would undertake forced marches every dawn. The needed provisions will overtake us, and besides, men if they must can fight on an empty belly. General Butler was correct. Every day General St. Clair doesn't advance, his chance of engaging the enemy with suitable numbers at his disposal diminishes accordingly. And if we can't bring the Shawnee to battle, we must destroy their villages on the Saint Mary's and establish a fort in their stead before retiring from the field. It is the least expected of us by President Washington."

With that sobering assessment, we grew quiet, and little else was said throughout our evening meal, the high points being the jug whiskey and Jared's freshly baked bread. I bided my time and finally had an opportunity to talk privately with Andy Young during midnight sentry duty, a chore Starkweather rotated among his troop regardless of rank. What I learned from Andy Young was to keep my nerves on edge the next several days, for as I had feared, Erin Green was not safe at Fort Jefferson, and the danger came from a totally unexpected quarter.

Our exchange began harmlessly enough with my asking, "Who rode into camp with Court Starnes?"

"The tall thin one with the bandaged jaw, Hookfin, and the stubby horse master, Val Dodd. The others I didn't recognize. No sign of your father or those in his direct hire."

"I was hoping Tap or Bear was with the pack train, and you might inquire of him how Erin Green's mother is faring," I admitted, my disappointment obvious.

"Or more likely Erin herself, huh, my friend?" the ensign countered.

Andy Young's head lowered, and even in the dark I could tell he was studying his own booted feet. Did he know something about the mistress he wasn't sharing? And if that were true, why was he being secretive? Had she been hurt or worse?

He was quiet for the longest of minutes. I stayed my tongue, afraid the simplest noise might convince him he should remain silent. Then, with a shrug of his shoulders, he cleared his throat. "Ethan, I must have your word that if I reveal what happened as I departed St. Clair's headquarters, you will curb your temper and not abandon your post. I must have your promise for your own protection. Starkweather wouldn't hesitate to hang an aide-de-camp for desertion. Do I have it?" Andy Young demanded, voice lifting.

I'd no choice but to honor his request, for he had me so het up, I was suddenly standing tiptoed. "Yes, damn it, you've my word! Now, tell me!"

And with a deep breath, Andy Young yielded. "First, let me assure you Erin has not been hurt or suffered harm in any way. But the thin one, Hookfin, was at the general's tent with Court Starnes. He saw me waiting outside and sidled over beside me. He has learned of our acquaintance, for he had an urgent message he wanted carried to you. Not wanting to appear rude, I'd no choice but to listen. It seems Starnes encountered the mistress at the Fort Jefferson spring, the same spring where the deserters kidnapped her, and he was taken aback by her beauty."

My tongue broke free. "He didn't—"

Andy Young raised a placating hand. "No, Starnes did nothing that offended or frightened her. Had he done so, I'm certain Hookfin would have been most happy to inform me in great detail and thus gain a measure of revenge for your unfortunate punching of him. What the miserable blade of a dog did impart was Starnes's bold brag that no matter the outcome of the campaign, he will have Erin for his own ahead of every man alive."

My heart thumped wildly, and I suddenly had to swallow. Starnes's boast couldn't be dismissed as a casual brag from someone overwhelmed by a woman's beauty, meaningless prattle spoken in admiration on the spur of the moment. Coming from Starnes, a brazen, powerful bastard capable of killing and maiming if he couldn't secure what he desired by sly, peaceful deceptions, such a boast was a serious threat to Erin's well-being, perhaps her life, if she resisted him, which she would, come what may.

"You haven't told Captain Starkweather?"

"No, I have not," Andy Young responded. "He has enough of a burden preparing the troop for what lies ahead to fret about matters occurring to our rear. Frankly, I believe we can warn the mistress by our own devices."

He was after what I craved the most, and my interest in what he was proposing swelled like wind filling a sail. "I'm all ears," I assured him.

"I'll be visiting St. Clair's headquarters before dawn for new orders on behalf of the captain. I will arrange for you to accompany me on the pretext you may need to do so alone in the future. On our return, we will seek out Val Dodd. I recall Tap Jacobs remarking that Mr. Dodd is trustworthy, despite the source of his pay. Is that not correct?"

"Yes, we can trust Val Dodd to do what is right by us."

"Excellent. We will ask him to not only warn Erin Green

and those guarding her but also convey our worries to Mr. Jacobs. Your friend wasn't with the Starnes train but should course past Fort Jefferson with the larger shipment Starnes described to General St. Clair."

Whether by oversight or design, Andy Young had not seen fit to make Paw aware of our private scheme to warn Erin, which was just as well in light of how my spontaneous rescuing of her had fostered the discord bedeviling the two of us. The worst eventuality would be for Paw to order Tap to steer clear of troubles not of his concern or making. At the bottom stair, given his undeniable fondness for her, I was counting on the old scout to keep some form of watch over the mistress till the army undertook its retreat.

Hobbled horses stirred behind us. We came alert, rifles at the ready, and two dragoons, our relief, emerged from the chill night. We relinquished our post with proper salutes, a requirement and not mere formality in a command as strict as that of Miles Starkweather.

The perpetual northwest wind was blowing briskly enough to bend tree branches, and we walked just as briskly to Jared's spent fire, a pile of bright embers and gray ash at this late hour. Morning drum wasn't far off, and Andy Young and I spared ourselves unnecessary good nights, slipping quickly into the servant's tent, accommodations we now shared with the captain himself. Starkweather was sound asleep in the upper portion beneath his wolf pelts, an amenity he refused to surrender. Jared flanked him, wrapped in a simple wool blanket and snoring merrily as always. Andy Young and I bedded down at their feet.

The ensign dozed off in a flash, his snores as rank and honking as those of Jared. Me, I lay awake for a spell, praying at length on behalf of Erin Green. I prayed over and over that the Lord would bless her above all others. I prayed an equal number of times that the Lord would watch over her and protect her against those who would take advantage of her till I could assume that duty myself.

A man need be careful of what he asks from his maker. I will never be so haughty as to intimate the Lord heard my prayers that late night and deigned to answer them.

Nevertheless, either at his behest or by a quirk of fate, I was to find myself in the presence of my beloved Erin Green sooner than I would have imagined possible, and in circumstances that imperiled both our lives.

Chapter 26

29 October till 3 November

To insure we intercepted Valentine Dodd before the Starnes crew took their leave, Andy Young altered our orders to proceed directly to St. Clair's headquarters after morning parade and rode instead for the packhorse camp. The ensign further surprised me by not stating his intentions to Captain Starkweather, who was occupied at that early hour updating his journal. The ensign's willful breaching of his orders was solid proof Andy Young loved the mistress no less than I.

We walked our horses south along the western perimeter of the main army encampment, passing the breakfast fires of the discontented levy battalions, the small bullock herd that had to date escaped the butcher's knife, then the haphazard collection of carts and wagons at the rear belonging to the hundred or so civilians still tagging after St. Clair's forces. The specter of women and children huddled in shivering clusters to ward off the morning cold reminded me again how grand it was Erin and her mother were ensconced in a snug, warm cabin downcountry.

The Starnes campsite butted against a thick copse of hickory shorn almost entirely of leaves. We arrived just in the nick of time, for the horse crew had extinguished their fire and were stringing out their animals for the day's journey. Val Dodd was at the near end of the line. Much farther along, at the head of the entire string, I could make out Court Starnes, mounted on a huge white-stockinged horse black of hair and rippling with muscle. The detestable Hookfin was nowhere to be seen.

Val Dodd's brief smile of greeting wrinkled his thin mustache. "Good morning, Monsieur Downer, and you, too, Ensign Young. To what do I owe your company this gray thing of a morning?"

Since we were out of earshot of the Starnes crew, Andy Young stated our business right off. "Mr. Dodd, we assume you are aware Court Starnes has bragged openly he will have Mistress Green for his own, despite any objections she or others may raise to the contrary. Is this so?"

Dodd's smile vanished and he glanced quickly in the direction of Starnes. "Yes, not from his lips, but those of Gabe Hookfin."

"Do you believe he would take the girl by force if that were required?"

"Yes," Dodd answered, head nodding slowly. "Starnes is a brute loose amongst what he counts a herd of sheep. He is a scabrous beast. His sole mission is to wreak vengeance on Ethan's father, the only man to nearly whip him in a fair fight. How better if he steals the beautiful woman holding the heart of his enemy's son, I ask you."

"But Paw doesn't know of my feelings for Erin," I objected.

"Perhaps, but thanks to his faithful puppy Hookfin, Court Starnes does, and he will act accordingly," Dodd replied. "He not only craves to destroy his particular enemies but all near and dear to them as well. Never have I witnessed hatred so monumental and unforgiving, never."

Dodd glanced down the long line of packhorses again. "Talk quickly, Ensign Young. We're about to have company."

Court Starnes, his features still showing the damage of his fight with Paw, was indeed bound our way. "Please call upon Mistress Green and warn her of Starnes's vile brag. She must not be caught alone and unawares. It would be most helpful," Andy Young finished hurriedly, "if you would alert Tap Jacobs as to her predicament."

"Consider it done, gentlemen," Dodd promised over the thud of approaching hooves.

Court Starnes reined his huge black horse to a halt. His swollen blue eyes impaled Andy Young and me. There was nothing friendly in the rigid set of his bruised Roman jaw or the musket slanting across his broad chest. His right hand was of such immense size that it smothered the whole of the musket's lock. "Trouble, Dodd?" he boomed.

"No, monsieur, just a chat twixt acquaintances," Dodd said softly.

"What about?" Starnes demanded, puffed lips slurring his speech slightly.

"Their superior, Captain Starkweather of the First Dragoons, insisted they inquire as to when our next shipment will arrive," the horse master lied. "Their captain is most impatient to move north and engage the Shawnee."

"He's a fool then, a dead fool he don't come to rightfully fear the redsticks. Tell your fool of a captain the largest pack train he's ever seen be three days' travel south of here. We're away, Dodd," Starnes announced brusquely, waving his waiting crew into motion.

With a farewell wag of his arm, Val Dodd obediently moved off, but Starnes sat his huge black horse, watching me closely. "You can depend upon something from me without your asking, Downer. I'll be sure and mention to a certain young red-haired gal soon as I see her how we met up this morning, it being sort of unexpected like and all."

His riling barb successfully launched, Starnes reined the big black abruptly about and rode after Val Dodd. I closed my eyes and held stone still, gripping the stock of my long gun so tightly my knuckles throbbed with pain. Had I looked after him or moved, I would have blown a hole plumb through his retreating backside then and there. "Never let me alone with him, Lord," I murmured, " 'cause fair or foul, I'll shoot the bastard in a heartbeat."

Fingers clasped my elbow. "I admire your restraint, Ethan. I thought of shooting him myself. But neither of us would be of any benefit to the mistress if we were to be hung, would we now?"

"No, that we wouldn't," I allowed, opening my eyes.

"Well and good. We have dispatched our warning, and we best hustle to the general's headquarters before we're tardy and incur the captain's wrath."

Our ride around the eastern perimeter of the main encampment out of Starkweather's sight did little to brighten

the melancholy that seeped over me. It saddened my spirits
that events had come full circle. I had started out rescuing
Erin Green from captors first red of skin, then white. Now
her association with me placed her in perhaps the greatest
jeopardy yet. Maybe I should have accepted Paw's punishment and gone home to Kentucky and been less of a bother
for all concerned. Just maybe.

My spirits did brighten a degree once we were caught up
in the bustle and gravity attending General St. Clair's headquarters. His marquee, centering a circle of smaller tents,
lacked the size and colorful striping of Starkweather's, but it
was evident from the constant comings and goings of officers
of high and significant rank that the truly important decisions
influencing the fate of our campaign were rendered beneath
that peaked roof. The marquee and its frontal environs endured a multitude of bodies, and my solitary glimpse of our
commander-in-chief was achieved quite by accident. A trio
of First American Regiment officers had just stepped forth,
and past their vacating bodies I spied General St. Clair and
witnessed the truth of his health. A wide swatch of bandage
circling his neck encased his left arm, and his coloring from
throat to forehead matched the sickly pallor of his frazzled
gray wig. The undersides of his eyes were black as midnight.
He was dressed in an unbuttoned vest, rumpled linen shirt,
breeches, and green slippers without heels. Two aides, their
faces puffing from strain and the efforts of one virtually
thwarted by the general's bandaged limb, supported his
bulky, unwieldy frame as he lowered himself onto a canvas
stool that sagged under his considerable weight. Major General Arthur St. Clair was most unimpressive this morning,
the farthest cry possible from the magnificently uniformed
and stalwart officer Tap and I had encountered on our ride
to the Ohio a mere twenty days before. Inexperienced I might
be, but it couldn't bode well for any army when its
commander-in-chief was too crippled with gout to sit his
horse.

A tug of my sleeve dispelled my stare and turned my
attention to other matters. Andy Young bore a bright smile.
"Major Hamtramack has confirmed we will march tomorrow
if the general's personal messengers signify the precise lo-

cation of the next pack train by evening today. He will accept but the word of his couriers, having lost complete confidence in the contractors. All companies, foot and mounted, are to be prepared to march on short notice. We best advise the captain. It's never wise to tax his patience."

I mounted Blue, and the ensign swung aboard his gray mare. "Can the general travel, bad off as he seems?" I inquired.

"Blessing, his servant, says he will be carried in a canvas sling twixt two horses, much like a corpse. The officers are betting as to how many of them will be required to lift him from the ground."

I chose not to embellish that unholy picture of absolute embarrassment for the general. "Any sightings of the enemy?"

Andy Young tugged his tricorn tight against a breeze warm and mild. "Yes, an infantryman of the Second was killed and scalped three miles from their tents yesterday morning. His hunting companion was shot through the body, but had the fortitude to flee and hide in the bushes till dark. Blessing indicated he would probably die of his wound. Nothing else of consequence."

The captain, sensing movement by the army was imminent, if for no other reason than to curtail a new spate of desertions, had already reversed the troop's schedule and dispatched foragers. At the conclusion of Andy Young's report, he declared the troop would rest themselves and their mounts the balance of the day. Out came the boiling pot and his Mahon razor, and we stripped to the waist in the warm air to shave and wash ourselves. Then, while Jared laundered and dried our shirts and breeches, we surrounded the fire swathed in our blankets and sipped jug whiskey. We exchanged tales of home and family, though the ensign and I did the gabbing, the captain content to listen and share in our laughter. Regrettably, that fine, unseasonably mild afternoon expired without my deciphering anything new as to the future romantic plans of Miles Starkweather.

A messenger of the general's delivered an express at dusk announcing the army would indeed march at nine in the morning, and we retired early. With the minds of the sentries on our pending departure, the night was mostly bereft of slain shadows and false alarms, and suffering no bad dreams, for once I slept soundly.

Despite it being the Sabbath, the army cast off on 30 October at the appointed hour, the Kentucky militia now at the forefront of the column, General St. Clair having decided they could provide some useful service after all by camping ahead of the column nightly, which positioned them to guard the advance fatigue party widening the road during the daylight hours. Though allowing he meant no vicious slight, Andy Young did remark in the hearing of the captain that it was somewhat more difficult to desert if those taking unbidden leave had to sneak past the entire army in full darkness, what with the Indians prowling about. Starkweather's concurring nod was reluctant but unmistakable.

The column slogged northwestward a full seven miles in pleasant weather marred only by a strong wind from the south. The country was level, forested, and poorly drained. Brackish waters shone in stagnant marshes on both sides of our path. Our progress was impeded by slow-traveling wagons and packhorses overloaded with personal stores and furnishings belonging to battalion and company officers. Abandoned baggage soon littered the edges of the narrow roadway. We would later learn some of the gear and equipment discarded to retain the possessions of officers included many tents of the Second American Regiment and the Pennsylvania levies, a discovery that fostered smoldering anger and resentment in the rank and file. And the dire events of that evening did nothing to soothe their upset.

The wind had backed around to the west-northwest and gained sufficient strength we were forced to lean against it while securing the horses to picket lines strung tree-to-tree. The erection of Starkweather's awning and Jared's tent proved major chores. A fire was possible only within a sheltering enclosure of logs. We dined scrunched together under the scant protection of the awning, husbanding the small reserve of water in our canteens, for the column had encamped on a poor excuse for a run, the water of which was insufficient and of poor quality. Conversation rendered nil by growing gusts of wind, we sought the shelter of Jared's tent at the first drop of rain.

We fell asleep guardedly, one ear tuned to the worsening elements beyond the canvas. Near what I took to be midnight, a stark bolt of lightning and a deafening roll of thunder brought the lot of us upright in our blankets. The wind, howling and shrieking, battered the tent walls, threatening to tear their pegs from the ground.

The captain threw his wolf pelts aside. "It's blowing a full gale, damn it!" he shouted above the ungodly din. "Roust the troop! We've got to see the horses don't get free!"

I'd no more cleared the entryway, clinging desperately to my helmet, when a sharp, ear-splitting crack behind the tent was followed by the crashing fall of a dead tree snapped at the roots. Once I touched solid earth again, .. circled rapidly among tents white as toadstools in the ragged blasts of lightning, shaking stockinged and booted feet alike, screaming, "To the horses! To the horses!"

It was a freak occasion that severely tested the prior discipline and training of the First Dragoons, and they responded admirably. Ignoring the danger of falling branches and flying debris, they struggled into their coats, fought through howling wind and spatters of frigid rain, and quickly gained the picket lines, there to bravely quiet and control animals whose sole desire was to lunge and kick free and escape the whole unrelenting uproar by fleeing into the night.

Twice lightning struck so close we smelled the stink of scorched wood. The slam of falling trees rivaled the thunder. Broken branches showered from the sky. It was a night belonging to the king of Hades and his minions, not to men made small and puny by the fury engulfing them. But just when we were thoroughly whipped from restraining the horses and swore we couldn't withstand one more ripping gust of wind or deadly strike of lightning, our nether hosts finally tired of their torment, and the gale relented.

At the captain's insistence, we stayed with the horses till the lightning abated entirely and the wind subsided. Through some miracle of providence, the troop suffered no significant bodily injuries, and we lost but a single animal, and that not by our own hand, a packhorse speared deeply in the flank by the limb of a toppling tree. As evidenced by the frequent cries for the surgeon drifting to us in the growing quiet, other army units had been less fortunate.

Dawn revealed the awesome damage wrought by the monstrous gale as Andy Young and I rode to St. Clair's headquarters, a venture necessitated by the failure of a messenger to appear at our fire with fresh orders. A freight wagon, bed and wheels collapsed by a downed tree butt, broken ridgepoles ugly as snagged teeth, lay in a shattered heap, reduced to firewood. Bloody, bandaged heads, slings, and splints were not uncommon sights. But the most shocking scene greeted us at the general's tent. Colonels, majors, and the squat, thick-bellied General Richard Butler sailed willy-nilly in and out of St. Clair's tent. The sounds of a heated confrontation hushed those watching and listening from outside. Andy Young, never one to be denied information, wrung an explanation in addition to cups of hot tea from Blessing, St. Clair's servant, whom he had befriended.

Blessing was stooped and his skin dark and wrinkled as the bark of the walnut tree, but his mind was sharper than a freshly honed sword. "Colonel Oldham was breakfasting with Sir General when an express came half his militiamens had deserted. He run off, then rushed straight back. Seems his officers talked all but sixty of his mens to remain. But thems that snubbed the flag swear they'll stop delivery of the provisions at Fort Jefferson. Sir General has summoned Major Hamtramack of the First Americans. He and his mens is ta trail after the wayward Kentuckians."

"God's bones," Andy Young blurted. "The First Americans are the most experienced corps in the army. Sending the whole corps after so few is nonsense. Captain Faulkner's riflemen are at Fort Jefferson waiting to escort the pack train here, and Court Starnes won't brook any interference from a gaggle of scruffy deserters."

"Maybe so," Blessing said with a practiced smile, refilling our cups. "But Sir General ain't often denied, be he?"

Andy Young was too wise to argue with the servant and perhaps forfeit his source of information. "Will we march today, Blessing?"

"No, Sir Ensign, yous won't. Sir General wants ta recover

the tents we threw away on the road yesterday, an' he won't sally forth less'n the larder be full." Blessing's almond eyes peered toward St. Clair's tent. "Sir Ensign Young, yous bein' beckoned."

Doing the beckoning was Corporal Thurston, the general's courier within the encampment. We relinquished our teacups to Blessing with sincere thanks, and the servant slipped off at Thurston's approach. The corporal, slavishly devoted to the importance of his task, offered neither smile nor salute, though we had spared him a ride to our fire. He held forth a sealed document and barked, "Orders of the day for the First Dragoons. To be initiated with all haste per Major General St. Clair." Andy Young took possession of the sealed document and saluted the withdrawing backside of Corporal Thurston out of pure devilment. A short laugh later, howsomever, we were in the saddle, knowing the captain would be wondering by now what was delaying us.

Starkweather's disgust with the contents of Corporal Thurston's sealed document was no less vivid than that he had displayed when Andy Young informed him the First Americans were being dispatched in pursuit of the deserting Kentucky militia. "We are to rove through the cow shit of yesterday's march and retrieve the tents neglectfully cast aside along the road. We have been given the quite magnanimous authority to commandeer a vehicle from the wagoners in the employ of the army. I may present a voucher to recover expenses, repayment of which will probably someday grace my palm, hopefully before my funeral."

But orders were orders, and the captain was an obedient soldier. While the troop prepared to journey afield, I accompanied Starkweather to the wagon park at the core of the army's encampment, where we hired Liege Canaday. A skeptical, crabby wagoner reeking of axle grease and horse sweat, Canaday was unwilling to commit his two-wheeled cart and skeletal nags to our cause till the captain fished a brace of gold coins from his purse. The wagoner's instant, toothless grin and bobbing head guaranteed he would follow the captain's bidding, whatever we demanded of his bony steeds.

We trekked south under a low, dull sky offering no threat of rain or foul weather, Liege Canaday's cart bouncing in our wake. Somewhere ahead of us on the same road traveled the Kentucky deserters and the Starnes pack string. The captain kept us doubly alert, on the lookout for lagging deserters as well as the redsticks. We searched through the discarded gear bordering the roadway in foursomes, two mounted dragoons holding the horses and standing guard over the two working afoot. By early afternoon, Canaday's cart was heaped with folded tents. Shortly thereafter, the fringes of the road yielded no additional enclosures for a mile, and the captain called off our search.

In the midst of blowing our horses before reversing direction, uniformed soldiers hove into sight from the south, followed by an immense string of packhorses. The soldiers were Captain Faulkner's rifle company. In the lead of the pack train loomed Court Starnes and his lackey, Gabe Hookfin. The beanpole's gloating smirk was visible above the dirty bandage wrapping his jaw and chin as he passed Andy Young and me. "Never miss a chance to wave their own flags, do they? Starnes will crow like a cock rooster in front of General St. Clair," the ensign predicted.

I eagerly eyed each passing packhorseman. No Paw, Tap, or Bear. But Henry Cross, Ira Fellows, and Paw's wagoners, Timothy and Thaddeus, were present and waved in greeting, raising the possibility I might later learn from them what had happened to those I sought. My disappointment was further tempered by the knowledge that Court Starnes was no longer bound for Fort Jefferson, a situation that would make it easier for Val Dodd to carry his warning to Erin Green without delay upon his arrival there.

"Two hundred twelve packhorses," Andy Young tallied. "Should be roughly thirty thousand pounds of flour. General St. Clair has no excuse now for remaining encamped."

We trailed after the pack train at a fair distance, Starkweather riding twixt Andy Young and me. "Captain Faulkner stated he encountered the sixty militia deserters on the road earlier. He was as appalled as I that General St. Clair would send the First Americans in pursuit of such worthless rabble." Starkweather rubbed his chin. "Gentlemen, I speak anticipating you may both be of higher rank in the future. I can only surmise the general believes stationing the First Americans on the road behind us will prevent the rifling of future provision trains by deserters. This decision comes when we are supposedly within forty miles of the enemy's villages. I, honoring the other tack, believe he risks his army to assuage the grumbling of weaklings. Perhaps for all our sakes, he will endure a change of heart."

It was hours later that we knew, but General St. Clair's heart remained steadfast. The descending sun a band of purple rimming the western horizon, we met the First Americans at dusk and once again conceded the roadway as we had with the supply train. Eight packhorses accompanying them, heavily laden with bloodstained pouches containing beef freshly butchered from the army's shrinking bullock herd, told the tale: the First Americans, three hundred strong, were expected to be away a number of days, perhaps as much as a week.

It was dark by the time Starkweather dismissed the troop with orders to sleep fully dressed with weapons at the ready. Andy Young went off to report to St. Clair's headquarters that the recovered tents were in the possession of Liege Canaday at the wagon park. I hobbled Blue and the captain's sorrel, then lugged our gear to Starkweather's awning, where Jared was busy at the baking oven and stewing pot, the pot smelling of beef, wild onion root, and salt. Corporal Thurston, brusque as ever, was just departing, and the captain held another of those sealed documents fresh from the general's quill.

The displeased scowl torturing Starkweather's lean face didn't bode well for my traipsing off to find Henry Cross or Ira Fellows, a sinking feeling confirmed by the captain's reaction to the document he crushed after reading. "For the love of God almighty, St. Clair's first states hoof rot is now felling the packhorses fast as starvation, then in the next stroke he suggests we dragoons dismount and use our horses to help transport the tents and entrenching tools. The worst thing imaginable would be to mix our mounts in with that fouled lot. Is St. Clair so sick he's blind to the obvious?"

Starkweather made to throw the St. Clair missive into the fire but then stayed his arm. "Ensign Downer, pass the word to the troop, every officer, that no dragoon is to stray from our fires for any reason. We shall question Ensign Young on his return and, if necessary, I will argue my cause at St. Clair's tent following the evening meal."

I completed my circuit of the troop's tents, and Andy Young appeared as Jared was serving the captain and me. He laid his saddle beside ours and accepted a plate from the servant. "Your report, Ensign, if you please," Starkweather urged none too gently.

"The general sent runners to spread the news about the recovered tents," Andy Young said.

"I assumed as much," the captain interrupted with an impatient waving of his tin cup. "Any mention of dragoon troops being dismounted to transport tents and tools?"

"Yes, sir. Your counterpart, Captain Trueman of the Second Dragoons, was there and argued most vehemently against doing so. Lieutenant Colonel Darke of the First Levy Regiment and Major Heart of the Second Americans supported Captain Trueman. Adjutant General Sargent opposed him."

"And what did General St. Clair decide?"

"For now, the First and Second Dragoon troops will patrol the flanks of our next advance," Andy Young said, provoking a brief smile from the captain.

"Thank the Lord. Be seated, Ensign," Starkweather ordered. He sipped tea and swallowed before inquiring, "Any word yet from those Chickasaws sent ahead to find the Shawnee?"

"No, sir, nothing. But their failure to locate the enemy doesn't seem to perturb the general in the least. He insists all the sightings to date have been merely hunters. Blessing, his servant, overheard the general tell his staff again just today that he is certain the Indians will retreat upon sighting our approach to their villages . . . or sue for peace."

I said nothing out of respect for the authority and sway of General St. Clair, but I couldn't help remembering the ten warriors I had witnessed in the night with Tap and the mistress. They had not been mere hunters. My silence did no harm, for the captain set little store by the general's opinion of the enemy's intentions. "I wish I shared his confidence. I might, if not for Ensign Downer's friend, Mr. Watkins, and the general's own scout, George Adams. Those knowing the redsticks firsthand doubt neither their will nor their courage." The evening breeze sawed at the flames of the fire, and the captain shrugged deeper into his coat. "We march at nine in the morning, will we not?"

"No, sir, we will remain halted another day," Andy Young answered quickly.

Caught in midsip, the surprised Starkweather choked, lurched forward, and spat into the fire. Flying tea sizzled as he wiped his chin. Anger brightened his eyes. "We have sufficient supplies, the weather is acceptable, and we do not march. I will never understand St. Clair's thinking," the captain concluded with a weary shaking of his head. "Gentlemen, finish your plates. We will retire early. If we must squander an otherwise fine day foraging for the animals, so be it."

The captain's prediction proved most true. On 1 November, we gleaned from Andy Young's daily visit to St. Clair's headquarters that Court Starnes, his fellow packhorsemen, and forty animals, escorted by a subaltern and fourteen men of the Second Americans, wended south for Fort Jefferson. From the ensign's observations going and coming, we learned the bulk of the army languished in its sinkhole of a camp with virtually no assigned duties. We dragoons? Why, we toiled the whole of daylight under the lash of Starkweather's tongue searching for forage in cloudy, moderate weather disturbed only by light southerly winds.

That night, the wind backed to the west and increasingly colder air crept into our tent. By the next afternoon, first rain, then fine snow fell. St. Clair's army, which according to Andy Young's beloved numbers now consisted of twelve hundred soldiers—regulars, levies, artillerymen, and dragoons, plus two hundred fifty militia, for a total fighting complement of fourteen hundred and fifty men—covered eight miles in the souring weather of 2 November.

It was a grueling, exhausting march across low, soggy terrain that turned to black, leeching mud at noon, mud that stuck to hoof, boot, and moccasin like color to skin. The ever-present Injun pathway spared us from total collapse, winding unerringly through the extensive swamps and clumps of towering beech timber on the best of the bad ground. The captain opined on several occasions that our line of march would be impassible in truly wet weather.

The army encamped in two lines on terrain marginally higher than that traveled during the day. The captain deemed it and the limestone run bisecting it tolerable for a single night at best. We clustered that evening around a fire that sputtered for want of dry wood, speaking only when necessary. The wind continued to circle, blowing after midnight from the north, never a favorable sign in late autumn. I slept deep and hard, content that Erin was safe at Fort Jefferson and probably informed by now of Court Starnes's brag. Taking no chances, I prayed earnestly and sincerely that night that the Lord watch over both Erin and her protector, Annie Bower.

Three November was no less gruesome a day. The dawn was a dreary blur of yellowish light and thick, hovering clouds. The northeast wind bore a small flight of snow throughout, but never heavy enough to blanket the leaves carpeting the woods. Our road, sufficient for two carriages abreast, passed small, sunken prairies for three miles, then rose gently, the beech forest giving way to thick stands of oak, ash, and hickory. With the advent of higher ground, the infernal mud petered out, and in its stead, small limestone brooks, not abounding with water at the moment, coursed hither and yon.

Excitement gripped the ranks about noon as small parties of Injuns, reputedly Shawnee and Miami, were spotted by the column's forward elements. We dragoons and the squads of riflemen on the flanks were dispatched after them, and though we stared behind every tree and bush, hoping to catch a glimpse of the enemy our ownselves, at their whim the redsticks melted silently into the forest without incident. Andy Young summed up my feelings by speculating, "Wonder how many there are that we haven't seen?"

During our pursuit of the elusive redsticks, the terrain leveled, then gradually descended to a small creek. The hour approaching late afternoon, and the army having advanced seven miles, a halt was called. The levies in the center of the line, hoping the day's march was complete, quickly kindled a large fire. From our parallel position on the flank, we sat shivering in our saddles and watched General St. Clair, surrounded by his staff officers, ride up to the blazing fire. A discussion ensued, followed by a cheer from the levies. But just as the general gave the order to disperse into our nightly formation, a hollow square, his aide-de-camp, Major Denny, and Quartermaster Hodgdon approached on horseback from the head of the column. After further discussion, the groans of the levies indicated the general had reversed his decision, and off we went again.

Impatient to learn why the general had resumed the march, Starkweather led a contingent of our troop rapidly forward. Two miles of hard pushing through wet, wooded marshes, and the captain had his answer. An elevated flat of ground approximately seven acres in size and fronted by a westerly running stream sixty feet wide spread before us. A considerable expanse of open woods, inclining gently upward, dominated the far bank of the stream. "Can't argue with the major general," Starkweather said more to himself than those in his company. "Rather a small site, but it's dry, with better water."

On the near bank of the stream a rider sat a gray horse with black mane, an animal I recognized from my travels with Tap as the mount of Colonel William Oldham, commander of the Kentucky militia. At least twenty of his sons of the bluegrass, yelling and signaling to one another with weapons and fists, prowled both banks of the stream and the open woods beyond it. Their feverish activity lured the captain onward.

Colonel Oldham twisted in the saddle at the sound of hoofbeats to his rear. Starkweather drew rein and saluted. "Trouble, Colonel?"

"Naw, redsticks quit the place just before we showed. 'Bout fifteen of them by their tracks, which be ripe and fresh," answered the militia commander.

"Hunters?"

"Not likely, Captain. Too many of them for hunting. I've sent a rider to tell the general."

The colonel twisted the opposite direction in the saddle.

"Sergeant Raney, how many recent fires did you count, those less than a week old?"

A lank-haired individual with red, peeling cheeks and toting a musket with a rusty barrel, flung snot with three fingers and dug into the mud of the bank with a moccasined toe. "More'n the cornstalks in our home patch, Colonel."

Oldham chuckled and swung his gaze to Starkweather. "The Injuns be here often and in large numbers, Captain. I suggest you guard your horses with great care tonight."

"That we will, Colonel, that we will," Starkweather promised. "Ensign Young, the day grows short. Fetch the balance of the troop."

With a farewell salute, the captain led his detail of eight dragoons west down the creek to the edge of the flat elevation, placing us on the left flank of the coming encampment. The balance of Colonel Oldham's militia trudged up the road and forded the stream, cursing the necessity of wetting their feet. Next came the five levy battalions. The first three, those of Major Butler, Major Clarke, and Major Patterson, aligned themselves from left to right along the near bank of the stream, forming the front line of our nightly hollow square. The remaining two levy battalions, those of Majors Bedinger and Gaither, and Lieutenant Colonel Doughty's Second American Regiment then did the same, forming the rear line. Seventy yards separated the front and rear lines. The marquees of ranking officers, the baggage wagons, and the carts of the camp followers filled the center of the square. Four hundred yards directly opposite the First Dragoons, our counterparts, the Second Dragoons and Captain Faulkner's rifle company, closed the far end or right flank of the hollow square. Captain Ferguson's artillery, split into two units of four cannons each, faced outward from designated points within both the front and rear lines. Detachments of sentries from the levy battalions and the Second Americans totaling two hundred soldiers ringed all but the creek angle of the square. Forward sentry duty was entrusted to the militia across the creek.

The captain being leery as ever of the hoof rot afflicting the column's baggage horses, every dragoon mount was hobbled and picketed a safe distance from those animals, which, out of necessity, were loosed along the rear of the encampment and left to forage overnight on their own. As an extra precaution against Injun thievery, Starkweather doubled the number of dragoons assigned to guard duty throughout the night. Thus, it was eight in the evening when we finally seated ourselves before the captain's awning to partake of the best Jared could muster.

We were spent and ate in virtual silence, what few comments we rendered centering on the immense amount of Injun sign located by the Kentucky militia. The red enemy suddenly seemed quite numerous and formidable, and battle with him in the near future more of a certainty rather than a remote possibility. And because of that growing certainty, just as suddenly I was lonely, afraid, and missing Paw and Bear and Tap something godawful fierce.

So it was mighty shocking to hear Tap's voice say aloud, "Lad always sees after his belly, don't he now?"

Bear Watkins's quick response was equally stunning. "That he do, my friend, that he do!"

I looked up from my plate, and my eyes fair leaped from their sockets. I hadn't lost my tree and taken to imagining things. They were there for real in the flesh, the one bowed as a stunted clump of pitch pine, the other solid and straight as the white oak, and they came bearing news even more shocking than their totally unexpected appearance from out of the dark of night.

Chapter 27

My excitement got the best of me. I came upright so fast I dumped my victuals, plate included, into the fire. My tin cup was spared a similar fate only because my finger was hooked in the handle.

Bear Watkins laughed softly. "Well, Ethan, lucky for you we've plenty of venison jerk with us, or you might starve after all," he said in that smooth manner of his, tossing me a bulky leather pouch.

Starkweather took up the conversation at that juncture, and I hastily regained my seat beside Andy Young, happy to escape everyone's attention. "Gentlemen, what brings you to our fire?" the captain inquired.

Bear accepted a cup from Jared, and the servant filled it with green tea. "We just finished deliverin' a letter to General St. Clair's headquarters from Caleb Downer, the lad's father, an' wanted to say hello is all."

"Curious," the captain mused. "Starnes seldom lets anyone but himself treat with the general."

"The letter wasn't necessarily Starnes's idea," Bear said. "Where Court's concerned, keepin' all but forty of the last train's horses for his own, places the blame square on St. Clair if'n future shipments are too small to feed the army."

"But Mr. Downer disagrees?"

Bear nodded and enjoyed a sip of tea. "Caleb thought it proper to warn the general straightaway how slim we are on animals. Less'n he returns some of the packhorses, it may be two weeks 'fore we can put together another train of sufficient size. The general needs to know, too, that the Ohio hasn't risen hardly a lick, an' flour shipments from upriver are arrivin' days late at Fort Washington."

The captain drank tea himself. "Mr. Downer is at Fort Jefferson with Court Starnes, I take it?"

"No, sir, he's at Fort Hamilton, tryin' to bring together quick as he can the flour an' other supplies that's dribblin' in piecemeal from the river. Caleb does have a shipment of ten thousand pounds of flour an' a drove of twenty bullocks on the way from there."

Starkweather drank more tea. "How did the general react to your letter?"

"Can't say, sir. He was already abed, but Corporal Thurston swore it would be presented to him yet tonight."

"You could do no more than that, gentlemen," the captain said with an understanding nod. "The two of you are to be commended for rising yourselves to deliver Mr. Downer's letter. Two white men traveling alone are mighty tempting to the savages."

"Well, we wasn't exactly without company," Bear admitted with seeming reluctance while staring forcefully at Tap.

The old scout, now sitting next to me on the dining log, rested the tin cup Jared had provided him on a bony knee and nervously cleared his throat. "It wasn't no choice of ours, but we had female company. Thankfully just the two."

Starkweather was horrified by this turn of events. "You knowingly endangered women heretofore out of reach of the enemy, Mr. Jacobs? How could that possibly happen? How could a man of your fortitude succumb to the demands of females wanting to heedlessly risk their lives overtaking a beleaguered army?"

I swung my head about and studied Tap, along with the others at the fire. The old scout twisted and squirmed but held his infamous temper in check. "They tagged along to tend a soldier badly hurt," he offered by way of explanation.

Apparently believing no woman worthy of his acquaintance would be so headstrong and misguided, the aroused captain demanded, "And who is this soldier these silly women risk their lives for?"

"Sergeant Tor Devlin of the Second Americans. He was

struck on the noggin during the big storm an' can't walk or hardly talk," Tap informed Starkweather.

Tor Devlin? My heart thumped and pounded. Were these women Erin and her mother? Good Lord, the mistress's mother had somehow departed her sickbed.

My thinking paralleled that of the captain. "Molly Green has made a remarkable recovery, has she not?" a disbelieving Starkweather ventured.

"She's not yet on her feet," Tap stated. I nearly dropped Bear's leather pouch, for I knew his next words before he said them. "Her daughter came in her stead."

My feelings swept two different directions at once. Erin was here, what I wanted most in all of creation. But being here when the army might soon engage the redsticks in battle exposed her to dangers from which I couldn't protect her.

"And who is the second woman?" the captain thought to ask.

"Bower. Annie Bower," Tap, keenly aware of Starkweather's dislike for the harlot, owned up. "Where the daughter goes, she goes. Ain't no way around it."

The captain accepted that, though not with any great pleasure. "How did the Greens learn of the sergeant's injury?"

"The soldiers of the Second who escorted Starnes's train back to Fort Jefferson told them."

"And what are Erin's plans?" the captain continued. "Surely she isn't intending to accompany the army?"

It wasn't lost on me how, unlike his evasive tactics in the past, Starkweather now openly referred to Erin by name, which I took as indisputable proof of his personal attachment to her.

Tap allowed himself a swig of tea. "No, she ain't plannin' to stay long. Bear gave her the loan of his gelding, an' she brung the family's cart. She an' Annie will care for Devlin on the return trip to her mama's cabin at Fort Jefferson. They'll set out at dawn if the sergeant's able."

The captain satisfied about Erin for the moment, the conversation then drifted to a discussion of vital information Tap and Bear had collected during their visit to St. Clair's headquarters. Of utmost importance was the general's proposal to construct earthworks on the morrow behind which the army would be stationed till such time as the First Americans rejoined the column. Me, I only half listened, lost in a private vision of red hair, blue eyes, magnificent breasts, and finely formed limbs, and the memory of a soft, trilling voice that ignited the best and the worst in a man. God forbid, I was so crazy in love with Erin I couldn't countenance not having her. I had to at least talk with her before she disappeared again, even if I had to desert the dragoons.

But bless my yearning soul, it was the captain, my rival for her affection, who saved me from that rank act. His discussion with Bear and Tap at an end, he stood and announced, "Gentlemen, I am retiring. You have my permission to visit at length with your young friend and stay the night. Since the army will not march in the morning, if you find it acceptable, the two ensigns and I will ride with you to the Green cart at dawn and extend a proper farewell to Erin and the unfortunate sergeant."

Tap and Bear, delighted as I was with the captain's hospitality, spread their blankets alongside the fire. Jared kindly brewed more tea before seeking his own bed. Andy Young, yawning heavily, soon joined them.

A chance to lay eyes on Erin assured, if nothing else, I quickly broached a second nagging problem to Bear and Tap. "How's Paw? He still furious with me?"

The two of them exchanged troubled glances. Tap spoke first. "It's blamed difficult to judge his mood, lad. He don't never mention you or ask about you."

Though it wasn't surprising, Paw's stark lack of interest in my doings since I had broken with him hurt me deeply while reaffirming the truth of our differences: He was a proud man who prized loyalty and devotion in his offspring. He held me at fault, and till I sought him out and apologized, I would have no standing with him.

I tempered the ache in my chest with the only remedy available, what I hoped were happier prospects. "How's Erin Green?"

Tap's seamed face drew near. "Didn't figure she was any concern of yourn, not with you bein' a fancy-sworded dragoon an' all now," he chided.

"Well, damn it, how is she?" I persisted.

The old scout slowly leaned sideways and spat into the fire, deliberately challenging my patience. My mouth sprang open to protest, and Bear snapped, "Tell the lad, you old codger, 'fore he jumps your creakin' bones an' does yuh harm."

Tap's head shook with regret. "Yuh ain't any more pleasant these days than a handful of wet dung, Bear Watkins," he accused huffily. But Bear's steely glare kept the old scout's tongue moving. "She mainly sees to her maw along with Annie. Afternoons, she often sits on the stoop, worryin' on somethin' or moonin' over somebody. I can't determine which. Either way, she ain't a terribly happy young lady, not liken she once was."

I wanted to believe Erin was mooning over me, but she was probably fretting about her mother's illness or pining after Miles Starkweather. I simply had no confidence that she could love a lowly ensign of dragoons, though I had twice risked my life rescuing her, for neither occasion had made me handsome nor lined my pockets with gold. And with the St. Clair campaign likely to wind down in two weeks or less, I would shortly be without employment and possess not the bulging purse of oblongs I'd anticipated but a slim packet that would sustain me by myself for just a single winter at most. I'd be fortunate if I owned Blue come the spring. There was, God forbid, the strongest of possibilities I would eventually have to crawl home and beg Paw's forgiveness to avoid starvation. By any measure, I had nothing to offer an ugly woman, let alone a beautiful one capable of attracting the most eligible man on the frontier.

Suddenly sorry I'd ever met Erin Green and gloomy as the hell-bound sinner, I took to staring at the fire, Bear and Tap forgotten. Wise and solemn, Bear granted me a couple of quiet minutes in which to appropriately suffer, then said, "Fess up your whiskey canteen, Tap. The lad needs his belly warmed 'fore I start speechifyin' for his own good."

As instructed, Tap retrieved an iron canteen from his haversack and poured liquor till my tin cup was overflowing. Not daring to defy Bear Watkins, I downed three large swallows, felt searing heat from throat to gullet, then dried tears with a thumb. Had I been situated an inch closer to the fire, my breath would surely have exploded.

Bear grinned, his teeth a yellow wedge above his grossly full beard. "Tap, wide as his eyes be, I do allow he's ready to hear me out. That tally with you, lad, or do you need another swallow or two?"

I wagged my head vigorously and wheezed, "No, I don't need no more. I won't miss a word, I swear."

Bear cocked his shaggy head and listened beyond the fire. "Much blunderin' 'round the perimeter this evenin'. The sound of muskets carries clear as the bugling of hounds on a cold, starry night. Hell's bells, it ain't midnight yet, an' the sentries have already wasted a night's worth of balls. But mayhap tonight there be somethin' out there besides shadows. Ethan, don't cowtail to the naysayers. The Injuns ain't gonna slink off without a fight. They'll lay into this army the first mornin' everythin' seems to favor 'em. They'll come in a zigzag wave, takin' advantage of every stitch of cover. You won't spy but a painted skull here, a banded arm there, a leather-clad leg yonder, an' then only for an instant. It won't be liken when they clumb the loft ladder an' yuh could kill 'em one after the other. Quicker'n lightning, they'll be everywhere, on every side of yuh. An' the redcoats have taught them who to down first—officers, artillerymen, and those on horseback, the dragoons—which puts you in the greatest danger from the first shot. But unlike when they jumped you an' the gal and killed Hardy Booth, yuh can't cut an' run an' save yourself the first opportunity. You're under the oath now, an' if'n yuh quit the field before a retreat's ordered, the army will brand yuh a coward an' hang yuh. No matter what, yuh got to stick with your troop an' abide by Starkweather's biddin'."

Bear paused to gather breath. "Now for what you must never forget, Ethan, or it'll be the death of you. In the frenzy of battle, yuh must fight with all the fury you can muster but still keep your wits about yuh. Keep up a steady fire an' don't get separated from your fellows. Always be ready to charge. Yuh lose your rifle or that new sword, don't hesitate to strip the dead. Remember, whether yuh win or be routed, only the upright depart the field. Yuh takin' to what I'm learnin' yuh, lad?"

I nodded more than once and told him so more than once. Bear Watkins had served in army and militia commands both large and small, spilled his own blood as well as that of the enemy countless times, and survived. He had me properly scared, but not so frightened I would flee before the redsticks at the outset. He had taught me in short order what was required to make a soldier of myself, and for that I was most grateful.

Bear thumped my shoulder with a fist. "I set great store by you, Ethan. An' thankfully, you ain't nearly as thick twixt the ears as your Paw be," he said with a wink. "Tap, where's that whiskey? The evening's not so late we can't imbibe a hair an' chew some of that jerk while we give our long guns their due."

Bear also spoke last that evening, just before I entered Jared's tent. "Fight first, love later, lad. A buried man ain't much use to a woman, be he now?"

Part V

Blood at Dawn

Chapter 28

Each minute of the brisk, star-blazoned night lasted an eternity. Despite Bear's wise admonition, whether tossing and flopping in my blankets early on or later while stamping about guarding the horses in the numbing cold of the hours before dawn, my thoughts were entirely of Erin Green. And thinking solely of what I might possibly say to her that wouldn't make of me a lust-driven oaf with neither brains nor manners was precisely what caused me to miss the most obvious of signs that something dreadfully out of the ordinary was unfolding all about me.

A half hour before dawn, fifes shrilled and drums rolled, but I barely heard Andy Young say beside me, "Reveille. Camp's coming awake." I continued to stare blankly across the dark waters of the creek while the troop shrugged free of their blankets behind us. All dragoons not on sentry duty then formed for morning parade, long guns held chest high. The terse comments of the reviewing Starkweather interrupted my silent reverie not at all. The captain then dismissed the troop for morning victuals, such as were to be had, sentries maintaining their posts till the troop sought their individual mounts after dining.

A sharp volley of musket fire erupted beyond the creek, far to our front, where the advance elements of the militia would be filling their bellies and warming themselves at their own morning fires. Distant yelling followed. "Damned undisciplined rabble," Andy Young snorted. "Probably shot a buck deer by mistake."

We were the dragoon sentries closest to the creek, and Andy Young, drawn by renewed though random musket fire, crept to the very edge of the near bank, which afforded him a view of the twenty-foot-high bluff bordering the opposite shore. I stood firm, rooted in my own private world of blue eyes, high cheekbones, and female lips full and red. "Mistress Green," I practiced under my breath, "it's a sincere pleasure to meet up with you again. . . ." No, that wouldn't do. Erin sounded so much more personal than the proper and formal Mistress Green. But did I dare greet her by her first name after all this while?

"Ethan!"

I ignored Andy Young's beseeching call. The random shooting by the militia had ceased, their officers undoubtedly having reined in their misbegotten charges with dire threats of the whip or worse. Besides, trees on the bluff across the creek were beginning to stand out in the gray dawn light, and the banks of the stream were populated only with the usual details of levies and militia calmly retrieving piggins of drinking and cooking water.

But Andy Young took to shouting. "What's that noise? It can't be horse bells! Damn you, Ethan, wake the hell up!"

I finally came fully alert, for the ensign had never before cursed me. I turned my head and slacked my jaw to listen, noticing as I did so that the water bearers on the opposite bank of the creek from us were suddenly staring behind them. The noise Andy Young sought to identify rose in volume and seemed to be advancing rapidly toward us. A close listen lasting a mere second and I recognized the high, keening howl for what it was. My hair didn't stand on end as some claim they experience when visited by acute fright, but my flesh crawled, a sensation much akin to having the point of a knife blade scrape across bare skin. I'd heard that same unearthly, wailing howl echo within the walls of our cabin as I waited at the top of the loft ladder with hatchet poised and waiting. I'd heard it again in the dark on the banks of the Great Miami. No sound ever emitted by a human throat was as utterly unnerving as the Shawnee war whoop.

"Holy Christ. It's the Shawnee, hundreds of them," I fair screamed at Andy Young, beckoning him to join me for a rush to Starkweather's awning.

The shooting resumed, and a virtual crowd of militia burst from the trees atop the bluff, in the main both hatless and weaponless. Consumed by fear and disdaining life and limb, they plunged down the sharp incline, falling, rolling, crawling, and scrambling through sucking mud, cattails, and bulrushes with the frenzy of fleeing, pain-maddened animals. Water spouted at their heels and, wheezing and gasping from shortness of breath, they escaped the creek and bolted into the ranks of the levy battalions trying to form into lines of defense against the screeching savages drawing ever nearer the far bank. I held fast long enough to witness the first of the painted heathens occupy the bluff the militia had so precipitously deserted, and indeed there were hundreds of Injuns in hot pursuit of the fleeing Kentuckians.

A ball whined past my ear, and I grabbed the sleeve of a stupefied Andy Young and pulled him toward the rear. The captain, I knew, would be looking for us to report to him. Flame lanced from the barrels of long guns along the bluff. A rippling crescendo of muzzle blasts swept along our side of the creek, and the boom of cannon shivered the air about us. Thank the Lord, we were returning fire.

Starkweather was aboard his sorrel, imploring the now-mounted dragoons to ignore the growing fight to our right and dress up their parallel lines. Jared waited before the captain's awning, in his black fists the reins of Blue and Andy Young's gray mare. We were most grateful the servant had already seen to their saddling and bridling. The ensign and I stepped into the saddle with diligent haste and joined Starkweather at the fore of the assembled dragoons. Bear and Tap were there, too, afoot at either stirrup of the captain.

Fear-crazed militiamen needlessly yelling the alarm flooded past our lines, craving refuge within the empty marquees of officers or beneath the beds of parked army wagons, and for the first time I feared for Erin Green. The repeated discharges of round shot and canister from the cannons raised an ear-splitting din and spawned a cloud of eye-obscuring smoke that enveloped the laboring artillerymen, then the levy battalions flanking them, then our position. Balls zipped past, not all from our front. "Hold steady! Hold steady!" Starkweather ordered, a command the sergeants repeated one after the other. The captain leaned sideways in the saddle to address Bear Watkins. "Your assessment, Mr. Watkins, if you please?"

Bear's response was loud enough it carried above the roar of guns big and small. "By the circular spread of the shooting, the red enemy has surrounded our entire encampment. If'n I'm hearing correctly, they're concentrating on the cannons."

The raptly listening Starkweather jerked upright, and a gloved hand flew to his left cheek. He winced slightly and the leather fingers of the glove came away bloody at the tips. "Close, damn close," he said as dispassionately as if he had observed a near miss of two stars in the night sky.

Starkweather's attention clamped on Bear once more. "Mr. Watkins, please obtain orders for the troop from General St. Clair or General Butler. We shall hold the flank till you return!"

Bear promptly disappeared into the writhing smoke. An increasing number of bullets, buzzing like angry bees, zinged past me. First a private, then a sergeant of the front line clasped their chests and slipped from the saddle. A chestnut horse behind Tap whinnied and settled to its knees. Though I could see none of the enemy, I knew where they were. They were creeping forward from tree to tree and stump to stump, hidden from mounted riders by the natural cover of the terrain and the ground-hugging smoke from the cannons and small arms. If we stayed stationary in the saddle much longer, we were in danger of being shot to pieces without ever shouldering our long guns.

Seven of the A.M.

Starkweather recognized our predicament. "Dismount! Horse holders to their duty!" He paused, granting the dragoons designated to control the horses time to gather the reins of those assigned to oppose the enemy from the ground, then shouted, "Kneel and fire at the ready."

I stepped down from the saddle, proud that I didn't entangle the long blade suspended at my left hip. Blue was led away, and I knelt quickly, thinking it would be safer once I presented less of a target. But my first peek under that lingering veil of smoke set my legs to begging, begging to flee, and I mean flee now!

Blossoms of expended gunpowder decorated every tree trunk, deadfall, and stump in sight. It was a severe strain to keep your legs still. And though I had just done so before dismounting, I couldn't resist hurriedly touching each weapon and accoutrement on my person again, be it horn, shot bag, Starkweather knife, sword, or the very rifle clasped tightly in my left fist.

"Draw bead!" Starkweather bawled, urging us into action. Personal dangers forgotten for the moment, I cocked my rifle, swept the barrel level, tugged the butt plate tight to my shoulder, and nestled my cheek against the smooth wood of the stock.

"Fire when ready!"

Instantly, rifles cracked to both sides of me, a startling development since, try as I might, I couldn't discern enough of a single solitary redstick to shoot at, leastwise not with any hope of success. When I did see any beadable hunk of him, he was lifting from the ground or stepping from behind a tree to advance against us, and his movements were completed so rapidly and furtively I could glimpse but the briefest flash of painted skin and roached topknot.

Gritting my teeth to keep fear at bay, I reverted to Bear's teaching and sought instead of bodily parts the black barrels protruding beneath those gray puffs of expended powder. I missed my first shot, but it repeated a telling lesson: Locate the enemy barrel, then patiently wait for it to fix on a target, for as Bear had preached, the skulking Injun exposed himself the most as he froze just before pulling the trigger.

Action bred resolve, and not worrying about hits or misses, I methodically poured, balled, rammed, primed, cocked, beaded, and fired. My shoulder came to ache from the constant slam of the recoil, but it was a welcome hurt, for it signaled I wasn't yet counted among the dead, the wounded, and the dying.

Moans and pleas for help told of felled comrades to both sides of me. The neighing and thrashing at my backside told me the redsticks had no compunction about mercilessly killing the horses of their hated foe. The relentless enemy shunned his own losses and crept steadily in upon our position. Despite our stout resistance, there was no denying the obvious: We were suffering heavy casualties, and less'n we regrouped, we were certain to be overrun, and soon!

About then, fingers gripped my upper arm and Tap said, "Get ready, lad. Bear's back, an' Colonel Darke's preparin' a charge an' we're to be part of it." The captain's voice rang out immediately thereafter. "Horse holders to the front! Dragoons, continue firing! Horse holders to the front!" he repeated. I fired twice more before the captain shouted, "Dragoons, cease firing! Stand and mount!"

I reloaded, came erect, and spun about to encounter not a horse holder but Bear with Blue's reins in tow, along with those of two other horses. He scowled at Tap. "Yuh can't run a lick, so yuh best ride. Yuh need a hand up, yuh bowlegged goat?"

With a snort of disgust, the old scout crouched and, defying his age, jumped astride with the litheness of the mistress. "Match that, Hair Man!" the incorrigible Tap challenged with an immense grin.

Simply thinking of Erin provoked a new rash of worry, worry greatly enhanced by the discovery that from horseback large contingents of howling savages could be spotted besieging the middle of the army's lines behind which the noncombatants had slept the previous night. I maintained an unyielding grip of iron on Blue's reins and cursed the oath that kept me from rushing to her aid. Damn my willful soul to hell, anyhow.

The remaining members of the First Dragoons, Captain Starkweather, and Ensign Young in the van, followed by Bear, Tap, and me, then the rest of the troop, angled southwest to join with Colonel Darke and rescue the army's beleaguered left flank. The Injun advance had almost reached the mouths of the cannons anchoring Darke's rear echelon.

Three hundred levies and regulars were massed and waiting. They parted ranks, and we galloped through, brandishing tempered steel now instead of long guns. After us flowed the massed levies and a spate of regulars, the regulars brandishing additional steel: fourteen-inch bayonets slotted onto the muzzles of their muskets.

The savages, having no taste for greater numbers, flying hooves, curved swords, and the equally dreaded infantry bayonet, took to heel. The First Dragoons pounded across a small run and pursued them toward the sparse timber flanking the creek. There the bravest of the redsticks made a stand, trying to slow our charge. A ball twanged metal on my helmet. Caught up in the pure excitement of the chase, I spurred Blue, and we sped into the scanty trees. A Shawnee rose before me. I slashed at his painted skull, but the wily devil proved no helpless bag of straw. He parried my blow with the barrel of his musket, nearly tearing my fingers from the hilt of my blade as Blue swept past him. Then Blue was leaping from the high bank of the creek. We hit the shallow water with a mighty splash, the gelding landing on his hooves without stumbling or falling, and at a flick of the reins, he was in motion again.

It was the opposite creek bank, not the enemy, that foiled our charge. We cursed and ranted and spurred, but our mounts couldn't overcome its cloying mud, thick bulrushes, and tangling underbrush. Sucking wind at every stride, the levies and regulars under Darke's command forged ahead, clawed their way up the bluff bordering the creek, and continued the pursuit.

His sorrel bucking and lunging, the captain escaped the clutching underbrush and herded the troop, clanging and clattering, into the narrow rocky wash at the base of the bluff. Tap, Bear, and Andy Young had, like me, survived the charge unscathed. But six horses with empty saddles wandered the creek bed, and my quick survey of the mounted dragoons surrounding me established the true gravity of our losses, thirty-two of fifty-eight effectives since the Injuns had won the bluff looming over us.

Our respite from the rigors of the battle lasted but a few deep breaths, for heavy, sustained shooting and wild whoop-

ing broke out in the direction of the army's rear echelon.
Starkweather's sudden grimace indicated he understood as I
did that our charge had carried too far. We had unintention-
ally granted the Shawnee not spooked by our horses the opportunity to assault full bore gravely weakened companies
lacking both discipline and courage.

The captain stood in his stirrups. "Mr. Watkins! Ensign
Young! Inform Colonel Darke we are returning without delay. Dragoons, after me in columns of two!"

I confess I was selfishly pleased with the captain's decision. If the Shawnee penetrated the rear echelon, Erin and
the noncombatants were in mortal peril. That familiar gnawing worry threatened to twist my innards into knots. I spurred
Blue forward and crossed the creek flush with the rump of
the captain's sorrel.

My worry was well founded. We emerged at the gallop
from the sparse timber shielding us from the army's hollow
square and were thoroughly sickened by the appalling car-
nage wrought by the diabolical Shawnee in twenty short
minutes. Uniformed bodies with skulls so freshly scalped
they steamed in the chill morning air sprawled everywhere,
their severed limbs and organs mere splatters of blood and
gory slop. The members of the artillery unit, slain to the man,
lay like heaped cordwood around their silenced cannons.
Dead and wounded deliberately thrown into breakfast fires
burned sluggishly, giving rise to a horrible stench that gagged
me anew. At closer range, Injuns could be seen running amok
behind the breached lines of the rear echelon, wielding tom-
ahawks and knives dripping with red. Female screams inter-
mixed with the triumphant scalp hello of the savages drifted
from the wagon yard, and I was suddenly terribly afraid Erin
had already met her demise.

Starkweather, splendid uniform still miraculously free of
dirt and blood, took it all in as did those galloping behind
him. He never drew rein. Sword held high, he rode smack
through the shattered lines of the rear echelon, yelling over
and over, "Roust the red bastards, dragoons! Roust them and
kill them!"

I veered toward the closest wagon. I screamed Erin's
name, but anticipating no response, craned my neck right and

left, searching for her. Blue's shoulder knocked an Injun aside. I slashed at the next and felt the solid impact of cold steel and enemy. I saw long, flying hair and a streak of white, reined Blue sharply about, and surged after what I believed was a fleeing female.

Blue shuddered violently and faltered. He regained his stride, blowing heavily through his nostrils. Then his legs deserted him. I felt him going down and kicked free of the stirrups. The gelding hit nose first. I loosed the reins and went sailing, struck ground hard as stone, and skidded sideways. I covered my head with my arms, but the back of my helmet slammed into the wheel of a gun carriage and I drowned in blackness.

Eight of the A.M.

I awakened to discover a pair of hazel eyes studying me. The brow above the unblinking eyes was reddish brown and coarsely grown. Runnels of dried blood drew my gaze upward to an oval of pink-tainted bone swarming with gnats. My innards roiled. I was staring at a white man who had been killed and scalped. I looked down and away to keep from retching and made an even more revolting discovery: There was nothing attached to the beard the color of the brow. The head had no body. Though it was unnecessary, I grabbed my chest and tried my legs to make certain I was in one piece. That done, I rolled away from those staring hazel eyes and peered out from beneath the transom of the gun carriage.

The movement added to the throbbing pain in my head, but I could see just fine. Legs adorned with shoes held together with thongs and patched with scraps of leather, levy-issue shoes they were, loped past. That sight and the virtual absence of the screaming and howling I'd heard before the bullet struck Blue meant the sweeping charge of the First Dragoons had temporarily flushed the enemy from the center of the encampment. But for how long?

I squirmed into the open, latched onto the wheel of the gun carriage, and levered upward. Once on my feet, the ache

in my skull diminished rapidly. I cast about and found my
sword a scant rod from the dead Blue. Averting my eyes to
avoid tears, I regained possession of my blade. I almost quit
on finding my rifle till I thought to search under the transom.
Sure enough, it was there, keeping company with the bloody
skull. Bullets thunked hollowly against the wooden trail of
the carriage, but refusing to panic, I sought the cover of the
dead bodies heaped alongside the off wheel and saw to my
long gun. I removed the dirt plugging the barrel with the
point of the Starkweather knife, then set and released the
cock, checked the flint, and primed the pan with fresh powder. With my rifle again in proper working order, I was ready
to rejoin the dragoons, my first duty now that the Shawnee
had renewed their assault, Erin or no Erin.

A solid gander every which way produced no sightings
of helmeted riders. The main defensive line of the rear echelon had receded to the outermost wagons and carts within
the army's hollow square, and I guessed the surviving dragoons, such as there might be, would be rallying within that
scattering of vehicles, the original object of Starkweather's
charge. That being the most likely place to also find one Erin
Green lent speed to my feet.

In spite of the renewed, constant, incoming hail of balls
from the enemy, I gained that which Blue and I had sought:
the closest wagon. The exertion riled the knot on my noggin,
and I paused to let the pain dull while I got my bearings.
What confronted me now was the havoc and slaughter per-
petrated by the Injuns during their brief penetration of the
rear echelon. The bodies scattered among the parked wagons
were mainly those of the drivers and women and children.
Not the length of a rifle from me reposed a slim, raven-haired
female that had been chopped in half. A child whose cleaved
forehead oozed gray brains clung to the lower portion of the
corpse with both arms.

Beyond the slain mother and daughter rested the overturned cart of the Green family, a sight that froze my blood.
The box of the overturned cart faced away from me, the
airborne wheel spinning slowly on its axle. Expecting the
very worst, I wound quickly among the civilian dead and
swept twixt the poles of the cart. Tor Devlin, skin white and

waxen, lay on his backside. A bloody bandage rested beside his scalped head. White-stockinged legs, partially hidden by the tail end of the cart, caught my eye. Praying Erin hadn't switched her male breeches for stockings and skirt, I inched past the remains of the sergeant. I couldn't help my relieved sigh. It wasn't Erin. It was the tallest of Annie Bower's friends. The harlot's torn bodice exposed ghastly wounds where the Injuns had cut away her breasts. Her tortured features indicated she'd suffered much before dying.

Where, though, was Erin? I felt an insane urge to start searching for her among the dead, and got a grip on the tailboard of the cart till it waned. With the Injun horde threatening to collapse the whole of the army's hollow square, there was no time to confirm the death of anyone, beloved though they might be. Besides, a moment's reflection told me that if Erin and her self-appointed female guardian were alive, I already knew where to find them. I trusted her and Annie Bower to seek the safest place for noncombatants at this stage of the battle: the very center of the ground still held by St. Clair's forces.

I shagged through the hodgepodge of wheeled vehicles separating me from that protected middle ground, eyes peeled for sign of either woman as well as the First Dragoons. I found dragoon sign first, two of the troop's horses, one prone, the other burdened with a profusely bleeding neck wound. Their riders, both privates, had been brought down, tomahawked, and scalped. It wasted precious time, but I couldn't leave the wounded animal to suffer. I shot him behind the ear and knelt to reload.

I was seating the ball when a great yelling sprang from white throats along the front echelon defending the near bank of the creek. This was no victory cry, being instead the harsh outpouring of what was now a thin blue line summoning every ounce of courage they could muster as they undertook a desperate charge. A tremendous firing arose, and I set off at a dead run, sensing that if Starkweather was sucking wind, he had those of his cherished troop able to lift sword or rifle plumb in the thick of that desperate forward push.

I cleared the last of the wagons and carts and encountered a vista as shocking as any previously witnessed. The crack and boom of small arms equaled the roll of thunder, and across the creek a cloud of fresh powder smoke formed atop the far bluff. Groups of blue-uniformed soldiers with bayoneted rifles, the Second Americans, scaled the steep incline and vanished into the expanding smoke cloud. But directly in front of my nose, a huge throng milled aimlessly, a throng composed of levies and militia who had thrown aside their weapons in abject fear. They drifted about the tattered tents of camp followers and elegant marquees of officers, begging aloud for mercy and deliverance from death. They paid no heed to their officers, unmoved by the threat of a bullet if they didn't return to the ranks. Most ludicrous of all was the bonneted, buxom camp follower chasing a cowering shirker from her tent with an iron skillet.

The fighting beyond the bluff eased, then the crash of small arms resumed fierce as ever. A blue-uniformed figure staggered from the smoke cloud. Their fear a raw stink, the milling crowd quieted. Suddenly, blue uniforms flooded the crest of the bluff, then just as suddenly dwindled to a trickle. I stared and stared, but no more bayoneted infantrymen appeared there.

An ominous foreboding weakened my legs. The charge of the Second had failed, and their failure signified the worst for General St. Clair. In the absence of the First Americans, the devastation of the only regular regiment engaged brought his army to the brink of total disaster. No surrounded force of arms could sustain the general's losses to death, wounds, and cowardice the past three hours and continue to resist a foe as intrepid and zealous as the Shawnee. Defeat would be a kind fate for the general's army, for it was threatened now with annihilation.

Nine of the A.M.

A new fear beset me, the fear that I might be associated with the shirkers. I pushed and barged through them, slamming with shoulder and elbow where necessary. Damn if I'd die thought a coward.

The cannon of the front echelon had ceased firing. The

lines of levies and regulars defending the creek were peril-
ously thin, and their rate of fire slackened by the minute. As
a consequence, the red enemy forded the stream in ever-
greater numbers. In an admirable display of bravery, portly
General Butler, wounded arm in a sling, popped above his
kneeling soldiers on horseback in an attempt to rally their
flagging spirits, only to be shot from the saddle. The last I
saw of him, he was carried from the field in a blanket by
four of his own soldiers.

The attacking Injuns seized the near creek bank, and many
levies and regulars already poised to withdraw scrambled to
their feet. At that crucial juncture, the Injun strategy of killing
officers first turned the tide of battle in their favor. Without
sufficient officers to enforce orders to the contrary, the standing levies and regulars began shuffling backward. Others
joined them. The emboldened redsticks rose from cover and
loosed a withering round of fire. The air sang with bullets.
Defenders crumpled, and the will of their lines crumpled with
them. A few war whoops, accompanied by another round of
shooting by the enemy, and the inevitable rout was under
way, St. Clair's untrained, undisciplined levy battalions abandoning their positions in bunches with the suddenness of startled deer.

I, too, was tempted to put sole to path and might have
but for the flashing sweep of a sword. I was thankful I hesitated, for it was Starkweather wielding the blade. He was
ensconced in the tents of Clarke's battalion, vainly trying to
staunch the flight of deserting infantrymen while a dozen plus
of his dragoons, all afoot now, continued to fire on the enemy. Tap was with the captain, shielding him from the enemy the fleeing cowards refused to fight. Bear and Andy
Young were nowhere to be seen.

Heartened by familiar faces, I dodged the terror-stricken
soldiers bound the opposite direction and joined with Tap
and the captain.

Tap's eyes bugged at the sight of me. "Damn my soul!"
he exclaimed. "Thought you was a goner, lad."

I clapped the old scout's shoulder and knuckled my forehead. "Reporting for duty, Captain."

Starkweather, always the officer, allowed me a nod of

recognition. "Dragoons, fall back in pace with me!"

We withdrew in orderly fashion to the innermost row of tents. "Sergeant Baker, form line abreast!" the captain bawled. Without a moment's delay, the sergeant and his companions swung about. The instant, unquestioned obedience of the sergeant and the last shred of the First Dragoons was a testament to the stern discipline Miles Starkweather had instilled in his troop. "Ensign Downer and Mr. Jacobs, after me, please!"

We heeled like hounds and stuck to the captain tight as cockleburs. I edged close to Tap. "Where are Bear an' Andy Young?"

Tap's head shook. "Don't know. Ain't seed them since they went off to deliver Starkweather's message to Colonel Darke."

Confusion held sway at our destination, the center of the St. Clair encampment. Swollen by the new arrivals from the front echelon, the crowd of shirkers now outnumbered those bearing arms. "Like sheep penned for the slaughter," Tap muttered disgustedly.

Starkweather skirted the burgeoning crowd and led us into the presence of St. Clair himself. The general was no less disheveled than his command. He was hatless, and his gray hair hung in strands about the shoulders of a rumpled, coarsely woven cappo coat, beneath which he wore only a linen shirt. In short, he looked what he was: an ailing general rousted from his sickbed to confront a day that had begun badly and worsened with each hour.

Corporal Thurston was just finishing a report, his tone dogged as usual. "Left flank has collapsed completely, sir. The heathen have overrun the contractors an' civilians there. We have hundreds dead an' wounded."

St. Clair's slow nod belied a racing mind. He addressed his listening officers with grave solemnity. "We will effect a retreat via the military road, gentlemen, and spare of this command what is possible. Have the drummers beat the command. Colonel Darke will lead."

Perhaps it was the finely tailored uniform, but the general spotted Miles Starkweather among his audience like a hound pointing the bird. "Dragoons will continue to support Major

Clarke so as to sustain the right flank during our withdrawal. Dismissed!"

Starkweather saluted, and we retraced our steps. "I ain't one to show disfavor," Tap said, "but where the general's road's concerned, them Injuns be thicker'n summer flies on bloody meat."

The captain grunted without eschewing a yea or nay regarding the opinion of the old scout. "We have our orders, and we will abide by them, Mr. Watkins."

Starkweather being the sole officer in our sector, he relinquished the narrow ground separating the tents of Clarke's battalion from a thin band of trees that ringed the entire right flank, thereby gaining for us a modicum of cover. I took a shine to the backside of a hefty gray beech that bordered on outright fondness. The pain in my head was by now a dull ache that hindered neither my shooting nor my brain. I stood solid with the others and did my duty but dwelled solely on the possible whereabouts of Erin Green. Somehow, some way, I had to conduct a final search for her before we were caught up in St. Clair's retreat, even if I had to disobey the captain or the general. Maybe it only made sense to me, but regardless of the seeming impossibility of locating her in the midst of a raging battle, if she were alive, she was expecting me to come for her. And I could not fail her, for if I did, I would loathe my every breath to the grave.

The remnants of Clarke's battalion and we few dragoons successfully shored up the right flank. Though our numbers dwindled alarmingly fast, we stubbornly gave ground a tree at a time. Tap, fresh from checking the progress of the retreat south via the military road, brought news that Colonel Darke's sortie to break through the encircling Injuns had collapsed, and the enemy was overwhelming the left flank and the rear echelon from the west.

A Shawnee ball struck above the captain, and tree bark rained on his cockaded helmet. "I should never doubt you, Mr. Jacobs," an unfazed Starkweather confessed. "What course should General St. Clair pursue now?"

Tap tugged at his beard. "Was I he, I'd retreat to the east. There be the fewest Injuns thataway."

The next tree over, Sergeant Baker lunged to his feet.

"Yuh best take note, Captain," he cried, pointing behind us. "The whole shebang's callin' it quits!"

Sure enough and for certain, as Tap had just predicted, a virtual tide of regulars, levies, militia, and noncombatants, every soul in the center of the encampment capable of walking, was gliding eastward, stumbling and falling over their own dead and dying. Starkweather hated such disorder, but evincing no dismay, adjusted his orders accordingly. "Gentlemen, we'll take station next to the wagon yard and delay the enemy's pursuit as long as possible. After me, if you please!"

Wanting to shout in thanksgiving, I hung at the captain's shoulder, eyes surveying the wagon yard for any flash of white shirt or red hair. Infantrymen plowed past us, many casting aside muskets and cartridge boxes and haversacks suddenly too burdensome. I wedged through the retreating infantrymen, bolted among the parked vehicles, and began calling for Erin at the top of my lungs. If the other dragoons thought me crazy, so be it.

Starkweather didn't yell for me to stop, and I ran farther into the yard, calling louder than ever. Wagons surrounded a circle of deserted fires still emitting smoke. I cast about wildly, saw nothing but a black horse tied twenty paces away twixt two of the vehicles, and cast about again. Something about that tied horse bit at my memory, and my eyes whirled back to him. He was a huge black animal, white-stockinged and rippling with muscle, and he wore a saddle, not a hauling harness. My feet were moving even as I remembered: The last time I'd seen that huge beast, Court Starnes had been riding him.

A squeal of pain sounded at the front of one of the wagons. I ducked under the reins tying the huge black horse, gained the corner of the wagon bed, and saw booted feet big as the black's hooves straddling a pair of slim legs encased in breeches and moccasins. Another step and I was looking at a broad male backside and the rear angle of a tricorn hat. This go-round there was no hesitation, no granting of quarter. I lifted my rifle and drove the butt plate into the bony crevice where the bottom of the wide skull came together with the nape of the neck.

The tricorn hat went spinning, and the broad backside tautened. Then, despite the tremendous impact of the blow, the wide skull slowly rotated, and I was staring not at the Roman jaw and Grecian nose of Court Starnes but a black-patched eye and a forehead centered by the jagged track of an old knife scar. The second blow of my rifle butt smashed Dyson Barch flush on the cheekbone under his patched eye. With that blow, his good orb rolled upward, and he flopped sideways.

And there, squirming from beneath Barch's heavy legs, was of course Erin Green. Her white shirt and frock coat were splotched with dirt, and black powder coated her chin and mouth, a disfigurement explained by the cartridge box belted about her waist. Tearing at paper cartridges with your teeth to load a musket was a right messy business. But dear God, even filthy Erin Green was stunningly attractive.

She scrambled to her feet, an accomplishment that, not surprisingly, loosed her tongue. "Well, now that you're finally here, you must save Annie, too!"

I should have guessed as much. In for one, in for the both of them. I wasted no time arguing, for redstick war whoops and the bang of small arms filled my ears to overflowing. The Shawnee were descending upon the very middle of the army encampment. "Where is the Bower woman?"

Erin gestured eastward in the general direction of St. Clair's retreat. "She cut Starnes on the throat with her knife, and he chased after her. He'll kill her if he catches her. Barch was to fetch me on Court's horse."

I untied the huge black. "Climb aboard. We don't have time to hunt them afoot." For once, she took no exception to what I proposed. I stepped astride the black, reached down, and lifted her up behind me. A mild thump of my boots against his flanks, and Starnes's animal answered the rein quite promptly. The gurgling Dyson Barch I left for the In-juns.

The black trotted clear of the tangle of wagons without our beholding Annie or Court Starnes, or more importantly to me, the First Dragoons. The black had to slow to avoid trampling infantrymen retreating now in a pell-mell dash. I was so busy seeking an open path through the dashing soldiers and the bodies littering the ground, the attack of Court Starnes, launched from my blind quarter, took me unawares.

Erin squawked with alarm as her arms were ripped from my waist. The next stride of the black, a substantial weight settled on his haunches and massive forearms engulfed me. Beefy fingers gripped the front of my coat while those of the opposite hand secured a purchase in the black's mane. The imposing bulk of the body accosting me left no doubt as to my attacker's identity.

The hand clutching my coat gave a series of powerful jerks, Starnes depending on the fist entwined in the black's mane for the necessary leverage to unseat me. I squeezed the black with my knees, but the burly Starnes was too strong to shrug off, and with my arms pinned to my sides, I could bring neither my sword nor my rifle into play.

Starnes felt me slipping from the saddle. He laughed and booted the black into a gallop. My downward slide, though, pressed the Starkweather knife against my rib cage and suggested a means of thwarting his desires. I pushed hard against the stirrups, butted backward with my head, and managed to flatten his nose with the metal spine of my helmet. Starnes's grip lessened for a fraction of a second. I yanked the captain's knife from its scabbard and stabbed at the only part of him readily available: that immense fist entwined in the black's mane.

The razor-sharp blade severed Starnes's thumb at the first joint and lopped off two adjoining fingers. Grunting with pain, he surrendered his hold on the black's mane, and I thrust upward with my left elbow, lifting his arm and exposing his left side. I stabbed with all my might, and the captain's blade sank to the hilt in the soft, yielding flesh below his ribs. Starnes's arms opened abruptly, and it required but a shrug of the shoulders to dislodge his heavy frame from the haunches of the black. He landed awkwardly on his right leg, and I heard the crisp snap of breaking bones. I slowed the black and reined about, but I needn't have worried. You know who was chasing me down afoot, and a quick snatch later, Erin was aboard again, this time before me where I could keep a proper grip on her.

Without delay, I booted the black toward the swampy

woods to the east. Had not untold numbers of the enemy halted to scalp and loot those they had already slain and had not Starkweather and his dragoons fired a volley from the closest trees, Erin and I would probably have perished before reaching those beckoning woods. As it was, we fetched up to the captain and his men with the black enjoying but a dangerously short lead on the pursuing Shawnee.

Ten of the A.M.

Starkweather waved us through his meager line of dragoons. I made to lift a leg, but the captain had other designs. "Stay mounted, Ensign. We will provide an escort for the both of you." At his behest, the dragoons closed up behind us, and we proceeded at double-quick time. There was no more holding of ground anywhere for the St. Clair army.

The captain, trotting at the black's stirrup, eyed the powder-smeared Erin Green. "We must proceed with all haste, mistress. The nearest site offering any semblance of safekeeping for you is Fort Jefferson," he estimated calmly. "Whatever happens, Ensign, do not permit your horse to be taken. If necessary, you may ride ahead."

I understood his reasoning. The woods about us teemed with wall-eyed soldiers. Their fright was so overpowering that even out of the sight of the enemy they continued to shun every attempt to establish order. A sergeant of levies was knocked aside and trampled when he vainly tried to block the path and form a rear guard. Other officers forswore their duty, succumbing to the panic gripping the rank and file. Three from the militia hammered by on a single horse and callously left the animal to suffer when it tripped and shattered a foreleg. St. Clair's army had become an undisciplined mob capable of any act that furthered its unmitigated desire to escape the scalp-hungry Shawnee, including setting the daughter of Molly Green afoot.

The rattling fire of muskets, the echoing war whoops of our pursuers, and the pitiful screams of those unfortunate enough to be overtaken by the redsticks, all of which carried with utmost clarity in the morning cold, assailed our ears every second. Discarded equipment, be it long gun, pistol, sword, bayonet, canteen, onion bottle, greatcoat, tricorn hat, powder horn, haversack, shot pouch, knife, hatchet, cartridge box, gray wig, unbuckled shoe, half-eaten loaf of bread, or silver snuff box, fouled the icy troughs of the pathway. Erin shivered at what she thought the wail of a terrified child, and with no potential mother in sight pleaded with me to investigate the source of that unsettling cry, but it proved impossible to disengage the black from the mass of soldiers cramming against my stirrups.

A mile and a half later, the path of retreat, angling south all the while, bisected the army's military road, and the way eased. Out of necessity, the pace of the breathless dragoons slowed briefly to a brisk walk, and Erin asked the captain, "Did you or any of your men see what became of Annie Bower?"

A gasping Starkweather seized the black's mane to keep his feet. "Yes, and I can state she is alive and well. She is somewhere to our front with Mr. Jacobs. She protested being separated from you, but I will not chance a female of any stripe to the butchery of the savages."

Erin's sigh of relief was quick in the coming. "Thank you, Captain. She is a woman worthy of your every consideration."

The genteel Starkweather offered no response to Erin's assertion regarding the loyalty she believed was due Annie Bower, and in the resulting silence, I inquired, "Captain, do we know anything of Bear and Ensign Young?"

"Neither man returned from carrying my message to Colonel Darke beyond the bluff," Starkweather related. "I fear they are among the lost."

I heard what the captain said but refused to accept his unfounded notion that the indomitable Bear Watkins had fallen at the hands of the Shawnee. For if I believed Bear dead, then Andy Young had most likely gone to meet our maker with him. It was imperative that Andy Young survive. With Cyrus Paine, Dyson Barch, and Court Starnes all shaking the hand of Satan, the ensign was Paw's last, solitary, wishful hope of avoiding the condemnation sure to befall every civilian contractor with the total defeat of St. Clair's forces. Andy Young, an officer of merit and solid reputation, was now the lone remaining individual who could swear from firsthand knowledge in court that Paw had not participated in the thievery and duplicity wrought on the army by William Duer and his henchmen.

Erin Green's poking elbow interrupted my personal ruminating. "There's Mr. Jacobs and Annie," she exclaimed, aiming a finger ahead and to the fringe of the crowded roadway.

Tap Jacobs had the resigned look of a man following the dictates of a female out of necessity, not choice. His smile when he spotted Erin and me aboard the black was one of deliverance as well as outright happiness. He tugged Annie Bower none too gently into the roadway, cursing those who didn't jump sprightly aside. They fell in beside us on the opposite shoulder of the black from Starkweather. "Damn glad you're here, young'un. They's both yours now."

Indignation twisted Annie Bower's haggard face. "Stop flappin' yer mouth, yuh ol' fart," she snapped, extending Erin a wooden canteen. "I ain't never been someone the likes of you has the least say about."

A passing soldier bumped the harlot. She stumbled but somehow regained her balance, avoiding a fall. I swung down from the black. If Annie Bower were knocked from her feet, she would be trampled, as had the levy sergeant earlier. Before she could object, I grabbed her about the waist and boosted her up behind Erin.

Starkweather did object, and quite vehemently. "Ensign, I ordered you to remain mounted with the mistress!"

"If she walks, I walk, Captain," Erin Green threatened, her voice trembling with anger. "No woman in danger receives less consideration than me."

The captain's handsome features slowly darkened. He swallowed hard and said, "I stand corrected, mistress. She may ride."

Another occasion, I might have taken some delight in Starkweather's discomfort, but more important matters intervened. A hubbub farther along the road preceded a parting of the fleeing throng of soldiers that yielded prominence to General St. Clair and the officers escorting him. The general, wincing with the pervasive hurt of his gout, was seated on a scrawny packhorse, an animal of far less stature and dependability than the black. "Push straight through with your horse, the women, and Mr. Jacobs, Ensign," Starkweather barked. "The two of you are to inform Fort Jefferson of the morning's events without delay. Understood?"

The captain's thinking was clear as the cloudless sky. The battle was lost, and the army's pell-mell retreat would continue unchecked for hours. And once the enemy was outrun, victuals of any kind as well as human comfort, particularly that warm and pleasurable, would be scarce as ripe apples in winter, and routed, despairing soldiers had been known to forcibly pilfer whatever essentials were available, females, attached or unattached, notwithstanding. Thus, any man truly loving Erin Green would want her behind the walls of the nearest stockade at the earliest possible moment, and carrying the alarm to Fort Jefferson provided a legitimate excuse to so situate her.

Rival or not, I trusted Starkweather as a commanding officer and took him at his word. I seized the black's reins and angled sharply into the mass of soldiers crowding past the general's contingent along the left side of the road. The gunfire and whooping behind us slackened suddenly, as if after a chase of four miles the Shawnee were growing tired of uncontested killing and scalping. Yet not a fleeing soldier other than the captain and his dragoons heeded the shouts of the general and his officers to halt.

Starkweather's arrival occupied the general and his staff for a brief half minute and we slipped by their position before any of his subordinates thought to commandeer for their poorly mounted leader the huge black horse carrying but two women. And soon as we regained the middle of the road, I urged the black into a near trot, as great a pace as Tap and I could sustain afoot.

One of the P.M.

In three hours of constant travel, we crossed ten miles of the rough-rutted military road with nary a break to rest and gather our wind. Even in the raw cold, Tap and I were sweating and huffing. Tap feigned resentment of any aid from Annie Bower, but when his canteen ran dry, he greedily gulped water as did I from the discarded vessels she had collected and stashed in the folds of her shawl.

The road grew less cluttered with soldiers each mile, and hardly another soul was about by the time we fetched up to the first sizable stream and halted to fill our canteens and blow the black. I helped Erin down but held the black shy of the bank for fear he might drink too much too fast and founder.

Erin bent low over the water, first cracking the ice and assuaging her thirst, then attempting to scour the powder residue from her lips and chin without benefit of soap. For all her earnest splashing and rubbing, she succeeded mainly in spreading the black stains to her cheeks. Though Tap's eyes were twinkling and leaping, the protective glare of the ever-vigilant Annie Bower stifled his amusement, and he glumly helped the harlot fill the canteens.

I let the black drink a few swallows and kept watch while Tap divided the venison jerk from his haversack into four equal servings. "T'ain't much, but it'll get us down the road a fair piece if'n we chew slow, and no one takes to bein' hoggish," he opined with a sly, skeptical glance at Annie Bower.

The harlot refused to be baited, and I was beginning to believe Tap and his funning had finally met their match. Paying no attention whatsoever to the old scout, Annie inquired, "It's fifteen more miles to the fort, ain't it not, Ensign Downer?"

I nodded, never surprised by how little Annie Bower missed of what went on around her. "You women are in for a mean ride. We must push straight through as the captain ordered. The First Americans may be at the fort, an' St. Clair's badly in need of relief to save what he can of his army and help with the wounded."

"Yep, he be," Tap chimed in. "An' not knowin' if'n the Injuns have truly quit the chase, we can't chance a fire along the way. So it's the fort or freeze yer toes tonight, ladies."

Erin Green rose from the creek bank. "Come Annie, I'll

give you a hand up. I believe these gentlemen are in a hurry."

The harlot giggled. "Yes, an' it's a goodly thing. A certain ugly ol' jasper can't hardly spout off a-tall when his feet's a-shufflin' right smartly, can he now?"

Tap was still fuming over being outjested miles later.

Four of the P.M.

The old scout and I trotted at either shoulder of the black, our eyes on the flanking woods more than the ruts and stumps of the road. There was no talking, no sounds except the pumping of lung, the squeak of leather, the jingle of bridle chains, and the pound of hoof and boot. As the miles fell away, we encountered a few individual soldiers traveling our direction. One sported a brow that had been crushed by the blow of a hatchet. The almost sightless levy refused any assistance from us, claiming his skull hurt too much for him to stand the jar of a moving horse. He finally accepted a canteen of water, after which he seated himself at the base of a big oak tree and waved good-bye as we left him to his own devices. His bravery wrung tears from both our women.

At what I calculated half the distance to Fort Jefferson, undisguised movement to our front heralded the approach of a mounted officer leading a twenty-man detachment of First Americans. Those marching regulars in their standard-issue uniforms toting muskets whose polished barrels winked in the late-afternoon sun were mighty uplifting to tired and beaten hearts, and we gladly relinquished the road to them.

The mounted officer in the fore raised a gloved arm, and the detachment halted behind him. His gaze roamed over Tap, Erin, Annie, and the black before fixing on my dragoon helmet. "Lieutenant Jeffrey Rodgers," he announced, touching two fingers to his tricorn. "We're bound forward, young man. Are you attached to a military unit?"

I promptly knuckled my forehead. "Yes, sir, I'm an ensign, First Volunteer Dragoons, Captain Miles Starkweather commanding."

The lieutenant reined his horse a step closer. "Stragglers reported to Major Hamtramack an hour ago that General St.

Clair has been defeated and his forces put to flight. Is this true?" he asked, voice held deliberately low.

"Yes, sir, every word," Tap interjected, "an' the general's in dire need of relief. Where be the rest of your regiment?" the old scout demanded.

Lieutenant Rodgers frowned. "For your information, Major Hamtramack decided that his best recourse in light of this stunning news was to proceed back to Fort Jefferson with the regiment, thereby securing the nearest point of refuge. My detachment is to reconnoiter the road as far forward as necessary to learn the truth of the general's plight. And I intend to carry out the major's orders."

"Well, you do that, Lieutenant," Tap said with a mildness that belied the sudden redness spotting his cheeks. "You won't learn anything yuh don't now already know, an' your detachment be too small to offer any real help to the general, but you'll be doing your duty, by God. Meanwhile, we'll carry out our captain's orders and report to Fort Jefferson with these here two women. That is, if'n you don't mind?"

Lieutenant Rodgers obviously minded very much, but his singular devotion to duty won out. He ignored the red-cheeked Tap and addressed me instead. "Ensign, please carry your confirming news to Major Hamtramack as soon as possible. I will brook no further delays," he said sternly, turning in the saddle. His arm lifted, and he shouted, "Detail, forward . . . march!"

Annie Bower smiled down at Tap. "Why, yuh old scapegrace, yer almost lovable when a lady least expects it."

Seven of the P.M.

We forded the creek above Fort Jefferson from the northwest by the light of the quarter moon ascending the eastern sky. Ahead, the evening fires of the First Americans glowed brightly on the wooden palisades of the garrison. Ahead, too, at the far edge of the eastern meadow, hidden by trees and darkness, was the Green cabin, the ultimate destination of our two female riders.

The black stepped from the creek, and Erin said softly

but urgently, "Ethan, I must get down. If I don't, I'm afraid I'll never walk again."

I halted the black with a tug on the bridle and helped her dismount, stirred as always by the mere touching of any part of her. Her first few steps were indeed wobbly, and I gladly lent her a supporting arm. The faint scent of rosewater hung about her.

"How 'bout you, Mistress Bower," Tap intoned. "Would you care to dismount?"

"No, yuh big tease," Annie retorted, "these skinny stems of mine are too old to cramp. I'll play the queen till the game's up, yuh don't mind."

My exhaustion faded, and my pulse quickened. With Annie lingering in the saddle and a tired Tap trudging at the black's hindquarters, I envisioned a few minutes alone at the head of that huge animal with Erin. Here at last was an opportunity to speak alone with her, an opening to express how I felt about her before she went off to care for her mother and my duty as a dragoon took me who knew where for how long. Whether it was the right time or the wrong time didn't matter. I had to find out if I had any chance with her. Not knowing was a fate worse than death.

Trouble was, I had no forewarning what a sensation our emergence from the shadowy woods along the creek would cause. Annie Bower was recognized the instant we could be seen by firelight, and numerous infantrymen abandoned their evening meal to welcome her with much shouting and hooting. Sentries flew upon the scene to investigate the swelling commotion, and their arrival dispelled any opportunity I might have had to speak privately with Erin Green.

"Halt and identify yourselves!" a hefty, bespectacled sergeant of the guard commanded.

Cursing my lousy luck, I set my feet and knuckled my forehead. "Ensign Downer, First Dragoons," I proclaimed over the clamoring infantrymen.

"And your business, sir?" the sergeant continued, staring boldly at Erin beside me.

"We're fresh from the battlefield and have vital details of General St. Clair's defeat we must share with Major Hamtramack," I said matter-of-factly.

My statement as to the origin of our travel and the fate of General St. Clair's forces tore the sergeant's eyes from Erin and ignited a near riot. The sergeant immediately dispatched a messenger to the fort and waved hurriedly for me to follow him. Curious infantrymen pushed in from all sides, yelling wild questions. The hefty sergeant screamed the loudest though, and his detail surrounded us, butts of their muskets poised and ready.

We gained the road leading to the gates of the fort, and the crowd grew so large we couldn't proceed. The sergeant grabbed my sleeve. "We'll never get through with the horse and everybody. Leave the others an' come with me. My men will stay with them."

Erin, clinging to my elbow, overheard, and her head began shaking. "No," she protested, "I will not be separated from him, not ever."

Overcome with joy and hardly believing my ears, I shoved the sergeant aside and pulled her against my chest. She came willingly, a longing and wanting showing on her beautiful, powder-blackened face that equaled my own. And this time, making sure I helped myself to a deep breath first, I kissed her, losing the pain and suffering of the whole nightmarish day in the warmth and taste of her.

The repeated call of someone to "Clear a path for the major" and the admiring whistles of the infantrymen sounded miles and miles away.

Epilogue

Eden's Fork, Ohio
16 August 1822
To: Phineas Augustus Trabue,
Owner, Publisher & Editor
Montgomery County Register & Gazette

My Dear Sir:

I am aware of your desire to acquire the St. Clair rec-ollections I have been compiling these recent months. I share as keen an interest in having my recollections of that cam-paign printed and distributed by a reputable sheet such as yours. Understand, I would not anticipate the receipt of any significant revenues from this endeavor. I would, howsom-ever, insist upon two conditions. First, you must present my recollections in their entirety without changes or deletions. Secondly, I must be allowed to complete additional pages that relate the fate of certain survivors near and dear to me whose following years were forever altered by their connec-tion with the bloodiest defeat in the history of our nation's military forces. Some of those involved, my dear sir, were unfairly judged at the time by military authorities and treated with an undeserved harshness by the general public. That record has yet to be put straight in the sake of fairness and proper justice.

It would not be a distillation of the truth to claim that my father, Caleb Downer, was first and foremost among those whose reputation and character was forever tainted and sul-

lied by the disaster of 4 November. The murder of Cyrus
Paine, the killing of Dyson Barch and Court Starnes by my
own hand, and the death of Ensign Andy Young during Colonel Darke's retreat on the left flank from the creek bluff left
no one alive who had witnessed the treachery of the Duer
men. And so thorough was the destruction of vital paper
documents, first by Dyson Barch and Court Starnes, then by
the Shawnee on the battlefield, no credible evidence was ever
found to prove conclusively whether my father did or did not
swindle the army with William Duer and his fellow conspir-
ators. Thus, Paw was never brought to trial or imprisoned,
but his punishment, for an innocent man, was no less severe.

In his rush to personally shed blame for the loss of hundreds of soldiers, General St. Clair conveniently forgot the
visit Paw and Andy Young made to his tent at Fort Jefferson
and condemned all civilian contractors out of hand. His condemnation gained great currency with a public terrified the
Shawnee would shortly besiege Cincinnati and Fort Washington. With no witnesses or evidence to the contrary, and
winter fast approaching, Paw had no choice but to return
home where my mother and sisters were in dire need of him.
His sudden departure from Cincinnati with the starving army
awaiting supplies from upriver, supplies he learned Quartermaster Hodgdon had never procured, was seen as another
sign that Paw was guilty of the charges leveled by the general.

By the time I arrived at Cincinnati in mid-December 1791
from Fort Hamilton with Starkweather, Erin Green, her
mother, Annie Bower, and Tap Jacobs, Paw had already departed for the Downer plantation in Kentucky. But in the
immediate days thereafter, while involved with the captain in
the forceful calming of the recently discharged levies and
restoration of order in the city, I heard rumors and falsehoods about Paw everywhere. And with each passing month,
as the enormity of St. Clair's losses in men and equipment
became common knowledge, those rumors and falsehoods
spread the length of the Ohio and forever branded him a
thief.

Each week I meant to write to Paw, but some demand or
event always seemed more important than the letter. I wasn't

*embarrassed about him or for him. He had hurt me griev-
ously the night he disowned me, and I was too mule stubborn
to forgive him as yet. Then the weeks and months became
years, and I was embarrassed, personally so, for being too
small of heart to forgive him earlier.*

*My beautiful, wondrous wife solved my dilemma before I
couldn't sleep at all. Erin Green had the habit of talking
with me at night in the privacy of our bedchamber while
sipping a glass of wine and wearing delicate fineries scanty
of layer. She was so successful with this ploy, she convinced
me in the winter of 1793 to employ the detestable Gabe
Hookfin. The penniless beanpole appeared in our dooryard
skinnier than air with his clothes and boots in tatters. His
jaw had healed crookedly, and he spoke as if talking around
a corner. He blamed my sucker punching of him for the woe-
ful luck and misfortune that had befallen him. He asked, he
contended, only for a bed in the stable and board in return
for tending the riding and breeding stock owned by the newly
promoted Major Starkweather and me. I, of course, slammed
the door in his ugly, slit-mouthed face, but that night Erin
did her female thing. She informed me that Hookfin was not
an animal to be sent off to freeze to death. And was I not
rejoining General Wayne's army on the morrow? Who else
was readily available to help Tap with the outside work in
my absence while she and her mother saw to the inn we
owned with Major Starkweather, the major's daughter, and
our own child? When I began disputing Hookfin's trustwor-
thiness, she simply smiled, sat her wineglass aside, and
snuffed the candle. Needless to say, I located Hookfin bright
and early the next morning. In his years of service he was
never a disappointment.*

*The same tableau unfolded the night she indicated she
wanted to journey to the Scarlet Knight in Cincinnati for the
New Year's celebration of 31 December 1799. By then we
had abandoned the summer heat, dirt, mud, and flying var-
mints of the city for the open country about McHenry's Ford
near Ludlow's Station, still operating an inn, farming, and
raising horses in conjunction with Starkweather. Erin ignored my arguments that the weather was rotten and that
she was just with child, our third, hopefully a son. Again, the*

glass was set aside, the candle snuffed, and the next morning we headed for Cincinnati in the sleigh Hookfin had built as a gift for her, the beanpole himself at the reins of our matching sorrels.

The sorrels covered the miles of frozen road without incident, and we swooped from the giant's brow down into the city in late afternoon. Already bonfires burned along the river and high-spirited revelers populated the trash-littered streets. We drew up in front of the Scarlet Knight, and Hookfin helped Erin from the sleigh. As was to be expected, her entrance brought forth the owner, Saul Bartlett, and he led us around the wide, square bar that squatted before the tall stone fireplace, Erin preferring a table on the rear wall close to where Cyrus Paine had sat the night of his murder.

The gentleman leaning on the bar with both elbows nearest our intended table looked strikingly familiar, even from the side. The ruffles of his shirt stuck from the neck of his broadcloth coat. He wore whipcord breeches, black riding boots, and a fawn-colored, flat-crowned hat stiff of brim. Damned if it wasn't Paw except for the iron-gray hair, the sunken cheekbones, and the white scar disfiguring the gentleman's jaw. Paw had been dressed thisaway the morning he and Court Starnes had come to our camp north of Fort Hamilton nine years ago.

At my approach, the gentleman's head turned and stopped my feet dead. There was no mistaking those fierce, deep brown eyes. I saw them every morning when I shaved. Paw's nod of recognition was extremely slow, like he was afraid I might bolt and run on him. His "Hello, Ethan" was a mere whisper.

I stood dumbfounded till nudged in the back from behind. I stepped forward one stride, then another, praying he was proud of his son, who was wearing at his wife's insistence his dress uniform, that of a captain, United States Army. Paw nodded a second time and stepped to meet me, his arms opening. I went into them, and suddenly I was crying on his shoulder. He embraced me, and I was home, home at last.

Later that evening, when we were alone in our upstairs room, that wondrous woman of mine shared with me the *letter she'd dispatched south to Kentucky the previous autumn.*

> *Respectfully awaiting your reply,*
> *Colonel Ethan Downer*

No one knows the American West better.

JACK BALLAS

❑ *THE HARD LAND*

0-425-15519-6/$4.99

❑ *BANDIDO CABALLERO*

0-425-15956-6/$5.99

❑ *GRANGER'S CLAIM*

0-425-16453-5/$5.99

The Old West in all its raw glory